They called me the Bitch Queen, the she-wolf, because I murdered a man and exiled my king the night before they crowned me.

Hurricanes destroy the villages and they call it senseless; the winter winds come and they call it cold. What else did they expect from my people, the Oren-yaro, the ambitious savages who created a war that nearly ripped Jin-Sayeng apart? I almost think that if my reign had started without bloodshed and terror, they would have been disappointed.

I did not regret killing the man. He had it coming, and my father had taught me to take action before you second-guess yourself. My father was a wise man, and if the warlords could've stopped arguing long enough to put their misgivings behind them, he would have made them a great king. Instead, they entrusted the land to me and my husband: children of that same war they would rather forget. The gods love their ironies.

BY K. S. VILLOSO

CHRONICLES OF THE BITCH QUEEN

The Wolf of Oren-Yaro

The Ikessar Falcon

THE
WOLF
OF
OREN-YARO

CHRONICLES OF THE BITCH QUEEN:
BOOK ONE

K. S. VILLOSO

www.orbitbooks.net

Copyright © 2017 by K. S. Villoso
Excerpt from *The Ikessar Falcon* copyright © 2018 by K. S. Villoso
Excerpt from *Queen of the Conquered* copyright © 2019 by Kheryn Callender

Author photograph by Mikhail Villoso
Cover design by Lauren Panepinto
Cover illustration by Simon Goinard
Cover copyright © 2019 by Hachette Book Group, Inc.
Map copyright © 2020 by Tim Paul

Hachette Book Group supports the right to free expression and the value of copyright. The purpose of copyright is to encourage writers and artists to produce the creative works that enrich our culture.

The scanning, uploading, and distribution of this book without permission is a theft of the author's intellectual property. If you would like permission to use material from the book (other than for review purposes), please contact permissions@hbgusa.com. Thank you for your support of the author's rights.

Orbit
Hachette Book Group
1290 Avenue of the Americas
New York, NY 10104
www.orbitbooks.net

First Orbit Paperback Edition: February 2020
First Orbit eBook Edition: July 2019
Originally published by Liam's Vigil Publishing Co. in 2017

Orbit is an imprint of Hachette Book Group.
The Orbit name and logo are trademarks of Little, Brown Book Group Limited.

The publisher is not responsible for websites (or their content) that are not owned by the publisher.

The Hachette Speakers Bureau provides a wide range of authors for speaking events. To find out more, go to www.hachettespeakersbureau.com or call (866) 376-6591.

Library of Congress Cataloging-in-Publication Data
Names: Villoso, K. S., 1986– author.
Title: The wolf of Oren-yaro / K.S. Villoso.
Description: First Orbit paperback edition. | New York, NY : Orbit, 2020. | Series: Chronicles of the bitch queen; book 1 | Originally published by Liam's Vigil Publishing Co. in 2017.
Identifiers: LCCN 2019027762 | ISBN 9780316532662 (trade paperback) | ISBN 9780316532631 (ebook)
Classification: LCC PR9199.4.V555 W65 2020 | DDC 813/.6—dc23
LC record available at https://lccn.loc.gov/2019027762

ISBNs: 978-0-316-53266-2 (trade paperback), 978-0-316-53263-1 (ebook)

Printed in the United States of America

LSC-C

10 9 8 7 6 5 4 3 2 1

To Dad,
with all the love
and most sincerest apologies
of a daughter who could have been anything
but chose to follow her heart.

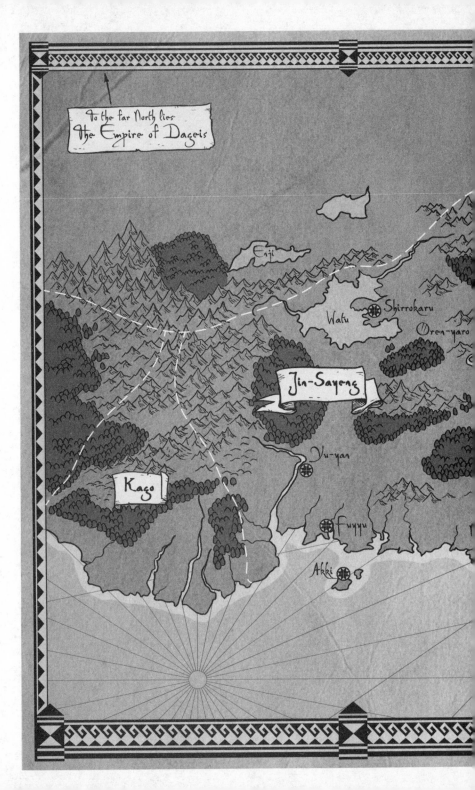

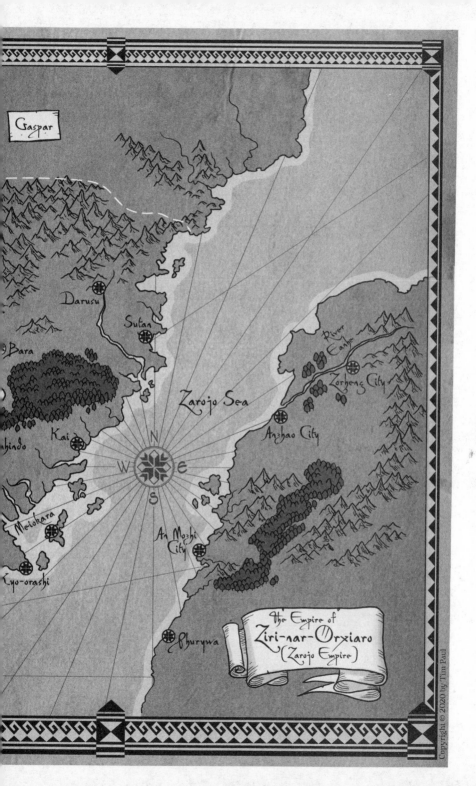

Gaspar

Darusu

Sutan

Bara

Kai

hindo

Meiokara

yo-orashi

River Eanzo

Zorheng City

Anzhao City

Zarojo Sea

An Mozhi City

Phurywa

N
W E
S

the Empire of
Ziri-nar-Orxiaro
(Zarojo Empire)

CHAPTER ONE

THE LEGACY
OF WARLORD TAL

They called me the Bitch Queen, the she-wolf, because I murdered a man and exiled my king the night before they crowned me.

Hurricanes destroy the villages and they call it senseless; the winter winds come and they call it cold. What else did they expect from my people, the Oren-yaro, the ambitious savages who created a war that nearly ripped Jin-Sayeng apart? I almost think that if my reign had started without bloodshed and terror, they would have been disappointed.

I did not regret killing the man. He had it coming, and my father had taught me to take action before you second-guess yourself. My father was a wise man, and if the warlords could've stopped arguing long enough to put their misgivings behind them, he would have made them a great king. Instead, they entrusted the land to me and my husband: children of that same war they would rather forget. The gods love their ironies.

I do regret looking at the bastard while he died. I regret watching his eyes roll backwards and the blood spread like a cobweb underneath his wilted form, leaking into the cracked cobblestone my father paid a remarkable amount of money to install. I regret not having a sharper sword, and losing my nerve so that I didn't strike him again and he had to die slowly. Bleeding over the jasmine bushes—that whole batch of flowers would remain pink until the end of the season—he had stared up at the trail of stars in the night sky and called for his mother. Even though he was a traitor, he didn't deserve the pain.

More than anything, I regret not stopping my husband. I should have run after him, grovelled at his feet, asked him to stay. But in nursing my own pride, I didn't give his a chance. I watched his tall, straight back grow smaller in the distance, his father's helmet nestled under his arm, his unbound hair blowing in the wind, and I did nothing. A wolf of Oren-yaro suffers in silence. A wolf of Oren-yaro does not beg.

Almost at once, the rumours spread like wildfire. They started in the great hall in the castle at Oka Shto when I arrived for my coronation, dressed in my mother's best silk dress—all white, like a virgin on her wedding day—bedecked with pearls and gold-weave, with no husband at my side. My son, also in white, stood on the other side of the dais with his nursemaid. Between us were the two priests tasked with the ceremony—a priest of the god Akaterru, patron deity of Oren-yaro, and a priest of Kibouri, that foreign religion my husband's clan favoured, with their Nameless Maker and enough texts to make anyone ill. They could pass for brothers, with their long faces, carp-like whiskers, and leathery skin the colour of honey.

My husband's absence was making everyone uncomfortable. I, on the other hand, drifted between boredom and restlessness. I glanced at my son. He had stopped crying, but the red around his eyes had yet to disappear. It was my fault—on the way to the great hall, he asked for his father as any two-year-old would, and I snapped in return. "He's gone," I told him in that narrow corridor, where only the nursemaid could hear. "He doesn't want us anymore." The boy didn't understand my words, but the sharp tone was enough to send tears rolling down his cheeks, a faint reflection of how I had spent the night before.

Now, Thanh rubbed his eyes, and I realized I didn't want to wait a moment longer. I turned to the priests and opened my mouth. Before I could utter a single word, the doors opened.

"Crown her," my adviser said, breaking into the hall. His face had the paleness of a man who had looked into a mirror that morning and seen his own death. His sandals clicked on the polished earth floor. "Prince Rayyel Ikessar left last night."

You could hear the weight of the words echo against the walls. In the silence that followed, I thought I could make out the rising heartbeats of every man and woman in that room. Not a day goes by that I am not reminded of what was lost to my father's war; even bated breaths could signal the start to that old argument, that old fear that I, too, may one day plunge the land into blood and fire once more.

Eventually, the Kibouri priest cleared his throat. "We must delay until the prince can be found."

"This day was approved by our order, set in stone years ago," the Akaterru priest replied. "It is a bad omen to change it."

"Every day is like any other," the Kibouri priest intoned. "You and your superstitions…"

My adviser stepped up the dais to face them. Both priests towered over him. His mouth, which was surrounded by a beard that looked like a burnt rodent, was set in a thin line. "Warlord Lushai sent a message this morning, congratulating Jin-Sayeng's lack of a leader. He will march against us by tonight for breaking the treaty if we do not crown her."

I didn't bother to pretend to be surprised. "Rayyel is hiding there, I assume," I said. It was such a bald-faced move: put me in a situation where I could not do anything *but* create trouble. Throw the wolf into a sea of sick deer—whatever will she do? Warlord Lushai once considered himself my father's friend, but daring me to make trouble in front of the other warlords was one step too far.

My adviser turned to me and bobbed his head up and down, like a rooster in the grass.

I gritted my teeth. "Get that crown." I didn't want to give them a reason to think I wasn't fulfilling my end of the bargain.

The Kibouri priest was closer to it. He didn't move.

"My lords," I said, looking at the warlords, the select few who were not too ill or infirm or couldn't find the right sort of excuse to avoid the coronation. "You agreed to this alliance. You all signed it with your own blood. Do you remember? Years ago, you all cut your arms, bled into a cup, and drank from it to mark the joining of Jin-Sayeng as one. Not even Lord Rayyel and I have the power to stop this."

There was a murmur of assent. A whisper, not an outcry, but I went with it. I turned to the priests. The Akaterru priest had already dropped his head, eyes downcast. The other eventually forced his knees into a bow.

They took the smaller crown. It was made of beaten gold, both yellow and white, set on a red silken headpiece. My father had it made not long after I was born, commissioned from a famous artisan from some distant town. I stared at it while the priests began their rituals, one after the other. I could have done without the Kibouri, but I didn't want to risk offending the Ikessar supporters in the crowd.

They crowned me with reluctance. No spirits came to crest a halo around my brow or send a shaft of light to bless the occasion. In fact, it was cloudy, and a rumble of thunder marked the beginning of a storm. I wondered when they would discover the body, or if they already had and were just too afraid to tell me.

Even after I became queen, the rumours continued. I was powerless to stop them. I should have been more, they said. More feminine. Subtle, the sort of woman who could hide my jibes behind a well-timed titter. I could have taken the womanly arts, learned to write poetry or brew a decent cup of tea or embroider something that didn't have my blood on it, and found ways to better please my man. Instead, Rayyel Ikessar would rather throw away the title of Dragonlord, king of Jin-Sayeng, than stay married to me.

It changes a woman, hearing such things. Hardens your heart. Twists your mind along dark paths you have no business being on. And perhaps it wouldn't have mattered if I hadn't loved Rai, but I did. More than I understood myself. More than I cared to explain.

———

I don't like to talk about the years that followed. Even now, pen in hand while I splash ink over my dress, I find it difficult to recall anything past the cloud of anger. All I know is that five years passed, quicker than the blink of an eye. I was told the anger could do that. That it could rob whatever sweetness there was in the passage of time, add a bitter tinge to the little joys in the life of an unwanted queen. "Will my father come?" my son would ask on his nameday without fail. Each year he would grow taller, stronger, more sure of himself, and each year the question would lose a touch of innocence, be more demanding. "Will my father come?" Soft eyes growing harder, because we both knew that wasn't what he was really asking anymore. *When will he be home? Why did you send him away? Why didn't you stop him?*

And each year, I would struggle to find an answer that wouldn't make the courtiers turn their heads in shame. They knew I couldn't have thrown him out—I didn't have the power to lord over the heir of the most influential clan in Jin-Sayeng. Yet I could not allude that he abandoned his duties. I could say it easily enough to the Oren-yaro, but not in court—not in front of his family's supporters. As if the weight of the crown wasn't heavy enough, as if I wasn't spending every waking hour fending the warlords off each other, off of me. After centuries of Ikessar Dragonlords, I was the first queen of Jin-Sayeng, and all the difficulties didn't bode well for my rule.

In late summer of the fifth year, I returned after an afternoon riding my horse through the rice fields, where I had been surveying the damage caused by last year's storms. There was very little a monarch could do about such things, but it gave people strength to see me, or so I liked to think.

Arro stood by the gates, waiting. I slowed my horse to a walk. It was always amazing how I could predict the future simply by my adviser's expression. If it was going to be a good week, he often greeted me with a smile, his eyes disappearing into the folds of his face. That meant most provinces had paid their taxes, there were no land disputes (or at least none that people had lost their heads for), and every single warlord was accounted for.

He didn't smile now. His lips were flat—not quite a frown, as if he wasn't sure he wanted to expend his energy all that way yet. I dismounted from the horse, allowing a servant to take her back to the base of the mountain to the stables. Arro wiped his hands on his beard and held out a letter, which had been opened. No doubt it was checked thoroughly by the staff, in case someone tried to poison me by sprinkling dust on the inside of the scroll that I might later inhale. The Ikessars loved to use such tactics—I had even lost a great-uncle to it during the war.

"What's this?" I asked, just as my dog Blackie appeared between the trees. I whistled, and he bounded to me, ears flopping while his tail wagged so fast it felt at risk of falling off. I patted my tunic before taking the letter.

I read it once, and then a second time. I could feel my heart pounding, my mouth growing dry. I wanted to ask if this was a dream. It must be. I had so many others like it before. The details were always different: Sometimes it would come from a messenger, his horse slick with sweat. Sometimes it would be a falcon with a note attached to its leg. Sometimes a hooded Ikessar would come bearing gifts before revealing himself to be my husband, years changed and begging for my forgiveness. In each dream, I had fallen to my knees and wept with joy. It felt odd that I now couldn't muster any emotion beyond cool detachment.

I looked back at Arro and found my voice. "What do you think?"

"The man who abandoned his position, who abandoned *you*, has no right to demand a meeting on his terms, let alone in a place as far as Ziri-nar-Orxiaro. I smell a trap."

"He insists that it is a safe place for us to meet. Anzhao City would be on neutral grounds, away from the warlords' meddling."

"Easy for an Ikessar to say," Arro grumbled. Blackie came up to rub along his leg, and he pushed the dog away in disgust. He tugged his rice hat back into place. "Take my advice, my queen. Ignore it. The man disappears for the better part of five years and then thinks that you will come running to him after a mere *letter*? Such arrogance."

I was silent for a moment. "The warlords..." I started. "A good number of them supported the Ikessars."

Arro snorted. "They did. And so? They are content with whispers in the dark. None have dared challenge your position."

"Not yet," I said. "Whispers in the dark are still dangerous. Did we not learn that in the days of the Ikessars' rule? They can roust the people, put ideas where they don't belong. All it takes is one warlord to decide he's had enough and get two more to agree with him. The rest will follow, and I will be yet another failed Dragonlord in this damned land's history."

"It's like trying to take control of a pack of dogs. Just bark louder than the rest."

"And you know a thing or two about dogs, do you, Arro?" I asked, watching him try to avoid Blackie's pestering tongue with a measure of amusement. Finally, I took pity on him and whistled. The dog returned to me. "The other warlords do not challenge me because Rai left of his own accord. They can say whatever they want... They have no proof I put a sword to his back and bullied him out of my lands. But it doesn't mean it will end there. Lately, they have turned to openly blaming me for his actions, and if word gets out that Rai wrote to me and I refused to answer, they will think I meant to hold on to the crown by myself. The idea of a wolf of Oren-yaro on the throne still frightens them."

Arro looked like he wanted to argue, but one of the things I appreciated about him was that he saw sense even when he didn't agree with it. He tucked his hands into his sleeves. "I will convene with the others," he said. "We will have to investigate this letter before we can make a decision."

"Of course," I said. "But this is the first time in years that Lord Rayyel has agreed to talk to us. Regardless of our personal opinions, he remains of importance to the royal clans. Don't do anything drastic—I will not have him frightened into silence."

He nodded, wiping his hands on his beard yet again. It was an affectation of his, a Zarojo mannerism. Arro had grown up in the empire, brought over to serve my father a long time ago—I would've thought he'd have jumped at the chance to visit his home after so many years.

I went up the flagstone steps leading to the garden, Blackie running in circles around me. I was doing a remarkable job at keeping calm. Only when I reached the fountain did my knees buckle. I sat on the edge, listening to the water bubble and the frogs croak.

"I told you to declare war on the bastards five years ago," a voice called from the gate. I looked up to see my father's general striding past the rose bushes. He must've been there when they first opened the letter. Although I knew it was a precaution, it irritated me that I was always the last to know, that other people were always making decisions for me. Taking a deep breath, I got up to face him.

Unlike Arro, Lord General Ozo never tried to hide his displeasure, especially his displeasure at *my* ruling.

He threw a staff in my direction, giving me only a split second to catch it before he charged with bamboo sticks, one in each hand. I stepped back and met his attack. Ozo was a big man, covered in hard muscle that had yet to go to fat, despite his age. Bamboo against bamboo clattered together. I staggered back.

"War," I repeated. "I told you before, Lord General Ozo. We don't have the resources."

He slapped the back of his head with his hand, his arm tattoos a deep black against his sunburnt skin. "I'm the one with the soldiers. I'm the one who can tell you we can crush the bastards if you just gave the order."

"And I'm your queen," I said as I tried to jam the end of my staff into his head. Just once, it would be satisfying to see his nose break.

He sidestepped, twirling the sticks in his hands. "Some queen. Your footwork alone..."

I bristled as I fixed my feet. "Is that insubordination?"

"That's honesty," he snarled as he charged me a second time. I spun on my heel, my staff slamming into his gut. But he only laughed it off. "This land is teetering on the brink of destruction because you can't make up your mind about what to do with that husband of yours." He continued to attack. "The other warlords laugh at you behind their cups. The peasants think you weak. You want to see the bastard? Order me to set fire to his holdings, and he'll come riding back to save his clan. I'll cut off his head, then."

"He's still your Dragonlord," I gasped, barely keeping up with his assault. I didn't know where the man still found the energy. He was old, too old to be sparring in broad daylight.

Sweat poured down his face as he finally grabbed my staff, dragging me up to him. "Uncrowned, like his uncle before him," he said. "I won't submit to it. He's no king of mine. And *you* won't be queen for much longer if you don't make a decision. You forget that *you're* Dragonlord, too." He spat on the bushes, a healthy globule that trickled down the leaves. My poor gardener was going to be livid. Then he pushed me away.

"Must this end in war?" I asked, relaxing my stance. "If I can find a peaceful resolution..."

"A peaceful resolution?" he asked incredulously. "*You?* You're Warlord Yeshin's. Yeshin the Butcher's daughter. The land will never allow *you* peace if you don't crush them under an iron fist first. You want our people to listen to you instead of their warlords, their clans, their families? Put them on a tight leash. Strangle their necks if you have to."

"Says Yeshin's general."

Ozo sniffed, flicking his sticks from side to side. "Or you can walk willingly into this trap for the sake of seeing your sorry sack of a husband and bring shame to the Oren-yaro. After everything your father has sacrificed, you would do this to him. And for what? The man has been nothing but trouble to Jin-Sayeng!" He lunged. The right stick smacked against my face before I could lift the staff to protect myself.

My skin prickled as I twirled the staff, jabbing him on the side. "You would say that, Lord Ozo," I hissed as I pulled back to jab him again. "You hate his clan."

"Hundreds of years under his clan's rule has brought us nothing but sorrow." He rewarded my efforts with another blow to my head. I reared back, shaking, and he gave a small grin. "You're the one with every reason to hate them. Their incompetence killed your brothers."

"Brothers I've never met," I grumbled, wiping my jaw.

"They were good men, and the Ikessars took them from us. Before your father's war, we had a Dragonlord who chose to wander the world instead of rule. And *his* father before him..." He spat again. "Shoddy rule after shoddy rule, and now this. Now you have the chance to prove to Jin-Sayeng we don't need the bastards at all."

My fingers tightened around the staff. "We don't, Ozo. But this alliance was my father's decision."

"A sorry excuse for an alliance. I've never seen an alliance where the other party slinks away and refuses to do their part for half a decade.

And if you *do* decide to go to the empire, what then? Do you know how corrupt their cities are? Their officials won't help you. As far as they're concerned, Jin-Sayeng is a land of penniless peasants, and they wouldn't be wrong. And all you've got is that cracked halfblood adviser of yours, and Captain Nor. Nor's Oren-yaro, at least—I don't doubt her capabilities, but she's not Agos."

"Don't start this, General. Not again."

He lowered his sticks. "He was the best guard captain my army had produced, and you threw it all away for nothing. Don't come running to me for help if you get in trouble." He started to walk away.

"Not another step, General," I said in a low voice.

"You've got a sword. Put me in my place if you want to stop me," he snarled.

I dropped the staff and drew my sword.

He turned his head to the side and laughed. "Now what? Cut me down."

"Don't test me."

"But I am," he said, laughing. "I am, and you're failing. You hesitate. You always do, pup, and I'm sure when the time comes, you'll hesitate with *him*, too. Your lenience will be the death of us all." With a wave of his hand, he walked off. If he was anyone else, I could've had him executed on the spot, but...he was still a lord. An elder. In many ways, his authority eclipsed mine.

My fingers trembled as I watched him disappear around the bend, the same way my husband had done all those years ago. *War.* The word twisted inside my gut. General Ozo had wanted it declared the eve of the coronation. War would bolster Oren-yaro rule...if we won it. We had the largest army in the land, but that meant nothing if the others united against us.

"Mother."

A second voice, one that most days would have calmed me. Today, it filled me with dread. I sheathed my sword, wiped my face, and turned to my son.

"I heard what the general said," Thanh breathed. He hesitated. "Is it true?"

"You really shouldn't be eavesdropping on grown-ups."

He cocked his head to the side, the way he always did when I called him out for things and he understood he'd done wrong, he'd just rather not dwell on it. I believe my father would've called it something like discourtesy. Defiance. I merely found it amusing. "But are you really going to see Father? You're going to bring him back?"

Up until that moment, I hadn't been sure what I was going to do. A part of me was inclined to set the letter aside. I had done it before. After Rayyel left, it took a whole month for his first letter to arrive. It was an angry letter, full of his misgivings about our relationship. I left it inside my desk, refusing to read the rest of it. I had hoped he would send another soon, that time would ease the anger, would allow us to speak without throwing barbed words at each other.

That *soon* became five years. The letter in my hands was his second.

"If I do go to Anzhao," I said, "I can bring you back a book, or a falcon. I've heard they breed such beautiful falcons in Anzhao City. A white one, perhaps. And they have these little dogs..."

"I want my father," Thanh said, his voice growing stern.

I stared at my son, at the way he held himself, firm jaw, straight back, more pride and dignity than most adults I've known. My beautiful boy, seven years old, aged by his father's absence in a way I couldn't have anticipated. I had watched him turn from that chubby-cheeked toddler calling impatiently for his papa to this calm, quiet child who could no longer recall his father's face. Do you know what it feels like to see your son looking back at you, waiting for an answer that would soothe away those hurts, all those years of crying for his father in the night? To know that your words could crush his hopes and dreams in an instant? The boy could break me.

I held my breath and spoke before I could even really think it through. "So I will," I said. "I'll bring your father back, even if it's against his will. I promise. We'll be a family again."

If they were lies, they were such beautiful lies. The rush of relief in his eyes sealed the deal.

———

I've never known a life outside politics.

I *have* been told that monarchs can have hobbies. The last true Dragon-lord, Reshiro, kept butterflies. But then again, he was an Ikessar, and only Ikessars would find interest in that sort of thing.

My words to my son ringing in my ears, I returned to my chambers to try to find that first letter. It was gone. The drawers contained other things—a rattle from when my son was an infant, various brushes and empty ink jars. Old books. A wrinkled piece of brown paper I had folded several times over for my son—it had been a boat, and then a hat, and then a frog that could jump if you pressed its back. No letter. It was odd; I was sure I had left it there.

I returned to the new letter and read it a third time. My husband's words were flat and empty, precise, as if he were asking to meet with any other official. He addressed it to my full name and ended with his, with no hint of emotion anywhere. As if I was nothing. Not his wife, not the mother of his son. Not a woman he loved.

You would think that last part wouldn't sting anymore. I had considered the possibility enough times in the past—years of silence could do that. He didn't love me anymore. He never loved me at all. But I knew thinking like this was wasted energy. I could unearth all my memories of him and turn them over in my head until I came close to madness, and I would still come to a different conclusion every time. That look in his eyes as he helped me down the steps when I was heavily pregnant with our son—was it devotion, or was it abhorrence over my weakness? Whenever he held my hand, was it because he wanted to, or because *I* wanted him to?

That old irritation returned. Assurance was not something I had ever received in my marriage, and it would be foolish to expect it now. I could just as easily shove the letter into my desk again and forget about it for another five years. Life was complicated enough as it was. Rayyel left us. Twist the words however you want; he was the one who walked away.

I sat on the edge of the bed and looked through the window. Out in the courtyard, I spotted members of the Queen's Guard busy with their daily exercise, the light drizzle cloaking their sinewy forms. Their faces were blank, determined. I doubted that expression would go away even if you threw them naked into freezing snow.

Unfaltering, dutiful, and loyal to a fault—these tenets are why the rest of Jin-Sayeng have labelled our people *wolves of Oren-yaro*, a term that started as an insult. These wolves, they like to say, these bloodthirsty beasts, these savages who would stop at nothing. But far from taking offense, we decided to adopt the title, bestowing the name *wolf of Oren-yaro* on all who fall under the shadow of our province. As a people, we embrace these tenets, regardless of clan, regardless of caste, setting us apart from the rest of Jin-Sayeng. It has created a unity never before seen in these lands. We know it. The others know it. It is why the Oren-yaro are as feared as they are revered; the strength of our resolution has toppled realms.

Let me tell you a story. A long time ago, five hundred and twenty-six wolves of Oren-yaro died protecting Shirrokaru, the Jin-Sayeng capital and Ikessar stronghold, from warlords who rebelled. The rebels numbered over three thousand. By the end of the assault, all our soldiers lay dead except for one: Warlord Tal aren dar Orenar. He stood in the middle of that battlefield, covered in the blood of friend, family, and foe, and held his position for over two days in case the enemy dared to return. When the Ikessar lord came to view the slaughter, Warlord Tal was still able to throw his sword aside and bend his knee before he died.

I had no intention of bending my knee, not to the man who had broken *his* vows. But I thought of Warlord Tal, for whom I was named, as I watched my soldiers out in the courtyard. I watched them go through the motions, their voices drowned by the torrent of rainfall, and thought that if Warlord Tal could do it—if he could fight a battle in the face of defeat and then stand strong between those corpses for the sake of never giving up his post—then I could do my part. I could learn to swallow the silence and face my husband again.

CHAPTER TWO

THE BEGGAR QUEEN

ᛏᚢᛘ

We made preparations to depart from Oren-yaro two days later. It was the dead of the night, and Thanh was asleep in bed. He had tried to stay up late to say his goodbyes, but the excitement had proved too much and his little body was worn out. I kissed his forehead, smoothing out his hair. He really needed to get it cut, and I made a note to remind his caretakers to do so—a request that would probably be ignored. Representatives from my husband's clan kept close watch on my son at all times, and they didn't like me. They would probably like me less once they realized exactly where I was headed; I had told them I was making an extensive survey of the rice fields and wouldn't be back for days.

I tucked the blankets tight around him. He whimpered before turning onto his side, his fist on his mouth. He used to suck his thumb, and all that was left was the shadow of that small habit. As I turned around, I saw Arro looking at us from the doorway.

"You have grown up so much," he said, a little wistfully.

"And by that I'm sure you mean I'm no longer getting in your hair."

He rubbed his balding head with a rueful expression before clearing his throat. "You should know that the empire is...not Jin-Sayeng. My queen, you need to remember to keep your wits about you."

"I always do."

"Not *as* you always do. You will need more propriety."

I sniffed. "Since when did you become an Ikessar?"

"For instance," he continued, ignoring my jibe, "they openly practice the forbidden arts there. Do not ask questions that can be misinterpreted down the road. If you show the slightest bit of interest in mages or magic or the *agan*..."

"You're the one saying these things, not I."

"It doesn't matter what I say. I'm not the queen—you are. Remember they will find whatever fault they want to find, and use it to bring you down."

"I know," I murmured. "I've always known that."

He cleared his throat. "We are ready when you are, Beloved Queen."

I gave my son one last kiss before I strode out to follow Arro. In addition to him, twenty guards, my captain of the guard, and a single handmaiden made up my retinue. We looked less like a royal delegation and more like an angry mob, but we needed to be able to blend in. The last thing we wanted was news of this journey reaching the wrong ears. Despite my trepidation, a part of me felt as if I was finally doing something to bring my war-torn land closer to peace. I told myself this was the important thing; my father used to say that a Dragonlord who wore his heart on his sleeve did not stay Dragonlord for very long.

And so I left Oka Shto, the mountain castle my father built not long before I was born. It was the only home I had ever known. My family had an ancestral keep down in Old Oren-yaro back when my brothers were alive, but I had never been there; it was beyond repair and contained too many painful memories for my father. We rode past the rice paddies, the terraced hills forming into flatlands behind us, and then later, tall mountains rising from every side. Several days later, we reached the port city of Sutan in the east, where I boarded a ship heading to Anzhao straight across.

The journey itself was uneventful other than a few bumps and bruises from the bad weather, several days of bland food alleviated with a stop at one of the islands, and an afternoon watching dolphins follow us from a distance. A good omen, Arro said on that last part; a bad one, countered Nor, my captain of the guard. I wondered if it was both.

Our arrival was a different story altogether.

A curtain of rain hung over the horizon just as the *Singing Sainsa* floated into the docks. One by one, we filed down the gangway and mingled with the rest of the crowd: passengers from other ships, fishermen, merchants, and sailors come home after months at sea. The crew remained on the ship, where they were to wait for us until after the meeting. We weren't expecting to stay for very long—a day or two, at most. Just long enough to see my husband. Long enough to convince him to come back home.

My heart tightened as we viewed the city. The streets were wide and packed with people. It reminded me of the old eastern cities in my own land, but with a scale that took my breath away. Out of all the places in the world, I wondered why Rayyel would choose this one. He hated crowds, hated people. The man's idea of happiness was a hermit cave in the middle of nowhere.

Arro came by with a cloak to wrap around my shoulders. I glanced at him, struggling with the desire to tell him what I felt. Admitting weakness in front of my soldiers was the last thing I wanted. They were Oren-yaro, and loyal to me, but people were always watching, always talking. There was nothing I did that wasn't torn apart and re-examined, hidden meanings wedged between my words, the shadows growing taller than the truth. I followed my retinue up the street to an inn. Red paper lanterns hung outside the windows. I narrowed my eyes, trying to read the lettering on them.

Arro left us to talk to the manager. I turned to Nor.

"Not much to look at in the rain, this Anzhao," I said, trying to break the silence.

"Rain would do that, Beloved Queen," she replied flatly, eyes skipping past me.

Straight as an arrow, was Nor, and dedicated to her duty like no other. She was an obvious choice when they were picking the staff to accompany me to the empire. She was also my cousin, an *aron dar* Orenar. After five years, you would think we would be on more familiar terms.

Nothing could be further from the truth. Five years my guard, and then years serving the province before that, and there was still this layer of ice, this impenetrable wall between us. Nor arrived in Oren-yaro not long before my father's death, where she studied directly under Warlord Yeshin's own captain of the guard. Nor, I soon came to understand, was something of a prodigy. Only later did I learn that she was also a royal, which explained the speed with which she climbed through the ranks. At only eighteen, she was leading her own unit, overseeing the city's security among the gnarly old men that were the remnants of my father's choices.

Choosing to join the guards instead of taking a clan-honoured title or finding a position in the army was seen by many as an unconventional choice. The gossip was ruthless: Nor had married another guard, so of course she joined only to be with him. He was not a royal, so her family wouldn't have approved otherwise. I couldn't count the number of times I've longed to find the source of such gossip and then throttle the life out of it, even with my reputation as tarnished as it is.

Arro returned to us. I looked at his face and sensed the bad news before he even opened his mouth.

"They denied us lodging."

"Explain," I said.

"They were full. Said they had rooms left, but they were saving those for Zarojo officials. They asked us to go to Dar Aso instead." He wiped sweat from his brow.

I cleared my throat. "So why don't we? My feet are wet and I want a warm bed, Magister."

"Beloved Queen, Dar Aso is the immigrants' corner. It's right beside the district of Shang Azi...the slums. It's a small, destitute area."

"They don't want to shelter Jinseins," Nor broke in. She closed her mouth as quickly as she'd spoken.

Arro didn't reply, but I could tell he agreed.

"Did you tell them who we were?" I asked. "Did you tell them to show some respect?"

"Remember, my queen—*we* are in their land. You cannot just insult the Zarojo into compliance. Besides, they won't believe us. People will say anything to get by, especially around here."

"The nerve," I said in a low voice. "Let me talk to them. Captain Nor—"

"It's probably best if we just try the next inn," Arro said, sneezing into his sleeve. "You don't want to cause trouble. We don't have enough guards."

"Trouble? They're the ones causing trouble!"

"This isn't the time, Beloved Queen," he said. "Our situation is precarious enough as it is. Let's approach this amicably. We can't afford a scene."

Amicably. I was so cold from the rain that I wanted to order him to *amicably* go back there and tell them to shove a stick up their behinds.

Arro led us to the next inn before I could make up my mind. Again, he went ahead. At the gates, I caught sight of the manager yelling at him—of Arro bowing, trying to appease her, offering his apologies. Watching my royal adviser grovel to a peasant made my stomach turn. He returned to us, his face unbelievably calm despite the torrent of verbal abuse he'd just received.

"Let me guess," I said. "They're also full."

"This is normal here," he replied. "My apologies, my queen. The Jinsein accent is still so strong in my speech. My mother's doing, and all these years in Jin-Sayeng has worsened the affliction."

"Why apologize to me? My accent is worse than yours. *They* should be the ones apologizing!"

He gave a thin smile. "And this is exactly why I'm not allowing you to talk. We have to remain respectful, regardless of how we feel. The Zarojo will respond poorly to your hot-blooded Oren-yaro ways. There's another inn." He bowed and left us again. I could tell, even before he could reach the door, that the response would be the same. The innkeeper had already barred the gate, yelling at him to go away, they had no room, none at all. What he really meant was *for people like you.*

We wandered around the city for the next hour or so. The movement, at least, made the cold bearable. But I was exhausted. Angry. And I couldn't think of anyone to blame but Rayyel. Was this what he wanted? To see a queen become a beggar? Maybe he was in one of those houses at this very instant, watching me through the curtains with a flicker of amusement on his usually expressionless face. The image was beyond irritating.

Our last stop was the governor's house, which a bystander—momentarily taking pity on us—pointed out. We were so sure an official of the city would recognize my position for fear of causing offense. The servants made us wait at the courtyard for a good hour before telling us that the governor had taken ill that night and couldn't possibly entertain us. We could, if we wanted to, go to the government building in the morning, where he would see us—if he had the time. It took a lot of patience for me to refrain from commenting.

As we left the grounds, I saw a man approach us from the street. "The queen of Jin-Sayeng?" he asked, bowing. "I was sent by Deputy Ino Qun to offer you lodging for your stay here."

"Who?" I asked.

"A deputy from this district," Arro broke in. "I've only seen his name in passing. How did you find us?"

"He only asks that I escort you back to his home before the queen collapses from hunger," the servant said. He wouldn't meet our eyes.

I glanced at Arro, who frowned. "I don't know if it's safe," he said.

"Do we have a choice?"

"We can return to the ship."

"I have to meet my husband tomorrow, Arro. I can't do it looking like a drowned rat. What would our enemies say?"

He considered my words for a moment before giving a resigned nod.

"Bring us to your master," I told the man.

We didn't get to meet the deputy that night. Servants fetched us, took our wet clothes and offered dry ones, and I was given a room, where I slept like the dead. The next morning, I opened my eyes and lay back against the silk pillows, listening to the whistling call of a bird not from Jin-Sayeng. A moment passed. I rolled across the bed so I could tug at the curtains. Before I could even reach the cord, my handmaiden rushed forward to do it for me. Light flooded the room. I had been queen for five years and a princess for twenty-one before that. Although I knew that the mere action of glancing at a window would produce a scattering of robes as servants rushed to be the first to do my bidding, I still attempted to wrest control of my life wherever I could. Only recently was I able to convince my council to let me eat without someone sniffing my food first.

My father had detested that sort of attention. Warlord Yeshin had grown up with less extravagance, a claim few warlords these days can make. Born the youngest son, he learned to master the sword and the horse before he was given his first guard: a half-blind, toothless soldier who had been rejected from another warlord's household for his over-fondness for coconut wine. Even after Yeshin outlived his brothers and became Warlord of Oren-yaro, he still despised the luxuries.

He didn't try to raise me that way, of course. I was his only living child, and circumstances did not allow him to let his rivals poison his children until only the best remained. So I had no fewer than five servants scrambling over me since the day I was born, making sure that nothing—not even a fly—could touch me. Perhaps he might have been more lenient if my mother had been alive, but she died in childbirth—that same, tired story of the ages. She had been only fifteen.

One good thing at least about being far away from Jin-Sayeng with only the one servant. While she was struggling with the curtains, I got up. Her face paled. I ignored her and began to get dressed.

"My queen!" the servant gasped in horror, contorting herself so she could reach me before I finished tying my belt.

I glanced at the frightened girl. One of my councillors had picked her up from a town on the island of Akki a few years ago. Traditionally, handmaids were other royals, younger daughters or cousins of the *aron dar*, offshoots of the main clans. But Yeshin preferred to hire commoners even for important positions. Loyalty to clan preceded loyalty to your liege, and even friendship wasn't a guarantee. The servants in our household were a clear sign of my father's cynicism about our people.

"How do you like the Zarojo Empire so far?" I asked.

She stopped, fingers hovering over my belt. I could see her ears turning red.

"My queen..." she stammered.

"Are those the only two words you know?"

Her mouth opened and closed. I think she could see her life flash before her eyes.

A burst of irritation ran through me. I tugged the belt away to finish tying it myself. I glanced at my boots, and she tore herself across the room to fetch them.

I wondered if knowing her name would change anything. Would she answer if I asked her then? It was an easy enough question, one she needn't have to think about. But I watched her slide the boots onto my feet and couldn't entertain the thought any more than that. Perhaps I could bring it up with Magister Arro if he was in the mood for my questions.

I didn't try to talk to her again, and we walked out of the room into silence. I think she had the same idea, because she kept a respectable distance behind me, her eyes on the floor. I turned my attention to finding food. I wasn't clear on what customs were observed out here, and no one had bothered to leave me instructions. By the entrance to the guest quarters, I was able to corner one of my host's servants and somehow—in my best Zirano, the language in that region—ask her if breakfast was going to be served or if they expected me to find it myself.

She told me, with a quick bow, that it had already been served; they did not wake me, assuming I was tired from the long journey. If I would present myself to the dining hall, the kitchen staff would see to my sustenance.

I noticed that she was not as frightened of me as my own handmaid was. A little intimidated, perhaps—understandable, given the authority I represented and what our arrival might mean—but not overly so. I noted that in Ziri-nar-Orxiaro, even the servants shaved their eyebrows thin and wore the pigment that allowed their lips to look so red and supple. In Jin-Sayeng the servants needed to keep their faces plain, to mark the difference between royal and commoner. It was something I had never thought about before.

In an attempt to kill my growing discomfort over this observation, I turned to my servant. But she continued to keep her eyes averted, her fingers laced nervously in front of her. I knew her from the castle, though it was the first time she had served me directly, and I couldn't understand her discomfort. Servants knew I didn't whip people for no reason.

I wondered if she was reacting to the new environment as I was. After the long journey in cramped quarters, and now in a household of strangers, the barriers between us seemed to have been ripped apart.

Captain Nor found us on the way to the dining hall. "My apologies, my queen," she said, drawing her thick brows together. "I was called outside to deal with a small issue, but I left a guard in my place. He shouldn't have let you—"

"I didn't see him," I said.

She glowered. "That's unacceptable! I will have the man sent for and punished."

"I think we could let it go this time. No one tried to assassinate me, Nor."

"Without discipline, our morals falter." Nor's expression was hard, the sort of hardness that my father approved of. The guard might be wise to never show his face again.

"Will you accompany me to breakfast?" I asked.

She paused for a moment before giving assent.

We reached the dining hall. Our host must've been informed of my arrival—a fresh plate had already been set out. Arro was tearing into a steamed rice bun while wiping his fingers on the table. He noticed me and bowed.

I settled into the most comfortable and expensive-looking stool I had ever seen in my life and allowed a servant to place my meal in front of me: steamed rice buns, some sort of tofu pudding garnished with mint leaves, and rice balls wrapped in bamboo leaves. I was about to touch the rice balls when Nor cleared her throat. I sighed, pulling back to let my handmaid sample a bit of everything first. I had forgotten that they had waived my rights to an uninterrupted meal throughout this entire visit. It was like being a child again.

"I trust you slept well, Beloved Queen," Arro said.

"Well enough," I replied. "Someone was playing the harp long into the night—"

"I will inform the host that such activities must cease immediately."

"I was only about to say that I enjoyed it. It gave me pleasant dreams." I glanced to the side. As my handmaid was still alive, and not crumpled on the floor with foam on her lips, Nor gave a nod, allowing me to finally eat my own food. I'd had only a small meat pie from the market the night before, and I all but wolfed down the rice balls. The pork stuffing had salted egg and bits of mushroom, all melded together in a sweet and savoury sauce that tasted faintly of black pepper and oysters. I don't care what the Jin-Sayeng consensus is about Zarojo food—the elders have preached against its richness and penchant for over-spicing—I've always found it delicious.

I washed the food down with cold melon tea before I turned back to Arro. He chewed nervously on his ratty moustache. "You might as well tell me now, Magister," I said. "I'm bound to find out soon enough."

His eyes darted towards me. "I learned why we were turned away from the governor's house last night. Governor Gon Zheshan was informed of our arrival well in advance. But he will not entertain us. Prince Rayyel is lodging with him."

"*Dragonlord* Rayyel, according to him," a voice called out from the other end of the hall. "We've spoken about this, Magister Arro." A thin, pock-faced man, dressed in ornate silk robes, approached us. An official's hat perched on his head.

"Deputy Qun," I guessed, inclining my head towards him. It was the best way I could hide my irritation at his refusal to meet us the night before. "I'd rather not insult your hospitality, but that is incorrect. Lord Rayyel was never crowned."

"A technicality that Governor Zheshan has no problems overlooking," Deputy Qun said, taking a seat across from us. He bowed. "Diplomatic reasons, Queen Talyien, and nothing but. I won't bore you with the details." He flashed me a smile.

I stared at him for a heartbeat, Arro's warning returning to me. No—this was *not* Jin-Sayeng. There was more behind his words. Perhaps they didn't want me near Rayyel until the official meeting—but if so, why?

I took a sip of melon tea to quell my nerves. "Please accept my gratitude, then, that the Jinsein people can call the people of Anzhao City *friend*." Propriety, Arro had said. I glanced at my adviser momentarily, wondering if he approved. But he was too busy observing Qun.

"I would not go that far," Qun said, nodding towards me. "But your candour is appreciated." A smile worked its way up to the corners of his lips. "As is my head."

So, I thought. *My reputation precedes me.* Outwardly, I only smiled some more. "If you continue to serve these rice balls for breakfast, you may keep it." Let him think we had an understanding. My father had taught me, early on, to detect ambition, and it was clear from the gleam in the man's eyes that he offered his hospitality only because he saw it as a chance to undermine Governor Zheshan's authority.

Or so I imagined; I had been queen for only five years, and the feeling of being thrown into an ocean I couldn't swim in prevailed. Before I could get the chance to be smug about this, Arro bent forward, his skin folds jiggling. "Don't try to fool us with your prattle, *deputy*," he said. "You could at least honour our request to gain a private audience with the governor. That you would imply that the queen of Jin-Sayeng must *beg* to be allowed to speak to a mere governor…"

"I am only doing my job, Magister Arro." Deputy Qun gestured at the food before us. "If the hospitality is not to your liking, I can recommend several excellent inns in the area. Until then, my abode is yours." He bowed before shuffling out of the hall.

"This is intolerable," Arro said through gritted teeth. "The insolence they offer Jin-Sayeng…"

"What would you have me do, Magister?" I replied, keeping my voice low. "Declare war on them? Bite them?"

Arro snorted. "Would that you could."

"I cannot even get my lords to agree to a single law without at least a year of deliberation and arguments." I plucked a mint leaf before pushing the pudding away. "I knew Rai must be out of his mind to suggest this meeting *here*, out of all places. The Kag would've made more sense—at least we wouldn't have to brave the sea to get there."

"And the Ikessars have more weight in the Kag," Arro ventured. "More connections. More...spies." He cleared his throat. "Unless he doesn't want his mother to know."

"So he's dragging the Zarojo into our business while he plays the wayward son. Whatever he wants to discuss will have this Governor Zheshan's scent all over."

"The Ikessars have always been sneaky. Even if he's doing this without his clan's approval, he'll always be one of them." He paused. "I think I know why Governor Zheshan is sheltering him. Prince Rayyel's clan's city has a pact with Anzhao."

"Why haven't you told me?"

"I didn't think they would actually uphold it," Arro grumbled. He cleared his throat. "It's ancient. We don't have the sort of relations with the empire we used to."

I mulled over the information while I sipped more tea. "Oren-yaro has a similar pact," I suddenly recalled. "It's near here. Zar...Zoran City?"

"Zorheng," Arro corrected before glancing behind him. Qun's servants stood right by the door. His face tightened. "We will not ask for help there," he said, speaking in the local Oren-yaro tongue, not the Jinan lingua franca. "You are queen of Jin-Sayeng. Never forget, Beloved Queen—"

"That I am my father's daughter and need not beg from anyone?"

That must not have been what he meant, but he lowered his eyes without arguing.

———+———

The rain didn't last long. Shortly before noon, the clouds receded behind the gabled rooftops, and the sun shone over the baked clay tiles. Something about the deep colour of the sunlight made me push open the latticed windows, allowing me to take a lungful of the rich, earthy scent of after-rain air. I relished in the warmth and forgot my troubles for a while.

I heard three knocks on the door before it opened.

My handmaiden arrived, bearing the silk dress we had brought from Oren-yaro. I had declined to bring jewels—the last thing I wanted was to lose them and bankrupt the Dragonthrone even more. She left these on the bed before accompanying me to the bathhouse. Arro may have liked to throw the word *insolence* around, but I think Deputy Qun had our best interests at heart. The bathhouse was empty on purpose. I removed my robes and stepped into the water, which rushed in from lionbeast-shaped golden spouts and was kept hot by steam funnelled from a separate building. I could see no way to control the flow, although the water remained at the same level and was just the right temperature. I lowered myself up to my ears and felt my body regain its composure.

I wondered if my handmaid noticed. I had tried to keep my fingers out of her sight—the last thing I needed was rumours of my instability, of my exhaustion from wearing the crown. It was not the rule that taxed me, but the uncertainty. My father taught me about diplomacy, just not the sort between husband and wife.

I rubbed my shoulder and tried to focus on the soothing effect of the hot water and the relief of having days' worth of stench fall off me. The handmaiden poured a small amount of oil and soap onto her palm and began to work up a lather in my hair. I stared at the bubbles. Would Rai notice if I fixed myself up for him? I still wasn't entirely sure how I wanted to react to everything. Anger would be...unbecoming for a queen, but it was the closest emotion I could muster after five years. No matter the circumstances, he owed it to me to look back that day he left. One paltry glance, given momentarily, to tell me he didn't really want to go, that he wanted me to tell him to stay.

If he had, I might've fought harder for him.

In the middle of my musings, I heard the door to the bathhouse open. I looked up, expecting to see Nor. Instead, an older woman in a robe appeared. My first instinct was to order her out, but I immediately stifled it. I was in a strange land, and the woman walked with a proud air that made me understand she was Deputy Qun's wife. Still, just in case, I dropped my right hand to grasp the hilt of my dagger, which I had kept beside me under the water. If things got hairy, I would at least have a reasonable chance of fighting my way out. Not that my rule had been this interesting, by any means—but if Oren-yaro's history was anything to go by, it was bound to happen sooner or later.

She walked past my handmaid's shocked figure and paused at the steps to the pool. "If you don't mind, Beloved Queen," she said.

I gestured, pretending that none of this bothered me. "It's your home."

She gave a wolfish smile and slid out of her robes to join me in the water. "Your guard didn't see me come in—we have more secret passages than we care to reveal. I'm not here to assassinate you, if you're curious. I just couldn't pass up the opportunity to speak with the queen of Jin-Sayeng. I'm told your Zirano is excellent."

"It is one of the languages Jin-Sayeng royals are expected to be fluent in," I said. Despite her words, I kept my hand on my dagger.

"And Kagtar?" she asked.

"We've had to since Dragonlord Reshiro Ikessar's creation of the merchant caste. A nation does not open trade to the Kag people without learning their languages. We can't expect the same courtesy out of them." I sniffed. "You've come to discuss trade with me?"

"Not particularly," Qun's wife replied. "Though it would be quite an accomplishment, wouldn't it? That Biala Chaen, a mere deputy's wife, could reopen trade between the Empire of Ziri-nar-Orxiaro and Jin-Sayeng, Land of the Dragons?"

"We don't have dragons anymore," I told her.

Biala's eyes gleamed. "I've heard otherwise."

I smiled. "You've misheard."

"Misheard? That dragons have returned to your western borders and are now—even as I speak—razing the Sougen rice fields, keeping your western lords on guard?"

"As I said, you've misheard."

She looked like she didn't believe me, but I didn't care about her opinion. My handmaid finished rinsing my hair. I gestured for my robes. "If we're done here, Lady Biala, I have an important meeting to attend. I'll have to apologize for the abruptness of our conversation."

Biala regarded me with detached coolness. Something about that unnerved me; it probably had something to do with how easily she had bypassed my guard. They had been standing *right* outside the door. "I've heard about that. You're seeing your husband, Rayyel, for the first time after his disappearance five years ago."

I clenched my jaw. "This isn't supposed to be common knowledge."

"My husband knows, so I think it's reasonable to assume..." Her eyes lit up. "Oh. I see. I *see*. That is not how you function in Jin-Sayeng?"

"I am a royal. Our duties come before our marriages."

"Loyalty to clan before anything else. I see now." She scooped a handful of water with a golden ladle and allowed it to drip over her head. "You probably wouldn't care to hear this, then."

"Hear what?"

"Anzhao City is not as indifferent to the plight of your people as the rest of the empire. Here, we listened to news of your wedding to Rayyel Ikessar with much anticipation. A story such as yours…why, many a maiden in Anzhao was starry-eyed at the idea of two people who found love despite the circumstances of their arrangement. And it's not every day that you hear about two Jin-Sayeng clans united in the same way yours were."

"Our clans were not united," I said.

"United enough, I would say. You weren't absorbed into the Ikessars, and your husband wasn't embraced by your clan. That your people allowed you to keep your title as lady of Oren-yaro *while* remaining queen of Jin-Sayeng was a bold move, and one we didn't anticipate after that ridiculous war of that father of yours. Here, a member of the noble class would've had his whole family eradicated for such treachery."

"My father did what he thought was best for Jin-Sayeng. If you are implying he was a traitor…"

"That was not my intent. I only meant that were he Zarojo, his actions wouldn't have been swept under the rug."

"Then I'm glad he was Jinsein." I pulled myself out of the bath, making sure to keep the knife hidden between my arm and my body, and stepped towards my handmaiden, who helped me into my robes. I took a towel from the rack and wiped my hands on it.

Biala drifted to the edge, stretching her arms over the stone floor. "You are not quite what I imagined you to be, Queen Talyien," she said. There was a coy look in her eyes.

I regarded her with what I hoped was a casual expression. "What do you mean by that?"

"Given what I have heard about you, I expected someone who would've put me in my place the moment I showed up in the bathhouse unexpected. Unpleasant things—a public execution, punishments involving ants…"

The ease with which she said such things didn't escape me. "Rumours you didn't believe, else you wouldn't have risked meeting me alone."

"I thought, seeing you that night you arrived…" She pressed her hands together and regarded me with the look of a cat about to pounce on its prey. "Standing there with your guard drenched in rain…"

I stared at her, waiting for what she had to say. But she simply smiled, as if that was enough. Drenched in rain, like some commoner, like an alley mongrel instead of a wolf. I wondered if I was supposed to kill her on the spot if she had said this. "You've misheard again," I said. "All you saw was irritation, masked by the glow of the dreariness you people call *pleasant weather.*"

She smiled.

We were interrupted by Captain Nor as she strode in, a letter in hand. I could tell by the look on her face from whom it came. I excused myself and walked out of the bathhouse.

"He's probably changed his mind about meeting," I said later, in the safety of my chambers. "He probably doesn't want to see me after all." I kept my words light, pretending that this wouldn't hurt if it were true. I used my thumb to scrape off the golden wax seal embossed with the shape of the soaring falcon that was the Ikessar crest. I recognized Rai's crisp handwriting immediately, penned in dark ink with a touch of red pigment. A familiar twinge of anticipation ran through me. I fought to suppress it.

Rai wrote to me a lot in the early days of our courtship. He was not particularly romantic—most of his letters read like daily reports from my staff: what he ate that evening, news from all over Jin-Sayeng, the price of rice in the common market. I can still recall the first one, word for word: *Today, I took a walk on the southern shores of the city. The rebuilding projects are going well. I am glad we made the effort to push through, after years of abandonment. Time has not been kind to the capital, but its people stand strong.*

But once in a while, a snippet of emotion would leak through. *Do not let Warlord Graiyo's words sting you. You are the Jewel of Jin-Sayeng, my future queen, and he must learn to respect that, or risk alienation from the other clans.* He was not given to strong declarations of love, but in those days, I relished his words just as much as if they came from a poet from the city of Kyo-orashi.

I stared at the third letter he had sent me in five years and felt my throat constrict. I calmed myself long enough to read through the first line. When I realized that the letter did not contain the vitriol that first one had, I was able to read the rest of it.

Nor stood beside me, waiting.

"He's changed the location of the meeting." I folded the paper, pressing at the creases with my finger. "A restaurant called the Silver Goose. I have not heard of this place."

"I believe I saw it on the way here," Nor replied. "My knowledge of Zirano writing is limited, unfortunately. I'll have someone confirm."

She walked out. I looked down at the letter and realized my fingers were shaking.

I observed the trembling digits with a measure of detachment. I found it funny how such a simple letter, devoid of emotion, could provoke such a response from me. Did I truly expect more from him? It was suddenly too difficult to ignore the truth: that I was a wife first, seeking to lay my eyes on my husband after so long. You could remove yourself from politics for a time, but when it came to matters of the heart? I was reduced to a mewling woman—to the girl who used to think her heart would explode simply because her prince glanced her way. My shaking made me feel like a weak-willed fool.

General Ozo was right. Some queen I was.

CHAPTER THREE

ANZHAO CITY, MARVEL OF THE WESTERN EMPIRE

ᒍᚠᗢᵞ

I was subdued for the rest of my preparations that afternoon. Biala's words carried a distinct message: the people of Ziri-nar-Orxiaro did not take Jin-Sayeng authority seriously. At the very least, they didn't find much in the idea of *me* as the figurehead.

I stared at myself in the mirror while my handmaid pleated my hair, brushed and oiled for the meeting. I had hoped that maybe, here in the Zarojo Empire, they would respond to my reputation in the same way the Jinseins did. That I could go in and out of this meeting with as little fuss as possible. It revealed clear naivety on my part: far from respecting me, the Zarojo found me *amusing*.

It was appalling enough that if my father had a grave, I would have *heard* him rolling in it. He could at least start clawing at the walls of his urn.

It also made me wonder how they saw Rayyel. Deputy Qun's choice of words made it clear this Governor Zheshan not only accepted Rai's claims of a pact but welcomed him into his household with open arms. I found it hard to believe that Rai used his charm to pull off such a feat—the man was about as charismatic as the bottom of a chamber pot. There were other forces at work here, ones that saw Rai as the true leader of Jin-Sayeng instead of his ferocious queen. Did he see it? Did he care? Rai had never been the ambitious sort.

My handmaid finished with her work. I donned my dress, which I promptly hid under an inconspicuous grey cloak. I imagined I looked as elegant as a sack of rice. I left the bedchamber and met Nor in the hallway. She gave me an approving glance. "We've mapped out this restaurant—Magister Arro is on his way as we speak. The guards are staggered along the road. Only I will accompany you closely if we're to maintain our disguise. Does this suit you, my queen?"

I nodded. We stepped out into the grounds, past the curious eyes of Deputy Qun's servants. Past his gardens, which were better kept than the one in my palace, with their long rows of cherry trees in pink and white blossoms. A small gust sent a flurry cascading around us like snow-fall. I quite liked the effect, but I wasn't sure if I had the patience to create such an addition for Oka Shto. "Leave the gardening to the Ikessars," I liked to tell the warlords when they commented on the wild nature of the surrounding land. "We Oren-yaro have better things to do."

The abandoned keep down at Old Oren-yaro didn't even have a garden. The Oren-yaro tended to prefer utility and function over aesthetics, and the old keep was nothing more than an outcrop of buildings and warehouses and a temple behind walls. My father only had the garden in Oka Shto built after extreme pressure by his advisers, who told him he needed a more presentable image if his claim to the throne would be recognized. There was more to being a leader than cutting down enemies: if one wanted to challenge the Ikessars, one needed to show the people that one could be cultured, elegant, and sophisticated. So he had the garden built, with a giant fishpond in the middle and jasmine, hibiscus, and frangipani flowers everywhere—local Jin-Sayeng flora and fauna, nothing imported. He liked the scent of jasmine, he told me once—it reminded him of his mother.

But that was it. After Rai's departure, I allowed the garden to become overgrown, and by now all the fish had probably eaten each other. I could be harbouring crocodiles for all I knew. The reality of ruling is complex, made even more so when you have a nation like mine, with empty coffers and people who hate each other behind polite words and empty smiles.

"How rich is this empire, really?" I asked, flicking a petal off my shoulder as I walked.

Nor looked up. "You were asking me, Beloved Queen?"

I nodded towards Arro and the guards, who were walking some distance ahead. "You're the only one within earshot."

She seemed completely unaffected by my candour. "I have not had the chance to educate myself on the numbers..." she began.

I gestured at the garden. "I was not asking for the exact figure. It's just that if a mere *deputy*—an elected government official, yes?—can afford all this, while my father had to run himself bankrupt to get our garden built..."

I deliberately trailed off to let her pick up the slack. But she didn't respond, her thick eyebrows drawn together in what appeared to be a permanent furrow.

"I would appreciate your thoughts on this," I urged.

Her jaw slackened. "My Beloved Queen is wise. You will best know the answer to your question."

"But your opinion..."

"Shall I call Magister Arro? He is best qualified to advise you."

"I think I can guess at what he'd say," I said. And then, because I was my father's daughter, I tried again. "How did your husband react to news of this trip?"

"Beloved Queen, it is my duty to go where the Dragonthrone demands it. Do you have any particular concerns I can address?"

"No matter." I saw her shoulders drop as she visibly relaxed. I wondered what it was about my questions that made them difficult to answer. I wasn't looking for an enlightening conversation—a mere acknowledgment would've sufficed.

Maybe it was me.

Rai once told me—during an argument, I think, though I can't quite recall the details—that I was too blunt. Which was an amazing observation, really, coming from the man who rewrote the rules on bluntness. The systematic breaking down of people's temperaments and how they could be used was one of the few traits Rai and I had in common. As I was born princess and last heir of the Orenar clan, so was he prince and heir of the Ikessars. Together, we tried to navigate the social awkwardness of our positions, of the customs and behaviours of the people around us. He was a scholar and always considered himself a little better than me, having studied many books on the subject; for my part, I thought he was severely delusional. If people found me blunt, then Rayyel aren dar Ikessar was an Akaterru-damned brick wall.

But not long after, I found myself echoing his words to a friend. I asked him how I could make myself less abrasive. "Speak your thoughts less often," he suggested. Easier said than done, I told him. If I didn't speak my thoughts at all, what was there to say?

"Nice weather," I blurted out.

Nor looked at me and then up at the sky. "Grey," she finally commented.

"Which reminds me, Captain," I said. "My handmaid—what's her name?"

"Has she done something wrong, Beloved Queen?"

"No—nothing like that," I said. "I just thought, since there's only so few of us in a strange nation, that I might as well get to know everyone."

She blanched. "All the guards, too?"

I resisted the urge to sigh out loud. "Start with the handmaid. She's been under my employ for several years now, hasn't she? She usually brought my meals."

"Kora, Beloved Queen. *Aset gar* Angjar. Priest caste. I believe she was deemed the safest candidate for this trip. I can request a report on her background and have it sent to you if you wish, though it might have to wait until we get home."

"I... that won't be necessary, Captain."

"We can't be too certain anymore. The guard I had assigned to you early this morning is still missing."

"I hope nothing bad has happened to him."

"I don't know what's worse—if he's gotten into trouble or he decided to abandon his duties. Shameful, for an Oren-yaro. Be on guard, Beloved Queen. I don't trust this country, I don't trust its people. They look at us and sneer. You would think we were nothing but animals."

Anzhao City was a port city at the western edge of the empire, a hub for trade with ships coming in from as far as Gaspar and Dageis. It was a long way from being the biggest city, a fact I found difficult to believe while walking through its bustling cobblestone streets, which teemed with vendors. They sold everything from pottery to clockwork dolls to rice coffee toasted in earthenware pots and sweetened with honeyed milk. There was food of all sorts: sweet cakes with mung beans and egg filling, fried pork dumplings drizzled with plum sauce, and barbecued eels, served with pickles over a bed of hot rice. The smell made my stomach tighten. Breakfast had been hours ago. But I wasn't about to risk getting my dress dirty and willed my hunger to go away.

I forced my attention to a different sort of hunger beginning to build inside me: a child's desperate longing for something she could never have.

The feeling started at the first sight of the drainage canals when we turned at a street corner, right after nearly getting run over by a harassed-looking rickshaw driver. They were running full after the noontime rains, but what I found fascinating was the shadow of a carp, easily the length of my arm, swimming along the bottom. It stirred the clear water with each effortless sweep of its strong tail. I paused at the edge of the street and noticed other fish of all shapes and sizes: orange fish with black stripes, black fish with enormous mouths and spiny tails that hung like icicles from the sides. There was even a ray with brown and purple spots drifting under the carp.

"These gutters don't drain fully," I said. "Not like back home. And there's no... there's no garbage. How is it that there's no garbage, Nor?"

"I would assume that's because people don't make it."

"Everyone makes garbage."

"They don't litter, then."

"But that's... how do you stop them from doing that?"

Nor cleared her throat. "General Ozo insists we need to cut a few hands off first, to make an example. Perhaps we can ask their officials, my queen."

Not far from us, a group of gangly boys were trying to catch the carp with makeshift nets. One boy, dressed in loose trousers and a light vest that showed off most of his tanned skin, decided to jump in, spear in hand. Raucous laughter followed.

The canals grew even wider as we continued down the street, broad enough to hold boats. Here, houses built right at the edge of the canal had balconies overlooking the green-tinged water. Behind rails of wrought iron, a lady sprawled on a comfortable chair, her servants hovering over her with trays of delicacies and giant paper fans. On another balcony, two lovers sat with their arms wrapped around each other. A man stand-ing on a barge, drawn by a pair of six-horned, oxen-like beasts the Zarojo called the *rok haize*, whistled to them, and the lovers waved back.

Signs of Anzhao City's prosperity went beyond the canals. The tall, stately buildings, with the same red clay rooftops as Qun's house, were well maintained, showing only signs of natural aging and the pleas-ant growth of moss. Not a single broken window or bent rail. There were street lamps, bearing banners in bright colours of red and green. I struggled to read the Zirano script, which bore only a slight resemblance to Jinan, and was able to gather something about a festival of lights three days from now. There was also the mention of a contest.

Envy was not an emotion I was prepared to experience during that trip. Neither was anger, the sort that had nowhere to go, that lingered deep inside my bones. I have been told, more times than I care to remem-ber, that Jin-Sayeng used to be a prosperous nation. Jin-Sayeng, they say, shone like pearls, its cities wonders of the world. She used to be so beauti-ful that other nations envied *her* instead. They stood in line to worship her, to admire her, to try to conquer her. If Jin-Sayeng would ever return to such grandeur, I needed to be her backbone. I needed to show the people I had the strength to unite her once and for all. And I had to start with my husband.

A child came up, interrupting my train of thought. He was shaggy-haired, ruddy-faced, and filthy only as a child who played outside all day could get. Even though he had chubby arms and looked well fed, my hand moved to my purse by instinct, but the only thing he did was look up at me with twinkling eyes and say, "You're not from here."

"I'm not," I said. "I'm from Jin-Sayeng."

His eyes widened. I expected an insult. He reached out to touch my arm, unaware that such an action might've cost him his head, and drew back, delighted. "I touched a Jin-Sayeng princess," he said, giggling as he returned to his playmates. I thought of my son, with his own bright eyes and that silly smile he reserved only for me, and felt homesick.

"Wild beasts don't have princesses," someone called. A scholar, books in his arms, stopped in front of me. His face contorted. Before I could react, he spat.

Spittle landed on my shoulder. One of my guards grabbed him by the arm, forcing him to drop his books.

"I'll call the city watch," the scholar hissed. "They ought to know there's Jins walking around in broad daylight. They…"

"Fucking *Xiarans*," my guard replied, using the derogatory term for the Zarojo people, the way *Jin* was for us. "You're half a century too late, old man. Do you know who you just insulted?"

"Let him go," Nor ordered.

The man blanched. "But Captain…"

"Let him go. We're not here to cause trouble."

The guard pushed the scholar to the side. "Count yourself lucky you're not in Jin-Sayeng, or your head would be in the river by now."

The scholar grabbed his books and scurried away.

"So much for maintaining our disguise," I grumbled. My guards dropped their heads in a bow.

"Our apologies," one guard murmured. But he didn't look apologetic at all. He looked like he enjoyed it. Was this how we were going to present ourselves in the meeting? Listen, or your heads will fly?

I remembered when I killed a warlord's messenger right before a summit, one that had gone like so many others before: warlords insulting one another, worrying about whose rump actually deserved to sit on the throne, or whether the worship of a different deity invalidated one's own beliefs. Over half the warlords didn't attend, because I had failed to address them by the decorative titles my father had doled out like candy after his war: Minister of Horses, Master of Archery, Commissioner of Arts.

The messenger had demanded the same thing—that I learn to show my respects. He elaborated on the slight his master felt, before proceeding towards the insults, things that should never be said to a queen. So I couldn't allow it. I killed him with my blade and told the crowd I had always wanted to use Secretary of the Dung Heap. No one seemed amused. I couldn't tell if the execution made the impact it should have. General Ozo later sent his various body parts to the absentees with a message that strongly implied more to come. The next meeting, not counting Rai, had full attendance.

If I did not have their friendship, I at least had their fear.

We reached the far end of the canal, where I noticed a crowd gathered in a small square. People were throwing angry glances and harsh whispers at each other. A couple of young workers, evident by the dust and sweat on their shirtless bodies, ran past me, chattering excitedly. I caught the word *prisoner* and found myself looking around in interest.

On a raised platform overlooking the canal, I caught sight of a handful of guards clad in the imperial regiment uniform: bronze-plated armour inlaid with a pattern signifying the rolling sea—both the colour and the pattern symbols of the Zarojo Empire's dominance in the continent of Lier. Rounded pouldrons that resembled horned-turtle shells, and elaborate helmets with a tuft of horsehair plume, dyed red, completed the regalia. They carried glaives with hooked ends, the handles of which were wrapped in what appeared to be alternating strips of leather and silk.

The guards were gathered around a man bound to a wooden post. The man's face was stricken with filth and tears, his clothes little more than strips. Bleeding gashes adorned his body. He looked like he had gone running through a field of thorns.

A long, drawn-out wail from the crowd caught my attention. A woman rushed towards the platform, weeping as she attempted to climb it. A guard grabbed her.

"My husband!" she blubbered.

The prisoner didn't respond.

The city official, marked by the colour of his robes and the same square hat that Qun wore, didn't even look up from the scroll he was reading. He adjusted the clasp of his hat around his braided beard and cleared his throat before continuing. "For allowing his associates to murder one of his master's housemaids, a cut on the right arm."

A guard, standing over the prisoner with sword drawn, obliged. The prisoner gave a strangled cry. I could smell the blood in the air, mixed with the scent of the sweat of the surrounding people.

"For wielding the sword that killed his master's stableman, a cut on the cheek."

The sword gleamed before it struck him again.

The woman gave a shrill cry as she heaved herself over the platform. The guard pulled her back.

"He doesn't have a wife," somebody in the crowd murmured.

"For raping his master's daughter..."

I didn't catch the rest of his words, but I heard a prayer, uttered repeatedly, like a chant. When the guard stepped away, the prisoner's ear had been ripped off. Blood was pouring from the side of his head like a waterfall.

I glanced at the stricken faces around me. It was clear why my sudden arrival in the streets of Anzhao City did not shake the officials one bit. Instead of running for the hills at the mention of my name, they shooed my guards; one even laughed in Nor's face, showing no embarrassment at flashing his smelly yellow teeth at the captain of the Queen's Guard. The household who did eventually take us in did it out of pity. Why would they find any reason to be impressed with my reputation when they were capable of just as much horror, if not more?

I didn't catch the official's next words, but this crime warranted the man's other ear. I stared, unblinking. It wasn't the sight of the blood that affected me. It was the anguish on the man's face, the look in his eyes, as if he was expecting the gods to intervene on his behalf at any moment.

"My queen," Nor whispered.

"The horse thief," I started. "The one who tried to steal my stallion a few years ago."

I saw her eyes flicker as she recalled. "He was caught red-handed, my queen. He deserved it. The practice of *t'che* is not for the offender's comfort. The purpose is twofold. First, it provides justice to the offended, that they may retain faith that the higher authorities have their best interests at heart. Second, it creates a warning to the people: stray, and you, too, will meet the same fate." Her eyes hardened. "We Jinseins picked up the practice from the Zarojo. The Ikessars had it abolished when they came into power, as such harshness offends their Kibouri philosophy and their Nameless God, but your father knew what he was doing when he reinstated it. Our people needed it, then. They still do."

She glanced away, and I felt a flush of shame over having brought it up in the first place. I was Yeshin the Butcher's daughter—why would the torture of a man concern me? General Ozo would probably have an answer, the sort that would deface my character and accuse me of being unworthy of my father's name. I resolved to keep my mouth shut.

I could no longer hear the man screaming, meaning he either had passed out or was dead. But the official was still speaking to the crowd, still laying out the man's sins. Nor took a deep breath. "If it makes you feel any better, my queen," she murmured, as if uttering words she didn't want anyone else to hear, "we killed the horse thief before we flayed him with our swords. He was not alive when this happened."

I had heard otherwise; I had heard that the man called out to the skies for justice, for the Jinseins' lost honour, the way the one I killed in my garden had cried for his mother. But it didn't matter. It shouldn't. I didn't want to prove Ozo right. I tore myself away from these thoughts and turned back to the scene before me. The prisoner was slumped on the ground in a pool of blood. The woman was still screaming. She threw herself at the guard, hysterical, and managed to remove his helmet. It clattered along the ground, disappearing into the crowd.

The guard tried to grab his helmet, the woman clinging desperately to him like a monkey. I heard someone call out that the prisoner—the dead prisoner, now—was innocent. The voice stood out against the accusations, an outcry in the dark. The desperation in it made my skin crawl.

Chaos erupted.

My guards reacted like Kag sheepdogs confronted by an unruly herd. Panicked people began to push back, weaving through the ones frozen in fear or shock or whatever it was that kept them rooted to the spot. I tried to turn to Nor, but before I could even catch a glimpse of the surroundings beyond the sea of bodies, the sky turned black for a moment.

I saw the Zarojo guards grappling with someone near the mangled corpse—I couldn't tell if it was the woman or someone new, but there was a sudden flash of blue. Cries of "Mage!" and "Blood magic!" ran through the air. I remembered Arro's words about the forbidden arts and backed away. I couldn't get involved in this.

"Captain Nor!" I called out. I couldn't see her anywhere.

"Beloved Queen!" she roared back. Somehow, the crowd had pushed her to the furthest end of the square. I could see her attempting to draw her sword, but she didn't have enough room. A fight broke out next to her, and she shoved a man out of the way. She hissed something, an order or a command that got drowned out. My eyes sought the other guards. I could count two, both too far away for me to reach. Why just two? Where were the others? I quickly lost sight of them as the sky flashed a second time.

I heard a voice at my ear, speaking in Jinan. "To the alley, Beloved Queen."

Taking it for one of the guards, I stumbled after him through the narrow gap between two buildings. The screaming behind us grew in intensity, followed by the smell of what could only be burning flesh; I began to run, nearly stepping over a dead body on the way.

Everything became a blur. The clatter of my boots on hard stone. The wind rushing through my ears. The acrid scent of the alley, of urine and dead things, a far cry from the Anzhao City I had envied less than an hour ago. Silence.

The silence told me to stop, whispered that I must have taken a wrong turn. Why didn't I look at where my guard was pointing before I took off? I turned around, heart pounding. I hadn't thought to take note of my surroundings, of the paths I had taken, because I had assumed the rest of my guard were behind me.

But there was nobody. I heard a rustle. "Nor?" I called out tentatively, but it was only a cat, jumping from the roof onto a pile of crates. It hissed and scampered away as soon as it saw me.

Someone grabbed my arm.

I was so disoriented that I almost didn't acknowledge what was happening at first. I stared at my assailant. It was a man with features that could've been either Zarojo or Jinsein in the shadows. That was as far as my appraisal went. My other hand found the dagger in my belt and I wrenched it up, catching him in the rib. The tip of it struck bone.

That I attacked at all must've been enough to shock him. I doubt he even noticed the wound, and I wasn't about to stay there long enough to watch him find out. I pulled the dagger back. My fist caught his jaw, and I fled down the alley.

I didn't hear any other pursuers, but I didn't trust my senses and kept running, darting around the tight corners and maze-like turns until it felt like my lungs wanted to collapse. As I exited into yet another street, a man, pulling out rugs to dry, paused to stare at me. Somehow, in my journey through the narrow alleyways and gutters, I had reached an entirely different part of the city.

If my attacker had friends, would they dare try something out in the open?

The panic left. I began shaking again and was glad Ozo wasn't around to see. I looked around and realized that I was in a part of Anzhao City that both Nor and Arro would have found unacceptable. Here, the buildings were crowded together, the alleys in between so narrow a body couldn't walk through them without hitting the walls on either side. Clothes lines hung from one balcony to the next. I could now see the broken windows with bent bars, cracked doors that didn't quite fit in their doorways, and loose roof tiles. The gutters overflowed with greenish water teeming with slugs and black, slime-covered lumps of garbage and human waste.

Revulsion stirred in the back of my throat. I bit it back; it wasn't the first time I had been in such squalor. I wasn't the sort of pampered royalty like the Zarojo princesses I've read about. Jin-Sayeng had known too much war and strife in all these years, and I've seen what these have reduced some of my cities to. In parts of the capital, you couldn't even walk through without a handkerchief pressed over your nose. But it was, I realized, the first time I had found myself alone in such surroundings.

It was the first time I had ever found myself alone.

CHAPTER FOUR

THE CON ARTIST AND
THE QUEEN

 $\vec{\omega}\hat{\omega}\tau\bar{x}\tau$

I almost wished that my enemy would catch up to me. My father had made sure I was trained to fight, and fighting—even when up against a big man like that—was something I could reasonably control. *Lost and alone* was different, wasn't something I knew how to deal with.

But I had to try. I swallowed and found myself approaching the man, the one with the rugs. His attention was still fixed on me. "I need to know the way to the Silver Goose," I said. "Could you show me?"

The man gaped. I wondered if he was deaf. It couldn't be that I had misspoken some words, could it? My Zirano, as Qun's wife had indicated, was excellent. I may have exasperated my tutors at times, but I had done well by them. "I said..." I started.

The man shrank back and quickly disappeared into his house. I stared at the creaking door, feeling slightly awkward at the turn of events. I wasn't sure if he was planning to come back or was hiding from me. Blatant rudeness was not something I knew how to deal with, either. I turned around and noticed another person. "You," I said. "Maybe you know the way to the Silver Goose?"

Something about my voice stopped the woman in her tracks. "What's that?" she finally blurted out.

"The Silver Goose. It's supposed to be a restaurant. I got separated from my . . . group."

There *was* something odd about how I was saying things. I could tell from the way she stared at me while I talked. I wondered if they spoke a different dialect in these parts. It didn't seem like it—I had understood the official's proclamations back in the square easily enough, and I couldn't have travelled that far.

"It sounds like a restaurant," the woman said.

"Yes," I replied patiently, resisting the urge to press my fingers over my temples. "Like I said. If you could show me the way—"

"There's probably five of that name in the city alone. Which one did you want?"

My knees grew weary. I should've asked for more details, but I had been so used to my guards and advisers taking care of everything for me that I had long ceased to pay attention to such things. "The nearest one," I said. It couldn't have been too far if Nor had found walking acceptable. She would've rented a carriage otherwise.

The woman pressed her lips together before breaking out into a grin. There was a gap in her teeth. "Fifty *rean*," she said, holding a hand out. "Fifty *rean* and I'll take you there."

To the queen of Jin-Sayeng, it was not a lot of money, but under those circumstances, it seemed like extortion. My insides balked at the idea that she would even dare ask. "I can find someone else," I said, my ears burning.

"Your loss," she chortled as I walked past her.

Mine? How could it be mine? I resolutely strode down the street, hoping to catch another eye. Surely there would be a kind soul somewhere who would offer to guide me to my destination for free.

I spent time—long enough that my throat began to burn from thirst and my hands itched from the dust—asking each person I encountered. Each reacted almost the same as the first two: they either outright ignored me or asked for money first. Both responses were confounding every time I encountered them. I told myself I would find a way to spin the conversation in my favour, but it seemed that I never responded fast enough. People might not think much of the Oren-yaro's penchant for ruthlessness, but I was taught never to turn my back on someone who genuinely needed help. Taking advantage of their situation was unthinkable.

I looked around. I had reached another intersection. Along the row of residences, I caught sight of a sign for what appeared to be a shop. Perhaps my mistake was in approaching people who weren't pillars of society in some way. A shopkeeper would be different. A shopkeeper would know things, be obliged to help.

I pressed my hand along the carved door and pushed. Little bells jingled overhead as the smell of dried herbs hit me like an over-enthusiastic dog. Boxes of them, along with jars of pickled meat and fruit, were stacked on shelves on one side of the wall. There were also various trinkets: children's toys, paper fans, amulets, tasselled mirrors, and clear vases with bamboo plants, some of which also contained small red crayfish.

"Good day," I said, tearing my eyes away from the assault on my senses. The proprietor regarded me with a dubious expression. I think he was taking in my flushed face and dirty clothes. I tried to ignore the feeling of having to justify my presence, let alone my entire existence. "I was wondering if you could assist me in joining my group. I was lost after a riot at the square."

"Does this assistance involve you buying anything from my shop?" he asked. He was a heavyset man, with a shaved head and eyes that seemed to want to pop out of their sockets.

I wasn't sure if it was his expression, the scent of his shop, or his words that made me feel ill. I had to pause to catch my breath and think about my next words. I managed to grumble, "How about just helping me?" in an exasperated tone.

"Pick anything," he said. "And I'll see what I can do."

"I just need to make my way to the Silver Goose. Even if you just gave me the directions." *Some water wouldn't hurt, either.* But I kept that last thought to myself—I was starting to suspect that these people would be just as possessive of their water as their goodwill.

The shopkeeper pointed at his wares. "One item. Or you can get out of my store and find someone else to entertain you."

"Do you even know who you're talking to?" I asked, my voice rising.

"Someone without any money, for sure. Buy something, or I'll call the city watch."

I turned away in disgust. In my hurry to get out of there, I nearly bumped into another man in the shop. I hadn't noticed him when he came in. He looked at me but didn't say anything. I felt like begging; the feeling did not sit well with me. I rushed out before I could give in and do something I would regret.

I walked as fast as I could from the shop, crossing the street to a small fountain surrounded by four street lamps. I gathered my courage and reached down to touch the water. The trickle was invigorating, and to my great relief, the water itself did not smell of urine. I washed my face. The cold water on my skin made my dry mouth itch, and I found myself swallowing. The sensation felt like sharp nails digging into my throat. I caved in, taking a handful to sip. I had gone from having my food tested in the morning to drinking from a public waterway in the afternoon.

I heard a footstep. My hand went to the dagger on my belt as I turned. A man stopped, hands held out in a gesture of appeasement. I recognized the customer from the store. "You followed me," I said.

"I did," he admitted. He had a deep voice, but it was also soft, with a timbre that rumbled slightly after he paused. Something about it made me relax my grip on the dagger, although I still kept my hand on the hilt. He noticed the movement, because he glanced down and smiled. "I should tell you that walking around with a weapon is...frowned upon here. Not exactly illegal, but the city watch will use just about any excuse to extort money from you."

"Do I look like I care?"

He pointed at the fountain. "That also isn't very sanitary."

I wiped my chin and tried to gather what remained of my dignity. "What do you want?"

"I think I should be asking you that. You need help, and I can offer it to you. In exchange..."

"Right," I said. "Always with the catch."

"I am not quite as barefaced as our friend the shopkeep. I merely need your assistance. Help me, and I'll bring you to the Silver Goose. The one with the dancers, am I correct? Roast pork that falls off the bone?"

"Help you with what?"

"I'll have to explain."

"No, thank you." I didn't want to spend another moment with these detestable *Xiarans*. I got up and walked away from him.

I had been lost before, in Shirrokaru.

Shirrokaru was the capital of Jin-Sayeng and had been since our people first proclaimed an Ikessar as Dragonlord, protector and defender of all, king in all but name. It was unique in that most of it was built after the Ikessars—whose ancestral lands were further east, in the mountains north of Darusu—were granted the throne. Before the Ikessars took over, it was a small town of no consequence, a hub of trade for the farmers of that region and the Gasparians near the border that sprouted along the shores of Lake Watu. The warlords contributed to the building of the palace at the northern end of the lake and helped fund the industries that would later propel Shirrokaru to growth.

Shirrokaru stood as a promise to the people of Jin-Sayeng, of peace and prosperity that was supposed to come as a result of the warlords dropping their quarrels against each other. It had, in those days, been a profound idea. The Ikessars were the ideal clan to rule—their leaders were charismatic and their scholars full of strange and exciting plans for the future. Furthermore, they lacked a proper army, which eased the warlords' hearts; it made it unlikely that this new ruling clan would try to wrest them from their own lands.

The day I got lost in the city had been my first time visiting it. My friend and I got it into our heads to view one of the pits they used to train dragons in. I had heard there was one near the southern shore of Lake Watu and begged him to accompany me.

We found the pit easy enough, after a boat ride off the palace district and a long walk from the southern guardhouse to an abandoned residential area. Years ago, a mad dragon unleashed by Dragonlord Reshiro's son, Rysaran the Uncrowned, had burned the buildings down. Shirrokaru had never been able to afford to fully rebuild it—the Ikessars lacked the funds and the warlords refused to assist, especially when Rysaran the Uncrowned disappeared after the incident. Huge sections remained empty, untouched.

It was the broken-down houses that ultimately held my attention, not the pit—which ended up just being a deep, rectangular hole filled with rusted chains and old animal bones. You could tell so much about the state of a land's rule by how easily such disarray could be swept under the rug. People blamed my father for throwing the land into chaos, but my father had started a civil war precisely because *nothing* was getting done.

My friend came up to tell me he couldn't figure out how we were supposed to get back to the southern docks. You couldn't see the lake from the distance, and unlike in Oren-yaro, Shirrokaru lacked distinct mountains that would've made navigation easier. My first instinct was to panic, but my friend's presence had always been such a comfort that I simply turned to him and said, "What do we do next?"

He told me to stay put while he climbed one of the buildings to find the lake. It took us some time to find one that was tall enough for such an undertaking—most of the buildings were in ruins. Even though it was getting darker, my friend took the whole situation almost matter-of-factly. Later, I would ask him if he was frightened at all, and he told me, "You learn to swallow the fear long enough to get things done. We're Oren-yaro, aren't we?"

If he had been with me in Anzhao City, I think things would never have gone this far. But he wasn't—he had been gone from my life for many years now—and there I was, walking briskly down an unknown street while a stranger went chasing after me. *Swallow the fear.* I stopped.

"What *is* your problem?" I said, turning to the stranger.

The man slowed down, a sheepish grin on his face. The grin stood out—it was one-sided, the look of a man who knew he was up to no good but couldn't be damned to do better. Without a word, he held up a purse. I immediately recognized the green-and-gold-patterned fabric.

"I couldn't have dropped that," I said, allowing the accusation to swathe my tone.

He nodded, throwing it at me. I caught it in mid-air. "It's empty," he said.

I coloured. "I know," I grumbled. I turned back to him. "But you tried to *steal* from me."

"Forget that little detail," he continued. "It's *empty*. No wonder you couldn't fulfill our dear shopkeep's selfish little request. Do you know how far you'll get in Anzhao City without both money *and* friends?"

"Not very, I'm guessing." I sighed.

He laughed. "At least you're honest about your predicament."

"So this is the Zarojo way. What ever happened to just doing the right thing?"

The man sauntered about to me. "The problem with that kind of thinking is that it allows people to take advantage of you. Anzhao has its fair share of con artists and thieves. You came into that store asking for help, but left when it was asked from you in return. The man wasn't taking your money for nothing—he wanted you to buy something. The shop *is* his livelihood. I'm sure he has half a dozen squalling children to feed. What if you weren't really some damsel in distress? The more likely scenario is that you're a vixen in disguise, trying to drag him to some unsuspecting street corner where your bandit friends could jump him."

I opened and closed my mouth, unsure of how to reply to this speech. I wasn't even sure he *wanted* me to reply, although I caught a glint in his eye that told me he might very well enjoy arguing his case if I did. "You're one to say that," I eventually said, "when you're a thief yourself."

"*And* a con artist," he said with a grin. "And I had you pegged for one, too, with your strange manner of speaking and the whole *don't you know who you're talking to* routine. One of the oldest tricks in the book: make them think you're someone important so they get swept up in not wanting to offend you. And then I caught you drinking from that fountain, and..."

I almost threw the empty purse at his face. "And then what?" I retorted hotly.

He scratched the side of his cheek. "And it occurred to me that Jinsein accent is real enough. Maybe you really are just a lost tourist—I don't know."

I took a deep breath, trying hard not to show how offended I was by his words. "If you bring me back to my people, I'll make it worth your while."

He shook his head. "See, a part of me can't seem to believe that. How do I know you're telling the truth?"

"Because I am! Isn't that enough?"

"This is what I'm trying to tell you. What if you *are* a con artist, and you just happened to be dying of thirst right now? What if you're from some other part of the city where they didn't piss in their fountains?" He smiled before handing me a waterskin. "Go on," he said. "I filled it up from a fresh spring this morning."

I hesitated, but my thirst won. I grabbed the waterskin and unscrewed the lid. The water was tepid, but it quenched my parched throat all the same. I returned the waterskin and found that I could think a little clearer now. "I take this to mean that you're still not going to help me."

"I didn't say I wouldn't. I just said I didn't know if I could trust *you*, too. Even if you say otherwise, everything about you is just—it's too strange. Look at your clothes."

I looked down. The dress underneath my cloak was streaked with dirt, but you could still tell it wasn't some peasant's.

"And the way you talk," he continued. "Who *talks* like that? You were neglecting your honorifics when you were speaking with the shopkeep. Why would someone who could speak Zirano so well deliberately ignore them? Either you really didn't *think* you needed them, or you were setting him up to make yourself stand out. Either way..."

"I think I understand you," I said. I also thought I wanted to hit him in the face, but not everybody appreciated knowing that.

"People need to know you're genuine before they waste their time. The Silver Goose is a good walk from here, and I still have unfinished business with our friend. Assist me, and you'll find that I'm a man of my word."

"A self-confessed con artist," I said.

He smirked. "Yes." He carried the smugness of one who knew I had no other choice.

I sighed. "Even though I feel like I'm going to regret this—very well. Tell me what you need."

"It's easy," he said, crossing his arms and walking around me. He paused for a moment to pat some dirt off my shoulder. "I just need you to return to the shop and confront our dear friend. We are, by the way, going to call him the *mark* from this point on."

"Wait." I held up my hand. "You want me to help you *con* him?" I couldn't contain the note of outrage in my voice.

"Yes," he continued cheerfully. "Please pay attention."

"Was that why you were in his store in the first place?"

He pressed his lips together and ignored my question. "He also runs a pawnshop. When you go back in there, you are going to show him your empty purse and admit the truth to him—you didn't have money, but you were too proud to say so. And then you are going to beg him to take this instead." He placed something in my palm.

I held it up against the light. It was a solid gold ring with a single gem in the middle. "This isn't fake, is it?" I asked.

"You know your jewelleries well. No, it isn't. It's real enough—crafted in the village of Anjishing, near the base of the red cliffs. Don't worry. You'll feel less awful about this plan when I explain the rest of it to you."

CHAPTER FIVE

THE RUSE

ย ร ย ว่

The Jinsein and the Zarojo share one thing in common: you can't really tell our ethnicity from looks alone.

There had been too many marriages between our people over the years. This man, the con artist, could've passed for a native Akkian—long-limbed, with sun-touched skin a shade darker than my own. But he also had narrow eyes that became thin lines when he laughed, the hallmark of a typical eastern Jinsein from a royal clan and a number of the Zarojo I have met. Despite the alarms that triggered in my head about what I knew of him so far—everything painted him as scum from the bottom rungs of Zarojo society—it was difficult not to notice how bright his face appeared when he smirked. I knew men who did it to deride, or for effect; he seemed to do it because he genuinely found something amusing. The contrast was confounding.

He was tall—almost half a head taller than me, and I am not a short woman, by any means. He also had the shadow of a beard, most prominent around his square jaw but creeping slightly up his cheeks, like he couldn't quite decide if he wanted to be clean-shaven or grow it out. His clothes were clean but plain. *That* made sense. If he was going to commit a crime, he would want to be harder to describe.

I suddenly realized that I was about to commit a crime, too. The thought made me ill.

"Another strange thing about you: you haven't asked me my name yet," he said as we sauntered past the damned fountain.

"I didn't see the need for it," I countered.

He stopped, rubbing the back of his head. He seemed to be thinking my words over. After a moment, he made a decision. "I'm Khine," he said.

I nodded. "Hello, Khine. I hope that's a fake name."

"I see what you're doing." He glanced around. "I don't think anyone can see us now, but I'll let you go on your way." He tipped his head towards me and drew back, turning at the next street corner and leaving me with nothing but my beating heart for company.

I turned in the opposite direction.

The dark street leading back to the shop felt like it went on forever. I found myself wondering whether Nor and the rest of my guard were busy looking for me, and getting angry that they hadn't found me yet. Even after Khine explained the particulars of our little ruse, I still wasn't sure what I felt about it. I knew I should just probably save myself the trouble and go straight to the city watch. They might bring me to the Silver Goose—if they believed me. After the last couple of hours, I was starting to doubt they would. Chances were good I would find myself in prison before the night was over, and the last thing I needed was news of my presence exploding throughout the empire.

I didn't realize how easily fear could drive you to desperation, to do things you would've never thought you were capable of. In the next instant, I was at those doors again, pushing them open, bells spinning overhead. The shopkeep, the *mark*, looked up. It was too late to back out.

"I don't have money," I announced.

He leaned on the counter, waiting to see what else I had to say.

I shuffled towards him, wiping sweat from my face. I took the purse and opened it, showing him. A puff of dust exploding from it in the sunlight compounded the effect. "I used it all up. Gambling at Monkey Hands down by the square. I'm supposed to meet my husband at that restaurant tonight, and he'd beat me senseless if he knew what I'd been doing all day."

I saw his eyebrows twitch at my story.

I placed the ring on the counter. "Please. A man out on the street told me you were also a pawnshop, so I came all the way back here for your help. That's my father's. I could never dream of parting with it, but I... I can't miss this dinner. I don't want to have to explain *why* I missed it. Especially after I dressed up so nicely for him."

"Should've thought of that before you went gambling," the shopkeep said, but it was clear that he was already intrigued. He sidled over to take a closer look at the ring.

I wrung my hands together. "I get bored at home alone. I didn't notice the time."

"You don't have children?"

I made a sound in the back of my throat. "I detest children."

The shopkeep grunted. "You shouldn't say such ill things. A child or two will keep you out of trouble, save you from your husband's hand more often."

I noticed him staring at my face. I remembered my assailant in the alley—the struggle must've left a bruise. I had wondered why it felt so swollen. I allowed myself to touch it self-consciously. "It's... it's none of your business. Will you give me money for that or not?"

"A hundred *rean*," he said. "With twenty *rean* interest if paid by tomorrow evening. Fifty *rean* if it takes until the end of the week."

"Highway robbery," I said. "Even if that wasn't a valuable heirloom, it should still give me five hundred, at least!"

"You just need the money to get to your husband tonight, don't you?" he asked, peering at me.

I blinked. "Are you implying I intend to gamble it away? That's—"

"You might. I know you types."

"I will not leave my father's ring in your hands for a paltry hundred *rean*. Do you think I'm an idiot? You might suddenly just close shop, and…"

He pulled a piece of paper out from under the counter and placed it on the surface. There was ink on it already. He began scribbling something else—I craned my neck and realized he was writing down the description of the ring. "I run this business legally," he said. He pushed the paper towards me, pointing at the bottom. "Sign there. I won't run off with your ring. Ask around."

"Two hundred *rean*," I said. "A hundred interest if I don't pay you by the end of ten days."

He took the ring and held it up to the window. "How bad are you at Monkey Hands?"

"I'm *good* at it, old man. I'd play you now if I wasn't in such a hurry."

"All right. I was just asking." He sighed, returning the ring to the counter. He picked up the brush, scratched out the number, and placed *two hundred* instead. I took the brush from his hand, dipped it in the inkwell, and signed it as Biala Chaen.

The name didn't seem to mean anything to him. He blew the ink dry before going to the back room. He returned with a small chest, which contained a number of coins, and began counting them out. After we reached two hundred *rean*, I scooped them into my hands and straight into my purse.

I left ten *rean* on the counter. "For my directions," I said.

He nodded towards the shop. "Buy something."

"I don't have time to…"

"Buy something," he repeated, glowering at me.

I sighed. I browsed through the shelves, cringing at the price tag of each item before I finally stumbled on something that cost ten *rean*—a small wooden figure of an armoured *rok haize*. I thought Thanh might like it. I placed it on the counter beside the coin.

"Thought you didn't have children," he said.

"I could pick something else," I retorted.

He shrugged. He took the item, wrapped it in brown paper, and handed it back to me.

"Go straight down and you'll see a fountain," he said, his eyes twinkling. "Take a right. Keep going until you hit the second intersection, and then you turn left. The restaurant is a few blocks away—you won't miss it. It's near Porlheng Bridge, by the canal."

"Finally," I grumbled. "Thank you." I stepped out of the shop just as Khine—who had swapped out his grey cloak for something in red, with golden cranes embroidered on the back—slid past. He barely glanced at me. My instruction was to leave him alone, so I did.

I returned to the fountain, wondering if he was going to succeed with his part. It didn't matter, anyway. I knew how to get to the Silver Goose and needed neither of them now. If I wanted to, I could start running and reach my guards before they could both cause trouble for me. I could forget that this whole debacle ever happened.

I paused to adjust my shoes. Running through the alleys had left them with dust and mud streaks, hardly the sort of footwear you're supposed to have on when meeting the Dragonlord of Jin-Sayeng. It was probably a good thing I didn't consider Rai worthy of the title, or it would have bothered me.

I heard footsteps.

"Madam!" The old shopkeep's voice was unmistakable. "Madam!"

I turned to him and narrowed my eyes. "What now?"

He stopped, panting, and gestured at me for a moment while he caught his breath. He finally pulled himself up. He was holding the pawn agreement. "I would like to buy the ring from you instead."

"No," I said. "It's my father's."

"Five hundred *rean*, like you said. I have the money here now. It's worth that much—you said as much yourself."

"No." I shook my head. "I said *at least*, if we're just talking about appraising it. I didn't say anything about selling it. It's all I have left of my father."

"Six hundred," he barked.

"Are you daft?" I asked. "Better yet, do you think *I* am?"

"Six hundred *rean*."

"Why?"

He looked at me, aghast. "You…"

"Did something happen? Why do you suddenly want to buy it?"

"My…daughter, we are making marriage arrangements. A proposal," he said quickly. "I just remembered. I don't have…for a dowry, you see." He pointed at the ring, not realizing he was babbling. "The make of this. Crafted in Anjishing, by the red cliffs. Rare enough to wow my potential son-in-law's family. Money would not have quite the same impact."

I pressed my lips together. "I don't think so."

"Seven hundred," he said.

"Something happened," I said. "That stranger in your shop…I'll have to talk to him myself…"

"A thousand," he gasped. "Please." He thrust the papers into my hand.

I stood there, taking all this in. What had happened? The man had been so proud inside his own store. To see him reduced to this…gibbering fool…was disconcerting. "A thousand," I mumbled. "I could pay my gambling debts."

He nodded helpfully.

I took a deep breath. "Very well."

"Your father will forgive you," he said as he counted the money out from his purse into mine. "If your husband learns of your gambling debts, he'll be furious."

"Oh," I grunted. "Don't even remind me." The last coin clinked into my purse. It was now bulging. I placed it in my pocket and tore up the pawn agreement.

"Thank you for your business," he said, turning away. I watched him walk down the street.

As soon as I saw his figure disappear into his shop, I ran.

Khine caught up with me two streets down. He had ditched the elaborate cloak and was clad as simply as when he had first met me. Laughter burst from his lips. His eyes were shining, and something about that made me chuckle in return. "Brilliant," he said, taking me by the arm and leading me down to an empty shop building. He drew the curtains closed. He turned to me and saw that his hand was on my waist. He dropped it and cleared his throat.

"That was...I didn't think it would go so smoothly." He couldn't stop grinning. "The way he talked about you—you didn't even give him space to be suspicious. How much did you get out of him?"

"A thousand *rean*," I said, showing him the purse, which I quickly returned to my pocket. "But I won't give it up until I get to where I need to go."

"Right," he said, clicking his fingers. He didn't seem like he cared all that much about the money. He peered through the curtains, glancing down at the empty street. "We'll wait awhile. If someone sees us together in the street immediately, it'll blow this whole thing apart."

I faked a sigh. "I knew it wouldn't be this simple."

"Might as well get comfortable," Khine said. He pulled an empty crate to the side and sat on it, his elbows on his knees. His face was still beaming. I couldn't help but smile back when he turned to me—his expression made it difficult to react in any other way.

"You're pleased it all worked out," I said.

He laughed again. "Yes. I didn't think everything would fall so neatly into place. I'd spent weeks working on this. *Weeks.* Paid people to scout out the best shops, the ones where this would most likely work. You needed a shopkeeper who is both honest and greedy, but in just the right amounts. You don't want someone who cheats his customers, or he would be suspicious from the beginning—he'd have to be, if he does the same thing to others. But you don't want him too honest, or he would've never taken the bait." The way his eyes lit up when he talked about his plan reminded me of the way my old swordsmaster would get when he talked about the way they made blades in Darusu, the *craftsmanship* of it.

"What did you tell him back there, anyway?"

His smile deepened. "He recognized me from earlier, but I told him I was on my way to a business meeting and forgot to buy something else. It's always easier to get them to trust you when they feel like they know you, you see. I noticed that he still had the ring out on the counter, which was good. I wasn't sure how I was going to convince him to take it out if it hadn't been—express an interest in buying rings, maybe. I don't know. But having it out there gave me a chance to point out, immediately, the rarity of such an object. I told him I had to have it, that my most beloved mother would appreciate such a gift from her village in Anjishing, which she has not been to since she was a child."

"Your *most* beloved mother? He actually believed that?"

He ran a finger under his nose. "I also said she was dying."

"Ah. Of course. The necessary detail."

"You never question a dying woman's wish, you know. Anyway, I offered two thousand *rean* on the spot." Khine showed me his purse, which was heavy with enough coin to have convinced anyone. "He told me you had it pawned. I asked if he knew where you lived and started counting the money out in front of him. He turned to chase after you."

"What would you have done if he had been less honest? What if he just sold you the ring outright?"

"Brought the city watch in," Khine said happily. "That's why you need someone honest enough to have done the paperwork for you in the first place. Then I can protest that the ring wasn't as valuable as he claimed it was, they'll ask him where he got it from, and then they'll discover that it was sold while under a pawn agreement. They'd have given me back my money, and since something like that would've invalidated your pawn contract, you could get the ring back and we'd at least be two hundred *rean* richer."

I couldn't help but smirk at his choice of words. "*We?*"

"We. Couldn't have done it without you. I can give you part of our catch if you ask nicely."

"You don't even know *my* name yet."

"I didn't see the need for it," he said as innocently as he could.

I burst out laughing. I couldn't help it. The ridiculousness of the whole situation was not lost on me. If you had told me yesterday I would be standing in an empty shack, having my words thrown back at me by a con artist and *enjoying* it, I would've called you a liar. Cut you down and thrown your head in the river, if my guards were around to add to it, the humourless bastards.

Perhaps it was only because I hadn't had that sort of conversation in so long. There was no one in court I could speak to in such shameless fashion—no one I knew who relished the flow of banter, instead of minding *their* honorifics and caring only about walking away with head still attached to their shoulders. I stopped to catch my breath and realized that Khine was looking at me with an intensity that was almost frightening. "Is there a problem?" I asked.

"Nothing," he said, breaking his gaze. The crinkle of humour in his eyes returned. "I was just wondering what *you* told him to get him to cough out a thousand *rean*. I didn't ask you to haggle. I would've been happy with anything over five hundred."

"I fed him a story about being a woman with a gambling problem, off to meet her husband before he decides to beat the living daylights out of her."

"That's..." He frowned. I caught him looking at the bruise.

"Only partly true. I *am* meeting my husband there. I've never gambled in my life, and as for beating me, nothing could be further from the truth." I looked away. "I'm...call me Tali."

"Tali," he repeated. "You're not from around here, are you?"

"Was it the lack of honorifics, or did I inadvertently do something more offensive this time?"

"You're Jinsein, and not one who lives around here, either. I've never seen you in the immigrants' quarter—I think I'd have remembered you if I did."

"And here I've been telling people it's impossible to tell from appearance alone."

"I've known Jinseins. Even been friends with some of them. You have a way of speaking Zirano that's difficult to ignore once you've heard it. Mix that with a few more clues, and then..." He folded his arms across his chest. "You came all the way out here to meet your husband?"

I nodded.

"Is he Zarojo?"

"No. He's Jinsein, too. I haven't seen him in years." I hadn't intended to say so much, but somehow, speaking with Khine made it easy for the words to come tumbling out.

"I see," he murmured. "I'm sorry to hear that. Are you hoping to reconcile with him?"

"I don't know," I mumbled. "It would only be right if I did, wouldn't it?"

He smirked. "It depends. Do you love him?"

It was a strange question, mostly because no one had asked me since Rai had left that fateful night. I have never been asked that question at all, actually. Was it because marriages between Jinsein royals are never about love? Or was it because no one ever cared to broach such a subject with me before? Surely they would've whispered about it in dark halls or crowded kitchens where I couldn't hear them; surely they would have asked if a woman who let Rayyel Ikessar go had loved him at all.

"Ah, talking about love with a brazen thief in some unnamed part of town," I said, pretending to brush it all off. "I've moved up in the world. And here, you, acting as if you know something about it, about love."

"You got me," Khine said with a laugh. "I've never been married. Wouldn't know how to get a woman's attention if I tried."

"I find that hard to believe."

"Really?" he asked, scratching the stubble on his chin.

I nodded earnestly. "You just convinced an *honest* shopkeeper, as you put it, to part with a thousand *rean*."

"*You* convinced him to do it. I just tricked him into thinking he could make some money off you without you knowing about it. Anyway, women's hearts are harder."

"And should, in theory, require less trickery," I said.

"A lot less," he agreed.

I was starting to enjoy the conversation a bit too much, which reminded me of where I was and where I was supposed to be. A queen's life didn't leave much room for such talk, for things beyond responsibilities. It was even less so with me, with what I had to carry. "I think enough time has passed," I said. I poked my head through the curtains. The street remained silent. "I don't hear the city watch."

He gave a quick snort. "I seriously doubt he would've called them about this. Too much trouble, too much investigating. The man can't be *all* that clean. Plus, he still has the ring, and he still doesn't know I have no intention of ever coming back. He'll wait." He got up from the crate. "I'll walk you there."

The way to the Silver Goose did not take as long as I thought it would. It was already dark—I could see the lights reflecting like stars off the canal's surface. A number of lute players were scattered on the outdoor patios of various establishments, the combined sounds of different songs lending a note of cheery chaos to the atmosphere. The air was thick with the scent of smoked meat and incense. The smell of it made my stomach rumble.

"Anzhao City's nightlife," Khine said distractedly. Then, as if noticing he had spoken, he craned his head towards me. "The kind they talk about, anyway. For tourists like you."

There was a sad note to the end of his sentence. I followed his gaze and saw a sign with the embossed image of a dancing goose. I caught sight of several of my guards standing near the door. It was clear from the harassed expressions on their faces that they were looking for me. The poor bastards had probably assumed the worst, and I could only imagine the harsh words Arro would've had for them when he found out what had happened. I would have to clear up with him that it was partly my fault.

And somewhere in that building, with its brightly lit windows of wrought iron and glass, Rai probably sat, waiting.

A lump grew in my throat. The excitement of the last few hours faded, leaving only more fear than I knew how to handle. But this man, Khine, didn't need to know that. I pulled the purse out and placed it into his palm. He looked at me in surprise, as if just suddenly remembering about the money. I closed his fingers around it with my other hand.

He opened his mouth to protest. "Don't," I said. "You've more than earned it."

"And are you sure about that?" he asked, nodding towards the restaurant.

"I don't know what you mean."

"That man in there. Your husband. Are you sure you want to go back to him? That he is worth whatever pain he's caused you? Is he worth fighting for?"

I had asked myself the same thing for years.

"Thank you, Khine," I said. I didn't stop to wait for what else he had to say and walked towards my guards. They saw me before I could even reach the path and rushed forward, my name on their lips. As they crowded around me, I glanced up to take one last look at Khine, but he was already gone.

I allowed my guards to lead me into the building.

CHAPTER SIX

THE SILVER GOOSE

ᛏᛁᛗ

I had the impression that my arrival broke a silence that had hung over the establishment for hours. Nor was standing by the entrance, a tinge of panic on her normally placid face.

"My queen," she said, stepping past the tank of brown and blue spotted fish and various potted plants to grab my hand and press it against her forehead. Her fingers were cold.

"We thought the worst," Arro broke in. His face was red, which told me he had been arguing with someone—quite probably Nor. "I told the captain she shouldn't have let you out of her sight. She—"

"I can take care of myself, Arro," I said in a low voice.

"Clearly," he replied with disdain, glancing at my dirty clothes. "But the captain better not let this happen again." He glanced back at Nor. "I can understand that circumstances aren't always under your control, but your guards are. You had twenty men, Captain. Not even an entire day in the empire and you already lost one—no doubt to the gambling halls or the whorehouses. I hate to say it, but Agos would've done a better job."

The criticism barely seemed to faze her. "I've reprimanded everyone, Magister. They're at their posts right now and have been for the past two hours. No one unauthorized will be able to get in or out of the restaurant. This won't happen again."

"Let's not argue right now," I broke in. "Is he here?" The very idea of speaking my husband's name made me want to lose courage.

Arro paused for a moment. "He is."

"Is he..." But I didn't know what I really wanted to say. Of course he was well; he was here now, and alive, wasn't he? And chances were that he looked better than me. If there was anything left to be sure of, it was that the last five years had treated him with more kindness.

My memory of what transpired after was lost in the flurry of excitement, the flash from the bright paper lamps hanging over the round tables, and the smell of fried meat—so deliciously distracting and now impossible to ignore. I was led to a private room upstairs, where entire walls were slid open to make way for my arrival. I found myself in a large room with a giant lacquered table. Sitting at the far end, directly across from me, was Rai.

A flurry of emotions descended on me like a hawk barrelling for its prey. Perhaps if we had been alone, I would've allowed myself the pleasure of perusing them for a more appropriate response. But I felt other eyes on me—Arro to my left, and then the unknown faces on both sides—and reached for anger instead. Anger and sarcasm I could do. I had built my reputation around them, after all.

I took a seat, even before a servant could offer it to me. The chair was comfortable, with a rounded back and smooth armrests. I looked at Rai, who remained silent, his eyes like hardened steel. Our gazes locked for a moment before he turned away. I could feel the weight of the last few years pressing on me. There was so much I wanted to tell him, so much I wanted to say.

A man beside him cleared his throat. "We have been waiting for hours, Queen Talyien."

"How appropriate," I said, craning my neck towards him, "seeing as I've been lost for hours. Was it part of the plan when you made such sudden changes to our venue? A little prank to play on a clueless guest? I should tell you that I had quite an adventure, one which would've been amusing under different circumstances. As it is now, though, I am merely irritated."

The man's face stiffened. "Is this your idea of a joke? You were the one who—"

"We must remember our respects, Governor Zheshan," Rai said. "She is still queen of Jin-Sayeng."

"Thank you, my lord," I said, unsmiling. He seemed to have interrupted that quick enough. Rai was always the sort of man who didn't like to admit mistakes, and if he'd made one with the restaurant, the world would fall apart before he would ever say so. Even now, he didn't respond, as if the slightest acknowledgment of my thanks would give him away.

Arro cleared his throat. "We are all pleased the Beloved Queen made it out of the streets safely. We will go through a review of our security measures later, but for now, perhaps, we can begin."

"I'll let Lord Rayyel start by explaining himself," I said. My eyes had never left my husband. I took a deep breath, telling myself to remember to keep my head clear. "You walked away from me, our son, and all your responsibilities on our coronation night. By all rights, you should have been rotting in the dungeons of Oka Shto years ago."

"For refusing to be crowned?" Rai asked. "What law did I break for such an action?" To his credit, his voice never rose an octave. I was the one struggling to keep mine steady.

"My father and your mother made an agreement. We were to rule Jin-Sayeng jointly. You abandoned your duties, my lord."

"I did not," Rai said. There was a scroll in his right hand. He gave it to a servant, who ran over to hand it to me.

I glanced at it. There were some numbers, names of cities and towns.

I detected a few villages from the mountains north of Darusu. "You've been managing the farms in your ancestral lands," I said. "Helped the price of rice go down for some of the cities."

"Oversaw trade between the Sougen and the Kaitan fields, directed the appropriate people to convince the rice merchants to give up some of their records for the Dragonthrone, and other duties I needed to fulfill within my capacity as Minister of Agriculture."

"And these people you've been dealing with never even thought to alert me of these activities?"

"I would assume they didn't think you'd care."

I struggled with the anger. There was, of course, an official proclamation that I sent days after the coronation, ordering Rayyel sent straight to Oka Shto if anyone came across him. Yet if he had been strolling through the countryside as he pleased, bartering with farmers and merchants and officials, why had I received nothing more than rumours that he *might* have passed through a certain city or town at a given point in time? "Such accomplishments—forgive me if I don't throw a feast in your honour."

"I am not trying to impress you," Rai said, his eyes darting across the room like he wasn't even talking to me. "I am merely giving you a quick account of my activities the past five years while you were busy with other things." He let the last word slide out abruptly, as if in place of something harsher. I could feel my temper rise.

"Busy fending the warlords off from each other, you mean?" I asked. "You know the difficulties of ruling Jin-Sayeng as much as I do. You cannot just run off and play King of Your Own Castle, my lord. The realities do not change just because you willed it." I noticed the map unfolded in front of him. He was holding a brush.

"These difficulties exist because too many of the warlords do not like the idea of Orenar blood on the throne. After years of the Ikessar clan ruling Jin-Sayeng without incident, your father's war has made their nightmare into a reality."

"*Without* incident?" I asked. "I'm sorry, do I need to remind you about Ziri-nar-Orxiaro's attacks on our main cities and the closing of trade—after *centuries* of goodwill—or the tyranny brought on by the Seven Shadows..."

"Heroes—"

"Who killed, in the dark, anyone who defied the Ikessars." I reached for a bowl of wine and swallowed. "Let's not forget the wonderful legacy your uncle Rysaran left us all to contend with: Oren-yaro and Shirro-karu both in ruins, and the dragons on our eastern borders threatening to destroy our towns and villages there, in addition to over half of Jin-Sayeng's rice crop."

"He had nothing to do with the dragons," Rai breathed.

"Yet it was his insistence at bringing the mad dragon into our lands that gave way to the others," I said. "He wanted to see dragons returned to Jin-Sayeng. And he got his wish! Untameable, blood-crazed beasts now swarm our lands, and if not for the efforts of the valiant people of the Sougen, it would be a lot worse. What have you done to control this plague and help our people? Busy with other *things*, indeed."

I gulped down more wine. The faint taste of plum stayed on my tongue, helping with the bitterness. "When you left, the warlords blamed me. The ones who didn't defy me in the open did so to my back. I couldn't create a single decree that wasn't outvoted in an instant. And the arguments between them...twice I've had to ride to stop Warlord Lushai from marching his army to take over Warlord Graiyo's lands. Ten villages raided in five years, and we still don't know who did what and what for." Despair hooked its claws as soon as I spoke up. There was more, so much more he needed to hear, even though I knew it would all sound like nonsense to him.

"Lord Rayyel does not disagree on the complexities that plague your nation," Governor Zheshan spoke up. I considered him for the first time. He was a short, squat man with a long beard, a shaved head, and enough fat on his body to live on for a year.

"Who are you," I said, "to get yourself involved in all of this?" I turned to Rai. "Why does an official of the Empire of Ziri-nar-Orxiaro speak for you? Did you suddenly lose your tongue? Maybe you left it at Warlord Lushai's."

"Governor Gon Zheshan is offering his assistance," Rai said, flushing red. I wondered if it was because he had caught on to my insult. He wasn't normally that perceptive.

"An outsider's look at what is causing these rifts in Jin-Sayeng." Governor Zheshan bowed towards me. "My intention is not to cause disrespect."

"You don't say," I drawled.

"These are issues we have all dealt with at one time or another within the empire. We know all too well the pitfalls that come with a federal government, especially when taken to the extremes your warlords have gone through."

"Are you proposing we strip them of their titles and their lands?" I said. "If so, be my guest. You can dole out the proposal for them in your best silks. They'll be your funeral robes, too."

"We are not quite so foolhardy," Governor Zheshan said with the sort of smile that could mean anything—appeasement or amusement, I couldn't tell. It made me distrust him even more. He turned to Rai, who knotted his thick eyebrows together before nudging the map closer to me. I saw the thick black lines running through it and felt my senses blur.

"You are not here to discuss how to return to Oren-yaro with your head intact, are you?" I asked. *You are not here to speak with me about what happened five years ago, either.*

Rai's lips formed a thin line. "Why ever would you think that, my lady?"

"Our clans had an *agreement*. A treaty."

"One which I am merely interpreting another way," he said. He turned to Arro. "Why is she surprised, Magister? I had requested that you get her acquainted with the terms before this meeting."

Arro looked uncomfortable. I held out my hand to stop him from replying.

"He tried to show me your terms," I said. "I declined and told him I would hear them straight from your own mouth."

Rai placed his hands on the table. "I need not speak. They are in front of you, my lady."

I glanced at the map, at the divided Jin-Sayeng Rai was proposing. The north and west would be his. He was giving me Oren-yaro and the south, running to the east, including the dragon-infested Sougen Plains. I stared at the letters that made up our clan names, *Ikessar* and *Orenar*, and wondered how my father could've done all of this without going mad.

"I will not do this," I said. "I will not. You spit on the agreement our clans made, Rayyel. You spit on everything that was sacred in our marriage."

"If it was so sacred," he began, a hint of a snarl under his breath, "then why, by all the gods, are we here now, Talyien?"

I closed my eyes and held my breath for a few moments to try to calm down. Why was Rayyel angry? Did he expect a different reaction? He must have known on some level that if he wanted to wrest me from the position my father had destined for me, he would have to do so over my mangled corpse. I noted that there were now more lines on his face than when I had seen him last, five long years ago. His shoulders were broader now, too, and he had grown a proper beard instead of the peach fuzz he'd carried all those years. We had been so young, once.

I think he wanted to say something to me, but he didn't want to look me in the eyes. "Magister Arro," he said, a layer of revulsion in his voice. "Why waste our time? If the lady did not even bother to read our terms…"

It irritated me that he was still playing this old game. "I was under the impression I would be presented with reasonable terms." I pointed at him with my fan. It was all I could do not to rush over and jab him in the eye with it. "By all the heavens, Rayyel, if you cannot even talk to me straight, we might as well end this meeting right here."

Something in my voice must've done it. He did finally turn, though slowly, like it was the most painful thing he'd had to do in his life. Eyes that once gazed at me with a flicker of affection now regarded me with detached observance. I suddenly had cause to wonder what he was thinking about—what the last few years had done to me, perhaps. I was not the soft, naive princess I once was.

"Perhaps if you would both set aside your differences for now…" Rai's other adviser, a woman whose name I didn't catch, took a long sip of tea before glancing in my direction. She was very pale, with a forehead that subtly reminded me of my horse Osga. Her robes marked her as a priestess of Kibouri; the sash around her belt marked her as a scholar. I found it amusing how even as far as Ziri-nar-Orxiaro, the Ikessars insisted on flaunting their perceived superiority.

"The only difference I see here—" I started.

"My queen," Arro warned.

"—is that Lord Rayyel is an idiot." I fixed another glare at Rai, daring him to respond in kind.

He avoided it by following the priestess's example and drinking the tea. "To be fair," he murmured a moment later, "the fact that you think so is not news to me."

"Oh," I said, feigning surprise. "So you *were* listening!"

His face remained impassive. "I've heard more than you give me credit for."

"Then maybe perhaps you've heard me call you a donkey's..."

"My queen," Arro coughed. "The matter at hand."

"Methinks your queen has been spending too much time with her soldiers," the priestess said, concealing a grin behind her tea.

I turned to her. "Too low, priestess."

"I was merely implying the manner with which you speak," the priestess said. "If you think there is more to it than that, it is your concern, not mine."

"Arro...off with her head."

"More wine," Arro grunted, glancing at the servants behind us. "Did you hear at all what I said?" There was a flurry of robes and footsteps. "It has been a long night, and we are all tired. Perhaps we should wait until we've sufficiently filled our bellies before we proceed with the talks?"

"We don't even know who's paying for this meal," I said, glaring at Osga. I made the mental note never to learn her real name. "Because I won't."

"We can afford to pay, Magister Arro," Rai said. "I take it this place was chosen for a reason? They serve both Jinsein and Zarojo food."

It was almost adorable that he was still denying it. "Maybe it's the only one that serves infants and kittens," I said. I flashed both Osga and Zheshan a smile. I liked smiles. In my world, they could mean anything: a hidden joke to a friend, a threat to an enemy. There are songs written about my smiles and what usually comes after them.

Those were, of course, the kinds of things Rai never understood. He didn't use to think twice, for example, of showing up to council dressed in the same robe he had slept in. It used to drive me mad trying to explain why this was inappropriate behaviour. He didn't at all understand that people judged him for how he looked. Even worse, he didn't understand that people judged *me* for how he looked. I wondered what he really hoped to accomplish out of this meeting. Did he really think I would agree to a divided Jin-Sayeng? Had he forgotten whose daughter I was?

The manager of the establishment arrived with the menu. "Our apologies," he said, throwing me a wary glance. "We are short on some of the items. It's been a busy night. We do not mean to offend."

"They're frightened of you already," Rai commented dryly.

"Feed us well and you may keep all your body parts," I told him. The man looked up at me and tried to smile, which his face seemed to have difficulties with.

"Our special for today is pork bone stew," the manager said.

"Pork bone stew sounds excellent," I said. "Rayyel could use a spine."

"Is heartless shrew on the menu?" Rai asked without batting an eye.

I laughed. The manager looked even more nervous than when he came in. He tried to clear his throat and looked at the ceiling. "We, ah, also have sweet beef with green beans, and steamed fish in banana leaves with a ginger sauce. I highly recommend the fish—it's freshly caught from the crystal-clear canals of Anzhao City just this morning."

"Let's try the fish," I said, glancing through the menu. I caught a scribbling that meant fowl of some sort—I couldn't read the subtleties of Zirano script as well as I thought—and ordered that as well. Arro wanted noodles with goat tripe, eggplant stew, and chopped pig snout, which they deep-fried and seasoned with onions, soy sauce, and vinegar in pale imitation of a Jinsein dish. Governor Zheshan ordered the roasted pork, the Silver Goose's specialty. I didn't pay attention to what Osga ordered. Oats or air, I don't know. Were priestesses even allowed to eat?

They returned with more wine to occupy us while we waited. I sipped, taking the time to look at Rai through half-lidded eyes. It hit me what was bothering me about him—he had taken the time to tie his beard and comb his hair before this meeting. He was also wearing very elaborate clothes: a black silken shirt, embroidered with gold thread at the seams, under a well-cut grey tunic. He had been silent for years and then all of a sudden decided he wanted to claim his part in Jin-Sayeng after all? And then he fixed his hair? Was Horse Face to blame? I didn't know what to make of it. This was what my father had warned me about ruling all those years ago: you can't rely on things to remain the same. You always have to be ready for change, to adjust the sails as the wind comes.

Rai, Akaterru bless him, had not had the education I had when it came to ruling. He grew up in the mountains, raised by Kibouri monks or hermits or some such, and did not set foot in Shirrokaru until he was fourteen. He could've been raised by badgers for all I knew. He exemplified all the traits the Kibouri religion praised: humility, subservience, compassion. I had never known him to have ambition. Where was he now getting the nerve to challenge me, and all groomed and perfumed, too? I glanced at Zheshan. Qun had claimed they had only just met days ago, but I suddenly found that hard to believe.

I realized that everyone had gone damnably quiet after the manager had left. It was all very disconcerting. "So," I said, drumming my fingers along the surface of the table. I had purposely spoken in Jinan to prevent Zheshan from interrupting. "Seeing anyone?"

Arro choked on his tea while Osga pretended to look at the ceiling. Rai coloured. "I don't see how that's any of your business," he snapped.

"No, it's not," I agreed. "But it might be fun to talk about while we wait." I stared at him, giving him my coldest smile. I saw him swallow.

"My queen, now is not the time," Arro murmured.

I waved him off. "Old men," I said casually. "Such prudes."

Rai cleared his throat. "I'll humour you," he said, in a tone that was one part factual and two parts loathing. "There was someone. A Zarojo *lady*." I caught on to his emphasis of the *lady*, although he himself did not seem aware of it.

"A Zarojo," I repeated. "So you *have* been hiding out here all these years."

"I went around. I did not see the prudence in staying in Jin-Sayeng when you have the Oren-yaro sniffing after me like angry dogs. Why do you care what I do, anyway?"

"*You* personally? I don't, to be honest. Go, be one with the whales if you want. I wouldn't have come here for your sake alone, except it's clear what you're doing. Have you gone insane? The last time the Zarojo got involved in our politics, it didn't end too well for everyone. Honestly, Rayyel, it's like you don't study history."

Rai's face remained blank despite my insults. "I've studied it more than you. It is generally agreed upon that it was the Oren-yaro's insistence on insulting the Zarojo court that resulted in those troubles. Feel free to consult a history book if you disagree with me."

"I think I see our food," Arro croaked out.

I rubbed my temples. "Does your woman appreciate such droll bed-talk?"

"Does your new man appreciate the sarcasm?"

"Which one? I've got a number. That's what you wanted to hear, isn't it?"

"Are any of them the true heir to the Dragonthrone?"

"No. I never needed one to rule."

"It *is* our food! Oh, thank heavens." Arro looked like he was on the verge of convulsions. I smiled thinly, a gesture that Rai did not return, and drew back as they placed steaming plates on our table. At the sight of food, I momentarily forgot my irritation. It had been a long night.

The food was divine. Each item came in portions big enough to feed an army, and with more than enough rice to satiate empty bellies. We shared the meal, hostilities seemingly fading in the background. I remembered what Khine said about the pork, which *did* fall off the bone, with a crispy exterior that leaked fat as soon as you bit into it. The flavour was very strong, a mixture of hot peppers and sweet sauce with a hint of lemongrass. I was quite taken aback. A number of restaurants specializing in Zarojo cuisine had popped up in Jin-Sayeng over the years, but they never could get Zarojo cuisine quite right—something to do with the availability of spices, which was made more difficult by the trade embargo Dragonlord Reshiro created against the Zarojo Empire. I was glad I had taken the time to learn how to use chopsticks properly. The traditional way of eating with one's fingers in Jin-Sayeng, while perfectly acceptable even for royals, was often seen as primitive elsewhere.

I didn't say anything during the meal. I didn't want Rai to get into the history of spoons in Jin-Sayeng. I wondered if the restaurant would divulge the recipe for the noodles and tripe. The manager came by to check on us, and I smiled and complimented our meal. Rai looked at me quizzically. I wondered what he was thinking. Was civilized behaviour really so beneath me?

I also wondered about his admission to having a Zarojo woman. Rai was not normally the sort who would say things to get a reaction out of me, so chances were good that what he said was true. But why would he say it at all? "Was," I said, realizing only too late that I said it aloud.

Rai glanced at me, perplexed.

"Your woman. You said *was*."

"As I said—it is none of your business."

"Isn't it? We are still married, are we not? Do these words not mean anything anymore?"

Rai's face tightened. "I did not realize you would want to go down this road. This is not an argument I want to have right now."

"It seems like it is an argument you would rather we never have at all."
I sighed, pulling back to allow the servants to take the plates away, and
gestured at the map. "We have made quite a leap from a misunderstanding to dividing the land five years later with *brushstrokes*. I believe you
were educated on the laws and principles of ruling better than that."

"That was how you saw that?" he asked. "A misunderstanding?"

"You never gave me the chance to explain myself," I said.

"And if I had?"

"I would have told you that I cared enough about my land and my
people to see this through. I came all the way out here, didn't I?"

He picked up his tea and looked away from me while he sipped.

"Let's return to the subject at hand," Zheshan spoke up. "I believe the
queen and my lord have both come to terms with each other?"

I laughed. "Not even close."

Rai grunted. He placed his wine bowl back on the table. I caught
a flicker of unease on his face. "My lord," I said, deciding to dig at it.
"Think this through. The warlords will not like the idea of a division."

"Do you truly know what your warlords think, Queen Talyien?" he
asked.

"I've spent more time at court than you have. I don't think you understand what you're saying. Jin-Sayeng isn't…it isn't *ours* to divide. We
were tasked to rule, jointly—"

"Which we will."

"But not like this! If an announcement like this doesn't create civil
war in the first hour, it certainly will by the end of the year. The warlords
will *never* agree to it."

Zheshan cleared his throat and tapped a pile of papers on his side.
"They will, if you care to peruse the details with them. We have it all
laid out here. It is a truly remarkable arrangement: you will be allowed to
keep your ancestral lands and remain queen to those who have supported

you, while ceding your right to oversee the warlords who have historically been more vocal against Oren-yaro rule."

"And how would *you* know which is which, foreigner? What dusty tome did you get your information from? Something you inherited from your grandmother, no doubt." I pointed at the map. "You have Bara marked for the Ikessars. I don't even know where to begin to explain the absurdity of this. Can I *please* watch you tell Warlord Lushai he has to bend his knee to the Ikessars?"

"You do not know Warlord Lushai as well as you think you do," Rai remarked.

"And you do, I suppose?" I asked. I didn't wait for him to reply—instead, I burst out laughing. "Right. My apologies...I've *forgotten* exactly why you don't want to talk about marriage and duties. Warlord Lushai—of course. He sheltered you the night you left Oren-yaro, didn't he? Where else could you have gone? Yet we sent riders there that same afternoon, only to be told you weren't there and that we were sorely mistaken if we thought Bara would ever offer help to a wayward Ikessar lord. He feigned *insult* that we would even dare ask." I sank into my chair.

"If this tires you..." Rai began.

I fixed him with a glare. "Or is that your plan? To wear me out so that I would willingly step down and take the mantle of some holy order or another? I am not your mother, Rayyel."

"Do not bring her into this," he murmured.

"You all bring my father into everything I do, and you don't see me complain," I replied. "Where does Yeshin end and Talyien begin? It's never been an issue. Jin-Sayeng should take precedence over *all* our issues." I turned to Rai and swallowed. "I know. I understand there are many. But this is the first time we have spoken in years. Can't we begin with something that doesn't threaten to throw our people into chaos?"

"My lady," he said before falling silent. He had always been good at deflecting topics he would rather not discuss with silence. It was heartening to find out that it still infuriated me.

I glanced at Governor Zheshan. "I haven't even started on how uncomfortable it makes me that we are discussing such drastic measures in front of a Zarojo official."

"We have a pact with the Ikessars," Zheshan said. "Lord Rayyel asked for assistance. We were only too happy to give it."

"Happy…" I nearly choked on the word. Deputy Qun had implied otherwise. The man's prattling was starting to get on my nerves. I returned my gaze to Rai. "My lord," I said, taking care to keep my voice as low as I could make it. "Come home with us. We will discuss a resolution properly, among our people, as we should."

He cast his eyes downward, as if he was suddenly afraid to look at me.

"He will do no such thing," Gon Zheshan broke in. "Likely you have assassins waiting for him as soon as he steps on your shores."

"Stop filling his head with nonsense!" I barked. "I see what's happening here. This is your doing, you bloated fart. Do you honestly think you can manipulate me as easily?"

"Enough," Rai snapped. "I will not have my advisers insulted."

"And this whole charade—you do not think it is an insult? To me, and to every warlord across these shores?" I got up. "I will not consider these ridiculous demands. I'm surprised you thought I would."

"How, pray, do you think the warlords will react when they learn that you had the chance to turn away the tides of war once and for all, and didn't?"

I curled my fingers against the edge of the table, resisting the urge to give in to my anger. "Is that a threat, my lord?" I asked. My eyes shifted towards Zheshan for a moment before returning to Rai. "You would declare war if I don't accept this? You, Rayyel Ikessar? With what army?"

"I only meant to imply that drastic actions may result from your refusal to heed all sense," Rai said. "Or are you telling me that the warlords do not strain on their leashes, that they are not gathering their own armies every day that they bristle under Oren-yaro rule?"

"They chose us!"

"Exactly. *Us.* Not you. If you thought every warlord has been happy with the five years Jin-Sayeng has been under the rule of Yeshin's bitch pup..."

"Now the insults start," I hissed.

"I am quoting," he said. "You need to stop taking things personally."

"I need a breath of fresh air." I stepped away, to Arro's protest, and stalked down the hall and through the main restaurant, which was quieter than when I first came in. Nor moved to stop me, but I ordered her to leave me alone. I kept walking.

The streets were empty outside the restaurant. A light blanket of rain had covered everything in a grey sheen. Exhaustion seized me. I stepped under the roof eaves for shelter, placed the back of my head against the wall, and closed my eyes while I attempted to gather my thoughts.

I heard footsteps. Thinking it was a guard, I ignored it. But then I heard the sound of his familiar breathing and turned to see Rai staring down at me.

"What do you want?" I snapped.

"This is not queenly, Talyien," he said.

"And what part of this is *kingly*, do you think?" I asked. I gestured at him. "The demands, the insults? I came all the way out here to humour you. You can't even give me the courtesy of acknowledging my attempts."

"I have given you plenty of courtesies. You'll do well to see them."

I began to shiver from the cold, but I ignored it. I wiped rain from my face. "How have we come to this?"

Rai took a deep breath. "I don't know," he admitted.

"And this is what you truly want, is it? Not something that Gon Zheshan pressured you into?"

"A divided Jin-Sayeng can still function as one. It is merely assigning the warlords under a ruler they can all agree with. From there, perhaps we can build and grow."

"The warlords will laugh at us."

"We are here to talk, not decide on anything. This proposal can be presented to them upon your return to Jin-Sayeng. I was not willing to do it myself when I knew your first reaction would be to order your soldiers to arrest me. I figured if you could be made to see sense first, then the rest will fall into place a lot faster."

I closed my eyes. "It would be easier," I said, "if you just came back with me. We haven't even tried to rule jointly yet."

"Yet we have been married, and if we couldn't even make that work..."

"Because you walked away!"

His eyes flashed. "Don't put this on me, woman!"

"You dare? You..." I resisted the urge to slap him. "Have you considered what this division will mean for Thanh? Or have you forgotten our son?"

His face tightened. My skin crawled when I realized he was purposely avoiding that subject, too. He had not, in five years, even *asked* about the boy. That, perhaps, was the most puzzling part for me of all. The boy had been raised with both our clans' tenets. He was a strong, thoughtful lad who was thoroughly devoted to his duties, as much as a seven-year-old could be. How could Rai find fault with *him*? Even if I wasn't his mother, I would've sung his praises anyway. He had our strengths with none of our faults.

"No," I said. "This will not do. I will not have Thanh inherit our problems. Do not make me have Nor bring you back to Jin-Sayeng in chains. And I *will* give that order if you don't step back from this madness."

The threat seemed to mean nothing to him. He turned his head, the rain dripping past his face. "After I left, you did not move to Shirrokaru," he said.

"You expected me to?"

"We were supposed to rule from there. You knew that the last thing we needed was to remind the land that they fell under Oren-yaro rule after all. Instead, you left Shirrokaru with an empty throne room. Five years, and the Heart of Jin-Sayeng remains crumbling. Your father's legacy persists."

"You have no right to scrutinize my actions," I said. "Not after what you did. I had no reason to leave my father's home without you. Did you expect me to live in a place where I'm surrounded by your clan's supporters?"

"You said this was about the land," he said. "Not you or I."

"I did," I murmured. "You asked me a question earlier—I'm going to throw it back in your face. Why are we here, Rai? Why aren't we back home in bed, discussing the state of last season's rice crop and the price of tea? Why, by all the gods, did we let it get this far?"

My words, and the ease with which I slipped to his familiar name, caused Rai's face to assume an expression that strayed from his usual stoic demeanour. That I was able to observe the momentary flicker reminded me of how much I had tried to learn to read him over the years. I've known men who twisted their faces into masks in an effort to hide their true thoughts from me. Not so Rai; his thoughts often seemed to be as blank as his expression.

It sometimes gave others the impression that he was a fool when I knew it was far from the truth. I knew what he was doing, which was assembling every little fact and bit of information in the back of his mind so he could later find a purpose for each—like gathering the pieces of a puzzle he couldn't yet see. It was an admirable trait, especially when compared to my hot-headedness, but it still left room for me to wonder what he actually felt about things. I still found it hard to imagine that he could muster nothing more than irritation over my reactions.

I do not know how to begin talking about Rayyel aren dar Ikessar without these old frustrations rising to the surface.

He was always like this. I find it hard to believe as an older woman that my memories of Rayyel Ikessar started from when we were both still very young, because he was always like this. When most boys were concerned with playing soldier or sneaking off to town to watch horsefights, he would be in his study, a book in his hand. Any attempt to disturb him would be met with either abject impatience or a sudden litany of facts he had learned in the past hour. The first time I met him, I was eleven years old. I had been young, impulsive. It felt like a lifetime ago.

I was no longer a child that night in Anzhao City. By then, I had known Rayyel for sixteen years, and it occurred to me as he turned to walk back to the restaurant—unable to respond to my questions, unsure of what to say—that he was probably just doing what he thought was best for Jin-Sayeng. It was one of the few things about him that I was sure of.

The thought proved to be more chilling than comforting. If all of this was Rayyel's doing because of some inconvenient ambition that flared up over the last few years, then all well and good—I could steer him in the right direction. But this man was the same stern-faced, unassuming boy I had known for most of my life. The man who would debate the finer points of harvesting wheat and the significance of it to the economy over a bottle of wine was, in my eyes, incapable of making these demands for his own gain.

Someone, somewhere, was behind all this.

I followed him back inside. By now, the main restaurant was empty, and the staff was busy at work carrying plates of uneaten food back to the kitchen and scrubbing down tables. They didn't look at us—they must've been instructed not to. "It's very late," I told Rayyel. "I think I'll drop dead if we stretch this out another hour. Let us go back to our lodgings and meet again tomorrow. I will not sign half of the land over on a whim, but I promise I will entertain another meeting, at least. I will not let you slink off into the night again. Rai—"

He paused by the stairs. I could see him wrestling with something. I followed him up the steps and carefully reached up to place my hand on his shoulder. At my touch, he flinched.

"I will honour your request," he murmured.

His words were promising, and the queen, the politician in me, should've been happy with the small victory. But they were not words his wife wanted to hear. I pulled away and watched him stalk into the room. I sucked my breath in before I joined him.

All three of our advisers nodded as we entered. Zheshan and the priestess were near the entrance, Arro closer to the window. The food had been cleared from the table, and Zheshan was in the process of unrolling the map once more. "If we can proceed..." Zheshan began. Rai bent over to him, whispering something in his ear. I observed a frown appear on Zheshan's face.

"Are you sure?" the governor asked.

"It is very late," I broke in. "You can hardly expect me to agree to such terms when I am not in the best state of mind. There is still the matter of the warlords. Just because I promised my consideration doesn't mean a damn thing in the long run."

"You are the queen," Zheshan said. "What you say ought to be final. If our emperor told us to jump from the cliff, why..."

"You really don't understand Jin-Sayeng at all, do you?" I asked. I wasn't even pretending to be polite anymore.

"On this, she is correct, Governor," Rai said. "Let the queen sleep on our terms." *Our terms*, I noted. I shook my head.

I turned to Arro, who seemed like he was about to keel over where he was sitting. His eyes were drooping. "We will set up another meeting, Magister," I intoned.

He made a sound in the back of his throat.

"Come," I said, my voice softening. "You look tired." I touched his arm.

Arro coughed, white spittle flying from his mouth. I watched in horror as he fell from his chair, his eyes rolling into the back of his head. On the ground, the spittle turned to blood.

My head swam. I could see Rai walking towards us, and I started to wonder if there was something in the food and if he was going to get sick, too. And then I saw the red-tipped dart sticking out of Arro's neck, and my eyes automatically shifted to the open window. A man dressed in all black stood in the shadowed corner.

I threw a chair at him.

CHAPTER SEVEN

THE BEGGAR QUEEN, REPRISED

The man flung his arm out to protect himself as the chair struck the wall, missing him by a hair's breadth. He drew two daggers and came for me.

From the other end of the room, I heard a scream. I didn't look—I couldn't. I had no sword to defend myself with, only the wretched dagger, one against his two. I would be doomed in a straight fight. Why didn't I have a sword? Arro had thought it was inappropriate, unbecoming for a queen in foreign lands. *They have laws in Anzhao City*, he had said. Ah, Arro, my poor tutor, the man who had been with me longer than my own father and husband combined. Arro was dead now. My mind didn't know what to focus on.

The assassin came for me, and I kicked another chair into his path while I tried to wrench the dagger loose from my belt. I didn't have time. He leaped over the chair, his blades swinging for the kill. I slammed my right hand against his wrist as he lunged, trapping him between my left arm and body as I circled to the left. I twisted his arm and managed to knock one dagger from his hand. He struck me on the jaw with the hilt of the other.

The room spun as I dropped to the ground, blood spurting inside my mouth. From the corner of my eye, I saw Rai wrestling with a second assassin. And a third? Governor Zheshan was nowhere in sight. I spotted the priestess's robes, but they were all on the other side of the giant table, and I couldn't see what was happening. I pushed myself up just as the assassin tried to strike me a second time. I managed to catch his wrist again while my left hand fumbled with the dagger. My fingers wrapped around the wooden hilt, and this time, I was able to pull it out.

But the angle was too awkward, and there wasn't enough room. I could only jab him in the knee before he freed himself from my other hand. He slammed his elbow into my throat and shoved me against the wall with a force strong enough to make me drop the dagger. It clattered next to my foot. He pressed his elbow harder, trying to cut the breath off from my lungs. My vision clouded.

I spat blood on his face.

He jerked back. Trained assassin or not, he closed his eyes to protect himself out of reflex. That split second was all I needed. I slid from his grasp and went straight for the chair on the ground. As he recovered and lumbered after me, I threw it once more. It struck his hip and he fell with a shout.

From the other end of the room, I heard Rai groan. I resisted the urge to run to his side. I couldn't help him, but I could take myself out of danger and call for help. I went past my assassin, who lashed out with his dagger and struck me deep in the leg. The blade went straight into the muscle.

I ignored the pain and vaulted out the window.

I had not escaped through windows since I was a child, but somehow, I managed to make my way down. Hot blood gathered in my heel, but I didn't have time to check it and could only hope that the blade the assassin used wasn't poisoned. I screamed for Nor and the rest of my guards as I tried to open the main doors from the outside. They were locked.

I heard the window above click. I ran back out into the street, into the rain. My guards were nowhere in sight.

My mind raced through my options. I wanted to save Rayyel. I couldn't if I was dead. I could see the assassin struggling at the window. The chair must've hit him harder than I'd anticipated. I needed to take advantage of that, but I had no weapons, my guards were missing, and the only thing I could do was run.

So I ran.

Rain poured as if upended from a bucket, hard enough that I could barely see through the thick rivulets. Every drop felt like ice—sharp, cold shards of it, washing away all the blood. My cut throbbed with every step. I tried to ignore the pain as my boots pounded on the slick road, tried to ignore the freezing blanket that seemed to have been draped over my skin. I suddenly remembered my missing guard from that morning.

Was it only that morning? I had only been in the empire a little over a day, and they were already trying to kill me.

I struggled to focus my thoughts. My missing guard couldn't have been a coincidence. I remembered, too, the chaos out by the canal, during the *t'che* execution. Someone had started it, and then someone had told me in Jinan to go to the alley where I met the first assassin. Also, Rayyel's party had denied that it was their idea to change the restaurant. Had someone else sent that letter? But it was penned in *his* hand, with his penchant for neat scripts, the way his brushstrokes ended slightly downward.

I remembered Biala Chaen's knowing smile.

I realized that I didn't know whom to trust. Nor? But I didn't know where she was—if she was fighting for me or had been paid by the enemy to step aside. The only other people I had been sure of had been in that meeting room with me: one was being strung along as a puppet by an unseen hand, and the other lay dead on the floor.

Two streets down, and then another two. The night seemed endless, swallowing the surroundings like a grey shadow while small, faraway lights dotted the black silhouette of the city. I ran until my heart threatened to burst from my chest. Only then did I stop, drenched from head to toe, my leg now starting to feel like a lead weight. Resigning myself to another fight, I turned to face an empty street. My shivering hands curled into fists, holding on to thin air like a lifeline. I waited, half expecting, half dreading the sight of the assassin stepping out from behind the fog, but no one came.

I swallowed. The silence was worse than the attack itself. Hand in hand with the darkness, it was a stark reminder that my father had not prepared me for this. Wolves ran in packs, and lone wolves didn't live for very long. However I looked at it, I was on my own.

It was amazing how fast the cold and the damp could diminish the dignity of a queen.

One moment I stood there, ready to fight to the death, down to tooth and claw if I must. The man who would claim the title of being the slayer of the first queen of Jin-Sayeng would not be free to walk away unscathed.

The next moment, I was slinking through the alleys, knocking on doors in an effort to find someone kind enough to offer me shelter. My earlier experiences out in the streets of Anzhao City stilled my expectations, but I had to try. I tried even when I saw them peer through the windows and then close both shutters *and* curtains, and I tried even when one opened his door only long enough to throw a rotten egg at me. He missed; I didn't bother to waste my breath. Turning me away at least meant that nobody was paying them to betray me. Small comfort to someone freezing half to death; I think my mind was starting to wear out.

I don't remember how long I wandered those streets, begging people for shelter. I think I've washed most of it away, those memories that filled me with a deep sense of helplessness and disgrace. What I do recall was that at some point, I was sitting in the corner of an alley, cloaked in darkness and grey rain. Tears crawled to the corners of my eyes. I refused to let them fall. Arro…Arro was dead, but I refused to let it ruin me. Rai was still back there. My guards…where were my guards? If there were more than the assassins in that room—if they couldn't get to me because *they* were in trouble—then I needed to do something. I was their queen, not some helpless damsel.

I glanced at my wound. It grinned at me like a foul creature, the flesh ragged at the edges. Sucking in my breath, I ripped part of my sleeve and tightened it around my leg as a makeshift bandage. The pressure alleviated the pain momentarily. Drawing another breath, I limped down the street, dragging my leg behind me.

The city watch precinct was right down the end of the canal. I remembered seeing it on my way to the restaurant with Khine, the sign emblazoned in my memory. If there were assassins behind me, the sight of city guards, at least, should deter them. The rain was falling so hard that I nearly ran into a vendor selling fried quail eggs.

"Watch it!" he screamed, hot oil sloshing on the wet road.

I murmured a half-hearted apology.

"Idiot woman…" he began. "What are you doing wandering around here like that? Where's your husband, eh?"

I wished I knew, too. I turned away from him. He tried to grab my sleeve to wrench me to the ground, and I pushed him away and stumbled into the nearest alley. Here, I heard groaning and saw barred windows at eye level. Hands poked out between the spaces, waving at empty air.

A watchman walked past to smack the protruding limbs with his spear. "Back in there!" he snarled, thrusting a lantern at their faces. "Back! And you!" He turned to me now, his face leering. "We'll have none of your services here. This is a clean district. Go home."

"I'm not—"

"Go, before I decide to arrest you!"

I swallowed, considering snatching the sword from his waist. He wouldn't expect it. But then what? What would killing a watchman do?

"There was a disturbance down...down at the restaurant," I managed. "The Silver Goose."

"Are you from around here?" the watchman asked, peering closer at me.

I swallowed. The damn accent. "No," I managed. "I'm...a...I'm a servant. My masters were killed. I barely escaped with my life."

The watchman's eyes narrowed as he crossed his arms. It didn't look like he believed me. Did my clothes give me away? But I was covered in mud and rain and blood, and it was dark enough. Still...

Someone whistled from across the street, an alarm.

"You stay here," he said, jabbing my chest with a finger.

"Hey, you," one of the prisoners called out as soon as the guard disappeared. "You!" He was speaking in Jinan.

I turned around.

"Oh, fuck me sideways," the man breathed. "The queen. The fucking queen."

I limped closer to the cell and grabbed his outstretched hand, twisting it. He slumped against the window. "Who the hell are you?"

He grinned. "You don't recognize me? And here I thought we had something special. Back on the *Singing Sainsa*, you told me..."

"To tie your boots properly," I said in a flat voice. "You're the guard Nor's been looking for."

"I'm guessing the captain misses me. How is the old mare?"

"We were attacked."

"I'm not surprised. About time someone put you in your place, you arrogant, conceited bastards."

The man tried to wriggle from my grasp. I twisted his arm some more, pouring whatever was left of my energy into the movement. "You left your brothers. You left us. This is treason."

He spat. "Fuck treason. Fuck *you*. I'm not Oren-yaro."

"You were the moment you wore that armour."

"Well, I'm not! I'm from Kyo-orashi, and if the warlord hadn't thrown me out of *his* army for gambling, I'd be back home. Then I met you bastards, you Oren-yaro. Captain Agos assured me you were different, and for a while I believed him. Well, you are and you're not. You're something else, acting like you're better than everyone. Making people think they're one of you when it's really all about you, isn't it? You royals."

I let him go. "You act like someone who wants to rot in prison."

"Like you could do anything about this. You've got no power here."

"As you said." I gave a small bow and started to walk away.

He ducked back into the cell and darted to the window ahead of me. "Hey," he called out. "Wait. Hey!"

"I have a name," I said between gritted teeth.

"Talyien. *Queen* Talyien. Can you get me out?"

I paused for a moment. "I don't see why I should take the trouble."

"Ah, don't do that. I'll make it worth your while. You want to know where the captain and the others are?"

I stared at him. "I didn't tell you they were missing."

"You didn't have to. You're alone, and Captain Nor wouldn't have allowed that. And I don't think she'd go down easily without a fight."

"We were separated."

He laughed. "Sure you were."

"Talk now, or—"

"Your threats don't work here, Queen. Get me out, *then* I'll talk."

I hesitated. I didn't trust the man. A coward who defected from his sworn brothers wasn't worth the air he breathed, and had we been back home, he would've been put to death by now. But I was also growing dizzy from blood loss. I needed to find Nor before I passed out on the street. Stifling a groan, I turned around and made my way to the entrance of the precinct.

The lobby was empty, which wasn't surprising in the dead of the night. A fish tank was propped under the window. Fat, ball-shaped fish floated along the surface of the glass, peering at me with bulbous eyes. I struggled to keep my composure as I strode down the hall, my clothes dripping with water. I could also feel something warm trickle down my leg. Blood, probably, but I tried not to think about it.

A single watchman was on the desk. "I'm here for someone," I said, leaning on the edge to stop myself from spinning to the ground. The guard was a blur—I tried to focus on the golden threads of the embroidery of his uniform, which was easier than trying to look at his face.

"The Jin," the watchman replied.

I didn't bother to correct him. "What's he in for?"

"Causing disorder in one of the winehouses down the river." He narrowed his eyes. "You know he really shouldn't be here? There's enough drinking to be had at Dar Aso. He acts like that, of course people are going to complain. I've got nothing against you folks, but antics like these don't help."

"If that's all he did, then let him out. I don't see why you'd need to waste food on him."

"You Jin women really are something," the watchman said with a chuckle. "What makes you think *telling* me is enough?"

"I don't see—"

He patted the desk before holding out his hand.

I flushed, remembering I had no money. I shook my head. It felt like a laborious task on top of trying not to pass out on the floor.

"Then I'm afraid I can't—" the watchman began.

The doors opened. Several others tromped in, wet from the rain.

"There's dead bodies in that restaurant. The Silver Goose," a watchman said. "We don't have a clue what happened, only that Jins were involved."

"No one to question?"

"The rest of the staff insists they saw nothing."

"Too many Jins." The watchman at the desk paused before pointing in my direction. "You. Stay there."

All eyes were on me. I wilted to the corner, knowing it was impossible to disappear.

They returned, dragging my guard with them. The traitor. They forced him to his knees and surrounded him, crows circling a dead man.

"You know something about those deaths, don't you?" a watchman asked, smacking his head with a spear. "What Jin conspiracy are we looking at?"

My guard spat out blood before laughing.

They struck him again.

"Talk, or we'll kill you!"

A second time, a third, and then I lost count of the blows. The smell of blood made me even more nauseated than I already was. Eventually, he crumpled to the ground.

He laughed again, the sound bursting out of him like a wet cough. He began to crawl towards me. "They're going to kill us," he said in Jinan. "Why did we go here? Didn't they teach you lessons about your father's war? Your own husband's clan had done a good enough job trying to eliminate *yours*. Everyone is your enemy, Princess."

"I'm your queen," I replied evenly.

"Right. I forgot. You were crowned." He tried to lift his body, and a guard kicked him back down. "Captain Agos asked me to keep an eye on you," he hissed, his breath wheezing into the floor. "I don't know why you banished him like that. I could understand you getting rid of your husband, but Agos? The man would carve himself like a roast if you just asked." He suddenly groaned, a spasm of pain overtaking him. The guards stepped back, as if giving him room to breathe.

I stumbled forward. The watchmen didn't stop me, and I found myself right next to my guard. He smiled again, white teeth standing out against the red that streamed down his face.

"He sent me to protect you," he repeated, "but how's a man to do his job around those assholes? If that Captain Nor had your best interests at heart, she would've doubled your men. Tripled. She would have never let you come here at all. I told her some of the guards were acting strangely. I told her they'd been switching shifts under her nose, disappearing during their watch. She told me I was overstepping my bounds by questioning her authority. And *I'm* the one at fault?" He laughed. "You want to know where she is? Where the rest of your guards are? Look at the docks. At the whorehouses. Wherever a Jinsein can spend his hard-earned money for selling you out—"

A watchman picked him up by the collar. "Are you done?" he asked before running a sword into his belly for one final stroke. My guard crumpled into a heap, blood pooling under his body. Now they left him alone, as if he were nothing more than a hunk of meat lying on the floor of a slaughterhouse.

"Funny a drunkard would say that," I whispered to the dying man.

"I never lied about what I am. Can you say the same thing for yourself?"

"I—"

"It doesn't matter," my guard whispered. "Your boy...you need to go home now. They'll kill your boy."

"What are you saying? He's safe with his guardians. His father's people won't let anything happen to him."

He laughed one last time, and then the smile grew still, the light in his eyes disappearing. I suddenly remembered his name: Saka. It shamed me that it took me that long to recall it. Saka. He had been in my guard before Nor took over duties as captain, had once killed an assassin attempting to shoot my son with an arrow during a parade. He and my old captain Agos had been close.

The watchman from the desk stepped close to me. I recoiled from his touch. He looked almost apologetic as he stood aside, pointing at the open doors. "Run now," he said.

I opened my mouth to protest.

"You're new here," he continued. "I'm going to give you a piece of advice. Don't ask for help, or they'll know you're helpless and take you for everything you're worth. This is a kindness I'm doing you here, woman. Run before I change my mind."

I stumbled back into the rain. Run? I could only limp. At some point, I found myself blacking out in the corner of the street even as my mind struggled, screamed at me to get up. The image of Arro, dead on the ground, flitted through my consciousness. I thought of my husband being beaten like Saka, his head flopping like a dying fish, his brains dripping into the floorboards.

I thought of my son in his bedroom back in Oka Shto, staring through the window down at the courtyard while waiting patiently, so patiently, the way he had all these years.

CHAPTER EIGHT

THE IKESSAR HEIR

ᛏᚢᚙ

Saka's words had the sharpness of a knife under my throat. I had thought my son's safety the least of my concerns. He was the crown prince, son of the Ikessar heir. Who could hurt him? Say what you want about the Ikessars—they were vigilant where it counted. His father had survived a civil war as a toddler, which included multiple assassination attempts by my own father. They were so frightened for his safety that I didn't meet him until after my father's death.

I could still remember that day. The entire palace had been thrown into chaos and excitement: the Ikessar heir, come to meet his bride-to-be at last. It was a story to be passed on for generations, one that people didn't want to miss for the world. We had been betrothed since I was born, a monumental day because it was also the same day my father ended his terrible war. After so many years, people saw the chance for peace at last.

So our first meeting was marked with a large celebration. There had never been anything like it in the palace before. Entertainers arrived from all corners of the land—singers from Kyo-orashi, fire dancers from Akki, jugglers from Kai. A tourney was held, with the best warriors from every province coming to compete at *Karo-ras*, an ancient form of fighting where warriors stripped down to a loincloth and fought with sticks and bare hands. Though no blades were allowed, *Karo-ras* battles were still bloody and sometimes deadly. My tutors did not like me attending the matches, reasoning that a young, delicate princess such as myself had no business watching men beat each other to a pulp.

My opinions did not align with my tutors'—they rarely did. The day the tourney started, I escaped through the window so I could watch the first few matches. My friend, Agos, was already waiting for me in the garden.

"Arro will be *furious*," Agos told me.

"A sleeping man can't say much," I pointed out, grinning.

"You didn't…"

I nodded. "Herbs in his coffee. He so dearly loves his coffee."

Agos gave me that look that told me he didn't quite know what to make of a princess who regularly attempted to poison her staff. I punched him on the arm. He was large and muscular, even at fifteen, but he pretended to wince.

Because the castle at Oka Shto was built on a cliff side, many of the celebrations were being held in the square at the base of Mount Oka Shto, between the barracks and the stables. I forged ahead, berating Agos for being too slow down the long, winding trail. A man dragging a wagon filled with supplies up to the palace paused to look at us, but I had taken care to dress myself in common clothes and he didn't recognize my face.

It was easier to get lost in the crowd once we reached town. I had never seen Oren-yaro like this—filled with music and strange faces of people from every corner of Jin-Sayeng. I even caught sight of Kag tourists, which would've never happened in the days when my father was alive. I stopped to marvel at their fair skin, paler even than a pureblood Ikessar's, and their long, delicate noses. My swordsmaster always talked about going for a Kag's nose first in a fist fight, because they break really easily.

The smell of smoke and meat was too much for me to ignore, so I went straight for the food stalls. We bought skewers of chicken intestine dipped in a sweet sauce and roasted over hot coals. It was the sort of food Arro never allowed into the palace, giving me all the more reason to devour it whenever I could.

We sauntered over to the tourney grounds, chewing on the rubbery meat. I could already hear the drums and the cheers. Agos whistled and pointed to the wooden platforms that served as seats. I caught sight of some of the royals in their brightly coloured ceremonial armour. "That's Lord Nijo, Warlord Lushai's son," Agos said, following my gaze. "Master Torong was just fixing up his horse's saddle this morning."

"And those boys in the corner..." I said.

Agos narrowed his eyes. "I don't know. I don't recognize their banner."

"Yu-yan, you think?" Yu-yan had not traditionally belonged to the royals until the War of the Wolves, when the Anyu clan of Kai decided to claim the surrounding land for themselves. They succeeded in making the rice merchants bend their knees, though not without shedding a lot of blood in the process. The clan was widely criticized for their actions, a stark reminder of the further disarray the land could fall into if my father's war continued. After my birth and peace was declared, nobody dared unseat the Anyus. "Let them deal with the rice merchants by themselves," my father had been fond of saying. "They made their bed—now they get to sleep in it."

"The twin sons of Warlord Ojika," Agos said. "I didn't think I'd ever actually get to see them."

"I thought Warlord Ojika was too scared to return to the east after what he did."

"Maybe he still is. I don't see him anywhere," Agos said.

"Strange. Did their father let them go alone?"

"Maybe they escaped, like you." I jabbed him in the ribs. He grunted, looking back at the platform. "That man beside them, that's Warlord Basho of Darusu. The mountains on his banner...this tourney is drawing the snakes out of their den."

"Careful with your tongue before they cut it out for you," I murmured. I scanned the rest of the royals, noting the various colours and markings of the banners above their seats. I glanced at the far end. My eyes settled on a black flag with an embroidered soaring falcon.

"Ikessar," Agos said before I could open my mouth.

I pressed my lips together. "It's too far away to see," I said. "Let's get closer."

"Why?" Agos asked.

I jabbed my finger in the air. "My betrothed will be there."

He scratched his chin. "I don't know about this. They'll recognize you, and then you'll get in trouble, and then *I'll* get in..."

I was already rushing through the crowd. I heard Agos groan behind me.

The match was starting when we reached the platform. A warrior, waiting on the sidelines, shoved himself past me. He was completely naked except for a loincloth and a corded piece of rope with a wooden amulet around his neck. I scanned the platform and paused. Two seats above the Anyu brothers sat another boy, solemnly observing the match. Even though he couldn't have been more than fourteen years old, there was already a line above his brows, and the downward quirk of his lips did not seem to belong to someone who was only starting to grow a moustache. Unlike the Anyus, whose faces were twisted into an expression of delight and cheer, he seemed almost unaffected by the excitement before him. For all he reacted to it, he could've been staring at a wall.

I breathed. The Ikessar banner and the priest of Kibouri yawning beside him made it clear enough: this was Rayyel aren dar Ikessar, my husband-to-be. I felt a lump the size of a fist in my throat.

"Hey, you! Away, girl!"

I barely glanced in the direction the voice had come from. I was not used to somebody speaking in that tone and didn't even realize it was directed at me until it was too late. A man reached down from the platform, his hand on my shoulder. I lashed out in shock, but my fists never connected as he shoved me aside.

"You dare..." I started.

The man clambered over the seats to face me. He was dressed in a royal's silks. On his breast was a pin with the falcon crest on it, marking him as an Ikessar man, likely a member of a minor royal family. "Do you not hear the words coming out of my mouth?" he hissed. "You don't belong here. This area is for royals only. Where are the guards? Do the Oren-yaro not know the meaning of *security*?"

"Let's get out of here," Agos said behind me.

"It's a shame to see someone from such an established clan as the Ikessars get into hysterics over a mere girl," a voice observed. It was the warrior from earlier. He pushed himself closer to us, lean muscles gleaming under the sun.

The Ikessar lifted his chin, his eyes blazing. "The future Dragonlord is sitting right above us. That *anyone* could just waltz in here..."

"What's she going to do? Spit on his shiny boots?" The warrior's Akkian accent was strong. He glanced up, staring right at Rayyel. "You, Beloved Prince. Why don't you come down here and fight your own battles?"

"Do not speak to the future king in such a way," the Ikessar said.

But the warrior's words seemed to make an impact. Rayyel got up and walked down the steps. "Beloved Prince," the Ikessar continued, bowing. "I was just asking the girl to step away from the platform. This area is for royals and contestants only."

Rayyel looked at me. My cheeks flushed from the attention. *My future husband*, I thought. I wondered if he was going to rush to my defense. Was he going to fall into a speech about harassing defenseless girls?

"There is a section for commoners right across from this one," he said. His voice was already deepening with manhood, but the flatness of his words took me aback.

I found myself stepping forward. "What if I don't want to go?"

"Let her stay," the warrior said. "She just wants to watch the match. The commoners' seats are hard to see from. I'll see to it she gets out when it is over."

"*Without rules, we are no more than animals,*" Rayyel intoned.

"That's the best you can do?" I asked. "Quote Kibouri?"

"Watch your tone, girl!" The Ikessar man wasn't about to walk away.

I felt Agos's hand on my shoulder. "Please," he murmured. "Let's go now." He bowed to the prince. "We're deeply sorry, Lord Rayyel—"

"See to it they are escorted out." Rayyel didn't even look like he wanted to hear Agos's explanation.

The Ikessar bowed. "My lord."

"You coward," I hissed. I didn't know why I said it. I think I wanted to see how he would react. He didn't at first. He took two steps before turning back to me, his face red. A smug grin slipped onto my face. "You're scared, aren't you?" I continued. "You're scared of looking weak in front of them, so you're going to do whatever's easiest. But that's not how you look strong. Doing what's expected of you—that's how you would rule?"

The warrior grunted. "Now, girl, I wouldn't go that far."

"No, you're right. I wouldn't want Lord Rayyel to waste breath on me," I snapped. I pulled away from the Ikessar, who was reaching out to grab me again, and made an elaborate curtsy. "I leave you to your festivities, my lord," I drawled.

Rayyel didn't say anything. I drew back. Agos started running, and I dashed after him. We heard somebody call out to catch us, but nobody made the first move; two peasant children weren't worth the trouble.

———

We spent the rest of the morning watching the matches from the rooftops while trading bites out of a meat bun. I wasn't going to let my first meeting with Rayyel spoil the *Karo-ras* tournament for me. Agos didn't talk about it, which was just as well, because I wasn't sure what I would tell him if he did. What *did* I expect, anyway? That he was going to be a dashing prince like the ones in the stories instead of the usual Ikessar lord with a stick up his behind? My father had made his own opinions of the Ikessar clan clear from as far back as I could remember. I should've figured that Rayyel wouldn't be an exception.

But I was a young girl, then, and like all young girls found it difficult to accept that reality could be nothing close to fantasy. I hid my disappointment as best I could. After the first break, when a warrior from Osahindo was declared victorious for nearly snapping the bone of his opponent's left arm with two sticks, I told Agos I needed to return to the palace. Likely Arro had woken and was looking for me.

We took the back road, the one that ran along the castle walls on the edge of the cliff. I stopped to pause at the view of the city down below, nestled between the terraced hills and stretching out as far as across the river in the distance. My father's legacy—and in exchange for keeping it, I had to give my hand to that despicable boy in marriage. It irritated me beyond measure.

Surprisingly enough, Arro was still asleep, and the palace staff, thinking I was busy with my books, had not noticed me missing. I cleaned the dust from my face and sneaked back into the study to wake the old magister. He didn't stir at first—I must've given him enough sleeping herb to knock out a horse—but when I screamed into his ear, his eyes snapped open. "What's that?" he stammered.

"Shouldn't I go? Won't the lords be here at any moment?"

"Yes," Arro blurted out. "You should get ready. You look—" He gave the resigned sigh of one who had been tasked to turn me into a *lady* and believed he had failed every step of the way. "Ask your maids to make you look presentable."

I batted my eyelids and went through the routine of dutiful princess. I cleaned up, put on my best silks, and did not argue with the servants at all, even when they insisted I have ribbons braided into my hair, a process that took well over an hour to accomplish. They were just on the finishing touches when a boy came running in to announce that the Ikessars had arrived.

I was led to the common hall. Minor clan leaders were presented to me one by one. I didn't pay attention—my eyes were locked on Rayyel at the far corner. It was only when that man, Lord Faro—who oversaw Shirrokaru as a regent of sorts—was brought forward that I forced my eyes back to the task at hand. The simpering fool took my hand to kiss it. I let him, noting he was blissfully unaware that I was the same girl he had been so eager to throw to the dogs earlier. What a difference clothes could make! I resisted the urge to have him arrested on the spot and waited for Rayyel to be brought to me.

"And lastly," Arro said, "Prince Rayyel aren dar Ikessar, son of Princess Ryia aren dar Ikessar and Lord Shan aron dar Hio, heir to the Dragonthrone."

The hall fell silent as everybody's head dropped.

I stood there, staring down from the main platform where later—much, much later—I would be crowned without him. I wondered at the expression of awe emanating from the crowd's faces. Rayyel aren dar Ikessar was *not* a direct male descendent of the Ikessars—none existed anymore. His uncle Rysaran, the last true heir, had seen to that. Yet the people regarded him as a symbol of peace nonetheless, a ray of hope that the Ikessars could still somehow save the land from the chaos my father had plunged it into.

I knew it was unfair for me to be critical. I was the last direct Orenar myself. It was one of the things that made our betrothal significant—the joining of two rival clans on the brink of extinction. A thing for stories, indeed. But at that moment, I could only regard him with contempt, the way my father must have regarded the betrothal agreement.

He looked up. Recognition flooded into his eyes.

I smiled, slowly.

Somehow, he was able to muster up the courage to pick up my hand and kiss it. His lips trembled. "Beloved Princess," he said. "It is good to meet you at last." To his credit, his voice sounded calm.

I refrained from uttering the insults brewing in the back of my mind. "It is good to meet you too, Beloved Prince," I replied sweetly. Emptier words have never been spoken.

A night of celebration followed, one that I was not allowed to see to the end, as Arro and the rest of my tutors insisted I stick to my schedule. Oren-yaro ways are difficult to bend, especially with almost every lord of the land up there watching us. So I woke up early, like always, ate a simple breakfast of boiled eggs in my room—away from the prying eyes of the warlords, most of whom had not seen me since my father's funeral—and then made my way to my study for that morning's lessons.

Rayyel was already there, his nose in a book. The first thought that came to mind was that he had been up long before I was. That made him even more irritating in my eyes. Not only had he *not* apologized to me about yesterday—he had not even thought to mention it, as if I could somehow forget the insults he and his man had thrown at me—he now had the audacity to act as if my home was his. It was *my* study. The least he could do was wait for me to be there first and *then* ask for my permission. The Ikessars must be the only clan who, despite lacking an army or resources to acquire such power, think they can get away with everything.

He must've noticed me staring at him, because he lifted his eyes from his book to regard me with an expression of curious calm. I think I could've forgiven him if he had apologized, then, but he didn't. So I didn't talk. Instead, I dashed in, grabbed his book, and sprinted out.

I honestly didn't expect him to chase after me.

By the time I heard his footsteps behind me, I was already committed.

I went straight for the hall leading to the garden. I glanced behind and saw him gaining on me, although his face was red from the exertion. I took a deep breath and plunged through the bushes, making my way past the back trail of the palace and off a fork that led into the woods. Here, I thought, he wouldn't follow. He was soft, raised in a temple—surely the woods would frighten him. I glanced up, welcoming the dappled shadows interspersed with golden sunlight, the smell of trees, and the feel of forest litter under my sandalled feet. I had played in these woods with Agos for as long as I could remember and knew every twist and turn by heart.

"You!" I heard him cry out.

I stopped. It was the first time he had ever actually spoken *to* me since the tourney, as opposed to the practiced lines his advisers must've prepared for him. I turned on my heel, holding the book loosely in my fingers. "Oh?" I asked. "Did you want something?"

He was panting. His face was *very* red now. "You're a wild child," he hissed. "Unfit to be queen."

"And you're a pain in the neck," I retorted.

"Do you think this is a game?" he asked. "Sneaking out of the palace, pretending to be a commoner so you could get a rise out of me? This is what you were taught about ruling?"

"Don't lecture me about ruling," I said. "What happened down at the tourney—no self-respecting prince would've acted that way."

"Pray, tell me. *How* should a prince have acted?"

I laughed. "Shown mercy. Isn't that what the Ikessars are known for?"

"Rules..."

"Exist, right. So let the tourney attendants see to that. You could've shown your generous spirit. Be the gallant prince, not some stern-faced official." I saw his face tighten at my words, like he didn't quite understand them.

"You're Oren-yaro," he eventually blurted out. "*Generous* sounds like such an ironic word coming from you."

"This is how you're trying to get to know me?" I asked. "By throwing my people's name in my face?"

"You did the exact same thing."

"I don't say *Ikessar* like it's an insult," I replied. "I'm not a fool. I know what you all think of my father."

"You say *Ikessar* like it's a standard, like I'm supposed to know better because of it," he said. "Not all insults have to sound the same." He held his hand out. "Give me my book."

"How about I throw it down the cliff?"

"You're not helping your case, Princess. *Give me my book*, or I'll march up to the council right now and demand they find me a better bride-to-be."

I laughed at his face. "You really *don't* know anything. Do you think this is *your* land alone, that you could tell them to do anything just because you wanted it?"

"I *am* the future Dragonlord," he said.

"An old title," I reminded him. "A formality. You are the future king who will have a *queen*, who will also, incidentally, be Dragonlord. We are to have equal power, Beloved Prince. It was written out, one of the first demands my father made when he allowed this betrothal to take place."

"A frivolous demand," Rayyel said. "Pointless. The scholars all agree."

"The scholars can kiss my behind. We could've won Jin-Sayeng," I said in a low voice.

"Your father gave in because he *couldn't* win."

"He could've, given time. And he would've killed your mother, too, and you, only he didn't." I waved the book at him. "We are ruling jointly, Beloved Prince, whether you like it or not. But I'm glad I know what you

really think. I'm glad all of this came to light. When I present the council with your treachery..."

Rayyel snorted. "My personal thoughts can hardly count as treason,"
he said. "Unless your plan is to sink us back into the rule of blood and
sword. He gave me the stink-eye, so off with his head?"

His tone of voice was becoming too much for me to handle. I turned
around and pretended to throw the book into the bushes. He gave a
sharp cry and rushed forward, exactly how my dogs would react when I
fooled them into thinking I had a stick in my hand. I laughed. *This is it.
I've given up all that my father worked for because I couldn't be patient with
a pimple-faced boy.*

Rayyel grabbed my shoulder and pushed me into the ground just as a
roar blasted behind us.

The surrounding air felt like the palace kitchens in the morning, hot
and muggy from the wood stoves. I tried to shove Rayyel away from me
and saw a dark, scaly form scurry past us. A nearby branch burst into
flame before wilting, and then I heard Rayyel screaming at me to get up.
I was in too much shock to understand his words.

He pulled me to the side a second time. A lick of flame surged from
the creature towards us, knocking a small tree to the ground. Only then
did my head clear up enough for me to form coherent thoughts.

We were being attacked by a dragon.

It was, I would later learn, a juvenile, a creature the size of a horse.
But it was enough that it could breathe fire and wanted to kill us. Confronted with the beast back then, I didn't know what to do. I wanted to
run, but the creature was standing in the middle of the only trail that led
back to the palace. The woods behind us led to the cliff.

Rayyel coughed. "I've got my ceremonial sword with me," he said in
a low voice. I wondered how he could be so calm. "I'll distract it. You
make a run for it."

"Don't be stupid. A ceremonial sword will break," I said.

"I don't intend to fight it. Only distract it long enough for you to get away."

"And then what?" I hissed. "You'll burn to a crisp before you get close! Then it'll chase after me and we'll both be dead, anyway!"

I could see a bead of sweat make its way down his face. He really hadn't thought it through himself. I turned back to the creature. It was shuffling around in a half circle, snake-like eyes bearing down on us. I could see fire bubbling in its mouth, small tendrils of flame licking past its sharp white teeth.

"It's making more fire," I said, glancing at its distended belly, which contrasted with its long body and whiplike tail. It didn't seem to like me looking at it and draped its wings over itself. Thick red veins throbbed through the blue membrane, which faintly glowed. Its eyes were golden orbs with thin black slits that never left us. I recognized the look of an animal trying to make itself seem bigger than it really is, and realized the creature was just as frightened of us as we were of it.

But that didn't reassure me any; it didn't make the dragon any less dangerous. I could feel a pit in my stomach. If we tried to run past it before it could finish growing its fire, it might just throw us to the ground and open us up with its teeth. I had not known helplessness until that moment. Rayyel must've felt the same way, because he reached for my hand. His palm was wet and cold.

We would've both died, two fool children who thought they knew more than they did. *Heirs of the Dragonthrone, killed by a dragon*, our tombs would say. The history books would laugh. Our ancestors once rode those same dragons, those trustworthy and intelligent beasts that made Jin-Sayeng's name in the world, until they eventually died out. Prince Rysaran was the one responsible for bringing the first grown dragon back, but it was a vile, crazed creature he couldn't control. That dragon destroyed parts of Shirrokaru and the old palace of Oren-yaro, and killed many people, including my own brothers, Yeshin's grown sons.

It was said that these new dragons were offspring of that old one, which flew away and was never seen again. Unlike the dragons from the stories, these were weak-minded, untameable. I hadn't believed it before. But facing that creature, seeing my own death in its eyes, I suddenly could.

The dragon jerked its head back. A man appeared on the trail, pike in hand. The dragon whirled, its tail whipping around as it lunged for him. The man shoved the handle of his pike into the creature's open maw.

Fire curled around the wood, but the man didn't seem to care. He pushed back against the dragon. Almost at the same time, he pulled out a small sword from his belt and, with a grunt, stuck it through the pebbled skin under the creature's neck. Steaming blood hissed from the wound. The creature clamped down on the pike, its body contorting. The man dropped the pike and stepped back as the dragon curled around it in its dying throes.

He looked up towards us. His face was streaked with sweat and soot, and his short, curly black hair was damp. He was built like a warrior— not a young man, but not too old, either. "Are you children all right?" he asked.

Rayyel dropped my hand. I swallowed. "We're unhurt," Rayyel said, stepping out of the woods. "We're not…"

The man's face flickered at the sight of us. His face dimpled, even as he frowned. "You're Prince Rayyel and Princess Talyien," he said. "Out for a walk without your guards? You could've been killed."

"We don't usually get dragons here," I said, trying to sound calmer than I felt.

"No, I understand that part," he said. He flexed his fingers, still staring at us. It was disconcerting. People usually bow when they see me, falling flat on their faces in their quest to throw flatteries my way. Rayyel, I have no doubt, had the same experience. But this man barely even tipped his head in our direction. I probably could have understood if he was a Kag, but he looked Jinsein. Perhaps he had grown up there; his Jinan had a tinge of a foreign accent to it.

"Is there a problem?" I asked.

He closed his mouth. "You shouldn't be out without guards," he said. "It's not just the dragons. Anyone with an interest in the Dragonthrone could try to hurt you. *Anyone.*"

"They wouldn't dare," I breathed.

The man's eyes narrowed. "Heir to the Dragonthrone. *Child.* I'm going to speak slowly so that you can understand. Not everyone celebrated the day your parents laid down their arms and agreed on your betrothal. There were talks, dark thoughts in the shadows. Pacts made to edge Jin-Sayeng closer to a more *desirable* peace. Your betrothal is not what it appears."

He looked at the still-writhing corpse of the dragon nearby. "That one is a mere mindless beast. I've been tracking it from the west for weeks. I don't know what drove it to travel all this way, but it was exhausted. I've never made an easier kill. But had I arrived a moment later, you would both be dead. How much closer, do you think, will someone with a mind to kill you get?" He spat to the side. "I'll walk you back to the palace."

He didn't say much else on the way. He took us straight to the gardens and stopped once we had a clear sight of the door. Remembering my courtesies, I wiped dirt from my lip and bowed towards him. "We are grateful for our lives," I said. "If we may know to whom we owe them . . . ?" I deliberately trailed off so he could pick it up from there.

The man's jaw tightened, like he was thinking it over. "Dai," he eventually said. "I am Dai alon gar Kaggawa."

"A merchant?" Rayyel asked. "What are you doing in the palace?"

I elbowed Rayyel. "Kaggawa," I repeated. "We owe peace to the work of two Kaggawas. Merchant caste, too. Are you related?"

"My grandfather and my father's sister," he murmured. "If you would call it peace. But with all this bickering…" He shook his head.

"You speak of shadows who want us dead," Rayyel said. "Would you know of these fools, that they may be brought to justice?"

Dai shook his head. "I cannot say. I will not say. I will not plunge this land into chaos so soon after the last." He placed his hand on his sword. "Remember my warning. And when you are crowned, do not forget about the west. Our lands in the Sougen are plagued by these beasts. If we are overrun, what you just saw this morning will become your entire life." He spat again before walking back to the forest.

I watched his figure disappear and heard Rayyel draw a deep breath. "Should we have him arrested?"

I looked at him, aghast. "He just saved our life."

"And threatened us while offering no courtesies whatsoever." He sighed. "I will let it be. It's been a long morning. Do you have my book?"

"We almost got killed by a dragon, and you're still thinking about that?"

"It's a good book. I don't have any copies of it."

"I think I dropped it back there."

He stared, as if this answer wasn't enough. With a sigh, I went back to find it. I didn't have to look very far; I had dropped it near the bushes right outside the gardens. I picked it up and dusted it off, which revealed the cover. *Memoirs from the Beginning of the Wolves' War* by Ichi rok Sagar, a known Ikessar supporter. It said much that Rayyel didn't think twice about reading such a book in *my* own castle. If you brushed the insult aside, it was a clear enough sign of peace. I returned to Rayyel and handed it to him.

He wiped the cover before tucking it under his arm. He turned to me, a thoughtful look on his face. "You're brave," he said after a moment. It sounded like he was talking to himself.

I swallowed. "As are you, my lord."

His eyebrows knitted. "He is right, you know. It will not be the last time we will face danger together."

I realized he was serious. I thought about Dai Kaggawa's words and nodded. "It's not like we can abdicate," I said, trying to keep my voice light.

"No." He patted my shoulder once before leaving me in the hall.

CHAPTER NINE

LOST IN SHANG AZI

ᛁᛏᛟᚢ

Ididn't know how long I lay in that mud, sleeping like the dead. A warm hand on my arm woke me. I bolted in shock, expecting an attack. Instead, I found myself looking into the kindly face of a plump woman.

"You'll die out here," she said, holding an umbrella over me. I blinked, staring at the first rays of sunlight seeping through the oiled yellow fabric. I wanted to tell her I had no money, but my tongue had forgotten how to work.

She tugged at my sleeve, urging me to stand up. My body obeyed. She led me into the street and down a walkway that ran under a mossy bridge, past a narrow section of the canal. I couldn't tell if it was still connected to the same waterway near the Silver Goose or if it was an entirely different one altogether. The water seemed dirtier here, murky. Instead of fish, I saw a dead cat bobbing amongst the rest of the refuse, its tail sticking out like a flag.

I had no time to think things through. I continued to stumble after the woman, heaving myself up a flight of slippery stairs. We crossed the street. My leg was starting to protest again. Before I could give voice to it, the woman stopped in front of a gate and inserted a large iron key into the lock. The gate creaked, opening inwards. She urged me past the threshold and into a damp courtyard surrounded by tall stone walls. She closed the gate behind her and led me through the closest door.

The feeling of warmth, after hours in the rain, was indescribable. The woman brought me to a small room, where I was relieved of my wet clothes and given a soft robe to wrap myself with. I stumbled onto a hard, narrow bed that smelled of mint and smoke, and for a while, it was all I knew.

I slept for a very long time. I had wild dreams of being chased by phantom assassins down the street, except this time I was down on all fours, paws instead of feet, tongue slavering down my open mouth. In most of the dreams, I was able to escape into the shadows, only to hear them calling me—soothingly, at first, like hunters crooning to their dogs. And then their voices would rise, the soft tones souring as they begin to threaten and call me names. *Come out, bitch*, they'd say, whistling, laughing. *We've got a nice boarhound for your thirsty cunt, and we'll even let you finish before we mount your head to the wall.*

Each and every time, their voices sounded like Rayyel's.

Sometimes, I didn't escape them. I would feel a spear end sinking into my chest, pinning me to a tree. I would reach out, snarling as the assassins-turned-hunters crowded around me. They would laugh, and I would try to snap at their long, curved nails and their faces, shaped oddly like the warlords' back home, and then I would die.

At some point, the dreams stopped, and I slept soundly. I woke to the sound of a rooster crowing. For a time, I stared at the patched ceiling, where a pink-skinned house lizard with beady grey eyes ran in circles chasing after flies. When it disappeared behind a beam, I sat up to notice that the swelling pain in my leg was gone. The gaping wound had been stitched shut with black thread and covered with a thick yellow salve.

My first real thought was that Arro was dead.

Arro, who had been by my side for so long that I couldn't even remember when he first came to court. My father had handpicked him, I was told, to oversee my education, but in the years that followed his arrival at Oka Shto he had become something more, easily rising to the rank of magister because of his work ethic and sound counsel. He had done his best not to become overly familiar with me, but he had been a fixture in my world, one of the few faces that had remained constant in a sea of changes.

The loss gnawed a hole in my stomach, and it bothered me that I could feel that way yet not muster a single tear. I am not heartless, you understand; I have bawled over dead dogs and horses like a little child. And I was sad about Arro. But all I could think of was my promise to my son. How I had been there, been so close to making it all right again. Except my pride... my damnable pride... had gotten in the way. If I had only swallowed it before I walked into that place, perhaps none of this would've happened. We would have agreed before the assassins ever got there, would have been on our way back to Jin-Sayeng together by now.

Now, I had nothing—not my husband, not my adviser, not my guards, not even my own strength. And my son—was he safe? He had to be. I *needed* him to be safe. If I was to survive even the next hour, I had to ignore that knife on my throat. I had to ignore it, or else it would bleed me.

"Oh! You're awake!" a voice called from the doorway, breaking my thoughts. A small, sprightly woman with a thin, freckled face and a button nose came towards me, holding a bowl. I smelled hot herbed rice porridge. My stomach tightened, my thoughts replaced by the hollow pain of hunger.

"The mistress thought I should check up on you, see if you're up, and she's right," the woman said, speaking a lot more quickly than I was used to. Flabbergasted, I couldn't think of a reply fast enough. She propped me up on a pillow, dragged a small table to the side of the bed, and placed the bowl there. She began to stir the porridge with a spoon. "Tashi Jhao thought you were going to sleep another day, because he gave you a sleeping draught to last that long, and Manshi Ziori—that's the mistress—said she's willing to bet you'd be up long before, what with your constitution and all. She's never met anyone who could be in that rain as long as you've been, injured leg besides, and still walk all the way here. They argued about it, actually."

She eventually seemed to pause to catch her breath, but it was only to blow at a spoonful of rice porridge. "I can feed myself," I said before she could push it towards me.

She paused. Was it my tone of voice again? I didn't know anymore. I reached for the bowl, which she willingly gave up. I placed a spoonful into my mouth. It *was* still hot, but I wasn't about to give her the satisfaction of being right and swallowed before my tongue could protest. The porridge was in need of salt and was laced with too much ginger. I resisted the urge to comment.

"So," she said, which was the least I'd heard her say since she first walked into the room.

I ate a few more bites before turning back to her. "I appreciate you giving me shelter and bringing me food. Thank you." I bowed. My father had not raised an ingrate.

She looked shocked. "You don't have to—I mean, it's the mistress who brought you in. I'm just doing what she asked. You've got a strange manner of speaking. Are you not from around here?"

There was no sense in denying it. I shook my head.

She clapped her hands in delight. "A foreigner! How exciting! I've never met a foreigner before. Well, the herb store owner's wife comes from the east of the empire, from the big city where the Esteemed Emperor lives, so she claims, but that's not even close. I've always meant to travel away from Anzhao City when I've paid my debts, maybe down south, to the Ruby Grove lands—the trees there, you know, all the leaves, *red*, and

An Mozhi City perched above the cliffs like a dream, all those bridges…
and here I've forgotten my manners. I'm Tati, and I've been working here
close to a year. How did you end up on the street like that? Someone
must've thrown you out. Was it your husband?"

"Miss Tati," I said carefully. "I would speak with your mistress now, if
she has time."

"Oh, I understand if you want to keep it a secret. Everyone here has a
secret. It's why we're here, after all. This isn't exactly a first-choice, first-
class place, if you know what I mean."

I think it was clear from my expression that I didn't. She closed her
mouth. "I think she's with the cook, overseeing today's meals. I'll go call
her now, tell her you're looking for her."

"Thank you." I bowed a second time. Tati pulled away. She seemed
perplexed, like she wasn't exactly sure how to respond to me, even though
I was pretty sure I hadn't said anything offensive at all. I heard her shuffle through the door and turned my gaze towards the window. The sun-
beams hurt my eyes, but after the seemingly endless dark dreams, I more
than welcomed the pain.

"Seems like the good doctor owes me fifty *rean*," a shrill voice said. I
glanced at the woman by the door, the same one who had found me in
the street, it seemed. I didn't really recognize her. Back in the rain, she
had been nothing more than a spectre leading me to the shores of the
dead for all I knew; now she was substantial, a woman whose painted
face barely covered her wrinkles and her frown. Her lips were so red that
it looked like she had been drinking blood. Had I only imagined the
sympathy in her expression from the morning before?

She was wearing a heavy fragrance. The scent of it, mixed with her
body odour, engulfed the room as soon as she stepped in. It made me
feel ill. "I'm Ziori Ashi," she said. No bow, I noted—she chattered
matter-of-factly. She strode to the windows and pushed them all the way
open. I cringed at the flood of sunlight.

She turned back to me. "How are you feeling?" she demanded. I don't think I'd ever heard those words used in that tone of voice before.

"Alive," I said, still trying to find my thoughts amidst her noxious scent. "I wanted to thank you. I would have died out there if you hadn't found me."

"Yes," she said, nodding. "You would have. And yours wouldn't have been the first corpse in the streets of Anzhao City that morning. You are far from home, I think. Your clothes were not Zarojo-made, and that Tati said you admitted you were a foreigner."

I nodded.

Ziori narrowed her eyes. "A foreigner would be something new. Try to stand up."

I blinked. "I'm sorry?"

"Tashi Jhao thought you shouldn't bear weight on that leg for the next few days, but he was wrong about how long you were going to sleep, and I dare say he's wrong about that, too. Circulation is good for your legs." She crossed her arms. I realized she was waiting.

In my court, her attitude was the sort of thing that would soon result in someone being dragged out of the castle in chains. In my father's time, they wouldn't even have thought twice about throwing her off the cliff. I don't even believe anyone had been so brazen to my face in recent years. But I was far from home, and the longer I stayed away, the harder it seemed for me to remember who I was. I wanted rest, and the faster I could get her to leave me alone, the sooner I could get it. I braced myself on the bed and placed my feet on the cold floor. My legs shook and the sharp pain told me my wound was more serious than I had anticipated, but I stood.

Just as quickly, I sat down again. Ziori cleared her throat. "Not ideal, but I suppose it will do. You can sleep it off the rest of the morning, but you have to start work tonight."

"Work," I repeated.

"Yes," she said, as if speaking to an idiot. "Work."

"I think you're mistaken," I said. "I'm not here to work."

"You are, if you know what's good for you," Ziori said. "You think I call on Tashi Jhao for his company? The man isn't cheap, and what he did for that leg of yours set me back a few thousand *rean*. Unless you can pay me back right now?"

I almost choked at her words. "I didn't ask you to call him."

"If I had known your leg was torn up that badly, I would've left you to rot on the street," she said in a low voice. "But you were already here when we saw it. I couldn't very well let you die under my roof. Do you know how expensive funerals get? It's not like I can just dump your body on the street, either. I had no choice but to call Tashi Jhao."

"If you'll help me return to my...people, we can pay you back in full." If I could find an official to trust, a swift letter back to Oren-yaro was sure to make all my problems go away. "And more, besides, for your help."

Ziori gave a weak grin, yellow teeth flashing through luscious red lips. "I found you penniless and alone," she said. "What makes you think I believe you have people to return to?"

I closed my mouth. *Did* I have people to return to? Did Rayyel make it out of that assassination attempt alive? I clutched at the sheets as my mind started running through the possibilities.

"So you'll work it off," Ziori continued, oblivious of my distress. She was going through her words with the practiced ease of one who had done this speech too many times. "I can arrange a client for you tonight, to start with. I've a man in mind who I think would appreciate..."

I turned to her, realization dawning on me. "What sort of work is this supposed to be?"

"Didn't know you were daft as well," Ziori huffed. "Isn't it obvious, girl? You're in a brothel. Although *girl* doesn't seem appropriate for your age. From the shape of your hips, you've already given birth, haven't you? Never you mind. The men don't..."

It took all my self-control not to hit her on the mouth, which was an easy red target from where I sat. "Whatever you think I owe," I said in a low voice, "I am not going to play *whore* for you, *mistress*. I will take this to the city watch if I must." I didn't really want to go back there, but she had no way of knowing that.

"The city watch?" She laughed. "I'll have Tati call you to give you time to get ready. Lo Bahn prefers—"

I pulled myself up and headed for the door.

She screamed after me, her bony fingers reaching out to grab me by the arm. I tore her off me easily enough and limped out into the hall, my leg tingling with a swollen, feverish sort of pain. I struggled against the urge to throw up and started for the most promising-looking door.

Ziori continued screaming. Two large men appeared from around the corner. "Out of the way," I hissed. They ignored me, grabbing my arms and lifting me as easily as if I were a child. I couldn't even swing out at them.

They dragged me back to the room, all but pushing me onto the bed. "Careful, now!" I heard Ziori exclaim. I could feel my wounded leg begin to throb.

"You're not leaving until your debt is paid." Her voice was wooden.

I turned to her. "This is extortion. Robbery. Your doctor's fees probably wouldn't even amount to half of what you're asking from me."

"There's also lodging fees, your meal, and the service I offered you in saving your life..."

"You run your whole establishment like this?" I retorted. "I can have this place collapse over your head. You can't have bribed the *entire* city watch. It hardly seems worth it for one night's profit."

"One night? Oh, no. To pay me back, you're going to be here for many, many nights, and mornings, besides." She gave a grim nod before stepping back. One of the men slid the door shut. I heard them barring it from the other side.

I slumped against the wall, my hands curled into fists.

There are people who find themselves in a precarious situation, believe themselves betrayed, and will do nothing but run their tongues ragged in criticizing the world for not helping them better. Like wailing dogs in the rain, they strain against their leashes instead of turning to gnaw their bonds to freedom, or sit on their piss and wait for pity.

The wolf knows better. I was raised a princess. I was not pampered. But people find it hard to see past the flocks of servants, and assume everything was handed to me on a silver platter. Only another child of Yeshin's would understand, I think, and they are all dead, cold bones under the ashes of Old Oren-yaro.

I made the mistake of saying "I can't" once. I think there was a lesson, a problem I couldn't solve. But I remember Yeshin's eyes turning towards me, the softness in them gone, a rage burning within.

"You're my daughter," he had replied. "Figure it out." There was no hint of threat in his words—despite what people believed about him, my father never threatened me. Instead, his voice was laced with the weight of expectation, one rivalled only by the standards he held for himself. A wolf of Oren-yaro looks at the circumstances and deals with them.

There was a barred window in that room, which I should have noticed when I first awoke. Bars kept thieves out and were a common sight in rundown parts of a city, but the way the iron was melded to the frame made it clear that here, they also served the purpose of keeping people locked in. Not long after Ziori and her men left me alone, I dragged myself along the floor to get closer to it.

The window revealed a street below. I looked down and noticed a man in a straw hat passing by, pushing an iron cart with a stove built into it—a moveable stall for selling fried food. I leaned against the opening and called for his attention. He looked up. His dark face, flecked with white stubble, broke into a toothless grin.

"Maybe if I sell enough fish balls!" he jeered. He tipped his hat at me before continuing on his way.

I bit my lip in an effort to keep my rage in check. Ziori Ashi would hang for this in my father's time. But here, locking women up in a brothel against their will seemed entirely normal. For someone who had lived her whole life within the confines of the law, I couldn't wrap my head around how someone could sink this low. I wasn't even sure if I was still dreaming.

I noticed the rusted hinges on the window. I took the spoon from my porridge and wedged it under the cracks. The frame lifted slightly, and I gleaned that with a certain amount of movement, I could make the nails creak with some effort. With renewed hope, I began to rattle it, hoping to loosen it enough that I could pry the window open with something bigger.

It was slow, excruciating work, which further taxed my already-exhausted body. But it helped me keep my mind clear, held my worries for Rayyel at bay. It was nearly dark when the window began to give way. I held my breath, trying to focus on the task at hand instead of how I was going to find my way through those streets again.

The door creaked.

I rushed back to the bed with such speed that the mattress was shaking a little when Tati walked in. "It's not so bad," she said softly. "I was scared my first time, too. Just look at the ceiling, count the lizards, and try not to breathe into their mouths. Some of them don't like that. If they want to kiss you, let them, but most don't expect that. This isn't like that fancy place by the docks. The men won't expect you to do things, either.

If they ask for too much, you just threaten to tell the mistress because it means they'll have to pay extra." She placed a folded dress beside me and patted my hand.

I wondered if I could knock her flat before she made a sound. But as if reading my mind, she craned her head towards me and murmured, "The mistress told me to warn you not to do anything funny. This man you will be with is not…well, you don't want to cross him. That's all."

I couldn't help myself. "And why is that?" I found myself asking.

She pressed her lips together. "I've had him before. He's a frequent customer. Powerful."

"Money?"

Tati nodded. "Lots and lots." I wondered what *lots and lots* meant in this world. I didn't have a frame of reference.

Violence wasn't going to solve this problem. If this was an important man, Ziori would've warned her guards to keep an eye on me. Also, I didn't want to hurt the poor girl, who looked almost hopeful now that I was talking *to* her. "Tell me more about him," I said.

Her eyes sparkled as she began helping me put on the dress. "He's not a bad man. Not mean or cruel, like the others. He's smart—really smart. They say he runs his business like a tight ship. He doesn't like me, because he complains I talk too much, but I think he likes the talk, so I don't really know what he meant when he said that. He goes here for his health, he says. He has a wife, but she runs him ragged, keeps him on edge. His favourite was Ganya, but she paid off her debt a few weeks ago and left with one of the other customers, which really made him angry, so I wouldn't mention her at all. If you become his new favourite, it will work out well for you. He'll pay for your time, exclusive, unless you want to work with someone else, and then you'll have to work it out with him and Manshi Ziori. You *do* get paid, you know. Don't think she's holding it over your head. Ten percent for every profit we make off a customer—the rest goes to the house expenses. She's just trying to help us. Anything the customer gives extra, you can keep. A good incentive, don't you think?"

She paused and took a deep breath, which gave me a moment to think. I realized, belatedly, that Tati had finished lacing the dress and was staring at me. "Is there something on my face?" I asked.

"What? No. I just—I thought, for a moment, that it didn't look right." She gently ran her fingers along my arm, on the long bruise there. I couldn't even remember where it came from. She made a sound of surprise. "Yes. See, that's muscle under that skin there," she said. "You're a fighter. I can tell. Manshi Ziori told me what you tried to do when she told you. Whatever you're thinking of doing when you're in there with him, don't. It's not worth it. It's over a lot faster than you think."

"Small comforts," I murmured. I glanced at the window. "Will I be... entertaining him here?"

"No. We've got a special room. Come."

I braced myself to stand up, my legs still shaking. She looked like she wanted to say something about that, but shook her head and was blessedly silent about it for once.

She guided me through the hall and past a larger one, with a ceiling that was two storeys high. I could hear noises emanating from the other rooms—angry grunts, faked moans, the sorts of sounds I didn't even think people could make in actual throes of passion. The hair on my arms stood on end, and it took all my strength not to give in to the desire to flee. We went down a flight of stairs and into a room just underneath the staircase. "Han Lo Bahn likes his privacy," she explained, almost apologetically, as she opened the door.

It was a large room, with a mattress that took up about half the space and was covered with silk sheets and several pillows. I noticed rope, a bucket of water, a chamber pot, and the smell of scented candles, though none were in sight. Tati lit a lantern by the window. This one was barred, too, and overlooked a fenced section that formed part of the courtyard. My last plan wasn't going to work here.

"I'll tell the mistress you're ready," Tati said. She dropped her head—not the deep bow of respect, but a slight incline of sympathy—and drew back, closing the door behind her. I heard her talking to a man, probably a guard. The sound of their voices quelled the last of my rebellious thoughts, and I found a corner where I could sit without bothering my wound.

I closed my eyes and focused on keeping calm.

CHAPTER TEN

LORD OF SHANG AZI

ᝢᝮᝥᝤᝮ

It helped that I was not a maiden and had a body that had already
borne the brunt of childbirth. I was also nearly eight years married by
that time (though five of those, admittedly, were without my husband).
The prospect of being around a man who expected more than conversation didn't frighten me. But it was yet another hindrance to escaping.
Could I club him to unconsciousness without anyone knowing better? I
scanned the room once more, hoping there was a table with legs I could
break. I didn't think I could smother the man with a pillow while he was
awake. Besides, what would killing him do? I could be stuck in the room
with a decaying body, which wouldn't improve the situation any.

My thoughts quieted down as the door opened, and a man in a loose
robe walked in. He looked at me, sliding the door closed behind him,
and began untying his belt. I took a moment to observe him—a thick,
grizzled face, with a trimmed beard that was several shades of grey. It
contrasted with his hair, which was still very much black and gathered
in a ponytail above his head. He had small eyes. Brightly coloured tattoos depicting various deities snaked up from where his robe fell open at
his chest. They went all the way to his throat. "Where are you from?" he
asked, noticing my attention.

I folded my hands on my lap. "Jin-Sayeng, my lord," I said.

He looked surprised. "You're far from home. What's a Jin doing in a place like this?"

"Gambling debts," I said easily. "My husband—but that's not important. You are named Han Lo Bahn, I'm told?"

"You know how to be courteous, at least," Lo Bahn said, nodding his approval. "Perhaps overly so. What's your name?"

"Kora," I said, trying not to think about my handmaiden. She had been left behind in Qun's home—surely she was safe. I watched Lo Bahn shrug himself out of his jacket. "It's early in the evening. What would you say to a game of *Hanza* first, and perhaps some wine? It will give us time to get to know each other, and I'm sure Manshi Ziori wouldn't deny either for her best customer."

He paused, a flicker of amazement on his face. "That's the last thing I'd expect to hear from a Shang Azi neighbourhood whore."

"I'm Jinsein," I reminded him. I craned my head to the side. "But perhaps you're frightened I would beat you. Yes, perhaps it's best we forget what I said."

Lo Bahn's nostrils flared. "Not likely. I've been playing *Hanza* since I was young. You think you've got a head for strategy, woman?"

"I don't know, my lord," I said. "We can find out."

He stepped out of the room in a whirl and returned with wine and a game board. He slammed the board on the floor, poured himself a bowl of wine, and watched as I arranged the pieces. This *Hanza* set used pebble-sized conch shells, painted and hardened with lacquer. There were two colours, red and white. He let me have the red side, as a gesture of goodwill; traditionally, red was the easier start, giving a slight advantage to anyone who knew what they were doing.

I used to play *Hanza* with my father. Not for fun, which was a hard thing for a child of seven to grasp. The warlords all dabbled in *Hanza*, and he told me that a simple game could reveal so much about how they thought—if they understood strategy or only tried to mirror my actions, and most importantly, whether they respected me or not. After he had died, I would practice with Arro, and then later, Rayyel.

Neither had offered the challenge that this Lo Bahn now posed. It was a challenge I hadn't encountered since my father, who never let me win unless I truly deserved it. The smug smile on my face slowly disappeared the further we got into the game. I had formed my own strategies around attacking someone hell-bent on self-preservation. Lo Bahn wasn't like that. He attacked decisively, capturing my pieces like a ravenous wolf. We didn't talk much during the game, as he spent more time staring at the board than at me.

He defeated me, but not easily. I poured him more wine. "Well played, my lord," I said. He drank deeply and wiped his mouth with the back of his hand.

"Let's have another," he said.

"You've defeated me without question. Are you sure...?"

Lo Bahn looked up at me, a layer of irritation on his brow. "I need to see if your defense wasn't a fluke. Someone taught you to do this properly."

I bowed. "I'm glad you think so. My father was an avid player."

"I see." He started putting the pieces back on their proper places and flipped the white side towards me. "Let's switch."

"Stacking the odds in your favour? How very noble of you."

Lo Bahn's lip twitched. "Less talk and more play, woman. You wanted this."

I bit back my amusement and started the game. He was fuming now, watching my moves as a hawk might watch a mouse.

My father had taught me that there are many different types of men in the world. Some believe that no one else can know as much as they do, desiring absolute control at the expense of everything. I had pegged Lo Bahn for this type from Tati's description of him, and so far, the game was proving me right. He didn't like that I was able to thwart his moves, didn't like that he had underestimated me from the beginning. He was upset enough during the whole game that he overlooked one of my attacks, which set into motion my own series of counteroffensives that eventually led to my victory.

His eyes were wide open.

"Luck," I reminded him before he could say anything. I fanned myself with my hands. "I'm sure, had my lord seen my formation from another angle..."

Lo Bahn reached for the wine and realized the bottle was empty. "You wait here," he snarled, gesturing at me. "We'll have another game." His words were slurred, his movement unsteady. I had been pouring his wine bowl to the brim while neglecting my own. He had been so intent on the game that he hadn't noticed.

He stumbled back out into the hall as I returned the pieces to the board for a third time. He returned, bleary-eyed, and we began again.

I wasn't really trying to win or lose. I was intent on making the next game drag on for as long as I could. I was starting to lose this one, too, but I threw all my pieces at him one by one while letting him mount counter-assaults that made him feel superior about his strategies. Each time he thwarted me, I made a soft sound of surprise.

"Just give up already," he snarled at some point. "You're losing. I've never met anyone who would draw out a losing battle the way you are."

"*Am* I losing? How do I know for sure? Maybe I'm actually winning and you're just trying to throw me off. An ignorant girl like me wouldn't know one way or another." I tried to titter, but I had never been very good at that and ended up coughing instead. I took a sip of wine. I was still on my second bowl.

He turned to me. I could already see the exhaustion creeping on his face. "How could someone be so stupid?"

"My apologies. Perhaps you can show how stupid I am by defeating me a little faster."

He snorted. I couldn't tell if he was amused or upset.

To his credit, he was actually a very good player, but the wine and his uncertainty of me made everything doubly difficult for him. After he finally defeated me, he pushed the board aside. "Enough talk," he said. "The last time I let a woman get to my head like this—let's start on what I'm paying you for here." He reached for me. I was eyeing the lamp, wondering if smashing it on the back of his head would kill him. I didn't want to, but given no other choice, I would do it in a heartbeat.

I saw him fumble. I placed a hand on his shoulder and murmured, "On the bed, my lord. I don't know the last time they swept this floor."

Lo Bahn laughed, a chuckle that reached deep into him. For all his words, I think he genuinely enjoyed the game. He crawled onto the mattress and grabbed me into a fierce embrace, his mouth making a line on my bare neck. "You smell so good," he grumbled. "A Jin. Hah! The others won't believe me. Lamang will have fits of jealousy when he finds out."

I let him pull me into bed and made the pretense of kissing him back, but I didn't even have to go that far. A moment later, I heard him snoring on my shoulder. I pushed him onto the mattress, arranging the pillows behind him, and removed the rest of his robe. I threw that in the corner and placed the blanket over him.

I was suddenly aware of my own exhaustion. Trying to keep the man on edge while plying him with too much drink had sapped all the strength from me. I crawled to the corner of the mattress, as far from him as I could, and closed my eyes.

I didn't sleep—at least, not deeply. My mind remained alert, occasionally waking me so I could scan the quiet room for signs of Lo Bahn stirring. It also replayed the last couple of hours with stark acuity, contrasting them to the times I'd played *Hanza* with Rayyel. He lost more often to me, and it upset him, too, but in a far different way.

"It's just a game," I had told him more times than I cared to remember. "Your monks and priests didn't prepare you for the subtleties. But it's not important."

"When I'm Dragonlord, they'll expect me to know strategy," he would fume. "A king needs to know how to make logical moves."

"You don't need this sort of strategy. We're not at war," I would remind him.

And each time he would look up at me, his eyes searching, accusing. Like everyone else, he was afraid of the Oren-yaro, even when she was his wife. It was something I had learned to live with all these years.

I was awake in the morning before Lo Bahn was, arranging the sheets, pretending to tame the disarray in my hair. I saw him looking at me, perplexed. "It was a good night, my lord," I said.

He scratched his cheek. I wondered if he believed me. But he didn't look like the sort who would admit to falling asleep before he could properly do anything with a woman, and I was happy to leave it that way. He reached for his clothes, which I had piled in the corner. I could tell, from the laborious way he put them on, that he had taken in more wine than he was used to. A single vein was popping through his temple.

"If I can ask a favour from you..."

Lo Bahn paused, his face tightening.

"I am not here because I want to be, my lord," I said. I kept my voice low on purpose, to avoid giving him more of a headache than it looked like he had.

"What's that to me?" he snapped.

"Take me away from here."

He frowned. "I don't think so. I've a wife, and this is where you belong."

"This is *not* where I belong," I said. I lifted my skirt up. Lo Bahn's eyes sharpened, even when I only tilted my leg to show him the wound. "I was running away from my husband."

"He did that to you?" There was a note of outrage in his voice.

I nodded, pretending to look away. "Mistress Ziori found me two mornings ago in the rain. I owe her my life, but the doctor's bill..."

"Tashi Jhao has exorbitant fees," he agreed.

"Tati told me you preferred someone *exclusive* to you. And after last night, I thought perhaps..." I deliberately trailed off, allowing his mind to fill in the blanks.

There was a moment of silence. "I could arrange that," he said.

"Could you arrange it elsewhere?" I asked.

"What do you mean?"

"I dislike the food here, and I will not be locked away here like an animal, forced to service whoever my masters please. I may have made mistakes, but I still want my dignity, my lord. Pay Mistress Ziori, but keep me elsewhere—an inn or a place of your own, where you can come and go as you like. Then we can have freedom and comfort instead of this dark room, where you can't be sure she's made me share myself with other men. Your wife need not know."

"You're asking for too much," he said in a low voice, but I knew I wasn't. You could tell from the look on his face that he was already thinking it over, that the thought of such an arrangement enticed him more than he let on. He wandered over to the door and eventually let his eyes fall back on me. The desire was unmistakable. I tried to hide my discomfort as best as I could.

He eventually strode out of the room without another word.

I waited, wondering if Ziori would agree to such a thing. How badly did she want to keep me? The novelty of the whole situation had become tiresome. I wanted nothing more than to order my guards to take all of them out of my sight so that I could go home and sleep beside my dogs in my own bed. Jin-Sayeng felt like a lifetime ago, and yet I had only been gone a few weeks. I couldn't have been in the empire for more than a week.

I heard two sets of footsteps. Lo Bahn stepped in first, gesturing at me. "Get your things ready. She has agreed to this arrangement under the express condition that you be returned to her at first sight of trouble. I would warn you now—if you are thinking of crossing me, don't."

"He is the most powerful man here in Shang Azi," Ziori added, fixing me with a glare that could mean anything. I wondered what she told him. "I would take that advice if I were you."

I bowed. They withdrew, and Tati came by in their place. She kept her chattering to a minimum as I got dressed. I didn't get my old clothes back—they were valuable, and Ziori must've decided to keep them. I didn't care. I couldn't get out of there fast enough.

Lo Bahn and his men were waiting for me out on the street. All thoughts of trying to escape *now* fled my system. I was going to have to be patient again and find an opening when they least expected it. Right now, out here in broad daylight and with my leg the way it was, I had no chance of getting very far.

Lo Bahn strode ahead of us. Despite his talks of having a wife, he didn't seem at all in a hurry to drop me somewhere and get home. I refrained from talking and focused on keeping up. The last thing I wanted was for him to lose patience and take me back to Ziori. I wasn't sure I could trust myself not to do anything rash if that happened; I had decided I would rather die than return to that despicable place.

We eventually stopped at a marketplace. Vendors and people swarmed around us like ants, and I began to look for a chance to get lost in the crowd. But one of Lo Bahn's guards whistled to me, and I saw that Lo Bahn was starting up a flight of stairs. I shuffled after him.

The stairs led to a platform with a series of doors on a large, decrepit building, so drab and grey that it looked like an enormous wall engulfing one side of the marketplace. Lo Bahn picked the last door. It opened up into a narrow staircase that smelled of rot and animal droppings. The tight space did strange things to the shadows—they leaped and loomed over us like branchless trees.

Chatter and music greeted us as we landed at the bottom of the staircase. My eyes adjusted to the semi-darkness, and I saw that we were in another market, one that stood inside the building itself. People hovered around various stalls, which contained wares from pots to paper fans, woven rugs, vases, colourful blankets and pillowcases, and clay ornaments. One woman was selling luck charms and beads "made from the finest black wood in the holy mountains, blessed by Saint Fei Rong himself." Other stalls seemed to be for gambling and games—I saw caged rats in one, and a table full of dice and markers in another. At the next stall, people pressed against each other to view spiders fighting on a stick. They were screaming and exchanging coin while the spiders coiled on top of each other. They had spider fights in Jin-Sayeng, too—I was told they kept them starving in dark boxes for days to make them fierce. Children loved to catch and train them, to fight amongst themselves or to sell for a good sum at the market.

My attention drifted back to my surroundings. The only source of light came from the beams of sunlight streaming from the three windows at the top of the far wall. One of the guards pushed me closer to Lo Bahn in an effort to keep me in sight. The smell of fried meat and rancid sweat formed a thick, nauseating musk in the air. I was relieved when we turned into an alley formed by several stalls, and entered another door into a room.

Here, the air was clear, if still stagnant. The walls were lined with lanterns and red rugs embroidered with golden thread—most depicting various forms of lionbeasts and other Zarojo creatures unfamiliar to me. A large table dominated the center of the room. Several men sat around it—rough, grim-looking men, the kind I'd been warned you didn't want to meet alone in a dark, empty street. They looked up as we arrived.

"You're late, Lo Bahn!" a voice barked. A familiar voice. My senses swirled.

Lo Bahn forced me into a chair before I could think. "A distraction, Lamang," Lo Bahn retorted. "One you wouldn't know anything about, I'm guessing." He squeezed my shoulder possessively before taking a seat himself.

"He wouldn't," another man laughed. "Lamang can't afford women even if they offered to suck his cock for a bite to eat."

"Ah, you got me there," the familiar voice said. "I'm so poor I had to go barefoot while the cobbler stitched up my boots the other day. You see why I'm here."

"You're here because you've got nothing better to do all day than play with yourself, and *that* isn't going to make you rich. Pah! Who knows? Maybe you'll win this time." Lo Bahn laughed. "I'll even cover you for a night at Ziori's. Not that it'll do you good, Lamang—nothing about you that a woman can fix. Besides, I already picked the best one there for myself." I flinched as he drew me to him for a quick embrace. The man he was talking to turned to me, and I saw his face.

It was Khine.

He recognized me as soon as our gazes locked. The smile on his face faded. I saw a line of concern, followed by confusion, and for a moment I felt relief at the thought of not being alone and friendless after all. But he quickly regained his composure and turned to Lo Bahn like he didn't know me. "I can see that you did," he said. "Gods damn it, Lo Bahn. Leave some for the rest of us. It's not like you've got the energy for them all in one go."

There was a bark of laughter from the table.

Lo Bahn grimly picked up a cup. "Are we yapping or are we playing?"

"I'm just trying to wear you out, Lo Bahn." Khine smirked. "Give a poor man some credit. I've got a mother to feed."

"You told us last week she was dead," a man called out.

"Dying," Khine corrected. "But still very much alive."

"And she'll have our hides if we don't bring anything back," the man sitting beside Khine said. He was young, with a thin beard that looked like it was in its first season of growth.

"I don't think you Lamang brothers know how this game works," someone called out.

"They don't," Lo Bahn sneered as he dropped dice inside the cup and began to shake it. "Or they'd have won something by now." He slammed the cup on the table and lifted it. "Two and four," he said.

"Liar!" Khine called out.

Lo Bahn pushed his dice to the middle of the table. Khine took one look and gave a soft groan.

"You should know by now. He *never* lies," the young man beside him said.

"Not true, Cho," Lo Bahn retorted. "He just doesn't know how the game works. At least he has balls. How about the rest of you cowards?"

They exchanged bids, and I lost track of the next round. Normally, I would've sat there and taken the opportunity to analyze how the game worked—I'd never had the chance before, as dice games were traditionally played by the common folk and not by royals. Winning by pure luck, without the thrill of strategy or outsmarting your opponent, was seen as a waste of time. I liked learning about such things—you never know when that sort of seemingly inane knowledge might be useful.

But strategy was the last thing on my mind. I was trying very hard not to show how much Lo Bahn's pawing irritated me, and I couldn't take my eyes off Khine. He was acting the fool *too much*, something the rest of the men around him seemed unaware of. He had them, though for what purpose, I couldn't tell. He seemed to be losing money faster than he could hold on to it.

"Lo Bahn's woman seems enamoured by Lamang!" a man observed.

I heard Lo Bahn growl. I quickly turned my head away.

"I *am* pretty charming," Khine said. "Lend me to her for a night, Lo Bahn. I'll pay."

"No you won't," Lo Bahn snorted. "You'll be penniless by the end of this morning. By the gods, you'll be penniless by the end of the *hour*. Are you purposely losing, Lamang, or do you have some trick up your sleeve you were hoping to use? Something, say, that would've been useful back when we first started?"

"No trick, I'm afraid to say," Khine said, shaking his head.

"He's just *really* bad at this game," Cho piped up.

I heard Khine give a sharp intake of breath. I turned back to him in time to catch him give Cho a quick glance, a look of reprimand.

No trick surfaced. Khine lost all his money and walked away from the table like a man in a lot of pain before the whole game was done. He all but stumbled to the door. There, he paused. "It's still early, gentlemen," he said. "Take a break. A stroll out in the sun will be good for your lungs. And you should feed your woman, Lo Bahn. She looks starved."

"She can wait," Lo Bahn grumbled. "If I win this round, I'll take her out for lunch."

"Piss and vomit, man, this is why your wife is a harpy and you have to pay to get your wick dipped." He reached into his pocket. Lo Bahn's guards jumped, and he shot them a look. "You bastards," he said, all the honey gone from his voice. He placed a paper bag on the table beside me. "Eat before you pass out," he murmured.

"You're not a doctor anymore, Lamang," Lo Bahn said distractedly. He was busy counting his winnings.

"Never got that far," Khine grumbled under his breath. Out loud, he added, "And you don't have to be a doctor to have decent sense." No one said anything, and his face tightened. "Fuck. Let's get out of here, Cho." He stepped through the door and disappeared, his brother at his heels.

I stared at the bag. After a moment, I peeked into it and saw a meat bun.

"He's pissed because he lost," Lo Bahn said, completely ignoring me. "Man's a sore loser, always has been. Six and four! I *told* you!" He jumped up, slamming his fists on the table. I was starting to dread the next few hours of my life.

———

The game lasted over two hours, maybe more. I can't remember ever being so uncomfortable in my life. I was a prisoner bereft of a sentence, a body hanging from the edge of a cliff that just wouldn't break. Twice, Lo Bahn ordered somebody to give me water and accompany me to the public outhouse; each time, I tried to find some means with which I could escape, but I couldn't. A couple of opportunities presented themselves— the tiny window above the outhouse, my guard becoming momentarily distracted by the line outside, craning his head away from me long enough that I could've grabbed something and smashed his ear in—but I found myself unable to move fast enough to take advantage of them. Something about the last few days had wrung all the fire out of me. I was hesitating, when once I wouldn't have thought twice about seizing what I could.

Before I realized it, the game was over and Lo Bahn was raking in his winnings. He was becoming chatty again—dicing and three cups of rice coffee seemed to have done much to improve his mood. "I have an apartment at the edge of the district," he said, giving me a look. "If you don't mind living next to a slaughterhouse, you can stay there for now."

I bowed. "That is very generous of you."

He snorted. "We'll see. I don't remember anything from last night—I think you owe me a reminder."

"Your performance was . . . exemplary."

Lo Bahn lifted an eyebrow. "You don't talk like a whore. I *ought* to remember. You're lying. I suppose I can't blame you for trying to spare my feelings. You gave me too much wine. You should see me when I haven't had any. You'll never forget it."

He rubbed his mouth with the back of his hand and whistled to his men. "Take her to the flat," he said. "I have things to do, gods be damned." He grabbed me by the shoulder, his rough hands caressing my neck. I thought he was going to force his lips on me and found myself stiffening. But he only looked into my face thoughtfully.

"I'll see you tonight," he grumbled.

"My lord," I said with a bow.

He snorted. Two men came forward to lead me away. One was big, barrel-chested with ham-like arms, but the other man hardly had muscle on him. The disparity in their structure made it clear that these were not professionally trained guards.

I had been warned by my swordsmaster never to engage in battle directly—most male warriors outweighed and outmuscled me, and I think he was worried about me making foolhardy decisions that he could get blamed for—but I think if my leg had felt a little better, I might have tried to fight them. I could've intimidated the smaller one into giving me quarter while the bigger one lumbered behind us. Could've found a way to immobilize them while I made my escape.

The thought distracted me throughout the entire walk. Before I realized it, the men were leading me up the stairs of a small compound. Clothes lines and potted plants crowded most of the view, but I noticed people staring at us and giving us a wide berth. It was clear that they knew these were Lo Bahn's men, and that—as Tati had warned me—he was not a man to be crossed.

We stopped in front of the door at the very top of the building. The men didn't say anything as they unlocked it and gestured at me. As soon as I walked in, they closed the door behind me.

I glided through the flat, pretending the neat furnishings interested me. There were various paintings of a distinct style—a combination of thin water paints and thick black ink—and colourful vases the size of barrels. I looked into one and saw blue fish with bright yellow fins swimming through miniature lily pads.

I absently touched the surface of the water, half-amused at the way the fish bumped my fingertips, before investigating the kitchen. There was a stone stove filled with burnt firewood and a small table fit for two people. I noticed a purple rice cake dotted with sweet sesame seeds and wrapped in lotus leaves. I opened it and sniffed—it was still fresh, probably no more than a day old, which told me that Lo Bahn lived in this flat as often as his own home. The realization did not make me feel better about myself. I needed to get away, and soon—I had *no* intention of becoming anybody's whore.

I ate the rice cake—still half expecting someone to scream in horror and tear it away from my hand—and contemplated my next move. Afterwards, I walked back to the door, opened it, and stared at the guards.

"There is no private bathhouse," I said, making it sound like the most tragic thing in the world.

The guards exchanged glances before turning back to me. "Did you, er, expect one?" one asked. I could see amusement dancing on the corners of his lips.

"I was promised one," I said. "Lo Bahn said I would have one. How am I supposed to get ready for him like this? He'll be back *tonight*. I don't want to smell like a slaughterhouse when he gets here."

The other guard craned his neck towards me and sniffed. "You don't smell like a slaughterhouse," he said helpfully.

I drew away from him in disgust. "And I'm supposed to trust you, when both of you seem to have grown up in filth? I noticed that neither of you were gagging in that wretched market."

"The nerve of the whore..." the first guard said.

I pointed at him. "Lo Bahn will hear from me. He promised comfort, not some pigpen with two slack-jawed idiots for company. Go on, try to hit me!" I added, noticing he was lifting his arm. "See if Lo Bahn lets you get away with it! I'll tell him! I will!"

The commotion was starting to draw attention, which made both guards uneasy. I think dealing with an angry woman was more than they had bargained for. "Calm down," the second guard—the larger, more cheerful one—said. "There's a public bathhouse just across from here. I'm sure Lo Bahn will let you go later. He'll probably even accompany you. He likes his baths."

I opened my mouth, pretending to be speechless for a moment. "You want me to wait for him while stewing in my own filth and then *ask* him to go with me to the bathhouse?" I paused, letting the silence fill in the blanks.

"Now that you put it that way..." the man murmured.

"There's a laundry pump somewhere in this compound," the other guard said. "Calm down for a moment, woman. You're making a scene. Look, I'll go ask the neighbour for some soap, and then maybe you can get yourself cleaned up a little in the meantime."

"A *laundry* pump? You expect me to get myself ready for Lo Bahn at the *laundry pump*? He didn't hire you for your brains, did he?" I crossed my arms. "Take me to that public bathhouse now, before he gets here. I can at least tell him you weren't *totally* incompetent."

"He told us to watch you," the guard growled.

"And he told *me* to get myself ready for tonight. We seem to have a problem. Do you see our problem? Tell me you see our problem." I rolled my eyes.

"We could go with her..." the other guard started.

"Yes, accompany the boss's whore to the bathhouse so she can complain we saw her backside one too many times. You think I have a death wish?" The smaller man tightened his face. "Go back inside. I'll head out and speak with Lo Bahn about this. Do me a favour and keep silent until I get back. If the boss hears you've caused a scene, he won't be happy."

"Don't take too long," I hissed.

He spat to the side of the landing before starting down the steps.

I glanced at the bigger man as his friend disappeared. "In the meantime, I need your help," I said in my best husky voice. "I'm sorry I didn't catch your name. What was it again?"

"Ning," he said.

I gestured to him, drawing back into the apartment. He cleared his throat. "I don't think..."

"I was injured two days ago. I need help with the dressing," I said, limping towards a small chair. "Please, close the door."

Ning hesitated, but eventually, I heard the door click shut. He stomped inside, scratching his head. I had already unwrapped my leg. The flesh around it still hurt, but I noted that the stitches were starting to shrivel. I caught him looking at the gash.

"What do you want me to do?" he asked.

"Look for bandages," I said.

"I don't know if he keeps any around here."

"We won't know until you look."

He scratched his head before sauntering over to the kitchen, his back to me. I glanced at the nearest vase. All my instincts were telling me to grab the thing and smash it over his head. It would be perfect if he passed out before he knew what was happening. The other guard wasn't likely to return any time soon. I could make my escape.

But I also considered what would happen if he *didn't* pass out. What if I missed? What if he had a hard head? I couldn't fight, not with my leg the way it was. He'd warn Lo Bahn, who would probably rape me for my insolence and then triple the guards. It would be a prison worse than the whorehouse.

"Would a dishcloth do?" Ning asked, tugging one of the cupboards open.

"I need bandages," I said.

I wondered if the other guard would return with Lo Bahn, or if Lo Bahn would actually let me visit the bathhouse. I could try to escape there—it had been my original plan, after all. I wasn't sure anymore. I wanted nothing more than to just get out of there, and my *only* guard had dropped all his defenses. *Rush in. Think later.* My thoughts had taken on my father's voice, and he was all but yelling them at me.

The vase, then the chair. *And then, if he doesn't pass out, I have to kill him. There must be knives in that kitchen, or a piece of rope I could strangle him with.*

I didn't want to kill him. It's different in battle, when you're just trying to survive. You don't focus so much on the killing but on the trying to keep them from spilling your guts on the ground. In every other instance, I had killed in response to a threat. But killing in cold blood— I had only done it that time in the garden, with that man. Years later, the sensation of guilt had yet to pass. I had little desire to repeat the process all over again. I swallowed.

But you have to kill him.

I placed my hand on the rim of the vase.

Someone started knocking.

I swore, although I was also relieved deep down inside. Ning rushed to the door to open it.

"You—Ning, I thought it was you! They told me you were here! The street near your house is on fire!" a familiar voice called out.

"Can't be," Ning said.

"Look out the window if you don't believe me."

Ning raced back inside, followed by Khine. He didn't even look at me. They pulled the curtains apart. I saw a tendril of black smoke rising in the distance.

"Spirits!" Ning breathed. "Lamang, you—stay here, guard the woman."

"I came here to warn you, not babysit for you," Khine said.

"I'll pay you!"

Khine scratched the back of his head and sighed. "Very well, but…"

Ning stepped out before he could even finish talking. Khine smiled, a wistful look on his face. Only then did he turn to me.

"You again," I grumbled.

"It's a small neighbourhood," Khine said. "We're all friends here."

"Some friend you are. You didn't really set his house on fire, did you?" I asked.

"Heavens, no. The man has children. I'm not a heartless bastard."

"Then what…?"

"A cart, filched from an unsuspecting vendor and set ablaze in an alley. Should kill some rats, at least." He rubbed his jaw. "I'm surprised it was just him. I was expecting two guards."

"I got rid of one. I was just about to get started on the other." I paused, letting the situation sink in. "Why would you want to help me escape?"

"Escape? Is that what you're doing?" He walked up to me. "I wanted to talk to you, that's all. Didn't think Lo Bahn would let me if I asked him nicely."

"He does seem to hate you."

"He's a sore loser." Khine's eyes twinkled.

I laughed. "Never mind. So you did all that just to talk to me? Were you about to lecture me on the folly of my ways?"

"I wanted to see how you were doing," he murmured. He was looking at my wound.

"Well enough," I said, pulling my leg to the floor and covering it with the hem of my dress. I swallowed. "Not as well as I'd hoped." I stopped, trying to read his expression, wondering if I could trust him. He had been so kind so far, but then, so was Ziori at first.

"If you want to escape," he said, as if he was reading my thoughts, "then you better start doing it now, don't you think? Now that both of them are gone?"

"You're here," I pointed out sweetly. The vase was still beside me. Khine was smaller than Ning—I was a lot more confident that I stood a chance against him if push came to shove. And I've been told I'm pretty good at shoving people.

"I'm not going to stop you. I can even help you if you want."

"Now you're being smug. I don't need your help. I was doing just fine before you arrived."

"I did notice that. The vase?" He pointed. I pulled my hand away, but it was too late. He shook his head, chuckling. "Not on Ning. Flowerpots, bottles, one time a house beam—I've seen him take them all."

"What about you?"

"Ah, my heart. You wouldn't hurt me."

"Why would you think that?"

"Because you wouldn't. Come." Khine strode up to me and held out his hand.

I looked at it.

"You don't have to trust me now," he said. "Just know that we only have another few minutes before Ning or somebody finds that cart, and then..."

"Oh, damn you," I said. I reached out. His face broke into a grin before he led me through the door and onto the street.

CHAPTER ELEVEN

THE CON ARTIST AND THE QUEEN, REPRISED

ย รษ จ

Khine draped a shawl over my head as we walked. "I take it your meeting with your husband didn't go well?" he asked.

"Not well at all," I said in a low voice.

He clicked his tongue. "That's too bad. And then he threw you out, and Lo Bahn found you?"

"Ziori did."

He turned to me, his eyes wide. "That hag. That explains everything."

"It does?"

His face grew dark. "She and that despicable Jhao…they've been pulling this trick for as long as I can remember. Some poor girl from the rural provinces might find herself out in these parts of Anzhao—I think she's even paid people from the city watch to make *sure* they end up here…and then she and the good doctor will help her out, fix her up, put a nice, warm meal in her belly. Only it gets expensive, you see? And she gives her no choice but to pay back her debt one way or another."

"That is *exactly* what happened."

He gave a grim smile. "And there's nothing they can do about it, especially since Ziori preys on the sort of women who come here with nothing and have no one to turn to in the first place. And there's no rules against it, as far as the watch is concerned."

"The paid watch?"

"See, it's nice when people pay attention." He patted my arm before leading me down a bend. I didn't know the streets anymore and couldn't even see the canal. After all that had happened to me, the unfamiliar surroundings seemed even more threatening than ever before. I wasn't pleased that I was following this man blindly, but I didn't know what else to do.

I stopped beside a small tree, one that was dotted with lumps of green fruit along its trunk. I took a deep breath. "Let's get to the point, Khine...Lamang, was it?"

Khine turned to me in confusion. "That is my name, yes."

"What do you want from me?"

"I thought I was just trying to help you."

"You were the one who told me not to expect help out on these streets without giving anything in return. Are you meaning to sell me back to Lo Bahn? To a higher bidder? Speak your price, Lamang, because I can make it worth your while. Anything you think they can give you, I can double. Triple." I tapped my foot.

He stood there, his hands at his sides. "Tali," he said.

I had forgotten I had given him my name. I swallowed, trying hard not to show how much hearing it—after days of being called by another name or *foreign whore*—affected me. "Tali," he repeated, holding his hands out. "Believe it or not—and this is the first time I've ever had to tell a woman this—I'm not going to sell you."

I cracked a smile. "I'm not concerned about what you want to do. I'm just letting you know that you have *options*, should you decide..."

"All right," Khine said. "Thank you for letting me know."

"You don't believe me."

"That's—"

"I know you could use money. You needed it when we tricked that shopkeeper. Don't tell me you've had a change of heart all of a sudden."

"*We* tricked him," he said. "Money was not forced out of his hand against his will. What Ziori did to you...that's different." His voice had dropped to a low rumble.

"Different how?"

"Do I really need to explain?"

"I see. The self-confessed con artist has morals."

His expression changed. "Yes, he does. The same morals which are helping you escape from your captor's clutches as we speak." The frustration was plain on his face. "My house isn't far away. We can argue here, wait until someone spots us and alerts Lo Bahn's men, or you can go now, maybe find your way back to your husband. Or we can debate about this over a cup of hot milk tea."

"Hot tea sounds nice," I mumbled. I turned to follow him.

Khine didn't say anything in reply. Nor did he speak at all as we went down one dirty street to the next, his face contorted as if he was in deep thought. It was strange to be in the company of someone who could go from being so talkative one moment to downright silent the next. After navigating a length of alley with an oversized gutter running through the middle, we eventually reached a narrow street with houses crammed together like books in a library. A person could reach out from their front door and touch the neighbour's window across.

Khine ushered me up some slippery stone steps, which led to a small door. He fiddled around with a key, unlocked the handle, and pushed. "Welcome to my castle," he finally said, his cheerful expression returning.

I stepped inside. There was a narrow staircase leading straight up from the door. Two bodies side-by-side wouldn't be able to fit through it. He kicked off his boots and climbed up. I started to follow him, but right before I could make that first step, he cleared his throat. I looked at him. He looked at my feet.

Embarrassment flooded my cheeks. I hoped it was too dark for him to see. I mumbled an apology and slid out of my shoes. I placed them against the wall as an afterthought. It's not that I was raised without manners—I always took my shoes off in temples or before entering bedchambers—but growing up in Oka Shto, you couldn't really go barefoot through the main halls. Too many came and went for the servants to keep the floors pristine. They tried, mind you, particularly when my father was still alive, but...

I realized that Khine was still staring at me. I went up, one hand on the rails for support. Walking on the flat street had been tolerable, but going up a slope still bothered my muscles. My legs were beginning to shake. I dealt with the pain as best as I could. At the top step, he handed me a cushion.

I took a seat at the first empty spot, near a shuttered window, and breathed a sigh of relief.

"Let me look at your wound," he said.

My first instinct was to refuse. But something in his expression told me he was going to insist if I did, so I sighed and pulled up my dress, revealing my leg. The wound was bleeding a little. I had walked so much that day that I wasn't surprised.

Khine came over, and after a moment's hesitation, he touched the puckered flesh with his fingers. "So you pretend to be a doctor, too?" I asked.

He grimaced. "Not exactly." But he didn't stop to explain what he meant by that. He got up, walking to the end of the room. "Doctor Jhao does a good enough job, but it's not the best and it's certainly not what he pretends it's worth. I don't know if he's involved in Ziori's dealings, but he must be. He certainly benefits from it."

Khine returned to me with a box from the shelf. I craned my neck to take a look. There were various metal implements, bandages, and a jar of dark paste. He cranked the jar open first and slathered the paste—which smelled like cow vomit stewed in spirits—on my wound. It tingled, and I found myself pulling away in protest.

"Do you want the damn thing to get infected and fall off?" he asked.

"Not particularly. I'm fond of that leg." I let him put more salve on and looked around the room as he bandaged it. It was small and cramped, with an open doorway that led to what I presumed was the kitchen. There was a ladder in the far corner, leading to a loft. The wall on the other side had a shelf lined with books.

The books surprised me. In Ziri-nar-Orxiaro, did thieves and con artists find time to read? I would have thought otherwise. I turned back to Khine, watching him finish wrapping my leg with practiced ease. "Now," he said, looking at his handiwork with satisfaction. "I promised you milk tea."

"With sugar," I said.

He grinned. "I can see why your husband got rid of you." But he strode over to the kitchen anyway, stopping for a moment by the doorway to get a ladle of water from a barrel. He disappeared behind the wall. I heard the sound of firewood being stacked, smelled smoke, and without realizing it, fell asleep.

This time, I had no dreams, a result of that sleepless night I spent beside the snoring Lo Bahn. But after the worst of my exhaustion had passed, I forced myself awake. I reminded myself I was not yet safe, that I didn't know if I could fully trust this Khine. I struggled to open my eyelids.

I was lying on a mattress, in a dark room that was not the same one I had fallen asleep in. There was no door. I reached out in panic and was about to start screaming when I heard voices below me.

"Why the hell would I lie to you, Ning?"

"Because you already did, you sneaky son of a bitch." I recognized Lo Bahn's guard's voice. "You said you'd keep an eye on her."

"You didn't tell me she was a horror. A little warning would've been nice. The bitch *threw* me out of there. Said something about my smell or she didn't like the way I look or something. Said she was going to throw a fit if I didn't leave. She nearly smashed one of Lo Bahn's vases. You know how much he loves those fish, right?"

"No more than he loves his whores, I'm guessing. Why didn't you come find me?"

"Gods, Ning, I tried to. Believe me. I ran down the street to get you as soon as I could. But then Tashi Oban came by, and I had to hide—you know Cho owes him money, and he thinks he can squeeze it out of me, but I keep telling him I don't have enough—I can barely keep everyone fed as it is..."

"What was that upstairs?"

"What was what?"

"I heard a sound coming from upstairs. You're not keeping her, are you, Lamang? Lo Bahn is furious. He'll have your balls for this."

"Why the fuck would you think I'm keeping her here? Do you think I have a death wish? Go and check if you want."

I heard footsteps and instinctively drew the covers over me, even though I knew it wouldn't help. I heard the floor begin to creak and the sound of a door opening. There was a pause, a sharp intake of breath, and then I heard the footsteps descending.

"You better not be lying to me, Khine," Ning said. "You know how bad this is going to be for you if you are. For both of us *and* our families."

"We've been friends for years, Ning. Why would I lie to you? Come back to check again if you want. I live here—I'm not going anywhere."

"Where are your sisters? Cho?"

"Cho went to visit a friend by the docks and won't be home for a few days. Thao and Inzali are working until tomorrow. You can ask them when they come back. Maybe they've seen something."

I heard the voices recede. After a few moments, there was silence.

I stayed on the bed, my heart hammering. The silence continued for a while. I wondered if I should try to escape, but I couldn't see a window for me to climb out of. I was also still very tired, and very hungry.

I thought of Rayyel. I wondered if he was alive and if he was looking for me. He ought to be. How does a queen stay lost for long? I tried hard not to imagine his body lying in the gutter outside the Silver Goose, cold and stiff under the rain, the way Arro's must have been by that next day. But it was difficult not to, and the fear was made worse by the fact that there was nothing I could do about it.

I heard the door creak open again and stiffened. The shadows jumped as light from a lamp flooded the room. I saw the wall move and realized it was merely a divider.

"It's amazing how lazy some people are," Khine murmured, walking towards me. He looked amused. "At least I didn't have to hurt him. Last thing I wanted to do, but if he was persistent, I wouldn't have a choice. How are you?"

"I need to return to the Silver Goose," I said. "Tell me how to get there."

His brow furrowed. "Why?" he asked.

"My husband—" I took a deep breath. "It's not what you think. It's not what you all think. I don't know if I can explain."

"Maybe you can try."

I looked at him, not knowing what to say. I *wanted* to tell him and get it over with: *I am queen of Jin-Sayeng, separated from my guards. There are people trying to kill me, and I fear the worst for my husband. Bring me to safety, and I will reward you beyond your wildest dreams.* But the words wouldn't come. I was frightened out of my wits, and pretending to look calm was taking more effort than it should.

I heard him grunt. "Maybe you can try over dinner," he said. "I cooked. You took your sweet time sleeping."

The promise of food worked to get me out of the bed. I followed him down the ladder. "How did you get me up there?" I asked.

"Not easily. Please ignore any strange bruises or bumps you may have." He pulled over a cushion for me to sit on and scuttled to the kitchen. He returned with two steaming bowls. They were filled to the brim with white rice, topped with scrambled eggs and thick yellow curry sauce. It was sprinkled with chopped green onions.

My first real meal in two days was heavenly. I couldn't even tell if Khine was a decent cook or not—I was just that hungry. It was a good thing he had included the chopsticks when he gave me my bowl, or I would've just dug in with my fingers and made a fool out of myself. I found myself asking for seconds, which Khine readily obliged. I washed it all down with the promised milk tea, which had since grown cold. It tasted faintly of jasmine and toasted rice.

"So," Khine said after I took my first big breath. "You promised to talk."

"I didn't," I pointed out. "You were hoping I would."

"I see. I suppose my cooking skills weren't enough to sway you."

"It'll take more than eggs and sauce to impress me."

"You do know how to wound a man's heart," he said, tapping his chest. He grew serious. "The Silver Goose again, you said. Are you sure? You must be sick of that place by now."

I nodded.

He frowned. "I won't leave you on your own. Not this time."

I gave a grim smile. "You don't even know me."

"We've been over that."

"Right. Morals." I clicked my tongue. "And for that, you would lie for my sake. Risk getting yourself into trouble. You *and* your family, from what I understand."

Khine smiled and got up without replying. I watched him return the bowls to the kitchen and wondered what sort of man my father would've decided he was. Lo Bahn had been easy enough. But someone who tricked people for a living and lied so well? How could a man like that be kind on purpose?

The harder they try, the more they want from you. My father's words came back to me, so vivid it felt like only yesterday that I sat cross-legged beside him, listening to him go through the day's meeting with me. Khine stepped out of the kitchen smiling, and the memory faded. I found myself returning the smile, not entirely sure what it meant.

Had I decided to trust him?

Or was I going to knife him in the dark, first chance I got?

It was only later, when we were back out in the street, that I remembered I no longer had my dagger with me.

Before my father's illness, it was a common sight to see representatives from various royal clans in the castle at Oka Shto. They pretended to want to strengthen ties with my father, but I think what they really wanted was to see what it was all about—a place built with every intention to displace Shirrokaru's Dragon Palace as Heart of Jin-Sayeng, though of course this was never said aloud.

I couldn't blame them. My father's ambitions had dragged the nation into the most terrible war it had seen in decades, and it was only right that they get a glimpse of the famous palace where Warlord Yeshin was said to have planned his most strategic attacks and executed his rivals' supporters. I also enjoyed seeing them parade about with their extended families and numerous servants—men, women, and children, all bedecked in bright silks, expensive embroideries, and colourful paper parasols.

I was especially fond of meeting the daughters. Growing up in Oka Shto, there were no other girls my age, and so I took what chances I could to have rare conversations with them. It was not always so easy. Many of the royal daughters did nothing but simper and praise me when I spoke, refusing to engage in anything beyond mere courtesies. Others were downright horrible—especially when they mistook me for a servant's whelp, running through the halls in plain cotton robes. One made a terrible scene when I refused to get her tea. And none, of course, wanted to be my friend. It was either courtesy or disrespect—never friendship.

"They're frightened of you," my father once said, watching me bawl on my bed after being rejected yet again by a potential playmate. "Get up and wipe your tears."

I had obeyed, choking back another incoming sob. I can remember him looking at me, his hard eyes searching, calculating. Later on, people would say I looked like him, that I retained nothing of my young mother whose name Yeshin would not even utter. "They're frightened of you," he had repeated, his breath coming out in a sort of hiss, like he had forgotten he was talking to a child. "And so let them. Empty-brained fools, they think of nothing beyond painting their faces and picking what dress to wear for the day. They'll bear children and be forgotten in the vestiges of time. You..."

You. I did not have the capability to form the right words to say it then—and even if I had, I never would have, not to Yeshin's face—but it shook me every time he said that, every time he said *you* and looked deep into me like he was molding me out of clay and breathing life into my lungs. As if, from the mere word alone, he was creating this image of him that would carry everything he ever was and everything he could never be.

I feel like I have to say this every time I tell this story—every time people ask me what drove me back out on that street on a bad leg, mere days after being chased through it by an assassin hell-bent on spilling my blood. Most think I should have taken my chances with the city watch again. There were other precincts. Couldn't I find someone to help?

My father would've scoffed at this logic. He believed that a person needed to make observations themselves before making a decision, and that relying on others because you could not be bothered was a form of cowardice. *Lazy*, was how he would actually put it, and how a man could seethe so much from a single word, I can't tell you. But I can tell you that my memories of my father eclipsed whatever fear I felt over having to return to the place where I was attacked and where Arro was killed. And they masked the rising panic over what I dreaded to find: knowledge of Rayyel's death.

My silence unsettled Khine, but he tried his best to hide it. It was, thankfully, a clear night—the first one, I think, since I had first stepped on Anzhao City's damned streets. We passed by a flock of people in deep prayer. Children led the group, carrying poles with giant paper lanterns shaped like boats and stars.

"Festival for Saint Fei Rong," Khine explained, pointing out the trail of orange-scented oil the group left behind on the street. "People dip their shoes in the holy oil before they begin the journey to pray to the deity Shimesu, the *rok haize* goddess of good, stable fortune, in various houses. It's supposed to bless the neighbourhood. But you would know that, living here, wouldn't you?"

I almost didn't catch that. He was sneaky, this one, despite his light words. "We didn't live in Shang Azi," I said.

His eyes gleamed. "They don't just do it in Shang Azi. This time of the year..."

"Yes, well," I grumbled. "I haven't been here very long." I was still looking at the prayer group, who were travelling up the hill now, away from the neighbourhood. I heard him chuckle.

"They're probably done with their rounds. The last stop is to light candles at the temple before going home to feast on boiled chicken and bland rice. We don't have separate temples to our deities like you do in Jin-Sayeng. One's enough. I'm sure the gods and goddesses know who we're talking to—the prayers say their names often enough. We have one prayer where we say *Shimesu* forty-nine times."

I couldn't help myself. "Does that number signify anything?"

"Not particularly."

"So why not fifty? Why stop at forty-nine?"

He laughed. The sound of it eased my nerves against my will. I gave a grim smile in return, one that faded quickly when I recognized the street we had taken just nights before. It seemed like a lifetime ago. I began to sweat. The sound of music and laughter made me nauseated.

Khine must have noticed my discomfort as we slowed down. "What happened here?" he asked.

I shook my head, unable to find the words. I looked up at the sign, *The Silver Goose*, twinkling under the lantern lights. I saw a man emerge from the door to speak with the customers on the patio and recognized the manager. He was laughing, chortling almost. *He was in on it*, I thought. He had to be. If the attack had caught him off guard, the restaurant should be closed. Or if he had to keep it open, the events should at least have numbed him to stillness.

But there was no mark of that night on his face. None. "Tali—" Khine began, and I shushed him.

He looked like he wasn't sure whether to be amused or offended.

"Into the alley," I said in a low voice. I dropped my head, hoping the darkness was enough to mask my face. *Or maybe he wouldn't recognize me.* The man never turned, though, and I was able to pass him. We reached the narrow alley to the left of the building. The other windows in that meeting room had opened to here.

I looked up and heard Khine breathe beside me. He was following my gaze. I let him, allowing, perhaps, that he might see something I had missed.

I couldn't peek into the room itself from that angle, and about half the windows were curtained closed. I struggled to contain that wave of panic again. It *couldn't* have all just happened in my head. I have been told that my imagination could get the best of me at times, but not like this, and certainly not after everything that had transpired.

"Place like that, you'd think they could afford to maintain their windows," Khine said.

My eyes immediately noticed that the shutters of the furthest one were bent outward, like they had been broken and somebody had tried to fix them by simply pulling the frame back in. I rushed to the section of alley the window opened into and felt my heart in my throat.

A pool of blood was congealed on the ground and in the gutter. It smelled like dead cats.

Khine saw it, too. He went past me to approach it, both fascination and revulsion on his face. "Is that from a human?" he asked.

"I don't know," I said, knowing it was. *But who?* I didn't want to think of Rayyel, hurt and bleeding in this alley. It had been different when he left me. His life had not been in danger, so I knew he could take care of himself then—whatever worry I had felt had been for our son, for how I would explain his father's departure to him. But in a situation like this... the man had been taught to fight, perhaps not quite in the way I had been, but he had never been particularly *good* at it. He was no warrior. The assassin wasn't trying to debate the finer points of an economic advantage, and he certainly wasn't trying to slit Rai's throat with a book.

"Do you see a blood trail?" I asked.

Khine swallowed, his expression torn between asking me what was happening and answering my question. "Whoever that was couldn't have survived that," he finally said, his face tightening. "That much blood—that person is as good as dead."

"Not a pig, you think?"

"They wouldn't slaughter their animals here," Khine said. "City regulations. They're bloodless by the time they leave the slaughterhouse."

"Human, then," I said.

"Seems like it." He touched my shoulder. "I'm sorry, Tali. Is this someone you knew?"

"Take me to the docks," I murmured.

"Now?"

"Yes, now."

He scratched his cheek. "It's a long walk."

I believe I had known that. I wasn't thinking very straight anymore. "It doesn't matter. I need to get to a ship. The *Singing Sainsa*. She's the ship I came in on, and I was hoping..."

"The *Singing Sainsa*?" he repeated. His eyes were wide.

I nodded.

"It's not going to be there."

I turned to him. "What do you mean?"

"It sailed that same evening we were with that shopkeeper. My brother, Cho, works at the docks, and he told me about this ship that smashed into two bollards on its way out. A Jin-Sayeng ship, the *Singing Sainsa*. The officials were livid, but they couldn't catch it in time."

That same evening. My hands felt cold.

"I'm sure there are other ships bound for Jin-Sayeng," Khine said. "We could ask around."

"There are no trade routes between Jin-Sayeng and the Zarojo Empire, and no passenger ships, either. We've never been on good terms since those attacks during Dragonlord Reshiro's time. You need a chartered ship, which isn't cheap."

"Sometimes fishing boats will go all the way out here from Jin-Sayeng," he said. "That's how many Jinsein migrants get here. You'd have to be patient, but if you find one heading home..."

I shook my head. I didn't know how to explain that what I needed was assurance that my husband was alive and well. I swallowed. "Your brother saw this, he said?"

"You can speak with him when he comes home."

"I don't know if I can wait that long. Can you take me to him?"

"Gods," Khine breathed. "I wouldn't know where to start. I don't keep track of all of Cho's friends." He placed a hand on my shoulder. Only then did I realize that I was shaking. "Let's go back to the house first so you can rest. Talk to me. You look like you've seen a ghost."

"No," I said. "But I wish I did." Then I would know whose blood it was, and I could lift the burden threatening to suffocate me. I shook my head, pointing at the pool. "Could—could they still survive? Whoever this was?"

"Not unless they had help immediately," Khine said. "And the right sort. In the far east, there's doctors who claim they can replace lost blood with tubes, but…the *Texts of the Undying*—the reference book the empire approved for use by all physicians—looks down on such practices." He scratched his chin. "I'm sorry."

"So you keep saying. It's not your fault."

"I'm filling your head with nonsense. Maybe they survived. Until you see a body, you can't tell for sure."

"You are being truthful. That is more than what's been given to me these last few days."

That took him aback, I think. But I didn't dwell on it. I was so very tired, and I agreed to walk with him back to his house. A part of me didn't like the idea of *waiting*, and I was almost tempted to stop and ask him to take me to Deputy Qun's instead. He could offer answers, if I was careful.

But the part of me that wilfully remained Yeshin's daughter told me it was sheer idiocy, and Yeshin's daughter did not get involved in sheer idiocies. To walk straight into a snake's den was out of the question. *Go back. Think on it. Breathe.* Easier said than done. All I could think of on the entire trip back to Shang Azi was the congealed blood in that empty alley and how it gleamed like a marble floor under the moonlight.

CHAPTER TWELVE

THE LAMANG SIBLINGS

TIM

The betrayal of the *Singing Sainsa*'s crew struck a deeper chord in me than I thought it would.

Our terms had been generous. For a month of their time, they were going to make more than their usual profit carrying silk, hemp, and tuna from the Jin-Sayeng city of Sutan to Nalvor in the Kag. I had even made the courtesy of writing letters to the inconvenienced merchants that made up their usual clientele, praising them for their service to the Dragonthrone. Such approval from the queen would've been very good for the businesses of all involved.

Arro had thought it was too much. "We're paying, they accepted," I remember him grumbling, giving me a critical eye that would've made me wilt if I hadn't been so used to my father's. As it stood, Arro's expression was amusing—almost comical—in its concern. "Let them grumble, if they want...you do not have to make them like you. You have to be harder."

"As hard as they say I am?" I asked him.

"As hard as they say you are," he agreed, his eyes softening, speaking what he dared not say out loud: *even though we know you are not.*

Had I been too kind to the crew? Had I smiled too much at them, been too concerned with making sure they knew exactly how much we appreciated their service? Or were they frightened of what my guards said behind my back—the very guards who seemed to have abandoned me?

I had not been on the Dragonthrone long enough to know the sort of queen I was. A hard thought to admit, coming from someone who had been born for that throne—who had been groomed for it. I had known no life beyond this, and so I had never once considered that I would be betrayed by my own subjects. My father had only trained me in dealing with the other warlords, in detecting false courtesies and hidden ambitions; I did not know how to react to the betrayal of mere sailors and my own guards.

What did they have to gain from it? Money? I could have paid them for information on anyone who tried to buy them off. Did they know that? I may have neglected it in my preoccupation with Rayyel. Among other things, my rule was marked by my husband's absence. I had done everything I was supposed to do—learned everything Yeshin had asked of me, married the Ikessar boy, borne Jin-Sayeng an heir, kept the warlords at bay, listened to my advisers on every policy and action...and for what?

To find myself alone in a stranger's house without the loyalty of a single man or woman?

I wondered whether Governor Gon Zheshan was responsible. He had certainly been a little too interested in Jin-Sayeng's affairs than he ought to have been. Yet he was in that meeting room with us—had spent *hours* debating his cause—and I thought I had seen his face white with fright at the sight of the assassin. Perhaps I had only imagined it? Perhaps he had scheduled the attack so he would be there to see it through, and he had just been caught by surprise over Arro's death. Anything was possible at this point.

There was also Deputy Qun, who had been less than truthful to me since I'd met him. It was under his roof that I lost one guard, under his roof where I received the letter informing me our meeting would be at the Silver Goose instead. That, and his wife's cryptic words, made him just as much of a suspect as Gon Zheshan. I had made the mistake of relying on him without cause, because he was an official and I had assumed when I came here that someone was going to stick to politics the way I had planned to.

If Rayyel was alive, which of them had him? He was too valuable a prisoner—he *had* to be alive. Perhaps they had asked the assassin to dispose only of me, because Rai was easier to manipulate. If only the fool man had not been so stubborn, we would have...

"Is there anything I can do to help?"

Khine's voice cut through the haze of my thoughts like a blade. I swallowed, noticing he was offering me a cup of tea.

"It's too late for tea," I said, giving him my best smile.

"That blood. You're worried it was your husband." He sat cross-legged beside me.

There was no sense in hiding that part. I nodded. "There's no way to tell for sure, is there?"

"Would that I were a dog and could tell with one whiff." He spoke so ruefully that I couldn't help but grin. The sight of that made him smile. "If someone had died there, the city watch will know," he added. "We can make the trip there in the morning."

"The city watch..." I began. I tried to find a sufficient excuse. "You said Ziori has paid men there. That means Lo Bahn would, too. If they see me..."

"I can go alone."

"You would do that?"

He thrust the cup of tea into my hands. "If it will help ease your worries."

I looked at the green liquid. He had not added milk this time. I took a sip and felt heat rush into my body. "You've already done so much for me," I said in a low voice. "I wouldn't know how to repay you." I watched his eyes as I spoke, remembering my father's lessons. *That one—see how he lights up when he talks about this land he does not care about. He will fight harder than the others over it, so I will speak in favour of him keeping it. Look at people when you speak to them, Beloved Princess—listen to what they do not say.*

But Khine's eyes lacked this light. Not expressionless, no—there was warmth in them, the sort I have not really seen in my whole life...not even in Rayyel, whom I had loved for so long. I knew I wasn't supposed to trust people this fast; I had already made that mistake with Qun and Ziori and the others. I shouldn't make it again.

"If you insist..." he said.

"I wasn't."

He laughed. "Fair enough. But I was just going to ask about your husband. I had guessed a fair number of things from what you're not telling me, and I'd hate to be presumptuous."

"All right," I said, running my finger around the rim of the teacup. "Tell me what you think so far."

"You had been apart from your husband for five years before we met that first time."

I was surprised he remembered. "I told you as much. Go on."

"You were to meet him at the Silver Goose. There, you had another argument, and he threw you out, but not before things became physical. You, er...you stuck a knife in him? And now you're afraid he's dead?"

I saw his eyes glance towards my hands. "I see. You're scared of presuming that I'll stick a knife in you, too."

He grinned. "One can't be too careful these days. I've been knifed by women before."

I nodded, as if this was perfectly normal conversation. "Were you, perhaps, being inappropriate?"

"Gods, no! There's just some very violent people in these parts."

He ran a hand through his hair. "If you did knife him, it's...well, it's understandable."

"The bruises, you mean?" I shook my head. "I told you before. It's not what you think."

"Forgive me if I don't believe you. I've heard that story often enough. *He's a good man, most of the time, when he isn't drinking.*" His face darkened.

"My husband. He's not...he would never lift a hand against me. For one thing, I would've never let him get away with it." I looked down at my tea. "He's a good man. For all his faults."

"So you say."

"When we were young..." I pulled my knees up, a wistful smile on my face. "Oh, all the other girls were madly in love with him. He was so stern and serious, but also handsome and thoughtful—the sort of man who opened doors for you not so you could praise him for being chivalrous but because he got there first and it was the right thing to do."

"Sounds like he was quite a prince," Khine said.

I looked at him, wondering if it was an innocent comment. Or was it a slip of the tongue, and Khine knew more about me than he let on? "He...was," I said, keeping my eyes low in case they gave my suspicions away. "A rare sort. I didn't like him the first time I met him, you understand. I thought he was too dull, too stuck-up. If men were swords, then he was the plain, unadorned one with the wooden hilt and a straight blade."

"That's an interesting image."

"And he loved books. So, so much. You ever wanted to jab someone in the eye with a finger just because he would rather read than pay attention to you?"

I saw Khine's eyes dance towards the bookshelf, with his own little collection of books. "The bastard," he said after a moment.

I laughed. "And the things he liked to talk about—economy and law and history. Oh, but you could fall asleep and wake up and he would still be talking about the perils of the lower classes and what that meant for the future of the nation's children, if it means they're going to choose to sail to foreign countries rather than staying at home and working on a trade that would better benefit the land." I smiled at Khine when I paused for breath.

"He sounds like a passionate man. A merchant, your husband?"

"You could say that," I said. I took another sip. "I didn't like him, not at first. But I grew to love him. Yes. I loved him. I still do. You asked me that before. I've never—I've never had to say it out loud. Not to anyone. Not to him. We were an arranged marriage, my husband and me. Our parents had promised us to each other since the day I was born."

"*The critical folly of arranged marriages*," Khine said. "A scholar from the capital said that, once. I believe he had other things in mind, but seeing as how talk of economy bores you…"

"No, I love it. Do go on," I drawled.

He snorted. "In my mind, the biggest folly is that marriages from the beginning are as businesslike a transaction as you can get. Arranged marriages make a mess of things. At worst, you decide that love doesn't play a part in it. At best, you take the love for granted—assume it is a given because married people are supposed to love each other anyway. You've never told him? Ever?"

"Where is this going?" I grumbled over the rim of my teacup.

"Nowhere important," he said. "You ever wondered if he needed to hear it?"

"Weren't you just telling me about how you'd hate to be presumptuous?"

"I get curious. I'm working on it, believe me."

I drew my shoulders into a shrug. "I guess I never did," I found myself saying. "I mean, why would he? It was our duty. For the good of our families…"

"So does he think you hate him, then?"

"He couldn't. I married him. I gave him a son, named him Thanh..."

"What?"

"Thanh."

He scratched the back of his head. "You're not, uh, saying that right."

"My husband wanted him named after a priest. A missionary, I believe, from somewhere in the empire. His, ah...his family are devotees of that religion. Mine...aren't."

"The Empire of Many Nations. Yes, I've heard of the man. *Thanh.* You Jinseins and your pronunciations..."

I stared at him for a heartbeat.

"I'm just trying to lighten the mood," he blurted out. "I apologize if I've upset you."

"I'm not upset," I snapped.

He gave me a look.

"Yes, I heard my own voice. Let's leave it at that." I took a deep breath. "If he's dead..."

"There is no sense worrying until you know for sure. We will find out in the morning," Khine said. His voice softened. "You should rest. You've been on that leg the whole day. Up the ladder, now. I'll be down here."

I almost didn't want to listen—I was sure that the tea was going to keep me up another hour, at least. But I nodded and went up the ladder, and to my surprise I fell asleep as soon as my head hit the pillow.

This time, I dreamed of my wedding day: of Rayyel in his pearly-white robes, his thin beard trimmed, his hair combed and tied neatly beneath a black silken headband. He had said the words perfectly, had declared he would honour and protect me to the end of my days. I had thought at the time that a girl could die happy, marrying such a man.

I still do.

I woke up to the sound of chatter downstairs. When I opened my eyes, I saw a ginger cat—a tomcat, I guessed by the thick scruff of fur around his neck and the mass of scars along his nose—sitting with his paws on my belly.

The sight of him made me miss the dozen or so cats we kept in Oka Shto to keep the rats at bay. I greeted him groggily, and he responded with a quick meow and purring deep enough to penetrate the darkness. I wondered how he had come in, and then noticed a small window above the bed. It was held shut by a small hook, which explained why I had not seen it the night before. There was a crack in the corner where the cat must have wedged himself through.

I stood on the mattress to push the window open while the cat weaved a circle through my legs, allowing a wave of muggy, after-rain air into the room. I had been expecting daylight and tried to contain my disappointment. We had left Jin-Sayeng at the end of summer, and the turn of monsoon must've happened just as soon as we arrived in Anzhao City. The rains were heavier here than back home. Arro had once told me that the mass of forest-covered mountains that sheltered the empire's western coastline had something to do with it—something about pushing at the air, or making the clouds thicker...I don't remember. Rayyel probably would.

Thinking about Rai reminded me of last night. Before the heart-crushing anxiety could begin again, I forced myself down the ladder. My leg felt better, although there was still a twinge of pain with every step I took.

A woman was dusting the windows in the common room. She turned to me as soon as I stepped off the ladder. "Oh, hello," she said. "You're finally awake. We thought you'd sleep the whole day, to be honest."

The tomcat greeted her first, bounding past me to direct his purrs towards her like a faithless lover. She laughed. "You've made Olliver's acquaintance, at least."

"Olliver?" I had not expected to hear a Kag name out here in the empire. The Zarojo detested the Kags—so much that Dragonlord Reshiro's response to the empire's attacks on Jin-Sayeng was to attempt to open trade with the people both our nations once swore against.

"Khine read it from a book," the woman said.

"I thought Kag texts were banned here."

The woman smiled. She had a round face, sharpened by well-placed angles from her brows and an admirably pointed nose. Her skin had the pallor of someone who spent plenty of time indoors. "It's interesting you would say that. He told me you were a little strange."

"Be nice, Inzali," another woman called out from the kitchen. She popped her head through the doorway. "Please forgive our sister. She was raised by stray dogs."

"I'd have better family members if that were true," Inzali retorted.

The other woman waved a ladle at me. "I'm Thao. That's Inzali. Khine told us about you. Said you fell into Manshi Ziori's scheme. I don't blame you. I can't even count the number of complaints about her over the years..."

"Thao," Inzali said in a low voice. "I can smell burnt rice."

"Stray *monkeys*," Thao said, glaring at her before disappearing behind the wall.

I turned to Inzali. "You were saying, about the Kag texts?"

"What? God, you *are* a strange one. No, they're not banned. Frowned upon, I guess you'd say. The empire is too powerful to use the word *ban* for nations as small as the Kags', or the Jins'." She pressed her lips together, like someone who was used to offending people and didn't particularly care one way or another. I immediately liked her. I was getting tired of people either fawning over me or downright ignoring me, and the sound of someone's opinion—sarcastic though it was—was refreshing.

"This *Jin* does not blame you," I said, emphasizing the shorthand term for our people that would've been downright offensive under different circumstances. "We have to share land with the Kag and saw the folly in our ways soon enough."

"Not without difficulties," she said. "Didn't you assassinate a king just for extending friendship to the Kags?"

I took a seat beside the folded blankets Khine must've used last night. "There were many reasons why Dragonlord Reshiro Ikessar was assassinated. Contrary to popular opinion, it wasn't because he opened our borders to the Kags, but because of the way he went about it and the many laws he violated in order to pass *his* whims. We still don't know, exactly, who killed him. It wasn't surprising, considering what he had to do to keep his throne during the merchants' upheaval. I..."

I noticed Inzali wasn't so much listening to me as she was looking at me with clear interest. I blinked back, suddenly self-conscious. Five years without him, and I was still speaking too much like Rayyel sometimes. I didn't know whether to be amused or horrified. "This is boring you, isn't it?"

"Not at all," Inzali said. "But it's clear why my brother would go out of his way to help you."

"Your brother is a kind man."

"I don't disagree," Inzali snorted. "Too kind, really. He has this irrational desire to help the wounded. Look at the stray rabble he picks up." She craned her head towards Olliver, who had wandered over to the kitchen to bother Thao with his yowls.

"I apologize for being stray rabble," I said.

"That's how we ended up with Inzali, you know," Thao broke in before Inzali could speak, peeking out again. "Khine found her in a garbage dump by the River Eanhe. Do you want some tea?"

"I would love some," I said.

"No milk in mine," Inzali added.

"You don't deserve any," Thao snapped at her. "Insulting our guest like our mother didn't teach you any manners." She returned to her cooking.

"Where is Khine?" I asked.

"He had to run errands. I think he's dropping by the city watch on the way back," Inzali said. I had forgotten that he had promised to ask around about the Silver Goose, and felt relieved that he remembered.

My eyes wandered over to the bookshelf. Now that Khine was not around, I was suddenly less self-conscious about attempting to read the Zirano script on the titles. I found the one I was looking for. "*Texts of the Undying*," I mouthed. I turned back to Inzali. "Is Khine a physician?"

"He would be now, if not for his soft heart and even softer head," Inzali grumbled.

"Inzali—" Thao barked from the kitchen.

"Are we not telling people that now?" Inzali asked. "Because the last time I checked, everyone in Shang Azi knew already."

"*She* doesn't."

"So I'm just getting ahead of it, see?" She shook her head. "Thao thinks it's a shame, a taint on our family, and that the less said about it, the better. I think the less we talk about it, the easier it is for Khine to pretend it's not a problem. He was studying to be a physician. Our mother scraped for years to send him to Anzhao City. He came and settled here before us—had managed to get into Kayingshe Academy, under Tashi Reng Hzi himself, if you can believe it. He had one year left. That same year, Cho and Thao found work and left our home in the village of Phurywa."

"I've not heard of Phurywa," I said. "That's nowhere near these parts, is it?"

"It's at the southern tip of the empire. We had to take a ship."

"I was wondering why your names sounded different."

"Phurywa is part of Lay Weng Shio, which the Empire of Ziri-nar-Orxiaro occupied some few years ago," Inzali said. "Before that, we were occupied by the nations from the east. Bones, to give to dogs. Nothing but bones. I wouldn't know where we belonged if you asked." She narrowed her eyes. "But as I was saying…"

I inclined my head to the side. "Please, go on."

"Cho and Thao followed him to Anzhao City. I had to stay in Phurywa for a few more months because I was tutoring the mayor's son. If I had been able to leave early…" She snorted. "Cho fell in with a bad crowd. Gambling. Khine stepped in to pay it off. He shouldn't have."

"They would've killed Cho," Thao said.

Inzali bristled. "They wouldn't dare. Does a dead goose lay golden eggs?"

"You're assuming that people from Shang Azi are as smart as you. Or have brains at all. I've seen some of those idiots smoke rat poison to get bleary," Thao said, stepping through the doorway with two cups of tea. She handed one to me. "A family shame, like Inzali said. We spoiled our brother, I think."

"You and Khine both," Inzali said. "A clout on the head or two would've fixed him. Now it's too late."

"He was the youngest," Thao said. She resembled Khine—darker than Inzali, thinner and smaller. You could see the muscle underneath her brawny arms. "Our father died before he was born, and he looked like him so much we couldn't help ourselves."

"*You* couldn't help yourselves," Inzali snorted. She sniffed her tea. "And so now look where we are. That debt has not yet been paid, and in the meantime, we find ourselves stuck here, unable to leave without the fear of Lo Bahn's wrath over our heads."

I grew light-headed at the mention of Lo Bahn. I swallowed some tea before speaking. "Cho owes Lo Bahn money?"

"Khine does," Inzali said. "Cho had small debts here and there. Khine was able to convince Lo Bahn to pay it all off. So now Cho can prance about the streets without a care in the world, while Khine owes Lo Bahn more than that last year's tuition, in addition to an interest that costs as much as if we were renting another flat altogether. He says he is paying it off slowly, but it's been two years. I think the debt grows with each passing season."

Her words stirred a feeling of dread within me. If Khine *was* keeping me here to sell me back to Lo Bahn, then the price was only going to increase the longer I stayed away. I looked at Inzali, who was complaining to Thao about the tea, and realized that she herself did not seem aware of where exactly I came from. If she knew, she probably would have something to say.

I kept my mouth shut and was silent for the rest of the morning. Thao wandered back to the kitchen to finish cooking, and Inzali left to visit the neighbours. I amused myself by playing with Olliver and trying to read what I could from the *Texts of the Undying*. Even if I couldn't understand much of it, the illustrations on the faded yellow paper were interesting. Zarojo medicine was decades ahead of Jin-Sayeng, and their knowledge of human anatomy was startling. It explained why so many of the best doctors in my nation were either educated by a Zarojo physician or were from the empire themselves.

I was so engrossed by the text that I didn't hear Khine come in. He stood above me and cleared his throat. I closed the book quickly, as if ashamed of having been caught with it.

He scratched his head, a thoughtful expression on his face. "Fancy becoming a physician?"

"I don't like examinations," I said, offering him his book back.

That made his eyes light up. "Where would you have taken examinations?"

I swallowed, remembering long afternoons in the study halls at Shirrokaru. "Just the idea," I said instead. "Sounds dull. Anyway, I can barely make anything out of your texts. How could you remember so many brushstrokes? I feel like a child repeating words from my tutor's knee."

"With practice," Khine said. He peeled the book from my hands, as if retrieving something precious from someone who might rip it to shreds, and returned it to the shelf. "I went to the city watch and asked around. No dead bodies near the Silver Goose, not since three weeks ago when that boy fell into the canal. I'm sorry."

"That can't be. They *knew*. They're lying." I studied his expression, wondering if *he* was.

"I don't know. I couldn't tell." He slumped down beside me and gestured at my leg. "Can I see your wound?"

"You seem awfully fond of it," I said. I showed him, anyway. I wanted the inconvenience of it gone.

"I was thinking of asking it to marry me." He got up to fetch the salve.

"Forgive my brother for his horrible jokes," Thao broke in.

Khine laughed. "Yes, I know. He was raised by sewer rats."

I watched him put the salve on, feeling less self-conscious now that I knew he had studied medicine. "How long do you think before it heals?" I asked.

"Stay off it a few more days, and it should be well on its way."

"I don't know how it works here in the empire," I said, "but back home, certain masters of a craft will teach a student for free if he's particularly skilled."

"A big *if*," Khine said. He craned his head back. "I see my sisters have opened their big mouths."

"Inzali did," Thao replied.

"You were up all night with the seamstresses. Couldn't you have stitched it shut for her?"

"I didn't know where I could find a needle sharp enough to pierce her thick skin."

Khine snorted just as Olliver came up to rub against his knees. "Hey, there you are. You need to visit more often, old fellow." He bent down to pick up the tomcat and drape the massive form over his shoulder before heading towards the kitchen to help Thao with the rest of the cooking. Inzali came back, only to go outside again to air out the blankets and pillows. She barely even glanced at me.

I felt oddly out of place. I had always known the world didn't revolve around me, but here was a world where other people lived their lives, and I was nothing but a passing afterthought. *Stray rabble*, Inzali had said. In that room, a spider would have had more presence.

I had never breathed so freely in my life.

For lunch, we had soured white fish with leeks and pig's-ear mushrooms on rice.

Sitting in a cramped room while sharing food with people exchanging light-hearted conversation was not something I had experienced in years. The last time had been before my wedding, when I was sent to Shirrokaru to be tutored along with other young royals my age. Many of the dormitories in the Dragon Palace had been torched after the War of the Wolves, so some of the royals had to share rooms. We would sometimes spend hours studying in these common rooms, making fun of our tutors and sneaking in bites of barbecued eel purchased from the vendors down by the lakeside.

Even then, the comradeship of those late-night meetings revolved around the shared hardship of our clans' expectations. Here was something else, something that stirred within me a feeling I couldn't name. It struck me, watching Inzali steal a piece of fish from Thao's outstretched chopsticks while Khine tried to choke down his laughter with a cup of water, that I had never actually shared a meal with *family* before. Not like this.

A meal in Oka Shto would involve a long ceremony, where the servants checked each and every plate for signs of tampering. The dining hall was easily ten times the size of Khine's common room, and we had no less than two servants hovering over each of us—snatching dirty plates before we were done picking at the food, or serving wine and tea before we could finish drinking. Conversations usually involved politics or the economy or whatever topic came up during court that day. Worst of all was the distance—more than an arm's length away from each other at any given time, so that I could never really reach out to touch anyone if I wanted to. It had been that way with my father, and so was it with Rayyel.

It was even worse in Shirrokaru, where Rai and I stayed for half the year after we got married. There, they had a giant, expensive table imported from the Kag, and we had to sit on chairs instead of cushions on the floor. I have nothing against the Kags, but the Ikessars have never made a secret of how fond they are of these foreign customs and strange ideas, and the arrangement only intensified the distance between my husband and me.

Then there were those occasions with my son—when I could wrest him away from his Ikessar guardians long enough to have meat buns or a glass of melon milk from the kitchens...but thinking about Thanh was worse than thinking about his father, so I pushed those memories away.

Halfway through the meal, we heard the main door open and footsteps begin the climb up into the common room. I recognized Cho, from the gambling hall, with his lithe figure and ears that stuck out a little too much. His mouth flew open as soon as he saw me.

"Outside," Khine said, dropping his bowl to grab his brother's shoulder.

"What's happening?" Thao asked.

Cho jerked away from Khine's grasp. "You're a moron. You're a fucking moron, Khine! You've doomed us all!"

Inzali came up and slapped him. "Start talking sense."

Cho rubbed his head, snarling at her, before pointing at me. "That's Lo Bahn's woman. They've been looking for her all morning."

Inzali narrowed her eyes and was silent for a moment. Eventually, she turned to Khine. "Khine, you fucking moron," she grumbled.

"You said you rescued her from Ziori," Thao said.

"I didn't lie," Khine replied. "Just—you know, there were more details I may have neglected to mention..."

"Lo Bahn bought her from Ziori," Cho said. "And Khine stole her away somehow. I knew it—when they told me she was missing, the way you *looked* at her that day in the gambling hall...you and your obsession with Jins—"

Khine shook his head. "Women shouldn't be bought."

"Even so! That's what he did, and that's what he believes. Do you want to tell him that? Discuss philosophy with him while he runs a knife through your heart?" Cho's face had turned red with exertion.

"Sit," Thao said. "Have something to eat first. Getting into hysterics won't help any of us."

"For once, I agree with her." Inzali sat down. When Cho didn't move, she grabbed him by the leg and dragged him with her. "You," she added, turning to Khine. "You're not off the hook here. Explain yourself."

"I don't know if I can," Khine murmured. "She was in trouble. Do I need more reason than that?"

"So you'd risk yourself—*all* of us—because she wasn't smart enough to get herself out of it?"

"I'm still here," I mumbled.

Inzali turned to me. "I hope you understand what's happening. This, on top of Khine's debts to Lo Bahn...he'll have him hung and quartered by the end of the day. Or we'll be watching an unofficial *t'che* ceremony and make ourselves famous throughout Shang Azi on account of our brother's most gruesome death."

"Did you learn this from Ning?" Khine asked Cho.

Cho grimaced at the food Thao placed in front of him. "Yes. He found me this morning."

"What did you tell him?"

"What *could* I tell him? I didn't know anything, I said. My brother wouldn't be stupid enough to do such a thing, I said. I swore on our father's grave and our mother's life. *Clearly* I was wrong." He started eating, looking for all the world like he wasn't even tasting his food.

Khine patted his shoulder. "Good. I'm guessing Ning isn't blabbing to the rest of Lo Bahn's men? He'll get into trouble, too."

"He said he's telling them she escaped through the window after Ben Taey left him alone with her. Says if he finds out you're involved, you'll have him to deal with. I'm not worried about him—it's Lo Bahn who can ruin us all with one word. She has to leave." Cho didn't look at me the whole time he was talking.

"I can't let her do that. Where would she go?"

"I don't give a fuck," Cho grumbled before shoving rice into his face.

"Please, Cho, show our brother more respect," Thao broke in. "If you had not gathered those debts in the first place..."

"I never asked him to get involved!" Cho said. "And this, I've got nothing to do with this." He gestured helplessly in my direction. "Thirteen hells, Khine, of all the women to save, why Lo Bahn's? This isn't just some stray that nobody's going to miss."

"She has a name," Khine said. His voice had dropped an octave lower.

"Yes. They said it was Kora..."

"Tali," Khine corrected automatically. He gave me a look, but he didn't say anything about it. "You really *have* forgotten to be respectful, Cho. We are talking about a person, not someone's property. The last time I checked, we didn't own slaves in the Zarojo Empire. She was tricked into this whole situation."

"But it's not a situation *you* have to fix," Cho insisted. "Are you sleeping with her now? Is that it? Gods, Khine, if you'd just told me you wanted a romp in the haystack—"

This time, it was Thao who slapped him. "Do you want us to send you back to Mother?"

"I'll leave on the first ship tonight if you all don't stop harassing me," he said, rubbing his cheek. "I don't know why you're all so angry when I'm just telling the truth. Bunch of bullies."

"He is, unfortunately," Inzali sighed. "Whether we like it or not. How long are you planning to keep her here, Khine?"

Khine looked at me. "We're working on that. She needs to get better first. She can hardly walk."

"If they find her—" Cho began.

"They won't," Khine snapped. "Because you'll all keep quiet about this. I'll figure it out. Tali…please accept my apology on behalf of my brother. Sometimes his mouth runs ahead of him. He is only concerned about our family's well-being."

"I understand," I said.

"Do you?" Cho snapped.

"Cho!"

He dropped his eyes.

Khine seemed to have the final word. The rest of the meal was subdued, and after all the dishes had been put away and Thao went in to finish cleaning up in the kitchen, Khine took Cho and Inzali upstairs in the loft, where I heard them arguing. Walls were punched and doors were slammed, though they didn't get into blows as far as I could tell. Later, when they returned to the common room, Cho immediately went out again. Inzali rolled her eyes before rushing after him.

"He won't be a problem." Khine looked down at the floor, scratching his cheek.

"I need to find my husband," I said after a period of silence. "I am not planning on taking advantage of your hospitality for very long."

He gave a grim smile. "It's not...they're just like that. Cho. He's harmless. Last week we were arguing about the dishes. He'll come around. In the meantime, I'll keep asking, see if someone can lead us to some answers. Someone must've seen something that night. Is, uh...you do not have anyone else here? Nowhere in the empire where you have someone to vouch for you?"

I didn't answer. I wasn't sure if I wanted to admit it. But I think my face gave it away, because he placed his hand on my shoulder.

"We'll get you home," he said. The warmth in his voice was painful to hear. I wasn't sure if I wanted to wait for him to betray me, too.

CHAPTER THIRTEEN

THE DRAGONLORD IN DISTRESS

Sixteen days passed without incident. Sixteen long days in which I did nothing but eat and sleep and try not to get underfoot while the Lamang family went through their daily routine. It wasn't easy. While my father had made sure I was sufficiently exposed to discomfort, cramped quarters, and plain food (most of it was delicious, but it lacked the variety I was used to in Oka Shto), the feeling of being *useless* did not sit well with me. I had not realized how truly busy my life had been until those quiet, lazy days.

Here, there were no early morning meetings with my advisers, no court appointments with the common folk, no lunches with the overseer, who kept me up to date with the conditions of Oka Shto and the general outlook of the staff. No afternoons with the council or my generals, or evenings going through palace security with my guards. No late-night reading in the study with Arro to find some detail of law I had missed or needed for the morning after.

Here, I was allowed some silence, time to stare at the falling rain through muslin curtains and contemplate. Thao and Inzali left early most days to work at a seamstress's shop, sometimes even before sunrise. Inzali also worked part-time as a scribe and helper for a children's tutor, so she was barely at home. Cho kept away for the most part—I only saw him a handful of times between his shifts at the docks, and he never stayed the night.

Khine didn't have steady work as far as I could see. He mentioned another mark once, and came home with money in his pockets and a plate of peppered noodles with boiled eggs and strips of roasted chicken from a restaurant for everyone. But he wouldn't talk about the job in front of his sisters, as if he was ashamed of being a con artist while they ran themselves ragged with honest work.

"They don't know," he had told me when I asked. "I think maybe they suspect, but they haven't confronted me about it. Cho does, but only because he caught me at it once."

"I can understand the secrecy," I replied. "So why do it at all? It clearly bothers you."

"It doesn't... bother me," he told me, rubbing his cheek. "Not that way. I told you that I pick marks carefully—they fall into the trap because of their own greed. *That*, I don't mind."

"Like stealing from the rich?"

"There are many rich people who wouldn't bat an eye doing the same thing," he said. "Power does that. It corrupts. Makes them think others are beneath them, so they can easily justify what they do to you. They may even convince you it's for your own good."

I paused, flooded with discomfort from his words. How would this man react to the knowledge of who I was? "I don't think everyone in power is like that."

He gave a wry smile. "Perhaps not. Painting humans with a broad brush... that would be foolish. But that sort of environment can render a person incapable of understanding the effect of their own actions. They've been given a hero's narrative, you see? And they will do whatever it takes to see the world play out to this music, even if it means hurting others. So maybe...maybe this is my way of fighting that. Of fighting back. You're Jinsein. You should know this better than anyone."

"What do you mean?"

"What they do to your people out here—it's like what they did to mine, way back when we *had* something to remember. Now I don't know if we do. I can't even call my name my own. We're mutts, mongrels with no place to call home. Zarojo mongrels." He snorted with disdain.

"And that's why you're so sympathetic to Jinseins?"

"You could say that."

"And here I thought you just liked Jinsein women."

He coughed and turned away.

"I suppose I still care about what my siblings think," he said, to change the subject. "Even if I *am* the eldest and I know they'll let me do whatever I see fit." An expression of resolve crossed his face. "No, it doesn't bother me—I make more money this way, and it gives us a chance to get out of this debt and maybe start working towards a life of our own."

"And let you finish your studies, you mean?"

Khine mumbled something incomprehensible in response. He didn't like it when I talked about his studies. Despite his sisters' hopes, it sounded like a life he had clearly left behind.

And because I was still a guest, I didn't want to push it. I told myself it didn't matter, anyway. My leg was healing remarkably well; by the eighth day, I could walk without pain, with only an itchy scab where Khine had pulled out the stitches. By the sixteenth, only a faint pink line remained, and my recollection of the events surrounding it had softened, the fading tendrils of a nightmare.

On that sixteenth day, I was alone in the house, browsing through Khine's books in an attempt to pick up more of that frustrating Zirano script. I realized that the one in my hands was a history book. There were detailed drawings of Anzhao City, the landmarks, even the cuisine. And then, tucked in the back of the book with such precision that it felt like a golden beam of light was shining down on it, there was a map.

I flipped it open. I could see the major roads outlined, including much of the western coast. I caught a marked road leading to a city above Anzhao and was starting to read it when I heard a commotion out on the street.

I closed the book, but not before taking the map and tucking it into my back pocket. I quickly went up the ladder into the loft and bolted the trapdoor shut before I peered through the window.

There were about twenty or so men gathered in the alley. They looked rough, with scraggly beards and swords in their belts. I saw one push at a stumbling figure and recognized Cho. He looked like a bristling pup who wanted to lash out and bite but knew better.

Someone began pounding on the front door. "We know you're in there!" a man called out. I didn't wait to hear his next words. I pushed the shutters back and slid out the narrow window and onto the first rooftop ledge. My heart sounded like a drum.

Rain crashed on the rooftops as I made my way down, each drop turning every step along the tiles slippery. I forced myself to slow down, to test every ledge—any faster and a patch of moss might be enough to spell my doom. At the end of the last ledge, I took a moment to look back and instantly regretted it. Lo Bahn was right behind me. How he had managed to squeeze through that window, I couldn't tell, and I wasn't about to stop and ask. I leaped onto the next rooftop and slid down to the alley.

As I landed on the street, a man looked up, startled. Realizing he was one of Lo Bahn's guards, I struck him on the jaw before he could react. He staggered back, giving me time to steal the sword from his belt.

The man grabbed my wrist, as if he expected me to just give it back.

He looked surprised when I drew it instead. The blade sank into his belly like butter. He stared with eyes wide open, blood gurgling from his mouth, like he wasn't sure exactly what was happening. He grabbed the hilt with both hands; I pulled the sword out and pushed him to the side. He took a stumbling step before falling face down on the street, a pool of blood forming under his body

"Woman!"

I turned. Lo Bahn stood at the edge of the first rooftop. Confusion danced in his eyes, but also a hint of merriment, like somebody watching a play and not knowing where the story was headed.

"That's not my name," I told him.

He smirked.

I heard the rest of his men hurtling after me from the adjoining street. I tugged the dead man's sword belt off and fled the other way.

"You can't escape forever!" Lo Bahn called. His voice was like the first crack of thunder before a storm.

Having the map in my pocket gave me confidence. I turned into the first alley and then immediately into the next, and then again in an effort to lose the men. At the end of one street, I stumbled upon a tunnel. Despite the torrent of rain, the rush of water was only knee-deep, which was not enough to obscure the small footpath on the side. I took my chances with it.

The footpath led to a series of damp, narrow steps. If not for the small holes near the tunnel ceiling, the entire sewer would've been obliterated in darkness. But I could still see far enough to know I wasn't walking over the edge.

It was a very long sewer. Of all the cities in Jin-Sayeng, only Sutan and Shirrokaru employed such structures, and both were of Zarojo make. Unlike the ones in Jin-Sayeng, this tunnel—from the smell of it—seemed purely for storm water. I had heard that flooding could be a problem along the western coast, which explained the separation from the sewers carrying human waste. I wondered if such a system could be applied to the bigger cities back home. Oren-yaro, in particular, needed better facilities.

Although part of me knew it was ridiculous, thinking about city infrastructure was a calming exercise. For a time, I even forgot that I was being chased at all. I smiled when I realized that; Rai would be so proud. I reached the end of the tunnel, which opened up to a part of the canal. The rush of clear water told me I wasn't in Shang Azi anymore.

I took the first flight of stairs up to the street. It was broad daylight, and I hoped Lo Bahn's men knew better than to try to nab me out here. I slowed to a walk and did my best to blend in with the crowd. As I lifted my eyes, I recognized the street and caught sight of Qun's walled mansion amongst the array of smaller buildings. It stuck out like a blooded stallion in a farmer's barn.

Something in me caved. I started walking towards it.

My intention was not to speak with Qun—far from it. But I needed to see the building, to ignite some spark of memory of the day before it all turned to shit. I think I needed to remember that I wasn't always just this lost soul, fleeing from one thing after another. I was not Lo Bahn's woman or that escaped whore...I was Talyien aren dar Orenar, queen of Jin-Sayeng, daughter of Warlord Yeshin, wife of Rayyel Ikessar, and mother of Thanh. I did not just dream these things—I had a life before all this. I wanted nothing more than to return to it.

I stopped. A girl was sweeping the street right outside the gate. It was Kora. My knees shook. I croaked her name, and she turned to me.

"My queen," she gasped. One hand on the broom, she dropped to the ground, her forehead scraping the dust. I pulled her up.

"I'm glad to see you safe," I said. It felt good to speak in Jinan.

There were tears in her eyes. "They told me what happened. The poor magister! I can't imagine how his wife will take it. I saw his body myself. I was so terrified for you, to think the same thing could've happened..."

Even though I saw Arro die in front of me, the confirmation still stung. I think a part of me still clung to the hope that I had been mistaken. "Where did they take his body? I was told the city watch is denying all of this."

"They had it carted off to . . . somewhere. They said they can't keep it here. Said the Zarojo citizens would be offended."

I placed my hands on her shoulders. "Do you know what happened to everyone else? Do you know where Captain Nor is?"

She shook her head. "Captain Nor—I don't know. I haven't seen her, or the rest of the guards, since that afternoon, when you all left to meet King Rayyel."

I bit back the inclination to correct her. "What else did they tell you?"

"That somebody tried to kill you, that Magister Arro was killed. That they think your entire guard betrayed you. Governor Zheshan paid them off. He took the king as hostage."

I watched her as she spoke. "Deputy Qun told you all of this?"

"His wife," Kora blurted out. "She told me the next morning."

"She seemed awfully sure," I said.

Kora shook her head at the sound of my voice. "They've been looking for you since you disappeared. They've been nothing but kind to me, my queen. They told me—if I saw you, that is . . . please, come inside. They will help." She tugged at my arm.

I looked down at her fingers and how they easily grasped my sleeve with such familiarity. You could've taken us for sisters, seeing us out there. Yet that same morning before the assassination attempt, she couldn't even look at me when I spoke. I pulled away. "I have a place to stay," I said. "I'll be back."

"My queen," Kora said. "It's not safe out there."

"I've been out there for days. I think I'll be fine."

"My queen . . ."

"Do not tell them you saw me." I watched her eyes flicker. Was that a bruise on her chin?

After a moment, she nodded. "I did not see you, my queen." The Akkian accent was strong in her speech.

I stepped away from her and kept walking down the street.

Governor Zheshan... took the king as hostage.

I was not surprised to hear it. Rayyel was many things: intelligent, well-read, well-spoken—if somewhat absent-minded and straight to the point—but he was also gullible, and so awkward I had seen him bump into a wall trying to go through a doorway that could fit an elephant. He was the sort of man who couldn't fight his way out of a wet paper bag, and to hear that he was alive was more than I had expected after days of uncertainty—the thought filled me with such relief that I could hardly breathe.

But the relief came hand in hand with dread. The surge of hope was nothing when I was still in the middle of Anzhao City, with no money and not a friend in sight. Rayyel was a *hostage*, no longer this Governor Zheshan's guest, which meant he was being held captive. I could not allow such a blatant insult to Jin-Sayeng to go unpunished.

I found myself outside a scribe shop, wondering if someone would know of a way to send word to Jin-Sayeng. If I had a safe place to stay, I could maybe wait for the next ship heading for Jin-Sayeng and then scrape up enough to pay someone to bring a letter to Oka Shto. But the idea made me ill. The *Singing Sainsa*'s crew had betrayed me, and they were all Jinsein. How could I expect more from a Zarojo crew?

I stopped at the next corner, remembering the map. I pulled it out and found what I had been looking at before Lo Bahn's men interrupted me: Zorheng City. It was northeast of Anzhao City, along a path marked as "the Golden Road." I had tried to speak about it with Arro back at Deputy Qun's, but he had deflected the conversation. I should've really asked him when...

I paused at the sudden flood of emotions and took a moment to regain my composure before heading for the marketplace. *Zorheng City.* I needed to find a way there.

The response was unexpected. No one would tell me why, but most of the wagon drivers blatantly refused as soon as I uttered the city's name, even when I promised they would be well-compensated at the gates. One eventually agreed, but at four times the usual price. The glint in his eyes and the uneasy way he kept scratching his bare belly told me I would be found dead and naked at the roadside by the end of the day. I couldn't walk away fast enough.

I paused between an outcrop of stalls to catch my breath and glanced out into the distance. The eastern gate wasn't far from the marketplace. The road beckoned to me. Could I make it there on foot? Even if I did, I would arrive bedraggled and covered in dust, and then I would have the same problem as I did in Anzhao. Screaming that I was the queen of Jin-Sayeng wouldn't do a damn thing for me—they'd throw out the madwoman before sundown. I needed a way to prove who I was.

Arro, of course, would know. I realized I had the answer right there.

"Hey."

I drew my sword and whirled around. Khine jumped to the side just as the blade flashed past him. I stepped back. "I almost killed you!" I snapped.

"I didn't know you were going to try!" Khine retorted. His face was red with exertion, as if he had been running.

"Why, by all the gods, do you keep following me?" I asked. "If you think I'm some helpless cat you can just drag back to your house, you've made a big mistake."

"You're not," he said. I couldn't tell if he was trying to keep his voice calm for my sake or his. "I know you're not. But I feared for your safety. I heard what Cho did, and got to the house just as they arrived. They said you fled into the streets, so I went looking for you. I saw you go into the storm tunnel and followed." He frowned and waved at the sword. "Can you put that thing away?"

After a moment, I sheathed the blade, but not without keeping my hand on the hilt. "Your brother betrayed me. Why should I trust you?"

"I should ask you the same thing," he said. "I heard you killed one of Lo Bahn's men. Anyone desperate enough would've, I guess, but when you just pulled that sword on me—you're not a stranger to sword fighting, are you? You've been trained. You're not just some housewife."

I didn't respond.

Khine took a deep breath. "I heard what the girl said. When she bowed to you out on the street."

He was lying. He had to be. How could he have understood what we were saying? Was he a Jinsein spy? Asking him directly probably wouldn't reveal any answers, and a part of me didn't want to know. "You've been following me that long?" I asked, trying to change the subject.

He shrugged. "I wanted to see where you would go."

"So you did," I said. "And?"

"I..."

"You feared for my safety, so you kept quiet to see what I would do?"

"I suspected you were more than you let on."

"And did you clear those doubts?"

"I'm not sure I believe it." He swallowed. "Who are you, really?"

"You know my name."

"Yes, but that's not..." He scratched his cheek.

"Go home, Khine. I can take care of myself."

He hesitated. "Come back with me. We can speak better indoors."

"Why would I do that? Lo Bahn is waiting for me there."

"We talked before I went after you. We have some time. He'll want to talk again, but he promised he'll listen. He promised he'll give you a fair chance to earn back your debt. One that doesn't involve..." He faltered, unsure of his own words. As if he hated himself for even considering it.

I braced myself. "I can't do that, Khine. I don't want to hurt you, but I will if you try to stop me."

Khine swallowed. I wondered if he was taking the threat seriously. "Where are you planning to go?" he asked.

"I need to help my husband," I said. "If you're not going to leave me alone, then you might as well be of some use. Take me to Dar Aso."

He looked startled at my request, but he recovered swiftly. I let him lead me to the immigrants' quarter, making him walk in front of me. I kept my hands on the sheathed sword, ready to draw it at any moment.

Walking into Dar Aso felt like walking into a different world. It was an assault to the senses—the spices of so many different nations mingling together in the air, along with smoke, along with piss and excrement. I didn't even know why it existed—the empire was already a mosaic of so many nations and cultures, many of which had been colonized and conquered over the centuries. But I suppose there was a difference between *old* immigrants and the new. The people of Dar Aso had fled their own nations for the comforts and privileges promised by the empire, whatever those may be. Looking at my surroundings didn't really give me much of an insight.

"Where are...we going from here?" Khine asked.

"There must be a mortuary here somewhere." I clicked my tongue. "You'd know where that is."

"I would?"

"You studied as a physician."

"Ah. You're too perceptive." He glanced back at me. "Are you thinking you'd find your husband there?"

"No," I said, and left it at that.

He wasn't in an argumentative mood. He led me past a bridge, and then to a wider road that fringed the edge of the city. I could see tall stone walls.

"Over here," Khine said, pointing towards a low building right at the edge of the wall.

We ducked under a beaded curtain as we entered. The smell had grown worse, now—a rancid scent that mingled with the smoke and strong herbs. A small suntanned woman met us. "Khine," she said, wiping her hands on a rag. She had a strong accent, one I couldn't place. "I haven't seen you in a while. What can I help you with?"

"Nothing this time, old friend," Khine replied. "I'm just playing the...er, tour guide." He glanced at me.

"Did you get men here?" I asked. "Two weeks ago. Jinseins."

"We did," the undertaker said. "They've been sitting there all this time, waiting for someone to claim them. *Are* you?"

"I'll have to see them first."

"It's a hundred *rean* to claim them. Otherwise, off to the mass grave they go."

"How many, exactly?"

"If you're thinking about the same men I was," she said, "there's ten of them."

I pretended not to be surprised. "Show me."

She gave a small bow and led us past the rows of opened corpses laid out on cold stone slabs. We went down a short flight of stairs to a separate room, which was below ground—the only windows were tiny slits right below the ceiling. The undertaker gave me a lantern. "Over there," she said, glancing at bodies that had been laid one on top of each other on a shelf, like loaves of bread in a bakery.

I swallowed and approached them. The first one I recognized was Arro. He looked...well. Nothing like he looked in life. Naked under a thin sheet, his eyes sewn shut, his face deformed by the preserving oil that had been rubbed all over his skin. The choking grief clung to me like a needy child, refusing to let go. This time, I let it envelop me.

CHAPTER FOURTEEN

THE MONGREL OF OREN-YARO

ᴛᴜᴍ

Ah, Princess." I could still hear Arro's voice in my mind, see the way his eyes disappeared when he smiled. "Can you not write without smudging ink everywhere? There's more on your fingers than on that piece of paper. Don't let the officials see you like that. What would they say?"

"What *would* they say, Arro?" Agos broke in, walking into the room without invitation. "They already say whatever the hell they want. Let them."

I heard Arro mutter something under his breath, but I barely heard it as I hurtled down to the doorway to greet my old friend. "Agos! They finally got rid of you!" I stopped a foot away. He had grown tall enough to dwarf me, which seemed impossible in the span of time since I last saw him.

"They've got no reason to keep me all summer," Agos said with a smirk. "It's not like they're sending me out."

"What do you mean?" I asked. "I thought they were grooming you for command."

Agos laughed. "A commoner's bastard—"

"Your language in the presence of the princess—" Arro snapped.

"—like me?" Agos continued, ignoring him. "That's just rumours."

"Lord General Ozo didn't seem like he cared. The man favours you."

"Doesn't matter if the other bannermen have anything to say about it. Command belongs to their sons and daughters, and that's a hill they're willing to die on. You damn royals. Lady What's-Her-Face was livid I even made it this far, when her daughter's still stuck manning the northern outposts."

"Lady What's-Her-Face," Arro repeated with a groan. He gestured back at the door. "You must have missed your way to the kitchens. The princess is busy right now. Go, see your mother."

"Already did."

"Then why in heavens did you think you can just barge in here?"

"I came to tell the princess the good news," he said, turning back to me and crossing his arms. "General Ozo's demoting your captain of the guard and putting me in charge in a few weeks."

"That's wonderful," I said. "It will be like old times! I can finally ride along the riverbank—the old snot wouldn't let me."

"Because I told him not to entertain that nonsense because you could break your neck in the process, so gods help me," Arro gasped, the exasperation plain on his face. "No—not *could*. *Would*. You would."

"You'd dare give my men orders, Arro?"

"I'd dare, and I'd do it again for your own good." He snapped the book on his lap shut and turned to Agos with a small sigh. "And I don't know what General Ozo was thinking promoting *you*, but that's news we could have waited to hear from his own lips instead. He should've given me a chance to voice out my opinions about his pick. Her guardsmen need to have *her* safety and best interests at heart, which, given your past history, has not always proven true."

Agos frowned. "Those are harsh accusations, Master Arro."

"You indulge her. If she decided she wanted to jump off a cliff, you'd be the first to encourage her."

Agos flushed. "But I mean... try stopping her..."

"*And* you overstep your bounds. You don't just walk in here to converse with the princess like an equal."

"Why not, Arro?" I broke in.

He looked shocked that I would even say such a thing.

"Because..." he stammered.

"I'm getting married in a few days," I continued. "I'm not a girl anymore. I'm a woman now, Arro, soon to be queen."

"That doesn't mean anything," he said in a low voice. "It doesn't mean you get to do what you want."

"Doesn't it? Then why give me this position at all?"

"I should go," Agos mumbled.

"No," I said. "You have to get used to this. Stay."

He shuffled his feet uncomfortably before slumping against the wall.

I took a step towards my old tutor. "Tell me, Master. *When* do I get freedom? There's officials down there waiting for me to discuss politics—why do I have to worry about how I look? Rai never does!"

"Because for all the harm they had done to the land, Rayyel Ikessar's clan is still loved by Jin-Sayeng. Yours isn't." Arro held his hands together and sighed. "Princess, I understand it is grating that they judge everything you do, but that is the hand you were dealt. Do you know what they're going to talk to you about down there?"

"Something about a pact with the empire."

"A pact made by Oren-yaro with a *city* in the Empire of Ziri-nar-Orxiaro years ago, which has been done by other cities in Jin-Sayeng in the past. Most of them are ancient—we have old ties with the empire, long before those old hostilities. Those ties are more than tradition—for centuries, our economy *relied* on the empire's goodwill. They never even tried to invade us until the Ikessars torched that relationship."

"I thought they didn't try to invade us because we had dragons," I said.

"*Had*," he repeated. "Need I remind you? You only need to look outside to know the truth of that, Princess."

I swallowed. In the old days, Oren-yaro had dragon-towers—tall, glorious spires that rose to the heavens, connected by bridges. They served two purposes: as landing platforms and holding cages for dragons, and to direct dragon-fire underground, providing a source of energy to the city. While the other cities had dragon-towers, too, Oren-yaro had the most. From a distance, they gave the appearance of castles in the sky.

Now, not much remained. There were slums along the river, sections of which had grown black and green from sewage. We called another part of the city *Old Oren-yaro*, which we had long abandoned. Without dragons, it made no sense to stay in those decaying buildings tainted by war and demon magic. For almost three decades, we had pushed our people back to more practical industries: rice farming (though Oren-yaro rice is grainier than the sought-after fragrant variety grown in the Sougen region), fishing, livestock. Which barely took the edge off hunger; we still dealt with famine, floods, and drought almost year-round. Just keeping people alive was driving the throne bankrupt, never mind providing and repairing infrastructure. Cities where peasants could rise to fortune if they worked hard enough had become little more than myths to entertain children before they went to bed.

"When the number of dragons declined, we needed the empire more than ever," Arro continued, his voice growing harder. "But the Ikessars chose to break ties instead and ally with the Kags, with their strange ways and their strange languages. They upheld the merchant class, insulting every other warlord across the nation. Why *wouldn't* they try to invade us? Your father understood this more than anyone else. During the war, when he had nothing else to lose, your father attempted to make ties with the empire. He was led to this city, Zorheng, where he later made agreements with the city officials."

"And they're all angry about that," I said. "Why? If other warlords have done it before, why do they care that my father did the same thing? He's been dead seven years."

"Exactly," Arro replied. He rubbed his beard. "They're going to frame it as something else, of course. This Zorheng is currently under the rule of Governor Ong, whose only daughter is married to Prince Yuebek Tsaito, Fifth Son of Emperor Yunan. Prince Yuebek holds no office, but they'll say the pact has everything to do with him."

"Is it because my father had ambition? As if every single one of the ass—"

He frowned.

"As if every single one of the *idiots* don't," I grumbled.

"They won't talk about that. It'll draw too much attention to them. It's Prince Yuebek's reputation they'll latch on to. The man's made quite a name for himself over the years. They say he's—but I won't speak of these things behind these walls. They're not proven, anyway." He dabbed the sweat off his brow.

Agos interrupted with a snort of laughter. "You mean the *agan*."

"Be quiet!"

"General Ozo can court-martial me if he wants," he retorted. "Every time you officials start mumbling about something, it's always about the forbidden arts and the *agan*. Forbidden my ass. It was an *agan*-mad dragon that ripped our cities apart! Wasn't it the Ikessars who brought it to Jin-Sayeng in the first place? That same dragon killed the princess's brothers and drove her father to start a war. But it's going to be *her* head on the plate if she so much as talks about it?"

"There's a reason you're a soldier and not a politician, Agos," Arro said. "Stay out of this. Princess—" He turned to me, his eyes softening. "I am only trying to protect you."

"You all say that," I murmured. "Who am I supposed to believe?"

Akaterru guide you, Arro, I thought, staring at his body with regret. I should have been kinder to him, should have asked for his opinions more. There were a great many things I should have spoken to Arro about over the decades, so many things left unsaid, and now he was gone. I never even knew the name of his wife. *May all the gods guide you. You have been good to me. Better than most. May you find yourself home at last. I will miss you.*

I tore my attention from him towards the others. Nameless faces at first glance, but some came rolling back towards me like Saka's had. Ikong. Fasio. Attaru. Peng. The rest...I didn't know the rest. It wasn't the queen's job to know her men. I noticed their throats were cut, long ragged smiles beneath their jaws. Ten others were unaccounted for, and Captain Nor.

I heard Khine clear his throat beside me. "Your people?" he asked.

I nodded, trying not to let the emotion show in my expression.

"I'm sorry."

"Don't be. You didn't do this."

"It's...just a figure of speech." There was a sliver of concern in his voice. "If you would prefer to be alone for now..."

"Please," I said.

He gave a small nod and walked away. Only then did I lower my head and shed the tears I had been holding in the past few weeks. A moment to mourn, I told myself. All I needed was a moment. After that, I could be strong again.

I wiped my face as I walked up the stairs to rejoin Khine and the undertaker. I cleared my throat. "Did they have anything on them when they were brought in? Their clothes, personal belongings..."

"There were some," the woman said. She motioned for me to wait as she disappeared into one of the rooms. She returned with a wooden crate filled with various trinkets—belts, laces, scarves. I found what I was looking for—a wooden seal that Arro always carried with him, which he used to stamp the wax on all official documents. I glanced at the woman as I picked it up.

"I don't have coin with me," I finally said.

"Go ahead and take it," she said with a smile. "I'm not in the habit of charging the grieving. I just have to pay the rent."

"How long are you keeping those bodies for?"

"Another two days. They're past their time, but somebody's paid me to keep them here until then."

I looked up in surprise. "Who?"

"Hell if I know."

"Governor Zheshan?"

The undertaker gave me a smile. "Is that all you needed?"

"Thank you," Khine said, a signal that the conversation was over. For whatever reason, he didn't want me to talk any further.

I remained silent as we walked out of the mortuary, my thoughts scrambling over each other. Here I was, in the middle of Anzhao City, with no money and not a friend in sight. Rayyel was a *hostage*, no longer this Governor Zheshan's guest, which meant he was being held captive against his will. An insult to Jin-Sayeng, if there ever was one. By all rights, I should be making my way to the nearest scribe shop and penning a letter to Oka Shto. I was queen. I had an army, as my general had so clearly reminded me before we left. I could use them. I could threaten an assault on Anzhao while demanding my husband's safe return, and then worry what to do about *him* once he was back home, even if I had to drag him back in chains.

But if the dead men in the mortuary could speak, they would remind me of the price for pride, one they had to pay. Such an action would result in war. The empire would retaliate. They'd done it before. The whole weight of their forces against such a small nation like Jin-Sayeng would be catastrophic. Arro told me my own father had seen the wisdom in repairing relations with the empire. Would I ruin all his hard work now?

I had to consider the ramifications of whatever I did next. I had been taught how to rule—now I had to show I could be a leader. I *was* queen, and that meant more than just trying to push my weight around. Arro had tried to teach me that all these years. Taming a wolf wasn't an easy task, and he must've gone to his grave thinking he had failed. His death was already on me; I couldn't taint his memory, too. And my husband— I couldn't let the same thing happen to Rai. Five years of regret has a funny way of fermenting inside someone—like wine, it had only gained potency over time. There were many things that Rai and I did not see eye to eye on, but none of it warranted this. I would have never, in all my life, wished him pain. And I had not gone to the empire against my council's wishes just so I could let some piss-faced Zarojo get the better of my husband.

I looked at the map and measured the length of the Golden Road from Anzhao to Zorheng with my thumb. I didn't even need to convince myself I could make the journey. The anger did that for me.

CHAPTER FIFTEEN

THE LONG ROAD TO ZORHENG

ꜩꜩꝏꝕ

Khine coughed, and I only then remembered he was still there. "What now?" he asked.

I supposed it didn't matter if I told him. "I'm going to Zorheng City."

His eyes widened. "Why?"

"I don't have to explain to you." I started walking towards the gate. I heard him curse under his breath.

"For my family's sake, please, Tali..."

I ignored him. He continued to follow me, although he kept his mouth shut. Eventually, the rigid silence began to grate at me, and I turned to him with a snarl. "What are you doing?"

"I can't show my face there without you," he said.

"Why not?"

Khine didn't reply. For the entirety of the walk to the eastern gate, he remained at my heels like a damned dog who couldn't tell he wasn't wanted. I didn't know how to make him go away. Creating an uproar might only bring the city watch running to us, and the last thing I wanted was more attention. So we walked in silence, with nothing but the sound of our boots on the dusty road.

"Do you know how long it will take us to walk to Zorheng?" he asked as the crowded city faded behind us. It was the first time he had spoken after what felt like hours. Ahead, I could see nothing beyond dead grass and stunted trees.

"The map says..." I began.

"Forget the map." He folded his arms and stepped towards me. It made me realize that up until then, he had been expecting me to turn back. "You've got no money, no supplies. There's bandits all over those parts."

"I think I can handle a few bandits."

"You think this is a game? A story?" He started to reach for my shoulder and froze about a moment before he touched it. The expression on his face was conflicted, although I couldn't see what for. Did he find me disturbed? Was he really concerned, or was I making a muck out of one of his well-plotted plans? "Let me help you," he said. He curled the fingers that hovered over my skin.

I realized, at that moment, that he believed I was—if not truly a queen, then at least *somebody* important. Only the familiarity of the last few days made it possible for him to talk to me in such a tone. Or maybe he was just that sort of person, one who remained unimpressed by titles. "This isn't about me," I said.

He looked at me, breathing. Waiting.

"My husband's in trouble," I continued. "I've been told that someone in Zorheng City may help."

"Whoever told you that was lying," he said. "You might as well just fall on that sword now and save us the trouble. I've told you the road is dangerous. Zorheng City itself—it's like a thousand Shang Azis put together. No one is worth going all the way to Zorheng City for."

"Rai is," I said in a low voice.

"You said he left you. Is this about getting him back?"

I snorted. "I've lived without the man for five years. No. This is about saving his life."

A pony and a rider galloped past us in a flurry of dust and hooves. I wondered if they were headed for Zorheng. "Rai," Khine said. "Rayyel."

I hesitated before inwardly admonishing myself for slipping. The man was a con artist, an expert at observing and trapping people. If he had been lying about overhearing me before, there was no point in denying it now. The look on my face would have told him everything.

"The famous uncrowned Dragonlord of Jin-Sayeng. And you're Queen Talyien, the first of that title in all of Jinsein history." I remembered his passioned speeches from days ago and wondered if he would turn on me now. But he only swallowed, giving a small, almost apologetic smile. "Tell me what happened to you. From the beginning."

"And I suppose I owe you that information for saving my life."

"I didn't save your life," he pointed out. "You did tell me you were doing just fine before I arrived."

"I..."

"Tell me," Khine said, "as a friend."

"I am grateful for what you've done for me, Khine, but get one thing straight," I replied. "We're not friends."

His face fell. I had never before seen anyone look so hurt in response to something I said, so I kept my mouth shut after that and let him continue to walk beside me without another word. If he was trying to fool me into feeling bad for him, then he was doing a damn fine job. I almost wished he were the sort of person who was clearer about his intentions, like Lo Bahn and Ziori. Then I could've killed him and been done with it.

We saw burning buildings about an hour down the road.

Khine hurtled over the fence like a man possessed, rushing through squawking ducks and barking dogs to stop in front of a farmhouse.

Flames licked around its roof, filling the air with thick black smoke. I turned up the path to walk towards him before I saw two men emerge from behind a shed.

They did not look like farmers. One had an eye patch and thin, bristly hair covering a sweaty head. The other was clothed in tattered robes, the sort that looked like they hadn't seen a laundry basin in years. Both had bare blades in their belts.

I drew my sword, which caused a burst of laughter from Eye Patch. I lunged before he could do anything else. The movement caught him by surprise. He was on the ground, bleeding from a cut on his knee, a moment later.

"Fucking bitch!" Dirty Robes cried, reaching for me. From the corner of my eyes, I saw his friends emerge from the blazing farmhouse. I pulled myself behind the gate pillar, hoping they were all incompetent swordsmen.

"Jiro Kaz!" Khine called out.

I saw the men stiffen at the sound of his voice. One, taller than the others, broke into a grin. "Tashi Lamang," he said, opening his arms. He grabbed Khine and enveloped him in the fiercest embrace I had ever seen.

Khine pulled away. He had that same expression on his face, the one I had seen at Lo Bahn's gambling hall. "It's been too long, Jiro," Khine said. "I was almost sure you and the Blue Rok Haize had retired from banditry." Despite his light tone, his jaw was tightened. "What's this all about? Have you gone and killed Farmer Bhat Lee?"

"Gods, no," Jiro replied. "On my honour—"

"As a bandit?"

Jiro chuckled. "The man went too far. He gave a false report to the village chief three days ago. I couldn't let such an insult go unpunished. You know our rivalry goes way back. Don't get all judgmental on me now, Tashi Lamang. I waited until he took his family to the mountains for a vacation."

"And his servants?"

"Casualties. It happens."

"I see." I could tell that Khine was trying very hard to maintain his composure. He walked towards Eye Patch, who was still crawling on the ground in a mess of his own blood, and bent over to take a look at his leg.

"Didn't know you've made it a habit to keep the company of violent women," Jiro said, crossing the road to join him. "Think he'll walk again?"

"It's a scratch," Khine said, getting up. "A bandage and some rest will do you good. It's too bad you killed all the servants, or you could've gotten help right away."

"Not all..." Jiro began.

"All," one of his men croaked out.

Jiro gave a smug grin before letting his eyes fall on me. He had a thick black beard, which made it look as if an animal had died on his face. He tugged it before he spoke again. "What do we do about her, do you think? We don't just let women skewer our own and let them walk away from it."

"It's a slash, not a skewer," I said.

Jiro's face flickered, like he wasn't used to people talking back to him. He glanced at Khine. "Where did you find this one?"

"She's escaping from Lo Bahn," Khine said. He got up, tucking his hands into his sleeves.

Jiro broke into laughter. "All right," he said when he finally found the space to breathe. "All right. I'll let her off the hook. Going to tell this story until the day I die, see if I don't. Bloody idiot's fault for letting a woman stick him with a sword, anyway. Get up, fool!" He kicked the wounded man before turning back to us. "You taking her up to Nam Ghun?"

Khine nodded.

"They're making repairs to the bridge some ways up it. I wouldn't use the northern road if I were you. Looters from Zorheng. Not everyone knows you, Tashi Lamang. Next time you meet bandits, you may not be so lucky." He whistled to his men before returning to the farm. They scampered after him like a pack of dogs.

My arms slackened. "You've got friends in high places," I said in a low voice.

He scratched the back of his head. "Tashi Hzi used to do free work around these parts for some of the smaller villages. He'd take his students—a good way for us to learn, and a nice change of pace from the usual gout and whorehouse diseases in Anzhao. Jiro Kaz was one of the patients. I didn't know who he was until long after I'd gotten to know him. I think he took a liking to me, and I got along well with his men. He would call for me, on occasion, even after I left my studies with Tashi Hzi."

"It doesn't bother you, helping out bandits?"

Khine grimaced. "Self-proclaimed lords, these men. Him and Lo Bahn, and others. They crop up in places like these, where the nobility have strained their welcome and the elected officials don't care much beyond lining their own pockets. But to answer your question—no. If somebody needs help, I'm obligated to."

"I read that in your *Texts of the Undying*," I said. "But you're not even a physician, nor a student anymore."

"Even so."

I stopped walking. "I don't know what to think about you, Khine Lamang," I blurted out.

His brow furrowed. "What do you mean?"

I took a deep breath. "The people I thought I could trust have betrayed me or died or were captured. I have no one else. I think you know this."

"I've got to admit, I haven't thought that deeply into it." He gazed out into the distance. "You did say we weren't friends," he said.

"I don't know who my friends are. Not anymore."

"Back home?"

"I have advisers. Guards. Servants. I had their loyalty, I think." One of my councillors had recommended the *Singing Sainsa*, had sworn the crew's loyalty on his life. I needed to have him executed when I returned. I shook my head. "I don't know," I repeated, mumbling. "It's true that you haven't given me any reason to doubt you, but I could've said the same for everyone else. You haven't given me a reason to trust you, either."

"Opening my home up to you and giving you the only bedroom for the last few days hasn't been enough?"

"I do sound ungrateful, don't I?"

"Very."

We walked silently, plodding on the road like a couple of oxen. The sun was sinking into the horizon, and I felt the weight of the entire day bearing down on me. I was hungry and starting to realize that I hadn't entirely thought this whole trip through. I turned to Khine. He looked agitated—arms crossed, a frown on his lips. The restlessness appeared at odds with a man who could act his way through a con so effortlessly.

"I do need you to come back with me to Shang Azi," he said, noticing my gaze. "Not to return to Lo Bahn, no. No matter your opinion of him, he is not an entirely unreasonable man. But he...he asked me to go after you."

"So you didn't follow me because you wanted to." I couldn't control the thread of anger in my voice. He suddenly looked even more sheepish than before.

"I didn't...I *did* want to. It's...it's not what you think, Tali. Gods, it's not like I meant to knock you unconscious and drag you back to him like a prize rabbit."

"I dare you to try."

"No thank you. I..." Khine grabbed my wrist. And then, realizing what he'd just done, he dropped it just as abruptly. "My apologies," he grumbled. "Listen, Tali. I will be honest. Lo Bahn...he took my sister Inzali as hostage."

"And she didn't try to claw his eyes out for that?"

He gave a grim smile. "She, ah—offered. It would've been Thao, otherwise. And she has a very low opinion of Thao's chances of survival around those men."

I breathed. "I'm sorry," I said. "I have to do this first."

"I know."

"And I will try to get word to Lo Bahn, to repay that debt. Perhaps he'll let your sister go then. But there is a life I have to return to, Khine. You have to understand..."

"I'm not trying to stop you," he said. "I've been told to bring you back, but understand that I'm not going to do that, not against your will. I just want to make sure you get where you need to go so you can help *me* after. And I think you'll agree that you do need my help. There's a roadside inn not far from here. Come on. I'll pay."

Hunger and exhaustion won. I nodded. He strode up ahead, and I followed him this time, my boots making small eddies in the rain-soaked dirt. I struggled to remember that once, I had been a queen. That I still was. What did Jin-Sayeng think of beggar royalty? The last Dragonlord, Rysaran Ikessar, had lived as a vagrant for many years in his mad quest for a dragon that would offer some scrap of legitimacy to his reign. I had never understood that. A dragon alone did not make you a ruler. A dragon did not make loyal followers.

Of course, I had neither. What did that make me?

———

The inn was roomy, quite unlike some of the places I've had the misfortune of staying at during my travels in Jin-Sayeng. It was more barn than anything else, with large roof beams surrounding the dining hall. The round tables were so far apart from each other that the conversations around us were garbled, like the buzzing of bees in the summer heat. Grainy mats under the low benches cushioned our feet. It was not comfortable, but after hours of walking about in dust and mud, I more than welcomed the relief of getting to sit at last.

A mousy-looking server brought our food: hot, sour soup made of beef leg bones, corn, and jackfruit; bowls of rice; and some boiled eggs. The beef bones contained chunks of fatty marrow that oozed into the soup when I tapped them with my spoon.

"You must really love your Dragonlord," Khine said. "For you to go through all this trouble…"

I glanced up from peeling an egg. "I suppose. He's been…longer in my life than he hasn't."

"Even without the five years?"

I allowed a smile to flit across my lips. "Well, maybe not."

"I did tell you I have Jinsein friends. I'm not entirely ignorant about those events." He wiped his lips and took a long swig of the nutty brown ale that the inn served in round earthenware pots. "Dragonlord Rayyel, on the eve of his official coronation day, abandoned his bride of three years. A mystery that has confounded many scholars."

"I don't see what was so confounding about it. Everyone I've met seems to have an opinion about why it happened. They usually blame me. Things I did, things I didn't do." I stared at the egg in my hand.

"You seem almost nonchalant."

"Now I am. Five years ago, I'd have cut your head off for even daring to mention it." I smiled at him.

"Queen Talyien the Decapitator. I've heard of that one, too. I can see why."

"That's surprising. Most men tell me otherwise."

"Flattery."

"So you're not trying to flatter me? That's a relief. People are either trying to flatter me or trying to run from me."

"I don't believe in empty flattery, and I've been around Inzali too long to be frightened of women."

"Lies."

"Maybe." His eyes danced.

I was silent for some time while I sat there, staring at the fatty lumps congealing at the edges of my soup bowl. "It's not what people think," I said at last. "It's got nothing to do with our clans or my lack of suitability as a bride, or *his* lack of suitability as a husband for the last direct heir of the Orenar clan. It was never about politics or tradition. He left because sometimes we make mistakes and we do things we can't ever take back."

It was strange to hear those words come from my own mouth. It was even stranger to have someone else listening to them. Until then, I had never told anyone these things. Even if I had wanted to, especially in the midst of the raw ache of the months after I became queen, there had been no one else who would listen. It was easy enough to admit now.

He looked at me, waiting for the rest of it. I stared at my ale and took a long drink before I unlatched the gate to the story that marked the beginning of what would eventually take me across the Zarojo Sea.

CHAPTER SIXTEEN

THE PRINCE AND THE PRINCESS

ᜊᜓᜄ᜔ᜒᜎᜒᜈ᜔

Our courtship started like a dance. A bow, outstretched hands, each step perfectly choreographed by others.

The incident with the dragon seemed to have been enough to erase the effects of our first, tumultuous meeting. I treated Rayyel as was proper, and he, in turn, seemed to have completely forgotten the words *wild child* and *unfit to be queen*. After he returned to his mother in the Citadel, in the mountains north of Darusu, he began to send me letters, each signed *Respectfully Yours*.

The sincerity of the gesture struck me. It wasn't as if I had a choice. All my life, my father had drilled into me the importance of this alliance. "You will marry that boy," my father had told me on his deathbed. "And you will try to love him. He is an Ikessar, raised in seclusion with all their strange ways. You may not want to."

I had promised, not realizing—young as I was—that I would reach a point when I didn't *want* to have a choice. There were too many stories of princesses sent to marry gout-ridden warlords twice their age, or ones shackled to sadistic men with yellowed teeth who would beat them before they bedded them, for me to be anything but grateful that I had an actual prince. Perhaps he was not eloquent, and his letters were a little too rigid to be considered romantic, but he had been willing to face down a dragon for my sake. Young girls find it difficult to forget such things.

I would write back, haltingly, trying very hard to keep my letters short and free of the nonsense that sometimes plagued my thoughts. Some letters I wrote and never sent for fear that he would think me weak-minded. We continued this for the better part of a year until I saw him again on my twelfth birthday.

Arro had arranged festivities for the occasion, including a long ride along the southern riverbank to view the Seven Waterfalls and its grove of silver *padauk* trees. We had lunch under the sheen of those silver leaves, staring out at the crisp blue water of the River Agos. I still remember the food: sweet *pako* cakes, smoked fish bellies, and tomato wedges. We had run out of conversation, so Rai read something for me from his book *The Wars That Shaped Jin-Sayeng History*. I had never been happier in my life.

I saw him a few more times over the next two years, usually around celebrations of patron deities. Although he followed the prophet Kibouri's teachings like most Ikessars, he had made a habit of paying his respects for the other clans' sakes. I never once saw his mother, Princess Ryia; I was told that she had taken a vow of seclusion after Warlord Yeshin's war for all the blood she had spilled trying to seize the throne for herself. My father had not lied about the Ikessars' strange ways.

When I was fourteen, my studies with Arro ended. I was sent to Shirrokaru to further my education. By then, a good part of the Dragon Palace's libraries and studies had been rebuilt, and the young royals were encouraged to pursue the tutelage of Ikessar scholars. It was Princess Ryia's pet project. She wanted to give us all a chance to learn of the world beyond our clans' borders, as well as strengthen the ties between the future rulers of the nation. After decades of war and strife, it was one of the first sure signs of progress.

———+———

What is it about Shirrokaru that inspires so many poems and songs?

My father once told me that people cling to hope like drowning rats on driftwood. Sometimes it doesn't matter if it's all going to sink, anyway. What wisdom had there been in ceding all the power to a weak clan like the Ikessars? My father couldn't wrap his head around the madness that drove our ancestors to such a decision. The resources could've been better spent strengthening our own. It was true that the Ikessars had many sound ideas, but my father thought that several Ikessar scholars, well placed throughout the clans, would've done more good. It would've certainly fuelled less resentment.

To Yeshin's eyes, Shirrokaru was a symbol of excesses—a city built on the debt of others, one that only grows over the decades. *Starving peasants in Kyo-orashi? But the Dragon Palace needs new drapes.*

They were, I had to admit, wonderful drapes. Black and silver, emblazoned with the falcon crest of the Ikessar clan. I couldn't stop staring at them when we first rode into the Dragon Palace. We had simpler curtains at Oka Shto, and the only place you could see the wolf crest of Oren-yaro was in the wood carvings in the great hall. What money did we have left to spend on embroidery?

I had known that Rai had been in Shirrokaru many months ahead of me, and wanted to see him immediately. But this old woman with a nasal voice told me, in scathing tones, that the prince was busy. I was so offended by her stench that I made it a point to walk past her and demand to be taken straight to the studies, where I just knew Rai was going to be. A quick reminder of who I was sent a guard scurrying down the hall. I flashed the woman a smug grin before turning to follow him.

Rai was reading. There was a girl, a young woman, draped on the arm of his chair. I stomped in and they looked up, startled. The smile died on my face. "Rai," I said. He looked like a deer cornered by a pack of slavering dogs. It was the first time I had ever seen his expression stray so close to panic.

He cleared his throat and closed the book on his lap. "Princess Talyien. I did not know you would arrive early. How was the weather? Was the journey difficult?" He was babbling. I had *never* heard him babble before, either. Usually he acted as if small talk was beneath him.

"The weather was fair. We pushed the horses further than we probably should've." I glanced at the woman, who gave me a quick bow. She was beautiful, with the soft curves of womanhood already showing on her body—the sort of woman who could turn heads anywhere she went and have men running to do her bidding with one flick of her little finger. I had never felt more conscious of my awkward angles and many scars. *This* was what a princess ought to look like. My hands drifted to my sides in an unconscious attempt to hide the recent sword cuts and dog bites.

I wasn't sure if Rai was aware of my discomfort. "May I introduce Chiha aren dar Baraji," he said.

"Warlord Lushai's daughter." I didn't know why I spoke the way I did. Ignoring my rudeness, she bowed a second time—elegantly, like a swan. I was reminded of a comment from someone who said that I bowed like a baby horse.

I tried to gather my wits. The last thing I wanted was to look like a bumbling fool, and the effortless way she greeted me sparked a fire from within. She hadn't done anything to me yet, but I was already annoyed with her. "Prince Rayyel, may I have a moment of your time? It's been a long journey, and I had been looking forward to spending some time with my betrothed." I said the last part very slowly for Chiha's benefit, like I was talking to an idiot.

If Chiha noticed me mocking her, she didn't show it. She stepped aside as Rai stumbled past her, walking as if he had two left feet. As an afterthought, he returned his book to his desk before gesturing to me. "There's a balcony overlooking the lake..." he started, looking down at me. I flushed. I was still wearing riding clothes, complete with muddy boots.

"That would be most welcome," I said cheerfully.

He glanced at the guards, started saying something else, and then seemed to decide against it. He led me down the hall.

The balcony *was* beautiful. Even though Lake Watu was an unpleasant grey at the best of times, it sparkled under the clear sky. In the distance, I could see the boats ferrying goods and people between the palace district and the southern rest of the city.

"My apologies," Rai said, breaking my thoughts. "The wind can be particularly strong near the lake."

"I like it," I lied, even as the wind whipped my hair into further disarray. I tucked a stray strand over my ear, knowing it probably didn't do any good and that my head still looked like something you used to scrub the floors with. "Chiha—" I started. "Why is she here?"

Rai looked troubled. "What do you mean? She was invited, along with many other royals, to study in Shirrokaru."

"You seem overly familiar with each other."

"We've known each other since childhood," he said. He cleared his throat. "She visited the Citadel for a time."

"Did my father know this?"

"I don't understand."

I took a deep breath. "Chiha is Lushai's daughter. You do remember Lushai? The man who started the war on my father's side—his closest ally, who then betrayed him at the last moment?"

"Those were unfounded accusations."

"Lushai meant to plant a dagger in my father's heart."

"Warlord Yeshin is dead," Rai told me. "These old grievances should remain in the dust with him where they belong. Remember that *your* father tried to get my mother killed many times."

"They were enemies. That's different." I swallowed. "Lushai wanted you for Chiha."

"I am aware of that."

"So you don't care that we're both in the palace at the same time?" I couldn't stop my voice from rising. I was a girl, and the seed of jealousy, once planted, is very difficult to dig back out.

His face remained straight. "I don't see the problem. She is not her father, Talyien. As I'm sure you are aware that you are not yours."

The implication in his voice was clear. I don't think he knew how much his words could hurt me. Being compared to my father had always stung; hearing it from his lips felt like a dagger. I drew away from him, and it took all of my willpower not to storm off in a huff. I don't think he noticed. When it became clear I wasn't replying, I caught him gazing out at the horizon with that unreadable expression on his face, the one that would vex me for years to come.

"I think I know where this is going," Khine said when I reached that part of my story.

I observed him through the rim of my cup. "Do you?"

"He was seduced by this other woman, ruining your belief that you—unlike others in arranged marriages—had found a love match. A tale as old as time."

"Ah. Then it seems it is unnecessary for me to speak any further. You've already come to a conclusion."

He gave me a one-sided grin. "I apologize. Was there more to it?"

"There always is," I said.

He grew serious, and I could tell he was suddenly fishing for words. Which was strange, because in the short amount of time I'd known him, he always seemed to have a ready response to everything. I looked at his face, at the soft, appeasing expression and his bright brown eyes, very different from the sharpness in Rayyel's darker ones. Different, but no less calculating. But I knew there was no way he could understand. He was a young man—younger than me by two years, Inzali had mentioned—and unmarried. What would he know?

I heard the clatter of dishes, the sound of someone dropping a tray. I turned my head and saw a group walking through the doors. They were led by a woman, who was wearing a short robe over cotton trousers. There was a certain swagger in her walk that made me think she was a frequent customer, someone who believed herself more important than she was.

I turned to Khine and realized that he was gone. He must've gotten up to make water while I was distracted. I turned my attention back to the group, noting the swords strapped to their belts, which explained the sudden silence in the hall. Their leader walked up to a serving girl. After a brief exchange, the serving girl shook her head.

The woman grabbed a mug of ale from the counter in response. She took a long drink before glancing at the other patrons. Her gaze skipped across the room and settled on me.

I saw one of the men elbow her and recognized Dirty Robes.

"You!" the woman cried, pointing at me. The men rushed forward. I flipped the table and scampered for the door. I dodged a pair of lovers entangled in each other's arms as I barrelled my way outside. The blasted rain was coming down again, but for once, I was actually pleased to see it—it was easier to hide behind the torrent. I made for the outhouse, hoping to catch a glimpse of Khine along the way.

But it was empty. The door swung wildly with the wind. There was no one else on the path except the men behind me. I continued running, leaping over the next fence and into the woods.

The sky was overcast, with no sign of the sun. I hid behind the bushes, torrents of rain dripping across my face and down my jaw. I clenched my teeth to stop them from chattering and shut my eyes. I thought I heard the men crashing through the foliage, but it must've just been the tree branches swaying in the storm.

Time passed. No one found me. The damp darkness felt like a shroud. I wondered if they would find my dead body by morning.

I tried not to sink to such thoughts. Thanh was waiting for me. I had promised him his father, not the loss of both parents. Imagining the look on his face if he received news of my death drowned all my other fears. If they learned of my death, my boy, the first heir of *two* clans in the history of Jin-Sayeng, would be slaughtered at first light. Or else ignite a civil war larger than my father's. I could not put that on him. I would sooner whore myself out to Lo Bahn and all his men than allow such a thing.

After I hid long enough, I willed myself to move. I hadn't seen any other buildings on that road, so I carefully made my way back to the inn. The rain must've been too much for the men, because the yard was empty. I approached a window and pressed my back against the wall. I took a deep breath before pulling myself up on tiptoe to peer through the edge. The woman and her group sat around three tables pushed together. I saw Khine standing near her. They were too far away for me to hear their conversation, but it was clear enough from the looks on their faces what it was.

I dropped back to the ground, my heart hammering in my chest. *How long until you learn?* So Khine wasn't planning to sell me to Lo Bahn— no. There were *others*. I should've known when I met Jiro Kaz, when I learned who he was, when I saw how familiar Khine was with him.

There were so many clues. But just like back in Anzhao City, back with my own damn people, I had ignored them all, and here I was.

Father, I thought, staring up at the sky. There was no answer—there never had been. The man who had dragged me into this mess should at least have had the courtesy to lend me some wisdom. But I imagined he would be less than pleased that I found myself in this situation at all. Why did I expect loyalty from a mere stranger? From *anyone*? I couldn't even keep my betrothed faithful to me.

Sometimes I wonder: What if time has no fixed point? What if everything is happening all at once, the converging memories as real as they still feel? I was twenty-six years old, shivering in the rain. I was also eighteen, riding for Shirrokaru on my best horse, the harsh words I traded with Arro still fresh in my mind. At least, they were then—such is the fickleness of time that now I struggle to recall why it ended the way it did, why I chose to flee instead of waiting for my temper to cool down. Decisions congregate with emotion; one moment you are certain of yourself, the next you are standing where you once swore you never would. And then you must pick up your life where it fell, dust it off, and pretend that you knew what you were doing. Pretend that profound wisdom can be somehow gleaned from pride.

The past few years in Shirrokaru had given me a familiarity with the road that I wouldn't have dreamed of. Although I was no longer required to study with the scholars—I had been home for over six months at the time—I still found myself missing the refuge of the lecture halls, where I was just *one* of the students instead of the future queen.

"We should head back," I heard Agos grumble behind me. His horse was nearly a head taller than mine, a thick-limbed creature that he really shouldn't have picked for this journey. But I had left in a huff and hadn't given him enough time to think things through. I had that effect on him—I always have. Call it an oversight, how much I had taken his devotion for granted in those days. I still don't like thinking about it.

"I don't want to. Not until he sends me an apology. He's my adviser, not my *father*," I bristled.

"What will Prince Rayyel say?"

"He can say what he likes," I replied. "I'm not going back until Arro apologizes." Secretly, I was excited to see Rayyel. That tense meeting on my first day in Shirrokaru was a thing of the past. Chiha left months after I had arrived, feigning an illness of some sort, although most of us believed that she simply didn't have the stamina for the rigorous studies the scholars put us through. She was old enough to be married, anyway, and was said to be busy entertaining suitors in Bara by the end of that winter.

Rayyel's own studies were formally done a year after I arrived, but by then, he had come to call the Dragon Palace his home and would visit me in the study halls as often as his advisers would let him. Here, we would share tea or sweets fresh from the kitchens while I went through history books and he busied himself with reports from the various provinces. Although he was not supposed to have authority until our coronation day, he had already started to serve on the council as Minister of Agriculture.

Sometimes, he would pause from his work and take my hand under the table without a word. The warmth of his touch, in contrast to his stoic demeanour, would flood me with emotions—a sense of belonging, of being wanted, of love. It was towards that feeling I rode. I think a part of me was convinced that I was heading home, even as I was riding away from Oka Shto.

I arrived at the Dragon Palace without fanfare, handing my horse off to the stables and declaring I would see Rai personally first. Agos stayed with the horses while I paced through the gardens. I paused long enough to pluck a white rose from the bushes. I had joked, the morning I left six months ago, that I would throw one at his feet if he forgot to send for me.

"Sometimes I wonder if I'm supposed to be a business partner or your bride-to-be," I had added after.

I still remember Rai looking at me, trying to digest what I was really trying to say. I knew I confused him. All young women did—he had admitted as much to me in the past. After a moment, he cupped my chin in one hand and kissed me.

The memory of that first kiss burned in my mind, and my cheeks, as I walked down the hall. I was wondering what I would say to him, imagining the look on his face when I threw that rose the way I said I would. My arrival startled a guard in the hall, but I paid him no heed and kept walking until I reached the doors. I pushed one open.

I saw the naked back of a woman on the bed. She was straddling my betrothed, her hands on his bare belly. His eyes were closed.

They didn't notice me. I quickly closed the door and stalked back out of the halls, back towards the stables. I left the rose in front of the door. I never spoke to Rayyel of that day, but he must've seen it. He must've known.

CHAPTER SEVENTEEN

WHAT THE FIREFLIES KNOW

ᝆ ᝓ ᝆ ᝋ

The hours drifted by. The rain was starting to turn into a torrential monsoon—heavy and unrelenting, with drops big enough to feel like pebbles on my skin. I knew I couldn't stay slinking around in the bushes for too long. Night would wear on and it would get much colder; even now, I was starting to shiver. I caught sight of a small hut at the far end of the field, which the inn must've been using as a storage shed. It was close enough to the main building that they were probably going to look there, too, but I didn't know where else to go. I sprinted towards the promise of shelter.

A figure underneath an umbrella appeared around the corner. "Tali!" Khine called, recognizing me. He must have been looking for me since I left the inn.

I ran from him.

He chased me into the hut. I reached it first and attempted to slam the door shut, the bamboo creaking with the force. But he wedged the umbrella into the crack and managed to push his body in. My hand went straight to the slippery handle of my sword. "Get out before I run you through," I hissed.

Khine frowned.

"Out!"

He hesitated before taking one step towards me, and then another. I pressed myself as far back to the wall as I could. "Leave," I said again. I had meant to throw as much ice in the single word as I could, but my voice only came out weary. He knelt beside me.

"You should keep it down," he murmured. "They're asleep, but one or two might decide to go looking for you. They're not all stupid."

"You disappeared, and then I saw you talking to that woman..."

"Anya Kaz," Khine said. "Jiro's wife. I left, hoping she wouldn't see me with you."

"One of the men recognized me," I mumbled.

"I figured as much. I'm sorry I told Jiro Kaz about Lo Bahn. I didn't think he'd care. Thought it was our best chance of escaping—anything to be a thorn in Lo Bahn's heel. But Anya, she had other ideas. She was always the shrewd one." He looked up. "Did you think I left you?"

I turned my head without replying. From the corner of my eyes, I saw him start untying his shirt. "What are you doing?" I snapped. The sound of my voice, like the squeaking of an adolescent girl's, took me by surprise.

He finished taking his shirt off and held it towards me. "You're soaked. Change into something dry."

I hesitated before taking it. "Look away," I grumbled. But I didn't even have to ask him that—his eyes were already fixed on the far wall. I took a moment to observe his tanned skin from behind, the lean muscle over his shoulders, coated with a thin layer of fat. Not a warrior, this man, but one who, at some point, had done enough hard labour to have marked his body.

I realized I was staring a little too long, and focused on shrugging myself out of my shirt. Goosebumps flitted over my naked skin, and I felt self-conscious. If someone walked in on us right now, they were going to think the worst. The question was, Did I mind? My reputation was tarnished enough as it was.

I put his shirt on and cleared my throat. He turned, took my wet shirt, and draped it over a broken chair to dry out. And then he tugged me by the arm, pulling me towards him. The movement caught me by surprise and I started to kick him away, but I was so exhausted that I allowed him to wrap his arms around me instead. "You're still shivering," he explained, apologetic. "You were out there too long."

His voice was so soothing, and the warmth of his body—after spending hours drenched in rain—was starting to lull me to sleep. *Gods*, I thought. I was a branch teetering under the weight of a rock. I wanted to snap, but I couldn't.

"Stay awake," he warned. "Tali."

"I'm awake."

"It's dangerous to drift off now. Talk to me about something."

"Do you do this for all your patients?" I murmured, my ear drifting to the slight ridge over his bare chest. I could feel his heartbeat.

"Only the pretty ones."

"I knew it. *This* is why you're not practicing. Someone filed a complaint against you with the Physicians' Guild."

"Guilty as charged," Khine whispered, chuckling. "Told me I ought to keep my hands to myself." Despite his words, he kept his hands slack.

We sat silently like this for a while, his breath tickling my hair. It was strange for me to be so intimate with a man I wasn't sleeping with. I had not felt anyone's arms around me in a long time, and I tried not to dwell on it. Loneliness and desperation can push even the best of us off the edge. My father had warned me often enough about the perils of such emotions.

"Would returning to Anzhao be the worst thing in the world?" Khine asked.

"And you were doing so well in not getting skewered."

"I *have* been told my mouth runs ahead of my wits sometimes."

"From the short time I've known you, I'd say more often than not."
I looked down at his hands, at the dark, calloused fingers, so different
from Rayyel's smooth, pale ones. I resisted the urge to trace them with
my thumb or do anything that would make me forget I was a married
woman. I had lived this long without making it a habit of taking lovers
wherever it was convenient. "I can't risk it."

"Because of your Dragonlord."

I nodded.

"With all due respect, after what you told me—"

"It's more complicated than that," I grumbled. "We have a son. He is
waiting for me to bring his father home. How am I supposed to face him
like this? If his father is killed because of my inability to work around
minor complications like these..."

"I wouldn't call getting involved with a lord of Shang Azi and the
Blue Rok Haize minor." He shifted his weight. "Your sense of duty...is
admirable."

"Coming from a man who hates the nobility..."

He took a deep breath. "Admirable. Uncharacteristic. Confounding."
I could feel him looking at my face while he spoke.

"I have no choice," I murmured.

"Are you sure?"

"I was born to be queen. No—not just. I was born to be *Rayyel's*
queen. Without our betrothal, Jin-Sayeng would still be at war. I've
already failed, letting him leave that night. I will not fail again." My
voice buzzed through the darkness of that shed. It felt disembodied, like
I was listening to someone else speak for me.

"And so for this, you will walk out of here and face the unknown." He
shook his head. "If only I had that courage. I would be a physician now,
my family away from Lo Bahn's clutches."

"I thought Cho's debts caused that."

"They did. But if I had passed the examinations before that last year…" He trailed off, letting the silence carry the burden of the unspoken words. "You did not fail your husband. He was the one who erred."

"It doesn't change who I am and what I have to do."

"No. I suppose not." Khine started to get up. "I will see if it's safe to leave. I asked the innkeep to ply her men with drinks…I'll be surprised if any of them got up before noon."

"A moment," I said, grabbing his wrist.

He drew a quick breath. "Not too long."

"No." I closed my eyes against his neck. He smelled like rain and sunlight and mud, a clean scent that reminded me of my dogs and horses. I soon fell asleep, though not before his lips grazed the top of my head.

I dreamed of Rayyel, of opening the door to a prison cell to rescue him. Of outstretched arms and apologies, dancing around me like fireflies in the night.

We left hours before the first crack of dawn. The rain had slowed to a steady drizzle, but it kept the air damp and cold enough to make me wish for a warm bed. We took provisions from the shed: some rice, dried vegetables, and plantains. Khine insisted he had already paid for the rooms and that it was a fair trade. I was starting to learn that he always had to say these things, had to justify his actions, even when I didn't care one way or another.

I still didn't know how much I trusted him, or whether I did at all. He was too good of an actor. I supposed I was, too. We tricked a passing wagon into providing us transportation for part of the way, feigning a clueless husband and a pregnant wife. As the last village faded into a blip on the horizon, I glanced at the man and wondered what it would be like to have his sort of freedom—to have failed to meet his family's expectations, yet still be accepted, even welcomed. It was a fleeting thought, one that I killed almost as soon as it appeared. This was not the time for me to face an existential crisis. I could indulge in something like that if I had been born an artist or a poet, perhaps, but I was locked into this life, one where every action carried consequence for another. I had already learned that the hard way.

We reached the next inn at the crossroads by mid-afternoon. Khine found it an appropriate place to stop and rest, claiming that the Blue Rok Haize's influence did not extend this far. It was a busier inn, twice the size of the last one, and teeming with a variety of travellers from different parts of the empire. Although I was relieved to get fresh clothes and a bed at last, I kept my hand on my sword the whole time. But nothing out of the ordinary happened; we were able to keep up the pretense of husband and wife throughout dinner. At some point, Khine found another traveller willing to take us to Nam Ghun in the morning, and bade me to get as much sleep as I could.

"Past Nam Ghun..." Khine said as I was on my way to the room. "The bandits I mentioned. Actual bandits. The pillaging, raping, slit-your-throat-in-broad-daylight kind." He gave a sheepish grin. "Zorheng City is supposed to provide guard patrols along the road all the way to Nam Ghun, but it's a duty that Governor Ong has neglected as best as he could. I just thought I should warn you."

"If you think this will dissuade me..."

"No," he said, scratching his head. "I think I've come to the conclusion that nothing short of death can dissuade you. You *are* a queen, or else a very convincing madwoman. I am helpless, either way."

He didn't stop to explain what he meant by that and turned to walk away. I took hold of his arm, drawing him so close to me that I could almost touch his lips with mine. "And you are," I said, "either the world's biggest fool, or the best con artist this side of the continent."

"I could be both," Khine said. He looked at my hand. I let go, but not without some difficulty. I wanted so badly to trust him.

"Goodnight, Khine," I said. "Thank you for everything."

"Goodnight, Tali." His eyes twinkled. I didn't think he suspected that I had stolen his purse.

I slept only a few hours. In the dead of the night, I slipped through the window, made my way to the stables, and stole one of the horses, leaving the purse in its stead. The horse was a skittish bay, smaller and flightier than I was used to. I calmed him as best as I could before leading him to the road. There, I mounted the saddle and promised the gelding I would try my best not to get him killed. I wasn't sure if he believed me.

After an awkward start—I wasn't used to balancing myself on a saddle with a lantern strapped to it—we managed to clop along the Golden Road without trouble. It felt good to be in familiar territory, even if that only meant being on horseback again. It was better than running around in terror in the rain, better than skulking in the shadows like a hunted animal.

I rode about an hour or two down the road before I found a quiet clearing. I tied the horse to a tree branch. As I fiddled with the saddle, I noticed that the sky was splashed with a faint blue light, and recognized it for what it was—a rip in the *agan* fabric, a common occurrence wherever they practiced the forbidden arts. I had read about it from a book in the Dragon Palace. That alone, if nothing else, was a clear sign of the rampant hypocrisy in my land. The Ikessars played with knowledge that would doom me if I displayed the same amount of interest in such things; Arro knew it all too well.

Still, looking at the *agan* seeping through the sky, I wondered why it was forbidden at all. It was difficult to consider such pettiness against the dizzying brilliance above me. The Anyu brothers had offhandedly suggested for years that we study it. The rip in the *agan* fabric in their lands was what attracted the mad dragons in the first place, they said.

Thoughts of the mad dragons reminded me of the sort of creatures that could be lurking about in the dark. I tried to remember if I had read anything about Zarojo beasts. I had heard of false basilisks here, but they were supposed to be confined to the swamps. There were also legends of lionbeasts, feline creatures with horns on their feet and heads who carried the souls of dying women on their backs, to take them past the *agan* fabric and into the underworld.

A succession of sharp gusts overhead broke my thoughts. The horse gave a snort of unease. I got up to stroke his nose. Just as I was about to reassure him it was only the weather, the dragon appeared.

I grabbed the horse's rope just as the first blast of flame toppled a tree in the distance. It was too dark for me to see much more of the creature than its dark, jagged shape, and I didn't want to stick around to find out. I jumped into the saddle and rode straight into the nearest grove of trees. Behind me, I heard a roar, followed by the shriek of some other animal. The dragon must've caught its prey.

I pulled the horse to a halt and turned around, my heart racing. I could still remember that man's cryptic warnings from my youth. We were children then, but he had given them to me and Rayyel with the full knowledge that we would rule Jin-Sayeng someday. And yet in the past five years, I had done very little, even after receiving reports of dragons plaguing the western plains. I didn't see the need. The plains were their natural habitat, and while we had lost the ability to tame them, the lords there seemed to be doing a good enough job controlling the problem. The dragons also had yet to move further east, as Kaggawa had predicted. I had been too preoccupied with maintaining peace between the warlords, too focused on licking my wounds.

But sitting on the horse in the dark, sweat dripping down my back despite the cold air, I wondered if it was yet another oversight. A bad harvest alone could cause unrest—what would dragons razing the farmlands do to a people already on edge? The longer I stayed away from Jin-Sayeng, the more these problems would grow, trapping my family between them.

I decided not to wait for sunrise. When everything had grown silent and the horse was no longer jittery, I rode back to the clearing to fetch my things and returned to the road.

CHAPTER EIGHTEEN

ZORHENG CITY

丅工㊉

I reached Nam Ghun and stopped only long enough to purchase food. I didn't want to stick around to see if anyone had followed me from last night's inn. No one seemed to be looking for me, which was a relief after days of evading capture. A vendor did squint at me while passing me some hot meat buns, but I think that was simply because my manner of speaking stood out. She made a sign as I left her, an involuntary reflex to avert danger. Or maybe she truly meant it; maybe there was something about me she found frightening. Even dressed as a commoner, I couldn't help myself—in sheep's clothing, I remained a wolf.

Hours down the northern road, I saw a wide stone bridge that looked like it had been struck by lightning. The entire middle section was crisp black, and there was a pile of rubble underneath. I paused, wondering what was amiss. I recalled Jiro Kaz telling Khine about repairs. I dismounted to take a closer look.

Parts of the bridge had dropped to the river below, but the weight of the stone and the shallow water kept them in place. I whistled to the horse, encouraging him to follow me as I crossed the rubble. He wasn't too fond of the idea—two or three steps in, he began to pull back, kicking his heels and rolling his eyes.

I turned to comfort him just in time to see a basilisk leap from the river and clasp its teeth around the poor beast's neck. Its scaled tail whipped through the rubble before it dragged the screaming horse into the water.

I swallowed my terror and raced for the end of the bridge, just as a second basilisk slammed into the ground behind me, narrowly missing my leg with a snap of its teeth.

My heart pounded up my throat. I tried to focus on running, ignoring all instinct to draw my sword and face the creatures. The habits of false basilisks were well-documented—they rarely left the water and had soft spots in the back of their heads, into which you could easily sink a blade—but I didn't want to take my chances. I had read too many stories of true basilisks, with their venomous gazes, to even think about it.

Further down, a *rok haize* and an upturned wagon were blocking the road.

I stopped to catch my breath. I could no longer hear the creatures behind me, but as I saw the grim-looking men step out from behind the trees, I realized my troubles were far from over. I drew my sword. The act triggered a snicker from at least half. One approached me with a spear, his mouth twisted into a foul grin. "You know what we do to women like you?" he spat.

"Nothing I'll feel, I'm sure," I snapped back. I dropped low and allowed my sword to skim his spear as I lunged. His movement was clumsy, and he didn't recover—I stabbed him in the rib, grabbed his spear in my hand, and slammed my boot into his groin.

My swordsmaster once made me meditate for two days for not fighting fairly.

The bandit roared as he fell, letting go of his spear in the process. I flipped it around and jabbed it through his throat. Blood spurted through the open wound, trickling down the spear and around my fingers. He was still gasping for breath as his friends caught up to us, murder in their eyes. They were no longer amused.

Three rushed towards me, swords swinging. I couldn't take all of them at once. I sheathed my sword and darted back down the hill as fast as I could run. My heart was pounding in my ears when the first one caught up to me. I turned as soon as I heard his footsteps get close, holding both sword and scabbard out as he lurched forward. I drew the sword right below his neck, striking him across the chest.

It wasn't a killing blow; the sword wasn't sharp, and I barely ripped his clothes. He grabbed my shirt collar with both hands, tight enough to constrict my neck, and I realized he wasn't going to kill me if he could help it. Not yet. I tried to tear myself out of his grasp, and he struck me on the head with the handle of his sword. A dull ache pounded through my skull. My senses darkened. I heard a second man come close.

The man lifted me from the ground, tightening my collar with his fists. His knuckles got close to my mouth. I bit them, hard enough to draw blood. I could feel his bone between my teeth.

He dropped me with a cry. I recovered and struck the second, unsuspecting man, shredding his bare legs with two strokes. He rolled to the ground with a groan. I regained my footing just in time for the third attacker to wrap his arm around my neck. I could smell his foul breath over my shoulder. This time, the sword slid out of my grasp, followed by the wooden scabbard. The first man approached, his face red. "You're making this too hard, bitch," he snarled. "It's easier if you don't fight."

I grabbed the third bandit's arm and tore myself out of the chokehold, diving for my sword an instant later. I turned just as the man bore down on me. The tip of it went straight through his belly. His body fell on mine, and I twisted the sword deep into his gut, ignoring the fresh flow of blood. I slid away from underneath the body, pushed it aside, and lifted my sword.

"Mother," the dying man gasped as the blade sank into his heart. I remembered the man I had killed the night my husband left, and took a step back, my fingers trembling.

The remaining bandit made the same sign the vendor had that morning before turning tail.

I returned to retrieve the sword from the body. I could barely lift it now—my fingers were coated in blood, and the last few seconds had drained the energy out of me. But the battle was far from over. I heard the sounds of swords clashing behind. I turned. A bandit was grappling with Khine.

I should have known he would follow me; I thought I had been sneaky enough, but he must have seen through my acting the previous night. My irritation was drowned out by the horror of his fighting stance. Why did the man think he could handle a sword? Rayyel would have looked more graceful. I found an opening and stuck his opponent while his back was turned. The man twisted to face me, and I finished him off with a sword cut across his throat.

"Can't you tell when you're not wanted?"

"It's a sickness, I'm afraid," Khine said. He looked relieved. I noticed the horse he had ridden on wandering the roadside. "You can't steal from a thief, Tali. At least not without him suspecting you would."

"It's time you leave," I said. "I told you I can take care of myself."

"Do you know what's waiting for me when I get back?" he asked.

"Lo Bahn's wrath. I *know*. But—"

"Not just that." He straightened himself, as if bracing for a judgment he knew was coming. "There's a saying around these parts: *you are forever responsible for a life you save.*"

"I'll make this easier," I said in a low voice. "If you had ever helped save me, then I absolve you. You owe me nothing, Khine Lamang. *I* owe you nothing."

"It's..." he stammered. "It's not you," he finally said.

I stared back at him. It wasn't the answer I expected.

"I see her in you. This Jinsein woman I once knew. A woman I loved. The woman I hurt."

Suddenly, that explained the look in his eyes in every instance of us seeing each other in the street. There was always that flicker of disappointment, always a marked contrast to how he acted or the ease with which he pretended to deal with things. I felt a momentary pang of grief. *It's not you.* Of course it wasn't.

"One," I finally managed, "has nothing to do with the other."

"Perhaps not the way you see it. To me, it does. I saved her life once, and then I ruined it. Which makes me a person who broke his oath as a physician and a rotten human being. And now—"

"You chase after every Jinsein woman you see. I understand."

"That's not fair, Tali."

Our conversation was broken as screams erupted in the distance. The remaining bandits fled into the woods. The *rok haize* uttered a soft groan at being left behind.

Four armoured guards appeared from behind the wagon. I recognized the bronze-plated imperial uniforms. They walked down the length of the hill towards me and stopped a few paces away.

They bowed.

"Queen Talyien," one of the guards said, stepping forward. "We've been told to keep a lookout for you."

"That's convenient," I said, my nerves hissing through my voice. "Where were you weeks ago? I could've used you in Anzhao."

They ignored my sarcasm. My own guards would've been in apologetic convulsions by now. "We've heard word of your travels. We have been tasked to escort you the rest of the way to Zorheng City." The guard pressed the back of his hand over his forehead, which I've come to learn was the imperial salute.

"And who *tasked* you, exactly?"

"Prince Yuebek Tsaito, Fifth Son of Emperor Yunan. His Esteemed Highness has been waiting for you, ever since he got word of your attempted assassination in the venerable Anzhao City. He was afraid you were dead."

The Fifth Son. The one who didn't hold office. And yet they were reporting to *him*? I glanced at Khine, who cleared his throat.

"Do we part ways here?" he asked.

"I will send word to Lo Bahn and make him free your sister," I said, keeping my voice detached. "I promise you—I will make it right."

Khine looked like he wanted to say something else. Instead, he bowed the deep bow of respect, the sort a servant gave to his master. It was the first time he had ever actually acknowledged I was a queen. I had spent over two weeks wanting that familiar mantle of authority returned to me, but now it felt like a burden. I forced the memory of the night in the shed far from my mind and allowed the guards to lead me away.

I had expected that we would continue on the road. Instead, we took a fork that doubled back to the river. I almost balked, remembering the basilisks. But there was no sign of them along the sandy riverbank. A covered boat was waiting, where a man in silk robes sat, wiping sweat off his face with a yellow handkerchief. At the sight of me and the guards, he bolted to the shore.

"Queen Talyien." He dropped to the ground in a bow. After he got up, he gestured at the boat with his handkerchief. "If you could please get comfortable, we will take you to Zorheng."

I eyed the boat dubiously. "My horse was taken by a false basilisk on the bridge," I said. "There were at least two. I'm sure there's more."

"A shame," the man said, shaking his head. "But Prince Yuebek's mages have covered the boat with protection spells. You will be safe from the basilisks, and the crocodiles, and whatever manner of foul creature lurks beneath the Eanhe."

"There's other foul creatures here? Wonderful," I grumbled. I ignored his outstretched hand and clambered into the boat myself. It rocked slightly as the guards followed. I wondered what the other warlords would think about me in a boat held up by the forbidden arts. I supposed

I could send the first one who voiced criticism all the way out here and make him swim that river naked.

The robed man folded his arms. "I am Governor Radi Ong," he said.

That was surprising. I turned to him in shock. "What are you doing out here?"

"It was a nice day to sail."

I glanced around. We were at the top deck of the boat, which looked big enough to hold twenty or thirty people. But apart from Ong, the servants, and the guards, I couldn't see anyone else. The room we were in was bare, save for the rugs and cushions on the floor.

The boat began to drift into the middle of the river. I picked a cushion and settled down as comfortably as I could. The governor took a seat across from me. A servant appeared, carrying a tray of candied fruit in gooseberry wine. I watched Radi Ong pluck the fruit out of the small glass and swallow the wine first, in one gulp, before eating it. He was a balding, thickset man—more muscle than fat, like someone who was once a warrior but had given in to life's excesses. He had a thick black moustache under a bulbous, pocked nose.

At the servant's insistence, I finally picked up a glass and pretended to sip. I wanted to keep my wits about me. The scent of wine flooded my nostrils. "If you had known all the events that transpired in Anzhao, why didn't you fetch me?" I asked.

Ong dipped his head in apology. "Our men tried to, after the attack. I was told you disappeared. We looked for you. It was only when you crossed the northern gates that the guards spotted someone fitting your description. By the time their pigeon reached us, you were well on your way on the road, but the prince...*we* assumed that you were heading towards us. And we were right."

"Why is the prince so interested in me?" I asked.

He looked perplexed. "Why wouldn't he be? You are Queen Talyien aren dar Orenar, the first wolf of Oren-yaro to sit on the Dragonthrone."

"Hardly. I've never sat on the damn thing. Too cold."

"I..."

"A jest, Governor Ong," I quickly said. The man appeared to be on the edge of convulsions. "I doubt the Ikessars and their supporters would've let me, anyway. I ruled from my father's home in Oka Shto in Oren-yaro." I cleared my throat. "I was given the cold shoulder when I arrived in Anzhao City. I trust this was not supposed to be the Zarojo Empire's official stance on Jin-Sayeng?"

"There is no official stance on Jin-Sayeng," Ong said, wiping sweat off his chin. "The complexities involved in ruling the Empire of Ziri-nar-Orxiaro..."

"I think I've heard that before," I grumbled. "So your Esteemed Emperor is not concerned that his people have inadvertently insulted my nation?"

"Does the spider concern itself with the struggles of a fly?"

My hand moved to the handle of my sword.

He shook his head. "My apologies. I am not trying to aggravate you. I am only pointing out the size differences, and why there is no official stance. We have to balance the needs and relations of half a dozen small nations that border the empire—Jin-Sayeng, Herey, Lay Weng Shio..."

"You've annexed Lay Weng Shio."

"Have we? It's hard to keep track. So many kneel because it is easier to kneel." He blinked. "Anzhao City dealt with you the way they thought they should. Prince Yuebek...we...*I* don't agree with it, but I have no say in the matter." He swallowed. "The prince extends an offer of friend-ship to you. As the Fifth Son, he has no power outside the capital, the glorious Kyan Jang where the Esteemed Emperor reigns, but he wants you to know that he will do what he can for you and your situation."

"Will I meet him?"

As an answer, Radi Ong turned his head to the distance. I followed his gaze.

A city, unlike any city I had ever seen before, unfolded before my very eyes.

Massive walls, giant grey slabs, reached up into the sky, the tops of them marked with red banners. I could see two rows of windows near the top and nothing else. It almost felt like I was heading to the largest prison in the world instead of a named city.

I turned to Ong. He wasn't seeing the same thing I was. There was a look of pride on his face, like a child presenting his mother with some strange creation and waiting for her to pretend to like it. "Those walls..." he began. "They're not man-made. Our mages pulled them from the bedrock under the river, crafting it little by little until we have what you see now. Those walls are impenetrable, impossible to breach. You could batter them with boulders or flaming arrows from a thousand archers, and they will still stand."

"Do you expect attacks from the River Eanhe often? A vendetta by the foul creatures, perhaps? I wasn't aware they could secure catapults or archers."

His face fell. I think he was expecting me to be amazed by the feat. I *was* intrigued—it was the first time I had seen something crafted using the forbidden arts. But what was more interesting for me was why these people thought it was necessary to have such walls in the first place. "The expense..." I started. "Unless you get attacked often, I just don't see the need for it."

"If they were built traditionally, yes," Ong said. "The material alone... you could build an entire palace or two. But because mages crafted it, we did not have to pay a thing."

"You didn't pay the mages?"

"They were happy to serve for free."

"I thought the Zarojo Empire didn't take slaves."

He licked his lips. "We don't. They were happy to serve for free."

Something about the look on his face was disconcerting. I turned away and focused on watching the boat sail to the gates, through a massive tunnel set right into the wall. It must've been a cave, once—I noted limestone stalactites hanging from the ceiling. I glimpsed the shadow of a bat passing through. At least—I hoped it was a bat. If what the Zarojo had in broad daylight was frightening enough, I didn't want to know what they had in the dark.

The gates dropped shut behind us, iron crossbars blocking the rest of the Eanhe. The thought of *prison* no longer seemed as funny as it had been. I would've felt better if Ong had admitted that they regularly fended off hordes of basilisks and river serpents from that gate.

The boat stopped. We had reached a small dock, where we disembarked. I followed Ong onto a raised walkway leading into a smaller tunnel, the walls of which were lined with lit torches. The ground below the walkway was completely drenched, teeming with dark green moss and small black bubbles. I spotted a white, frog-like creature with no eyes and suppressed a shudder.

Eventually, the tunnel opened up into something more pleasant: a small pond, lit by sunlight seeping through a crevasse in the ceiling. Leafy vines with tiny blue flowers crept along the walls. I turned to Ong, who was busy humming to himself. We stopped in front of a wall with a wooden lever sticking out. He pulled on the lever. A door swung out from behind the vines, revealing a corridor with brick walls.

"After you," he said. He was the most polite official I had met in a while. But perhaps my perception was dulled after my experiences with Governor Zheshan and Deputy Qun.

We reached a courtyard. There were no windows anywhere that I could see, which made me feel as if I was inside a stone box with the lid open. There were more ponds here, held inside intricate structures decorated by rectangular statues that were supposed to represent something about the nature of the human soul, or so the signs indicated. It all flew by me, although I'm sure an Ikessar would happily spend weeks analyzing such concepts. Water trickled from some of them, which looked pleasing, at least.

"Let me guess," I said when I caught Ong looking at me. "More mage-work?"

"Our mages have perfected it into an art form," he said.

"What about the fish? Did they make those, too?"

"I don't, ahh . . . think that's possible." He scratched his chin, probably wondering whether I was insulting him or not.

I tried to appease him with a small smile. "Forgive my candour. We're ignorant about such things in Jin-Sayeng, you understand."

He nodded. "So I've heard."

"Enlighten me. I didn't hear much about mages in Anzhao City." Not without people screaming about it in panic, anyway, but I wasn't going to show him all my cards.

"It's because Anzhao is so provincial," Ong explained. "Mages are sanctioned by the Zarojo Empire, hand-picked by the Esteemed Emperor himself. Prince Yuebek's interests in Zorheng allowed us to use his connections. Many of his closest friends have what the Dageians would call an affinity to the *agan* fabric—mages, walkers between this world and the other side."

"As I said, we don't know much about the *agan* in Jin-Sayeng."

"Your warlords are stubborn, and temperamental."

"They prefer to stick with what works. It's a sensible approach. The *agan* has done more harm for my nation than good." At any other time, the idea that I would find myself defending our warlords would've made me laugh my fool head off.

"It is precisely your lack of understanding, and your lack of a formal body of mages, that makes it such a dangerous thing," Ong said. "Were you aware that many of your dragonriders of old did, in fact, have this affinity to the *agan*? It is common knowledge here in Ziri-nar-Orxiaro."

"Never say that in front of the other warlords. You'd have your head rolling around their feet before you could finish talking."

He giggled nervously. "I'll try to remember that."

"As it happens, I've heard about it. That our dragon-towers were built explicitly to channel *agan*, because dragons are both attracted to it and can be controlled through it. I don't know. We don't ride dragons anymore. When the occasional afflicted child is discovered, they are taken to the temples, and the priests or priestesses will have them sent to the Kag or Dageis or out here, where they have a better chance at life."

"I've heard…"

"I know what you've heard," I said. "That we throw them to the fishes. If the practice is done, I've never condoned it." Inwardly, I wondered if that was true. It was not something I had looked into over the last five years. Between warlords debating about rice and land and grazing rights, family inheritances, road maintenance (particularly who should pay for them), and the balance of power in Jin-Sayeng…

"Here in Ziri-nar-Orxiaro, of course, we don't have such…" I guessed he was lingering between the words *superstitions* and *stupidity*. "Practices," he finally decided. "The use and study of the *agan* is widely accepted. We have not perfected it as Dageis has, but Emperor Yunan has allocated a healthy amount of funds for the mages that, in time, we may catch up—even exceed—their prowess. We have an airship route, do you know? Powered by the *agan*, drawn by skilled mages forming part of its crew. It's the first of its kind in the empire. It starts in An Mozhi and goes all the way to the southern coastal cities."

"You sound like you idolize Dageis."

"*Idolize* is such a crude word. They inspire us. Of course, there are a lot of things we do better. Our systems, our government…we think their idea of an elected emperor is extremely…shall we say…risky?"

"You have elected officials," I pointed out.

"Minor government officials, elected by respected individuals, not the common people. A citizen of Dageis has *too* much power—they can buy themselves into society without anyone batting an eye. Ziri-nar-Orxiaro's government is like a system of pulleys. An interconnected system that doesn't allow any one of us, even the Esteemed Emperor, too much power."

"That is how Jin-Sayeng is structured, too." I caught a look of amusement on his face. "Are you going to say *not quite*, Governor Ong?"

"Pardon me. I did not mean to offend."

"Speak your mind. It is a sorry day when a ruler decides to hear nothing else but her own words."

"Your nation…your warlords have too much power. Yes, it makes it difficult for a single one to wrest control of the entire nation. But it also makes it difficult to get anything done. You know this, I think." He gave me an awkward sort of bow. "It is only an opinion. There are many solutions to such a problem as yours, but it is not one I am qualified to address. In any case, the other cities find it unfair that we have such valuable imperial resources as mages at our beck and call, but it is only natural for Prince Yuebek to want beauty in his surroundings, don't you think? Zorheng City has been his home for far too long, now. Ah!"

We had reached the end of the courtyard. A group of guards were standing along a long flight of stone steps. I saw a figure hurtle down from the top of the landing with such speed that I thought a basilisk or some other beast had appeared behind me.

But the figure had his hands on my arm before I could snap out of my stupor. A pale face, fringed by oiled black hair and a thin, curling beard, appeared. "Queen Talyien!" the man said with the eagerness and excitement of a small child. "You came! You actually came!"

I gave Ong a glance. He was on his knees, forehead pressed on the ground, hands outstretched. I turned back to the man.

"Prince Yuebek," I said. I wondered if I should bow. It was difficult to with his fingers firmly clutching my sleeve. I managed an awkward nod.

"You must've had a terrible journey," Yuebek said. "Absolutely terrible. Those roads...I don't even travel there anymore. I keep telling Ong to get it fixed. Ong! Why haven't those roads been cleared of bandits yet?"

"We don't have enough guards to spare," Ong said, without lifting his head.

"Excuses, excuses," Yuebek said, clicking his tongue. "That's all he does, you see? It's why he doesn't have a son. Weak man like that..." He jeered at Ong, who remained prostrate, before turning back to me. "Come, now. I will show you how the empire treats its royalty. Music!" He snapped his fingers at the crowd.

The faint sound of a lute began to play.

Yuebek turned to me with an eager smile, which I felt obligated to return. He held his arm out. After a moment's hesitation, I took it. He wrapped my hand around his elbow and gleefully led me up the stairs.

CHAPTER NINETEEN

THE FIFTH SON

The prophet Kibouri once said that Jin-Sayeng's royals would be her downfall.

He said a great deal of things, actually, most of which Warlord Yeshin thought were bullshit. But I always found his texts that dissected the structure of the Jin-Sayeng royal clans interesting. He had gone on a two-hundred-page tirade on the Oren-yaro, for instance, criticizing our ideals and calling them too difficult, *too rigid*, and arguing that the common people would find it difficult to relate to us and, thus, forever separate our will and theirs.

There is a great deal to be said for perspective, even if coming from a man whose insolence would make you want to throw him off a cliff.

Being inside Prince Yuebek's palace in Zorheng reminded me of home, and Kibouri's texts, simply because of the contrast. In Jin-Sayeng, respect was expected for the royal clans, especially heads and heirs, but not mindless grovelling. Walk into a room with a dozen warlords and you'd be lucky to get out in less than an hour without an argument. Even as queen, every decision I made was questioned, weighed, analyzed, prodded. I couldn't even have my breakfast tea without at least one person remarking about something I said.

When Prince Yuebek and I entered the main hall, all I could see were the backs of people's heads as they dropped and remained, unmoving, on the ground. The lute music faded behind us. As the guards outside pushed the doors shut, I heard nothing but the clicking of Yuebek's clogs on the marble floor.

We reached the center of the hall. Yuebek released my arm and looked around, an expression of annoyance on his face. "Is this how we greet our guest?" he said. "The queen of Jin-Sayeng? Liven things up a little!"

He snapped his fingers. People scattered; I noticed most avoided looking straight at Yuebek. He turned to me, grinning from ear to ear. "I can't recall the last time we entertained someone of importance in these halls," he said. "Ong, Governor Ong, he has the most droll visitors. Isn't that right, Ong?"

"A necessity in my service to your esteemed father, Esteemed Prince," Ong said from behind us.

I heard music again, this time an ensemble of three or four different instruments and the shrill singing voice of a young girl. Yuebek's face broke into a grin. "That's more like it!" he said. "Now, you must be hungry. You've not tried Zarojo cuisine until you've eaten in Zorheng. I made sure to hire the best cook in the empire—a native Herey, can you believe it? From my father's palace! Come!" He took my arm again, even when I instinctively tried to shrink back. Subtlety was not this man's style.

The fanfare—singing girl and all—followed us all the way to the dining hall. There was a long table, with giant, plush chairs. Yuebek seated me right next to him, never once taking his hands off me. A servant greeted us almost immediately with plum wine and tureens of cream-coloured soup.

"Really, Esteemed Prince, this is all too much..." I began, intending to be polite.

His face suddenly twisted into a frown. "Is it?"

I drew back, unsure of how to respond to the sudden hostility. He gave a short bark of laughter. "Perhaps it is!" he cried out. He turned around and pointed at the girl. "Cut her tongue out."

I heard the indrawn breaths of almost everyone in the room. The girl broke off from her singing and fell silent. She was pale as a sheet.

Yuebek broke into a giggling fit, slamming his hands on the table. "A joke. A joke! You people are too serious. But really," he added, tightening his jaw, "take her away. Find someone better."

Two guards came for the girl. Yuebek turned to the musicians. "Why did you stop?"

The music started again, like a funeral song.

I realized that Yuebek had, during the whole exchange, forgotten about touching me. I dropped my hands under the table, wondering if he would notice. He didn't—his attention was now occupied by the arrival of a mound of steaming crayfish on a large tray.

"Fresh from the river!" he exclaimed. He clapped his hands and turned to me. "Have you ever seen anything like it?"

"No," I lied. We had crayfish often enough from the River Agos, but I was starting to realize that honesty was the worst approach with this man. "Zorheng continues to amaze me. Governor Ong was just telling me about all the work your mages have done for your city. It is quite remarkable, Esteemed Prince."

He seemed pleased with my response. For the next little while, he did not attempt conversation as we ate. That table was large enough to have seated an entire army, but we were alone—I didn't notice Governor Ong anywhere. In the back of my mind, I remembered Arro telling me that Yuebek was married to Ong's daughter. Yet I had not seen her anywhere, and no one, so far, had thought to mention her.

The entire situation was so unsettling that I couldn't do much except pick at my food. When Yuebek was finished eating, the servants came, swooping away the empty shells and bringing in large bowls of water for us to clean our hands in. "I assume you know why I came here," I said, wiping my hands on a towel. I dropped them back down to my sides, hoping he wouldn't try to grab them again.

Yuebek looked surprised. "You didn't come here to see Zorheng?"

"I... of course I did, Esteemed Prince," I said. I fished for the proper words. "I had wanted to see it since we first arrived in Anzhao City. I had heard such great things from those who would speak about it. Most seem too in awe to tell me much." I wondered if he would pick up on the thin insult.

He didn't. He broke into a wide grin. "Good! Good. It is a marvel, you know. A city forgotten by my father, run into ruins by such officials as Ong, but when *I* arrived, I set them straight, showed them the error of their ways. I made this all happen. I... the rice cakes!" He clapped his hands as the tray of desserts arrived. "You must try the rice cakes! They've been working so hard in the kitchens."

I took a purple-coloured one sprinkled with a kind of white cheese, and nibbled politely. "As I was saying, Esteemed Prince, visiting you had been in the agenda. But I needed to speak with my husband, Lord Rayyel, first. I believe you're aware of how that turned out."

"I am," Yuebek said distractedly. He dabbed a handkerchief over his lips. "A travesty. Such a thing would've never happened in Zorheng City."

I glanced at the guards standing behind him. "I can believe it."

"But let's leave the past in the past, shall we?" He pushed the dessert tray away and pointed at a servant. "Bring more wine. Make sure the lady gets her fill."

I grimaced but didn't protest when a servant bent over to refill my drink.

"It's delicious, isn't it?" Yuebek asked. "We only get the best in Zorheng. We have our wine delivered straight from Lay Weng Shio, where they have the sweetest plums. Why else would my father have wanted it for the empire when he first took over the throne? It is such a dull little nation otherwise—so rustic, so unrefined. A little like your

Jin-Sayeng, almost, at least before you decided to rub elbows with us. Now, about your husband." He shifted in his seat, turning so that his entire body faced me. "I believe you were discussing terms concerning his abdication?"

I blinked. "No, Esteemed Prince."

"So you were trying to reunite with him? Bring him back to face his responsibilities?" The contempt was clear in his voice.

"I had hoped...we would make a decision for the betterment of our nation," I replied. "Regardless of events, I wanted to move forward. The last thing Jin-Sayeng needs is its rulers rising against each other once more."

"A wise thought," Yuebek said. "But flawed. What does your husband bring to the table?"

"I don't understand what you mean."

"The purpose of a marriage is to unite two parties. Power to power, royal blood to royal blood. What is strong can only be made stronger with the addition of *something* of value. Entire empires have been built because of this. Can you imagine trying to carve out a nation like Ziri-nar-Orxiaro from the ground up? Our lives are finite. So what did marrying your husband bring? I've heard he has no army, that his clan number less than fifty—minor families with muddied blood. I've heard his mother has cloistered herself inside this temple she calls *the Citadel* to make it sound more important than what it really is—a stinking hovel in the middle of the mountains. That she bathes in goats' blood and makes love to all her priests under the moonlight." He smiled. His eyes were very dark, almost black. Before I could frame a proper response, he turned to his servant.

"Ong," Yuebek said. "Where's Ong?"

"I will fetch him at once, Esteemed Prince."

"He shouldn't have disappeared in the first place!" Yuebek fumed. The servant fled, like a whipped dog.

"Our betrothal brought peace to the land," I said when Yuebek turned back to me. "The people hold the Ikessars with high regard."

"The common people? Who cares about what the common people think?" Yuebek laughed. "Oh, my father will say, mind you, that the common people keep the world turning. But common people need to be led. Their opinions are often misguided. I've studied your politics. The Ikessars represent the least threat to the warlords. All of you—you Oren-yaro included—know that as soon as one of you are able to gain the resources, you can easily dispose of them and seize control of the entire nation. Isn't that what your father tried to do?"

"His hand was forced," I said. "The land was in peril. In those days, we had no king."

"You had a regent. Your father killed him."

"An unworthy man. The Ikessars were starting to dabble in the forbidden arts." I took a deep breath. "But I am not here to argue politics with you, Esteemed Prince. My husband is in trouble. I've been told he's in Governor Gon Zheshan's dungeons. What Zheshan wants with him, I don't know, but..."

"Let him rot there," Yuebek said. He looked up just as Governor Ong arrived. There was more sweat on him than back in the boat, although the air in the dining hall was reasonably cool. Yuebek greeted him with disdain. "There you are, you lazy fart. Get my collection."

"Esteemed Prince?"

"In my room. Do I need to repeat myself? Have you gone deaf?"

Ong shuffled away.

"I'm afraid I can't do that," I said, trying not to let the whole exchange distract me. "I will be courting civil war, otherwise."

"That wouldn't be a problem if you had a big enough army."

"Oren-yaro might have the biggest army in Jin-Sayeng, Esteemed Prince, but we cannot hope to hold against an entire nation rising up on us. My father learned that the hard way."

"You're not listening to me, Queen Talyien," Yuebek said. "You need a big *enough* army. Larger than what you have now. I can help with that." Ong reappeared. He was carrying a silk pillow. It was filled with an assortment of jewellery and gemstones.

Yuebek picked one piece up. It was a golden brooch, shaped like a dragonfly and inlaid with the largest diamonds I had ever seen. You could buy an army with such a thing. "This one," he said, clicking his tongue. He turned to Ong. "What do you think?"

"You know best, Esteemed Prince," Ong replied, keeping his eyes averted.

"I do," Yuebek said. Without warning, he turned to me and pinned the brooch to my chest with such force that the tip dug into my skin. He grinned. "Yes. A dragonfly. Hovering over the others, bright and colourful. It suits you. I can give you an army large enough to strike fear in the hearts of all your enemies. Marry me, and you can have it all."

I thought I could feel blood running down my chest as he said that. I swallowed and stared at the man, who was breathing through his teeth while he waited for an answer. Behind him, Governor Ong had his eyes down, his hands folded as if in prayer. I reminded myself to be very, very careful—this was not someone to be trifled with. Sometimes, the way a man acts is not enough for you to make a decision on his character—you have to look at the people around him, how they walk around as if on hot coals.

"I'm flattered, Esteemed Prince, that you would extend such an offer to me," I said. "But I am married—"

"An inconvenience we can easily rectify," Yuebek snorted.

"—as are you, as I recall." I tried to draw Ong's attention back to us, but he seemed unaffected by my words.

"Another inconvenience. She can be set aside." The grin was still on Yuebek's face, but his eyes were turning hard. "What's the matter?" he asked. "Do you not think I'm handsome?"

"That's not…"

"I'm more handsome than your penniless Rayyel. I certainly have a lot more money, and power that he can only dream of." His voice had taken a turn. I saw him fingering a ruby-studded dagger among the jewellery and wondered if he would lunge for me. "Give me a good reason why this would make a poor match."

I fumbled for an answer. "I'm old," I finally said. "Too old to be a prize bride. I'm sure a son of the Esteemed Emperor deserves far better."

Yuebek began to laugh—a tilted, hollow sound that rang through the entire hall. The servants fidgeted uncomfortably.

"Esteemed Prince," Ong said, clearing his throat. "Queen Talyien has had a long day. Perhaps once she's had a good night's sleep, she can give you a reasonable answer tomorrow morning. We must not forget to show the hospitality of Zorheng City and the respect befitting a queen."

Yuebek turned sharply towards him. I thought he would strike him for interrupting. But instead, his jaw slackened, and he gave a soft, almost childish giggle. "Yes," he said. "You're right, damn you."

"We've prepared the Sun Room for the duration of her stay," Ong said. "I can escort her myself so the Esteemed Prince can also have his rest." He bowed. "If you think it is appropriate."

"The Sun Room. I know where that is."

Ong gave me a look. I got up immediately and gave a sweeping bow of my own. "Your Esteemed Prince is too kind."

Yuebek dismissed me with a wave of his hand. I followed Ong out into the hall, where I was able to breathe freely for the first time in hours.

As soon as they left me alone in my quarters, panic descended on me like a wake of vultures heading for a corpse.

Radi Ong's assurance that there would be guards outside my hall did little to ease my fears. I slid the lock into place and dragged a desk in front of the door so that someone trying to barge in couldn't open it. Only then did I realize that the dragonfly brooch was still on my chest. I pulled it out and looked under my shirt—it *had* broken the skin. There was a thin trail of dried blood running towards my belly.

I dropped to the ground with my back to the desk. Arro had tried to warn me. Blessed man—he knew *everything*. Yet I seemed to have made it my life's habit to rebel at every turn. If he were here now—if he were alive, and I had somehow been able to convince him to make this long trip against his will—he would've found the appropriate combination of words to get us out of this mess. Something about the pact between Oren-yaro and Zorheng City prohibiting marriage, perhaps.

I turned towards the window, which was barred. Of course it would be barred. And anyway, this wasn't the whorehouse in Shang Azi, where I could've dropped onto the street below without problem. The Sun Room was on the fifth or sixth floor, so unless I had decided to kill myself, I had to come up with another plan quickly.

Ong had been right about my exhaustion, because I didn't get very far with my thoughts. I crawled into bed and fell asleep, one hand on my sword, which they had somehow neglected to remove from me. Some-time during the night, I heard the desk rattle. My eyes snapped open. Someone was pounding on the door behind me.

As I struggled to contain my wits, I heard the sound of jingling keys. I saw the lock slide out right before my eyes. The door cracked open, but the desk barred it from sliding in fully. I heard someone breathing on the other side. It reminded me of a hound snuffling after its prey. I quickly rolled off the mattress and rushed to hold the desk in place with my body.

"Talyien." It was Yuebek's voice. I wondered if he could see the outline of my body through the darkness.

I considered answering, to feign a headache or come up with some other excuse. But it occurred to me that the man was used to getting his own way and that excuses would fly right over his head. So I kept my mouth shut, even when he tried to put all his weight on the door. I decided that if worst came to worst and he broke it down, I would kill him, consequences be damned. But as I turned to look for my sword, I realized I had dropped it in my haste. It was on the bed, too far for me to reach. I was afraid he would be able to push the desk out of the way if I left my post. I still had Arro's seal in my pocket—the top of it was pointed. Could I stick it into his eyeball and crush his brains that way?

He gave up before I could do anything so rash.

I listened to the sound of his receding footsteps and found myself thinking about Rai. I hoped his prison was a lot more pleasant than mine. Governor Zheshan may have been a snake, but he at least seemed to possess a rational mind. And Rai would not have to spend all night trying to protect his virtue—at least, I hoped he didn't.

Morning came. I heard the soft, polite knock of a servant and pushed the desk aside. She stared at me in confusion, but I offered no explanation, choosing to pretend that nothing was amiss. On the way to the bathhouse, I assured her I had slept well, throwing empty praises about the serene air of Zorheng City and other such nonsense she clearly didn't believe while she assisted me with washing up. When I returned to the room, a woman was waiting for me with a dress.

"The prince wants you looking your best," she said, holding the garment up to the window. It was white, made of a fabric so light it shimmered with the slightest movement.

I considered the woman. She was young and beautiful—likely my age, perhaps even younger. She was not dressed like the other servants, and her manner of speech was similar to Radi Ong's and Yuebek's. But she didn't introduce herself, and I wasn't sure if it was polite to ask, so I kept my mouth shut as she held the dress up to my chest. "It looks good on you, don't you agree?" she asked.

"I don't know. Did five peasants work their fingers bloody to make it?"

"Ten," she said. Her lips quirked into a smile.

"In that case, how can I say no?" I stood still as she helped me disrobe and put the dress on. As an afterthought, she pinned the dragonfly brooch near my breast, gentler than Yuebek had. When she was content with its placement, she patted my shoulders, a distant look in her eyes.

"You've got too much muscle for a young woman in Zarojo society, but you're tall, at least," she said. "You'll look good beside him."

"I don't think..."

She pressed a finger on my lips. "Think. Don't say." Her eyes flickered towards the door, where the servants stood waiting for us. "I'm glad I picked this material," she continued loudly. "Your shoulders are too broad for some of the dresses. The current fashion in the capital is to squeeze yourself into as little fabric to make yourself look as much like a bamboo reed as possible."

"That sounds like hell."

"It's appalling, but it's all the young women will talk about. I'm not sure I understand it entirely myself." She drew away. "Come. He doesn't like being kept waiting."

"You..."

"Come," she repeated, a little more urgently.

I frowned, but I turned to follow her. She saw me pick my sword up from the bed and clicked her tongue in disapproval. "Leave it there," she said.

"I always wear my sword in Jin-Sayeng," I lied. "I'd feel naked without it."

"It doesn't look good with the dress. I'll keep it safe for you." She held her hand out.

I sighed and handed the sword to her. She took it with a look of carefully hidden disgust, like she didn't know how to hold it but didn't want to offend me, before nodding towards the door. I stepped out, and the servants drew closer to accompany me to breakfast.

We didn't go straight to the dining hall, as I had expected. Instead, they led me to the other end of the hall and up a wide wooden staircase that gleamed like an old man's bare head. It opened up to a rooftop terrace. I paused to consider a giant wall on one side, blocking my view of the city with the same blue-flowered vines I had seen the day before down in the tunnels. There were servants lined up in a row, holding yellow paper parasols for shade. The other side of the terrace was clear, with a full view of the River Eanhe.

"It's a beautiful morning, isn't it?" Ong said, greeting me with a graceful bow. He seemed to be in a more cheerful mood than yesterday. "On windless mornings, you can see the shadows of the creatures down below."

"That sounds...very unpleasant," I replied.

He smiled. "Ah. I can see how you'd think so. But if you consider the relative safety of where we are, I'm sure you'll soon agree that it makes for a very entertaining show. It's even better if we have prisoners slotted for an execution—the creatures can give them a good, clean death and feed their bellies besides. If you're interested, I can check with the guard captain to see if we can arrange a demonstration for you." He gestured towards a table, where Yuebek was seated on a wide-backed chair covered in velvet. The prince was wearing an impressive purple robe with silver trimmings. No less than twenty peasants worked on it, I'm sure.

Yuebek greeted me with a straight face. The eager smiles of yesterday, the childish enthusiasm was gone. I had wondered if he would acknowledge what he had tried to do last night. If I had any authority here, he would be the one getting fed to those river creatures. As a guest, I had no choice but to bite my tongue and smile my horrors away. I took a seat.

"I hope you had a pleasant sleep," Ong said, filling a porcelain cup—rimmed with gold—with tea. He set this beside my plate, which was heaped with meat dumplings and preserved duck eggs the colour of coal.

"Very," I said. "I slept too deeply, I'm afraid. The world could've ended last night, and I wouldn't have stirred." I picked at the duck egg, pursing my tongue around the strong, creamy flavour of the jellied whites, and smiled at Yuebek. Did he realize I was offering him a way out? I didn't want him to think I was directly antagonizing him. Until I figured out what to do, I needed him to think I was on his side.

Yuebek tapped a spoon on his bowl. "Have you considered my proposal?" he asked.

"It's very tempting, Esteemed Prince," I said. "More than tempting, if I can be honest. How big of an army are we talking about, exactly?"

"I have two thousand garrisoned in this city alone," Yuebek replied with a snarl. He had taken my question as a challenge.

I tried to smooth it over by pretending to look surprised. "That is highly unexpected and very impressive, my lord. Only remember that, once rallied, Oren-yaro's can surpass ten thousand. On a good day, mind you, and the ranks will be bolstered by conscripts and volunteers—most of them farmers and villagers with bent swords—but…"

"I have twenty thousand in the capital," Yuebek continued with a straight face. The shadow of my insult remained. "Tried and true soldiers, not a single doddering peasant among them. My father's gift. I do not get the privilege of inheriting the throne, and as a Fifth Son, he ran out of provinces to give to me. So he gifted me with an army." He gave an unsettling smile. "I don't get to use it, of course. I would've conquered half the continent by now if I had them. Even now, if I make a request to send for them, he will question it, find ways to hinder me. But as a marriage gift to *you*, Queen Talyien, I'm sure my father will make an exception. I'm sure he'll be ecstatic that I came up with such a grand idea in service of the empire. Don't you think so, Ong? Why have we never married into Jin-Sayeng before? Remind me."

"The Esteemed Prince possesses wisdom beyond his years," Ong said.

Yuebek smiled at the empty compliment. "Twenty thousand," he repeated. "And a ship to take you home."

Two nights ago, I had to steal a horse. And now someone was offering me not just passage back to Jin-Sayeng, but enough soldiers to make the warlords sweat themselves to death. I could be forgiven for being tempted for a moment, couldn't I? It was the most prestigious marriage offer I had received in years.

I saw the woman, the one who had presented me with the dress, appear from the doors. Ong took a step forward, taking the woman's arm in his. "May I introduce my daughter, Zhu," he said.

Yuebek scowled. "I thought I told you to stay away."

"I came to fetch my father," she said, bowing. She turned to me. "Queen Talyien. I hope you are pleased with our hospitality so far. The Esteemed Prince should show you our gardens once your meal is finished. I—"

"Silence," Yuebek commanded.

Zhu dropped her eyes. She obeyed him so well and was so still that for a moment, I thought I could hear the river-monsters swirling down below. I reached out, taking Zhu's hand in mine. "That sounds lovely," I said, squeezing my fingers together.

She gave me a small smile.

"I have heard," I continued, turning to Yuebek, "that this remarkable woman is your current wife. Please correct me if I'm wrong."

"Current," Yuebek said with a smile. "Are you worried about her? Don't be. A minor inconvenience . . . we have laws that can allow our alliance to proceed forward."

"Laws that allow you to set her aside," I said. "I'm aware. It is not as simple in Jin-Sayeng. Divorce is not an option in my nation. Our gods do not allow it, and even the Ikessars' Nameless Maker frowns upon setting a marriage aside for no good reason. You will not easily find a priest who will absolve our marriage, never mind get the people to accept the act. Dissolving a marriage can happen, but it will take time and sufficient reason."

"That problem can be solved with a knife to the throat."

"Are you suggesting I have my husband assassinated, Esteemed Prince?"

"Are you suggesting he hasn't tried to do the same thing to you?"

His question took me aback. I closed my mouth and reached for the cup of tea. Behind me, I could hear Zhu and her father walk away. Before I could form a coherent response, Yuebek clapped his hands and dismissed the remaining servants with a sharp gesture.

I swallowed hot tea and placed the cup back on the table. "Lord Rayyel wouldn't," I said.

"Are you so sure?" Yuebek asked. "This Lord Husband of yours left you for some whore, I've been told. Some other warlord's daughter."

"A rumour."

"You don't think he'd rather have you out of the way, inheriting your land and army while he rules with his new queen? Are you really that naive?"

"It doesn't work that way. My clan has not accepted him as their own. My son is the heir of both Oren-yaro and Shirrokaru. And Rai wouldn't...he—"

"Loves you?" He said the words as if it was something vile, a child's fancy.

I smiled at him. "He is a devoted man. In any case, the assassination attempt in Anzhao targeted the both of us. I saw it with my own eyes. As I told you yesterday, he ended up in Governor Zheshan's dungeons while I managed to escape."

Yuebek's eyes flashed. He started laughing, a horrible grating sound that set my already-frayed nerves on edge. When he caught his breath, he slammed both his hands on the table, sending cups and plates rattling. "What would he be doing in Zheshan's blasted dungeons if the assassin was targeting you both? Foolish woman—can't you see a trick when it plays out right in front of you? To think that he managed to get away from an assassin, only to find himself in the clutches of the man beside him! It's beyond absurd."

"I did find it irregular," I said. "But I'm sure there's another explanation. It's why I decided to seek your assistance in the first place. If we can rescue him, perhaps we can come to an arrangement. Jin-Sayeng treats her friends very well, Esteemed Prince, and I'm sure..."

Yuebek reached out from across the table to grab my hands. His palms were cold and sweaty, a sure sign of a nervous temperament, or so my father liked to say. I wasn't so sure anymore. Revulsion stirred in my throat. I tried to pull away, but he kept a firm hold. "You've heard my offer more than once, now," he said. "Do not insult me like you did last night."

"Last night?"

"Don't play dumb, woman. You may be queen of Jin-Sayeng, but I am a son of the Esteemed Emperor Yunan of the Empire of Ziri-nar-Orxiaro. It would be very bad for you to ignore the weight of such a title." He got up, pulling me towards him. I could smell his breath, which had a stench masked only by the perfume he wore. "Come. To the gardens, as my dear wife suggested. Perhaps a walk will clear your head."

I didn't know how to refuse him without further infuriating him. I agreed, though I did manage to wrench my hands back to myself. We left the rooftop, going all the way back to the courtyard where I had come in the day before. This time, he led me through a small gap in the eastern wall, which led to a short maze of hedges. I found myself in another part of the courtyard, surrounded by a dazzling array of plants and flowers. On all sides were walls taller than I could see over, covered with vines and running water.

I touched one of the walls, watching the water spread over my hand. The wall itself had flecks of gold imbedded into the stone. "Why are your garden walls so high?" I asked. "You can't gaze at the city like this."

"Questions, so many questions," Yuebek said, but I think he looked amused. "Although I suppose it's to be expected, coming from a native of a backward nation like Jin-Sayeng. Do you want to know where the water comes from, too?"

"I'm guessing the Eanhe," I said. I instantly regretted speaking; his face assumed a dark expression. It was more unsettling than his usual mad merriment. I found myself bowing. "My apologies, Esteemed Prince. I suppose someone so *backward* wouldn't know the intricacies of such a system. If I had insulted you..."

"You already have, more times than I can count," he said. He placed his hands on my shoulders. "Do you not see me as a man? Is that why you flaunt your rejection to my face? I could have changed your mind last night. I would have had you mewling on the sheets like a cat, begging for more. You would have wanted to be wed within the hour." His nails dug through the thin dress and into my skin. If he assaulted me and the guards came running, would they kill me before I got the chance to kill him? I watched his darting eyes and the rapid rise and fall of his chest.

"I just don't see what you have to gain from the alliance, Esteemed Prince," I said in a low voice. "I have no intention of insulting your... manhood."

"I am *Fifth* Son of Emperor Yunan," he said. "If I had not married Governor Ong's daughter, I wouldn't even have Zorheng."

"I beg your pardon. My impression is that cities like Anzhao and Zorheng are city states. The governors that rule them and the surrounding regions are elected by Emperor Yunan himself."

His eyes flashed, and he pushed me away, as if suddenly disgusted. "Don't dare lecture me on what my father does and doesn't do," he murmured. He pointed at me. "If you do not see what good our marriage can do for *both* of us, then you are a lot less intelligent than I gave you credit for. An army of *thirty thousand* will go uncontested."

"You want to rule Jin-Sayeng with me," I said, answering my question for him. "That's... my lord, as flattering as that sounds, do you even *know* anything about my nation?" It was becoming more and more difficult to balance my courtesies with the outrage I was feeling. Sooner or later, I was going to snap and do something I would regret.

"People bend to power," he laughed. "That's all you need to know. Or perhaps your father failed to teach you such a basic thing? Is that why you're here, begging me to help your pauper of a husband? Is his cock *that* big?"

I found myself unable to reply properly. I realized that my upbringing had made it difficult for me to relate to people who didn't understand the concept of honour or duty. And while I had heard enough crude language from my soldiers and in the few days I had spent in Shang Azi to last me a lifetime, hearing it from the mouth of an emperor's son was more than I knew how to deal with.

To my relief, I heard footsteps. I turned to see Zhu approaching us with the tentativeness of a mouse crossing a kitchen floor while the cat was still about. The distaste became plain on Yuebek's face. Why did he hate her, and why was he so willing to set her aside without a moment's thought? She was beautiful enough to write poetry about. She reminded me of Chiha Baraji, only without the sly smiles and furtive glances. There had been a time when I envied such women and their graces. I used to think that if I had such elegance and refinement, Rayyel would've respected me more.

"My father requires your counsel, Esteemed Prince," she said. "The officials are arguing. Deputy Wanhe is creating a scene."

"It's like the old man can't function without me," Yuebek replied. But he seemed pleased at the notion that the governor of Zorheng City deferred to him. What did the emperor think of their strange arrangement? Or maybe it wasn't so strange at all—corruption was a thread that ran everywhere, and I shouldn't have been so surprised it existed here.

"Take her back to her room," he said before turning with a sweep of his robes.

Zhu waited until he had disappeared around the corner before walking towards me. There was a calm, almost serene expression on her face, a stark contrast to how I think I would look if I had to spend my life with that man. "*Do* you want to marry him? Is that why you came here?"

"No," I blurted out, resisting the urge to outright laugh at the notion. "I had no intention of making him think such a thing. I apologize if my presence has caused strain to your relationship."

"Oh," she said. "That's not...he does this." She gave the sort of smile I had seen people give when they don't want to talk ill of someone. It deepened the dimples on her cheeks and the lines along her eyes. No, not just beautiful enough for poetry—I could imagine she was the sort of woman kingdoms would clash for. "And will you consider his proposal? It is impressive, is it not?"

"It is. How much truth is there to it?"

"The army was indeed his father's wedding gift to us. The truth is a little more complex than that. The troops have been assigned to various outreach programs near Kyan Jang, helping the common people during the typhoon season and other calamities. The Esteemed Emperor calls it *Yuebek's Boon*, which was his way of keeping the Esteemed Prince from entertaining other...thoughts."

"Like taking over the empire, you mean?"

"He couldn't do that with twenty thousand men," she said with a smile. "But he could try to seize control of one of his brothers' provinces, which would create a very bad situation all around. We don't like civil war in the Zarojo Empire, not like in your nation."

I gave her my own practiced smile in return. "Believe it or not, we don't like it, either. I've spent most of my rule trying *very* hard to avert it."

"I didn't mean it that way."

"I know." I took a seat on a stone bench near one of the waterfalls. "Indulge me, Lady Zhu. This proposal—does it provide a way for Prince Yuebek to extract his army from Kyan Jang? He seems convinced it will, but I would like to hear your opinion on the matter."

Zhu dipped her head forward. "I shouldn't speak of my husband that way."

"We are not doing that at all. I need to know what he wants so I can present him with a different proposal. One that, perhaps, doesn't involve marriage at all. If he wants power, I'm sure we can come to a reasonable agreement. We can always open trade between our countries again. Something exclusive to Zorheng City, perhaps? Such a thing could do much for your city and uplift him in his father's eyes."

"You don't understand how his mind works," Zhu said. "When it comes to getting what he wants, he is relentless."

"I think I can relate."

"No. No, you can't." She looked troubled as she sat down beside me.

"Lady Zhu, please understand. I need to get help for my husband, who is in Governor Zheshan's dungeons as we speak. If I can invoke the pact that Zorheng made with my home city of Oren-yaro, we need not even look at marriage."

"My father told me of that pact. It was made hundreds of years ago. Your city has a pact with Zorheng, not *Yuebek*." She pressed her hands together.

"That is incorrect," I said. "This was a recent pact. I remember my tutor telling me. They made a big stink about it back home."

Her eyes flickered. "If that's true, then you need to be more worried. Yuebek is not a Zorheng official, but nothing happens in this city without his approval. My father is nothing but a puppet." She paused. "You don't know what's happening in your own kingdom, do you?"

"I know enough."

"You think you can talk him out of it—make him see reason—but it doesn't work that way. Prince Yuebek may be like a child, but his mind works like a sharp knife. Sometimes I believe he acts the way he does to throw people off guard, to make them think he is less than what he appears. He may seem unhinged, but he is also extremely focused, Queen Talyien, and this is the important part you have to remember: he *always* gets what he wants. It is the only thing that ever matters to him." She took my hands, pressing a key into my palm.

I felt the weight of the cold brass and turned to her. "What are you saying?"

"Go," she said, pointing at the wall beside the waterfall. I saw a keyhole etched into the stone. "Leave now, before it's too late."

CHAPTER TWENTY

ZORHENG CITY, REPRISED

ᛏᚢᚫ

"I'm tempted," I said. "But…"

"But not as tempted as you are with the Esteemed Prince's promise of twenty thousand men?"

"I don't need twenty thousand. Fifty or so should be enough to ensure my husband's safety. It is all I came here for." I looked down and realized I was gripping the key so hard that my knuckles were turning white.

"Fifty or twenty thousand, it doesn't matter. What he wants from you won't change. There is no talking yourself out of this, Queen Talyien. I'm trying to save you."

"I know." I still didn't move. She yanked the key out of my hand and without another word stepped towards the keyhole. She slid the key in and turned. There was the sound of shifting gears inside the wall before it retracted, revealing a narrow path between two walls.

"If you change your mind—no, but you will see for yourself soon enough." She took my hand and led me down the path. The gate shut behind us as soon as we crossed the threshold.

We reached the end of the path, which opened up into a dank, dirty alley with a gutter running right through it. The contrast to the pristine surroundings of the palace caught me by surprise. The alley led, abruptly, to the beginning of a tight street blocked by a rail on one side. Zorheng City unfolded in front of my eyes in a choking grey light.

I could see an enormous wall lined with windows. It took me two breaths to realize that it was actually a building, and that this building *was* the city. I could see clothes lines hanging from the guard rails, which were built so high in front of the windows that they looked like cages. Sunlight streamed down onto a street below, but everything was so crowded and covered in shadows that I couldn't see exactly what was down there.

Zhu pulled me to the side to let a man through. He was carrying a pole with two baskets hanging from each side, calling out, "Cat meat! Cat for sale!" Bile built up in the back of my throat, and I wondered how it was possible that I could still find air to breathe. Whatever was streaming into my lungs was so muggy and thick I could have scooped it with a spoon.

"Welcome to Zorheng City," Zhu told me. "The true *Yuebek's Boon.*"

I could barely make out her words from the buzz of people around me. I caught sight of a mud-covered child crying in the middle of the street. He had a rotund belly and was naked from the waist down. People passed by him without a second glance.

"This isn't in the guidebooks," Zhu continued. "The emperor forbade scribes to record what is happening here, even as he does nothing and continues to turn a blind eye to what both my father and his son have done."

"I don't understand," I said. "You have all that land around the city. Can you not make it bigger? Move the people further out so it's not so crowded?"

"The river lands are too soft to build on," Zhu said. "The surrounding hills are too rocky."

"But surely the empire would have foreseen a way to stop a city from turning into this."

"Zorheng was never meant to hold so many people. It was originally built to defend the mountain pass from invaders seeking to march against the empire. Those days, of course, are long gone, but when my father was assigned to his post, Zorheng was still an important outpost, the last great city before the weeks of treacherous journey ahead. And then I married Yuebek." She leaned over the railing, a wistful look on her face.

"How old were you?"

She seemed surprised that out of all the things I had reason to wonder about, I would choose to ask such a thing. "Twelve," she replied. "The Esteemed Prince was twenty. Why? You think it is too young? I already had my moon's blood by then, a woman in every way. I heard you were eighteen when you married *your* prince. We thought it was too old. Why wait so long when you had been betrothed since birth? He is very close in age to you, too, from what I understand."

"We see marriage as the final step. Until we can fully commit ourselves to our duties, we don't marry. I had to finish my studies in Shirrokaru. Others who do not have such concerns might marry younger."

"You Jinseins are a strange people," Zhu said, trailing her fingers over my arm. Her nails were painted with a bright, colourless sheen. "We marry young so we can carry children, as many as we can give our husbands. It has always been this way."

"How many do you have?" I asked.

She shook her head. I suddenly understood.

"I turn thirty this year," she continued, gazing out into the distance. "*This*—this is Yuebek's only child. His legacy, he likes to say. Our marriage was an opportunity for the Esteemed Emperor to send him away. He was to be the Esteemed Emperor's arm, far out into the west. I think he secretly hoped that governance would set Yuebek on the right path. Only…"

"He seized control of the city instead."

"I wouldn't say it that way. On paper, my father is still the governor. But Yuebek leaves people little choice except to indulge his strange ideas. Preventing citizens of Zorheng from leaving, for example, unless they pay an exorbitant tax, one which most poor families can't afford. When people complained that Zorheng was running out of room and threatened to walk out, he petitioned for builders and mages from Kyan Jang to construct up high. He also got them to set up those massive walls, to keep people inside. Anyone caught trying to escape will be publicly executed."

I tried to see how high the city went. I counted fifteen levels before giving up. There were streets on every level, and even from afar, the filth was unmistakable. I turned to see that the crying child was gone. I hoped his mother had picked him up, but the hostile, sideways glances from every soul around us gave me little hope of that. Was that vendor from earlier *just* selling cat, or was there anything else less appetizing on the menu? I had heard that cannibalism could be rampant under such conditions.

"You tell me this," I said, "*while* trying to convince me to escape."

"I am telling you," she said, patiently, "that there are other options you can consider. Find your way to Deputy Wanhe's home. It is in the middle of the market district. People should be able to point it out."

"Deputy Wanhe—this is the one you said was creating a scene?"

"He dislikes Prince Yuebek. Resents him, even. He will assist you, if only to stop the Esteemed Prince from coming into more power. But also, he is obligated to, because he is a government official and you *do* have a pact with Zorheng." She pulled me into an embrace. "If Yuebek finds you anyway," she whispered into my ear, "kill yourself first." She lifted her long, elaborate sleeve, revealing the sword she had taken from me earlier. She pulled it out of her belt and handed it to me.

"Come with me," I said.

She shook her head. "I will not leave my father with him."

"Then get him. I'll wait. When we get to my people, I can give you whatever help you need."

She shook her head. "I cannot. I am not a fighter, Queen Talyien, not like you. And Yuebek...for all his faults..." She looked up at me. "Would you abandon your husband, given a way out?"

"That," I breathed, "is completely different."

"Is it?" She drew away and returned to the alley, her robes fluttering behind her. The stark contrast of her faded yellow garments to the looming shadows made me think of a canary in an iron cage.

Me, on the other hand? I slunk through the bustling city like a rat in a maze. Hunched, I tried to blend in as best I could, which was difficult when I was still dressed like I was going to a dinner party. People stared at me as I walked right past their front doors; some stared a little too hard.

I had learned over the years that the best way to find the market district is to follow your nose. This was not as easy in Zorheng as I thought it would be—I could barely detect anything beyond the smell of the urine-soaked alleys and walls. I reached the end of the street, which turned into a winding stairway. Down I went, past a beggar with stumps for legs, rattling his coin cup, past two filthy boys sitting on the edge of the railing, who whistled at me, and onto a ledge where several men and a woman with a child on her hip were playing cards. Eventually, I dropped to the bottom floor, which was lined with cracked stone. Here, I caught the unmistakable sight of market stalls in the distance.

The smell didn't improve when I got closer to the vendors. The scent of roasted meat did not mix well with that of feces and dead rotten things, and it didn't help that I could distinguish what sort of meat I could see the vendors chopping before me. A pile looked like rat hindquarters, hairless tails hanging out like noodles in a row. The vendor dipped these in a bright orange batter before frying them in a vat of oil. They were served on sticks, drizzled with plum sauce. At least, it looked like plum sauce. Chances were equally good that it was something else.

I elbowed my way through the crowd and eventually found a man who appeared to be a city guard. He was standing beside a decrepit fountain, which struggled with a trickle of brown water like an old man attempting to hack out phlegm. I hoped that my disappearance had not yet been noted in the palace. "I'm looking for Deputy Wanhe's house," I said.

The guard blinked at me.

I crossed my arms. "I don't want to stay out here a moment longer than I have to, so if you don't know, at least show me someone who does."

He grumbled under his breath before lumbering forward. It wasn't a long walk. We stopped in front of a building with walls of a slightly different colour than the rest—a light shade of grey, compared to drab grey. I didn't have anything to pay the guard with, so I gave him my best smile before knocking on the door. I saw a window creak open, revealing eyes that fiercely stared back at me.

"Who is it?"

"I'm here to speak with Deputy Wanhe," I said. "I know he's up in the palace, but if I could wait here until he returns…"

The door opened. An old, bent woman ushered me through the hall, clicking her tongue to remind me to take off my shoes. They were covered in street muck, and I was glad to be rid of them.

I entered a common room that was larger than I expected. "Who sent you?" she asked.

"I have a pressing problem, and Lady Zhu told me Deputy Wanhe might be able to help."

"I didn't know Lady Zhu was acquainted with him," the old woman said. "You said he was in the palace? You must be mistaken. He doesn't go to the palace very often. He's up in his office now if you want to speak with him. Do you want some tea first?"

"No, thank you," I said. "I would like to speak to him now, if possible." I wondered how he had managed to get back before I got there. Lady Zhu had said he was in the council meeting with Governor Ong.

"Up the stairs, first room to your right," the woman said. "Be polite. He doesn't like being disturbed when he's busy."

I bowed and went up. The staircase was very narrow—two people wouldn't be able to squeeze by each other—but I think for a Zorheng apartment, this place was meant to be luxurious. I reached a hall, lined with various paintings of deities. There was an alcove at the end with a figure of Saint Fei Rong on a little platform. A string of dried lilies adorned his neck.

I knocked on the first door and waited. There was no reply.

Downstairs, I heard the old woman whistling. I recognized the tune, though I couldn't remember where I had last heard it. In Jin-Sayeng, we have childhood nursery rhymes twisted from songs brought from the empire, derogatory songs I would never acknowledge in front of polite company. But I didn't think hers was one of them. This was something else, something that went deeper than memory.

I knocked again before that age-old impatience flared. I pulled the door open.

Deputy Wanhe—or at least, someone I assumed was Deputy Wanhe—was on his seat. He didn't greet me. He couldn't—his throat was slit open. His skin was extremely grey, and there were flies buzzing around the wound. He must've been dead for hours.

I ran down the stairs. The woman turned to me. "Is everything all right?"

"He called for you," I said, placing my fingers around my sword hilt.

She went up without hesitation. As I slipped back into my shoes, I heard her scream and decided she was not the enemy. But someone else was. I barged through the front door, back out into the street, and saw guards approaching Deputy Wanhe's house from the distance.

I turned to run down the other way. I saw Yuebek appear. My first thought was that he had found me *really* fast. Then I saw Zhu beside him and realized what had happened.

Or at least, I thought I did; before I could throw hurtful words her way, I saw Yuebek's hand on her twisted arm. She was walking with a limp. Halfway into drawing my sword, I heard Yuebek click his tongue.

"I don't think so," he said. He dragged Zhu forward and bent over to squeeze her jaw with his fingers. "This one. Such loyalty. Such *devotion* to her husband. Upset as I am over what you did, Queen Talyien, I think you could teach *her* a thing or two about duty. Did she actually think she could trick me? *Me?* She should've known better. Using Wanhe as an excuse when I knew he had been dead in his house since this morning. I'm always two steps ahead of everyone, Queen Talyien. *Remember that.*"

Zhu uttered a low moan.

"Let her go, Yuebek," I said. "Your quarrel is with me."

"Is it?" Yuebek hissed. He pushed Zhu to the ground and pulled out his own sword.

I lunged at him.

He made a fumbled attempt to defend himself. But he didn't look worried—the guards were coming closer, and we both knew that if I killed him, I would be dead, too. I worked on pushing him away from Zhu while I got closer to her. I stopped, poised to defend, and helped her to her feet.

Yuebek laughed. "Are you sure you want to do that? She betrayed me and, in doing so, unwittingly betrayed *you.*"

"Why should I blame her for anything? You were the one who tricked her. You killed Deputy Wanhe before the meeting, didn't you? But some-how, you'd convinced her he was still in the palace."

He looked pleased with himself. "A well-placed rumour in the halls can do so much."

"You wanted her to think she was the one tricking you to give me time to escape." I swallowed. "Is this about me? You wanted to see how trustworthy I was?"

"I wanted to test *her* trustworthiness," Yuebek said, sneering. "Guess how much you failed, woman? You and your father both, filling my head with talks of how utterly *devoted* you would be to me... the perfect wife... and I believed you, all these years. I *believed* you!"

Zhu wasn't even looking at him. Her head was bowed, and there were tears streaming from her eyes.

"She returned to you, Prince Yuebek. I asked her to come with me, and she refused. Out of loyalty to *you*, though I can't for the life of me see why. There are crocodiles in the River Agos with more redeemable qualities."

"It is hopeless, Queen Talyien," Zhu murmured. "Please. You do not have to speak up for my sake. He is right. I did betray him. I betrayed him, and my father. I failed my duties. Your words cannot change that."

I turned to her. "This is ridiculous. He disregarded you, yet you were still supposed to obey blindly?"

"Blind obedience was all that was ever asked of me," she whispered. "And I failed."

"You didn't," I snapped. She attempted to walk towards Yuebek; I grabbed her by the arm and pulled her back. "You didn't," I repeated. "You can live without the man, Zhu."

She stared at me, her face pale, as if recognizing the truth in my words. But then she swallowed. "You went all the way out here to save yours."

"Your husband is a vile waste of air. How can you possibly love a man like that?"

She gave me a sad smile. "We didn't marry for love, Queen Talyien." She stared back at Yuebek. I saw the fear in her eyes as she took a step towards him, and then another.

"Daughter," Ong broke in.

She didn't look at her father, though she heard him. "I'm sorry," she mouthed to someone unseen. The movement seemed to give her a wave of courage, and suddenly she was running. I screamed, reaching out to stop her, but she slipped from my grasp like the wind.

Yuebek met her, arms wide open. For a moment, I was almost sure she was going to him to beg for forgiveness and that he was willing to give her a second chance. My heart leaped to my throat. And then he twisted his sword, the blade sinking deep into her belly. He left it in her as he kicked her to the ground. Blood pooled on the pavement.

"The inconvenience has been taken care of," he said, turning to me. "Shall we start making wedding preparations, my love?"

I spat on the ground. "Go to hell!"

He laughed. The guards closed in.

CHAPTER TWENTY-ONE

THE LEGACY OF WARLORD YESHIN

ꓕꓷꙊꙄ

My memory of what happened after Yuebek killed Zhu was hazy. Though I tried to fight the guards as best I could, there were too many, and my head met too many blows from gloved fists and at least two clubs. The nauseating blackness took much of those memories away. I do recall Yuebek climbing on top of me, his breath stinking of wine as he pawed at my thighs and tried to rip my clothes off. Before he could succeed, someone dragged him away, screaming. I recall the blood on his clothes, Zhu's blood, and how it soaked my dress, and how Zhu's dead eyes stared back at me as the commotion exploded around us and the darkness set in.

When I came to my senses, I was in a prison cell that had so little light, I could barely see beyond my own fingertips. A guard came to slide a tray of gruel and water through the door. No one else came to visit.

The shadows were comforting for a while, a welcome respite to the madness that had transpired out there with Yuebek. But the hours began to drag on, and when the guard returned to bring more food and empty the bucket, I reached out in an attempt to talk to him. I had barely said a word when he turned and struck me across the jaw with a gloved fist.

Solitude, it seemed, was to be my torture.

I counted the days by the coming and going of my guard, whom I no longer tried to speak to after a third clouting. And then it reached a point where I lost track of it and stopped. It could've been weeks. Months. But it was starting to feel like one long, stretched-out day, one that repeated itself over and over. My thoughts and dreams mingled until I could no longer tell which was which. More than once, I woke up expecting to be back in bed, back in my castle, and see my husband turned to the side, his back toward me. I sometimes saw myself reaching for his shoulder to wake him, to tell him to wake *me* up... *please, Rayyel, please.* I was still convinced he held the key to end all of this.

In other times, it was memories that plagued me: of my childhood in Oren-yaro, those long lessons with Arro. Hearing my father screaming at him for not teaching me the right things, or teaching me the wrong things, or not teaching me *enough.* The look on Agos's face whenever we would get in trouble. *You indulge her,* Arro had told him. Was it his fault, then? If he had gone with me to the empire, I wouldn't be here. I should have never sent him away.

I woke up screaming these things in the darkness and realized my mind was slipping. This was what Yuebek wanted—to break down my walls, to turn me into a helpless, babbling woman who would see marriage to him as preferable to madness. I couldn't let that happen.

So I focused on reciting every text, story, and poem I knew by heart, forcing myself over every word to occupy my mind. I went through my usual training exercises in the darkness and ate diligently, telling myself I needed to preserve my strength in case an opportunity presented itself. My survival depended on my sanity; the last thing I needed was permission to slip.

A day came when the guard arrived with no food. I thought this meant that Yuebek had decided I had learned my lesson and would be more cooperative. But instead of leading me out, the guard grabbed me by the collar and pulled me up close to his stinking face. He pressed his fingers over my cheeks, forcing my mouth open. I tried to bite him. He hit me.

Once I was on the ground, reeling from the blow, he straddled me and forced something into my mouth—something that smelled of herbs and dried bile. I gagged, struggling to spit it out. He hit me again. The substance—whatever it was—emitted a hot sensation that started in my tongue and spread across my body. I saw a flash of blue before I lost consciousness.

—————

When I woke up, I was on a soft mattress in a strange room. I was wearing different clothes—clean, plain clothes that still smelled of soap.

I didn't know how long I had been asleep. I smelled of camphor oil and mint, and I didn't feel as sore as I expected to be. My whole body had been scrubbed clean, and even my hair smelled as if it had been washed. I touched my forehead and noted a bandage on a cut I didn't even know I had.

The sound of music drifted to my ears. It was so faint that I had to strain to hear it. I rose, finding a pair of comfortable shoes in my size on the floor, and realized that I had been sleeping on a four-poster bed. The dark, heavy linens on the mattress, the frilly curtains, and every other piece of furniture in the room were of Kag make. Even the rugs were Kag—red and velvet, set above a floor of dark, polished wood.

I pulled the curtains back, to see if I had somehow magically been transported to western Jin-Sayeng or somewhere else where such trappings were common. The windows were stained—I couldn't see anything through the glass. I tried to open them, but the frames wouldn't budge. Trying to break the thick glass didn't work, either, even when I tried to throw a shoe at it.

I gave up and walked to the door, a giant carved slab of hardwood hinged in Kag fashion. I turned the knob, slowly peeking through the crack to see if I could hear anyone out in the hall. But the silence that welcomed me felt louder than the music itself. I stepped out into a large well-lit chamber. Chandeliers hung from the ceiling, the candle-light casting dancing shadows on the walls. In the middle of the room, I caught sight of the source of music: a piano, similar to the ones I had seen in some of the royal houses in western Jin-Sayeng. It had been a fashion lately for royal children to learn the instrument. Skilled tutors from the Kag could make good money in provinces where the warlords were more lenient.

I wondered if it was normal for the thing to play by itself.

There was nobody on the piano. The keys depressed on their own, cranking out a haunting melody that seemed to deepen my solitude. I placed my hands on the cold ivory, figuring there was probably some sort of mechanism inside. Something you wound up to make the song loop, maybe. I pressed my palm on one of the depressed keys, and the music stopped. I chuckled, but before I could lift my hand, the song began again in a more upbeat tune. It was being played from the other end of the piano, where I wasn't interrupting it.

A chill descended on me. I backed away from the instrument. When I turned around, I thought I saw a shadow flit across the mirror on the wall.

I chuckled again. Louder. "If there's someone out there," I offered, "come out and talk. I don't bite. Well—not hard, anyway."

My voice, hoarse after weeks of silence, sounded strange to my own ears. I spotted a table a few feet from the piano. I was beginning to get hungry and wondered if someone had the courtesy to leave some food for me, at least. I still wasn't sure if I was a prisoner or a guest, but surely both have to get fed.

Instead of food, I only saw a *Hanza* set on the table. It was an

expensive set—made of carved and polished wood, each piece meticulously painted. The pieces were arranged mid-game—a losing game,
with the red surrounded on all sides by the white. I saw a note beside
the game, penned out in Kag writing. It said: *The hungry wolf devours its
own.*

I frowned and left the table alone to view the rest of the room. There
were sofas on the other end, arranged to face each other. Vases full of yellow and white flowers lined the walls. I touched one and realized the petals were made of cloth, which explained the vibrant colours. There was
also an aquarium with a single inhabitant: a silver bonytongue the size of
my arm. I was glad to see one other living thing, although it wasn't much
company—it stared back at me through faded, glassy eyes. I noted that
its water was dirty, but not overwhelmingly so, as if someone checked
up on it at least once a week. Its scales were scratched. I wondered how it
could have happened—the aquarium was bare.

I found two doors, but both were locked. The only other door led
back to the bedroom.

I sat on one of the sofas, pretending I wasn't disconcerted by the
music, which paused long enough for a new, more sorrowful tune to play
out. I twiddled my thumbs. I stared at the fish and named it "Sparky."

Eventually, I crossed the room again and sat down in front of the
Hanza game. I read the note a second time before pulling back my
sleeves. I played the red, just because, and studied the board. I realized
it could be won in two consecutive legal moves as the red if you sacrificed your king. *Hanza* is scored in the end by the number of pieces you
have remaining, but it is commonly acknowledged that you also need
the king piece intact.

"Subtlety really isn't your style, Yuebek," I said out loud. Shaking my
head, I moved the red pieces in the proper order and then pretended I
was the white player and took out the king. With one red piece, I demol-
ished the rest of the white pieces.

As soon as this was in place, I heard something click. I looked up in time to see one of the doors swing open.

I felt that chill again. I found myself licking my lips in response. *So,* I thought. *This is how Yuebek wants to toy with me. Very well.* I strode towards the next room and found myself inside a small library. The walls were lined with shelves filled with books and scrolls. The only light source was from a lantern on a desk in the middle of the room, so I couldn't see how far the shelves went—the furthest corners of the room were cloaked in shadows.

There was an open book beside the lantern. I guessed that it must be another puzzle and sat down to read the page. It was a story.

Once, there was a soldier whose king was on his deathbed.

The soldier was utterly devoted to his king and swore he would remain by his side until the very end.

He stood guard at the door. He no longer had a sword, so when wild dogs came, he fended them off with his fists. But there were too many, and they ate his knuckles.

When the crows came, he beat them with his stumps and his elbows. But there were too many, and they made off with his nose.

When the vultures came, he smashed them with his head. But there were too many, and they pecked out his eyes.

When the king's enemies came, he had nothing. He charged at the voices, but they only laughed and walked past him and they killed the king.

What is the moral of the story? The moral of the story is that...

I heard a crash. I turned to see a dark figure emerge from the shadows and come straight for me. I hurled the book at it, grabbed the lantern, and rushed for the door.

Too late, I realized that I had sprinted for the wrong wall. Instead of the main hall, the door opened up to a dark staircase. I saw the figure halfway across the room and decided to take my chances. I slammed the door shut and slid the bar, locking it in place. Something struck the other side. I watched the wood heave slightly before the banging started, a sound that reminded me of someone beating the tip of a broom inside a cellar. My skin began to crawl.

I fled down the stairs. They were made of stone and slippery. I tried to slow down to keep my footing and saw that they led not to a room but to a basement of some sort, where the air was damp and musty. I held the lantern higher and saw cell doors along one wall. The basement must have once been another dungeon.

I heard a groan and saw something move behind the bars, something big and heavy. There was the sensation of hot breath, and I imagined I could see steam rising in the darkness.

Still a dungeon, I corrected myself. I wondered if it was the same dungeon I had been in. The doors looked different. The cynicism I imagined my voice held kept me calm enough—I was at least still aware of my own actions. But I avoided staring at the cell doors while I scanned the shelves and the tables for anything that could be used as a weapon. I picked up a rusty fire poker and made an experimental swipe in the air.

The groaning intensified. I saw dark hands grip the bars and didn't want to wait to see what face they belonged to. I rushed back up the steps, removed the bar, and kicked the door open, preparing to fight.

The library was empty. I checked each dark corner, just to be sure. There was a shelf turned on its side with books spilled on the floor, which told me that I had not just imagined the apparition. I stepped over it and tugged at the door to the main hall. As soon as I opened it, I heard a different melody coming from the piano: a rendition of a nursery rhyme from Oren-yaro, I recalled they sang to me on hot, sleepless nights. Each chord was so perfectly timed that I imagined I could *hear* the singing now. *Sleep, my little darling, father went off to find a deer, soon he'll be back, soon he'll be home, soon he'll be warm by the fire.* The hair on my head stood on end.

I fought to keep the fear in check as I tiptoed towards the center of the room. The piano was not playing by itself now. There was a young man sitting there, his thin fingers gliding deftly over the keys. He must've heard me approach him, but his face remained fixed in concentration, his lips mumbling through the tunes. He kept playing until the song was done.

"Who are you?" I asked, lifting my makeshift weapon.

He turned to me now. He was smiling, which had the effect of scrunching his eyes and making them appear smaller than they were. "Should I ask you the same thing?"

I closed my mouth. He had spoken in Jinan, with none of the markers or tics of somebody who had learned it late in life. On second inspection, his face appeared familiar. Perhaps the sound of the language and the way his face moved with the words reminded me of someone back home.

"Maybe it doesn't matter," I said. "Why did you attack me?"

"I didn't," he said.

"Someone did."

"Did you get a good look at his face?"

I grimaced. "No."

"His clothes?"

"A bit. They were dark."

"So nothing like mine, then." He indicated his white robes with a flourish.

His smugness was irritating. I couldn't keep the annoyance out of my voice. "Tell me where I am."

"You are in this room," he said, gesturing with his hands.

"Smart fellow," I snorted. "Would you be as smart with a piece of metal in your eye?"

"Were you raised to use violence as a first resort? Come, now. I think you've got more sense than that. Besides, I am willing to bet you can't hit my eye from that distance. Not with *that*, anyway."

I lowered the fire poker. "Maybe you're right," I said. "It'd still hurt, though."

"Oh, I don't doubt that."

"So are you going to give me any real answers?"

"Only if you ask *real* questions," he said.

"Yuebek and his men attacked me on the streets. They left me to rot in a prison cell, and then I was drugged by the guard and woke up here. What for? If he just wanted to speak to me, why hasn't he done so already? Am I still even in the Zarojo Empire?"

He held out one hand. "I should have said *one* real question at a time. Maybe you can answer them yourself. Have you lost weight?"

I looked at my arm. "I don't think so."

"Then you weren't asleep for very long. A couple of days, perhaps. Is a couple of days long enough to transport you out of the empire?"

"I guess not."

"And the closest city, one that could contain a building that could have rooms this big?"

"Maybe, if they put me on a horse..."

"And do you have any recollections of riding on a horse?"

"No." I swallowed. "So I'm still in Zorheng. I don't know how that will help me."

"Sit down," the young man said, indicating the sofas.

I heaved myself into one with a sigh, though I didn't release the fire poker. The young man noticed that, but he didn't comment—he only smiled. He sat across from me and observed me for a few silent moments.

"You are Queen Talyien of the Oren-yaro," he finally said. There was a hint of amazement in his voice.

"So what if I am?"

The young man cracked a smile. "Did that sound rude? I didn't mean for it to be rude. It's just amazing how far it's come. In the old days, we didn't have true queens. The Dragonlord's wife held no power—to have given it to her would've been an insult to the other royal women. The Ikessars were chosen to lead, but his lady could have come from any clan, even a minor royal house, and so she bore his heirs and did no more. But you—they chose you."

"You speak of Jin-Sayeng with much passion," I said. "Have you been away for very long?"

"You could say that." He was looking at me with an intensity that made me uncomfortable.

I cleared my throat. "Your clan..." I began.

"Oren-yaro," he said.

I tried not to show my excitement and relief at speaking with someone I shared something with. "But which one?" I asked. "Which specific family?"

"It doesn't matter. Like you said—I've been away for very, very long. Before you were born, I believe."

"Then you must've been a child, because you don't seem that much older than me."

He scratched his chin, a playful glint in his eyes. "The Oren-yaro hide their age well. Everyone knows it. It's why we rarely lose clans to other warlords."

"Well, of course. We have to dupe them *somehow* into offering their allegiance."

"Indeed. And of course, the word *Oren-yaro* was made to refer to both the city and the people, all the clans and commoners who kneel before the warlord of said city. We call ourselves *Oren-yaro* to remind us—not just what we are and what we are expected to do—but that we belong, a feat that no other ruling clan dare match. Outside of Oren-yaro, you could be of the Onni clan, kneeling to the Barajis of Bara. Or Shero, raising your banner for the Ikessars. But the Orenars think beyond that. We are swords first, servants first."

I swallowed. "We." He was an Orenar. But who was he? The last male *aren dar* Orenar had died when my father did.

"We," he said. The smile faded from his face, and he looked almost sad for a moment. He got up, patting his knee. "Follow me, my queen."

I had never heard anyone give me an order with such contrasts before. A soft voice, but an air of command about it, like he didn't expect me to say no. And he acknowledged my title. But of course, he was an Orenar, and perhaps such subtlety was a given with the weight of that name. I racked my brain to recall where else I had kin, and if there was mention of any who had travelled to Ziri-nar-Orxiaro as a child. He had to be an *aron dar* Orenar, an offshoot. But I had long thought that other than Nor and her sisters, the few relatives I had under that name were aging, toothless men my father had left in charge of the rice villages in the hills around the city. I wasn't even sure if they were still alive.

I realized he was leading me back to the library, and then to the door that led down to the dungeons. I dropped the fire poker but hesitated. "What are you doing?" I asked.

"Are you afraid?"

"Don't be ridiculous. I'm just saying that I've *been* down there. There's nothing to see. If you want to talk…"

"You are Queen Talyien of the Oren-yaro," he said.

I sighed. "Yes. So we've established."

"Then why are you frightened?"

"In case it's not obvious, my title didn't give me the ability to stop imminent death," I said.

"We can go back for your fire poker, if you wish."

I bristled. "If you're just going to make fun of me..."

He chuckled. "You've got to admit it's amusing."

I sighed. "Let's get this over with."

He made a sweeping gesture, and we continued down the steps. I heard the movement from behind the cell doors again and glanced at the young man to see if it bothered him. He strode straight towards the doors, and it suddenly occurred to me that what lay behind them was the very thing he sought to show me.

He stopped in front of the first door.

"Who's there?" a hoarse voice called from the other side. A familiar voice. I had not heard it for a very long time, but I would know it anywhere in the world. I would know it until the day I died.

The young man opened the cell door. "Father," I said to the old man who sat, cross-legged, in the middle of the filthy floor. If I had not held his hand as he died—if I had not felt the frail fingers grow limp and cold to my touch while I uttered long prayers into the night—I would've found it easy enough to fool myself into thinking Yuebek had him captured, locked up here all these years.

He looked at me, eyes sharp as ever, with a face that had not aged a single day since his death. His pure white hair was bound in a bun. There was no layer of dirt on his skin. "Father," I repeated, entering the cell. "We burned you in a pyre. I know. I was there. I lit it myself with a torch. I watched the fires claim you." I didn't dare take another step closer.

Yeshin's face broke into a white-toothed grin. "So you did," he said. "Smart girl. Did the Ikessars ask for me to be buried, like some Kag miscreant? I hope you told them to go to hell."

"I..."

"Of course you didn't. You let them orate at my funeral with that Kibouri filth, didn't you? And the Ikessar brat didn't come. You'd think he would've, given I kept his head from being paraded around on a spike. Never let them tell you that pious education is the Ikessar's defining trait—it's ungratefulness. Why is your mouth open, girl?"

"You're dead, Father."

"And the dead aren't allowed to speak, is that it?"

"I'm sorry." Only Yeshin could still frighten me into a stupor, even as a ghost. Or perhaps I was merely dreaming. Or perhaps... "Am I also dead, Father? Is this why we can speak?"

"The Ikessars would love that, wouldn't they? To have gotten rid of you so easily. And you—fool girl—you let them. You *let* them." He pointed a finger at me. "You fell in love with the brat."

I considered the tone of his voice. "I thought—I thought I was *supposed* to, Father. You said..."

"Do not tell me what I said. I know what I said. I *thought* I raised you to fulfill your duties."

"And I did. I was crowned queen, even after he left."

"And you did not let that little thing distract you, did you? You ruled with a clear head, made it clear to the land that what the boy did was treachery and that the Ikessars were not made to rule after all? Did you try to change their opinion at all, girl, to secure your claim on the throne?"

I swallowed, trying hard not to let it show how much the sound of disappointment in my father's voice could tear holes through me. "My duties entailed that I remain loyal to my husband. He is, for all his faults..."

Yeshin spat. "That's what that fool woman said, wasn't it? The governor's daughter. Before he knifed her in the gut."

"Zhu Ong," the young man offered helpfully.

Yeshin turned to him. "And now *you* speak up. Did you tell her, Taraji? Did you remind her which of her many duties come first?"

Taraji was my eldest brother's name. Despite the fact that I was convinced that *none* of this could actually be happening, I glanced at the young man to take in the features of his face. I had never met him in my life—he was dead long before I was born. He smiled knowingly at me. "We are swords first, servants first," he said, repeating his words from earlier. "The land comes first. Jin-Sayeng."

"I know that," I said. "And I did everything I could to hold it together. It wasn't easy, father. Every year, Lushai would come up with some odd reason to pick a fight with me in front of the Dragonthrone council. The Jeinzas remain tight-lipped and indifferent, and the river-land lords continue to argue amongst themselves as if they do not even *belong* to the nation. Lady Bracha is at her wits' end, trying to get them under control. And you know how the Orenar foothills rely on trade from the Osahindo River lands to keep going."

"So why are you here?"

"Bringing Rai back would help with the peace."

"I thought you've said, more than once, that you do not *need* him to rule."

"I don't. But—"

"So *why* are you here?" Yeshin thundered. I lowered my eyes. "Is he like Rysaran's dragon, and the only way you can see yourself at peace with your rule is if you have somehow brought him back, complete with ball and chain?"

"You already told her the answer, Father," Taraji murmured. "She loved him. Is that not reason enough?"

"For a simpering daughter of some other royal clan, perhaps," Yeshin snapped. "Not *my* daughter. Not the heir of the Oren-yaro. Love? What foolish notion is this? Who *taught* you to be so weak and risk all I have worked for simply because of the whims of your emotions?"

"It is not entirely her fault," Taraji said.

"No. Not *entirely*. If you hadn't gotten yourself killed by Rysaran's mad dragon, we wouldn't be here. But you did, and we are, and so…" He looked at me. "And so we have a queen who cannot even acknowledge when a man has betrayed her, a man who isn't worth a single drop of the tears she has shed for him. If I had been alive when this happened, he wouldn't have lived to see another day."

"Too bad you were too old." Taraji grinned. "Rotting away. Too dead to see the loathsome Ikessar boy marry your precious daughter."

Yeshin ignored him, reserving his anger for me. "Instead, you gave him a second chance, fool girl. And then a *third* chance, and now here you are. Why are you looking at me like that? Of course I meant that you could've had him deposed *that first time* when you caught him with the Baraji slut. That snivelling Lushai—I wouldn't be surprised if her own father put her up to it."

"Father," I said. "I thought…that you would've wanted me to carry on with the betrothal. You had agreed to it, after all."

"A betrothal I was *forced* to agree to!" Yeshin snapped. "Do you think I wanted it, my own get breeding with an Ikessar whelp? The very thought disgusts me. The fool brat offered you a way out, but like some feather-brained wench, you ignored it. Twice. What did you need to take action, some shining signal from the heavens?"

Taraji's hand drifted to my shoulder. It was solid, but the warmth you would expect from such a touch was absent. "Have you run out of insults now, Father?" he asked.

By the look on Yeshin's face, the answer was *no*. "You could've called his own guard. Caught him in the act. Trumpeted the deed from the tip of Shirrokaru, and all the way to Kyo-orashi and Akki and every other dusty corner of Jin-Sayeng. But you kept your mouth shut. You chose loyalty and love for the brat over loyalty and love for your nation. He broke his oath. Instead, you made a son with him, another pawn for the

Ikessars to get their grubby hands on. And I thought Taraji had been the bigger idiot, parading around with his foppish friends and that peasant woman he wanted to marry. The gods must have cursed my loins."

"Father," Taraji said. "Enough."

Yeshin licked his lips, but he did fall silent for a moment, giving me time to gather my thoughts.

"What would you have me do, Father?" I asked.

He fixed me with a stare. "Can you not make decisions for yourself, girl?"

"I thought I did," I said. "You've just pointed out all of them were wrong."

"Let the oath breaker rot in his own filth," Taraji said. "Return to your duties. Show them what it means to be a wolf of Oren-yaro."

"If I'm dead, it's too late," I said.

"Don't be ridiculous," Yeshin snapped. "You're not yet dead."

"*We* are," Taraji said, a mournful note in his voice.

"Forget this madness," Yeshin said. "Go home, child."

I blinked, with the sensation of having fallen asleep and then awakened only a second later to a clearer mind, like the morning after a long night. I was still in the cell, but there was no one else with me. Yeshin and Taraji were gone.

The emptiness came at me like a wave. Yes, they had lectured me and insulted me, but for someone who had spent so many years alone in a sea of polite faces, solitude had become unbearable. Even the overbearing company of family was preferable to the grating echo of my own heartbeat in my ears.

I decided that Yuebek's guards had rattled my head loose during my capture and that my addled brain had conjured the phantoms. When

I walked out of the cell where I had just moments ago spoken with my father and brother, I saw the shadow appear by the stairs, and I prepared to greet it with a smile. And then I saw the glint of a blade in the near darkness, barely perceptible in the faint lantern light. I held my arm out as the shadow flung itself at me. The blade cut through my sleeve and sank into my flesh. The hot sting of pain and the iron tang of my own blood were real enough.

I smashed the lantern into the side of my attacker's head and watched as its clothes caught on fire. It gave me time to slip from its grasp. The figure was still blocking the door, so I ran towards the other end of the hall, hoping I wouldn't hit a dead end.

I didn't. It led to a tunnel formed from a crack in the wall. One step in and I would be in total darkness. I heard something crash and realized my assassin was still alive and probably very, very angry. I wrapped my torn sleeve around my wound before plunging into the shadows.

I could hear dripping water all around me, and then, unmistakably, the howling of the wind, with the hollow ring of a sound coming through a pipe. That I could feel fresh air in my lungs—at least, air a little fresher than in that damp basement—gave me hope that the tunnel opened up to somewhere. I groped around blindly, letting the wall be my guide.

Behind me, I heard movement.

I stopped walking and pressed against the wall. The sound of heavy breathing was followed by footsteps. I couldn't see much, but I could make out a faint silhouette that lumbered past me. It paused a few steps away.

I had been holding my breath this whole time, and I experimentally let a small huff loose. The figure turned.

I leaped to the other end of the tunnel just as the figure sprang to where I had been standing. Just as swiftly, it leaped towards my new position. I realized its hearing was too sharp to outwit and dashed down the tunnel, hoping I was at least faster than it was.

The darkness faded into a faint grey. I saw faint specks of sunlight dancing in front of me from the grates above. The assassin was gaining on me—I was *not* faster—and I decided to stop, bending low and bracing myself. The abruptness caught the assassin by surprise. A lean body crashed over me. I gripped the extended foot.

I heard a soft grunt, confirming my suspicions: the assassin was a woman. It gave me the confidence to heave myself over her figure and smash my fist into her exposed jaw. But she had tougher skin than I thought, and an even tougher head. The blow barely rattled her. She struggled underneath me as she tried to reach for her dagger.

I grabbed her wrist. She smashed her skull against mine, her teeth sinking into my shoulder. I smelled burnt flesh and leather as I tried to twist the blade from her grasp.

She tore into my flesh like a deranged dog. Blood and saliva dripped down my skin. I forced my thoughts away from the pain, dulling it as I focused on slamming her blade into her own thigh.

She let go of my shoulder. I kicked myself off her and started down the tunnel again. I could see the light, and if I was going to die fighting, I wanted to do it out in the open.

I reached the end of the tunnel, all but bursting through the darkness to a gate swinging against rusty hinges. The assassin must've come through the same way. I strode out and found myself in a field fringed with dead trees and low, grass-covered hills. I picked up a rock just as the assassin reached me, then I turned around and smashed it into her head. Hard as it had been, the rock was a whole deal harder. She collapsed on the ground, reeling from the blow. I picked up her dagger and sank it into her throat.

I watched her blood throb over the golden grass as I slumped to the ground. My whole body was shaking now, not just my fingers. With rattling teeth, I turned the assassin's body over and ripped off her mask.

An unfamiliar face greeted me. I tugged her belt loose. There was a purse. I opened it, saw coin, and figured my assassin was not as professional as I thought she had been. What assassin would risk having coin clinking around in her possession? She had certainly been clumsier than the ones who had attacked me in Anzhao City.

As I pocketed the coin, I saw a small piece of paper and unrolled it. It was a message, likely sent by bird from the shape of the roll. The message said:

You will find it most profitable if you can take care of the target as soon as possible. She must not be allowed to return to Jin-Sayeng. We are generous, and a clean job will be amply rewarded.

There was no signature, nothing to indicate the source of the message to the untrained eye. But I didn't need clues. The blood drained from my face as my eyes skipped over the words again, the crisp, clean handwriting I had known for far too long. It was Rayyel's handwriting. Rayyel. Rayyel had sent the assassin.

I shoved the letter back into the purse and into my pocket. I closed my eyes. I thought of my phantom father's words. *You fell in love with the brat.* My downfall, so it seemed.

I didn't wait there for very long. The smell of the blood was starting to attract a frightening number of crows. I could see them watching me from the branches of the leafless trees with their beady black eyes. "All right," I said out loud, getting to my feet. "Greedy bastards. You can have her." I had to get out of there, anyway. For all I knew, she was not the only one.

I thought of Zhu, of her sightless eyes and the knife in her gut, and said a prayer under my breath.

I could only hope another might do the same for me.

CHAPTER TWENTY-TWO

THE RETURN TO ANZHAO CITY

ᬳᬗᬧᬶᬭ

I found a road not far from the field and kept walking. I dared not look back.

The worst of the rains seemed to have come and gone since my captivity, leaving behind a grey wasteland of withered trees, the branches crisp with frost. In nothing but a thin dress and wooden sandals, every step was agony. Blisters burned my toes; if I paused for relief, the cold crawled on my skin and became unbearable. Behind me, Zorheng's shadow bore down like a predator on the prowl. Even from the corner of my eyes, the city's dark silhouette filled me with dread.

It was finally the grip of hunger that tore me back to the present. I could see a village at the edge of the river. Was dying from the elements better than grappling with bandits? Before Zorheng, I would've scoffed at such hesitation. But the knowledge that my judgment was not as good as I once thought had left me a hollow shell, and I stood on the edge of the road so long that I began to shiver. I finally crossed my arms and stepped towards the first hut I could see. I had a dagger; I could still defend myself.

The door to the hut was swinging against the wind. My shadow had barely grazed the doorway when I knew something was wrong. By now I should've heard a dog or two barking, or seen chickens, ducks, maybe goats. And even in this cold, there ought to at least have been a group of children defying nature by the riverbank.

Nothing but silence greeted me.

My stomach grumbled again, and I went straight inside the house while I thought of a ready speech about my intrusion. I could repeat the same lines I had given in Shang Azi, even as the thought of saying the words *my husband* made me want to throw up. My husband.

You fell in love with the brat.

The house was empty. I took my liberties and went straight for the pile of blankets in the corner. A tattered woolen one served to keep me warm, and I wandered to the kitchen as I wrapped it around my shoulders. There was no wood on the stove. I glanced at the corner and noticed there wasn't firewood stacked anywhere, which felt strange given it was clearly the cusp of winter. With a sigh, I checked the shelf. I found nothing but a moldy piece of taro root and half a jar of rice grains.

I went out with a pot to gather water from the river and noticed the dead bodies at the other end of the yard. Skeletons, actually. They were still covered in rags that were once clothes, but the flesh had been pecked clean by wild animals. From their position, it looked like they had been struck down by arrows. I glanced at the rest of the village and knew I would find others if I looked. It seemed as if I would dine with the dead that night.

I fetched water, found wood in a neighbour's shed, and returned to the hut to start a fire. I cut off the moldy pieces from the taro root and mixed it with the rice and water. And then I sat down to wait for it to boil, watching the crackling flames dance against the freezing air with a sense of having just lost a fight. A strange thought, considering I was yet still alive. But my senses felt dim. The thought of the letter in my purse filled me with cold rage.

My husband wanted me dead.

I had thought we had left such things in the past, in the days of my father and his mother's war. We were supposed to be symbols of a brighter tomorrow, wiser than our ancestors, enlightened. Why kill the first Oren-yaro who had studied in Shirrokaru's halls, who had offered the Ikessars more respect than they could have ever dreamed of? And this, coming from the boy for whom so many had died, the last shining star of the Ikessars?

He is the heir of a rival clan, I thought desperately to myself. *Why are you surprised?* He must have sent the other assassins, too. Else why did he survive that attempt? Half my guards died. He must have paid the rest off, including Captain Nor. Saka had warned me. I was a fool for not seeing it sooner. My blind faith in the Oren-yaro was nothing compared to the wily ways of the Ikessars. Did the assassin pay Yuebek's guards to look the other way? They were wise enough to wait until the weeks had worn me down. No wonder escaping the dungeons was so easy. The Ikessars were experts in subterfuge, and it wasn't a secret that they resented how they had to cede part of the rule to my clan. If they killed me, Rayyel could attempt to take the throne for himself. This whole affair was meant to separate me from my people, to tear me apart before they could cut my head off.

Ozo had warned me, hadn't he? He had, and I was foolish enough to dismiss him. And now I was having hallucinations of my dead father and brother to remind me exactly why I failed. *You followed your heart and not your head, Tali.* Even if I thought otherwise. I didn't *need* him. When he left, I didn't stop him, did I? I didn't stop him and in doing so, held the key to the nation in the palm of my hands. I could have then done what Ozo had been begging me since the beginning—I could have seized control and put everyone in their place.

I placed another piece of wood into the fire and took a deep breath. I could still do that. It wasn't too late. I had enough coin from the assassin's purse that I could easily make my way to the next town. Surely not every official in the damn empire was corrupt. There had to be cities, perhaps a smaller town, where I could find an honest person who could help—someone in a trusted position, who would find it more troubling *not* to assist a queen than anything. They could betray me, of course, but it wasn't as if *trying not to get betrayed* worked. This must have been the logic my father's ghost wanted me to embrace. I could forget trying to save Rai. Governor Zheshan could be using him for his own sake, but if I found a sympathetic ear, I could begin the process of renouncing him while I made my way back to Jin-Sayeng. The warlords would know why, and it wouldn't matter. I had the assassin's letter, evidence enough to damn him.

I could very well be damning myself, too, but at least I would be home with my son.

"By all the gods," I murmured. The thought of Thanh felt like a blow to my skull. My promise to him—ah. Maybe that was what my father was trying to tell me. You could not be queen and wife and queen and mother at the same time. There were always sacrifices to make, and none of us can be more than one person. Something had to give.

The smell of rice wafted from the pot. I pulled it from the fire and ate in silence, the night stretching out around me. And then I tried to catch what little sleep I could.

The second assassin came early in the morning.

I sat with my back to the wall, eyes half-closed, dagger in hand. He came tiptoeing through the front door. The way he walked, I could tell he thought I was sleeping. I found his incompetence remarkably irritating for some reason. Rayyel could have found better assassins. His entire family's reputation was *built* by assassins. He had already shamed his wife and son; was he going to shame his ancestors, too?

Still, even an incompetent assassin could be dangerous. I waited until he stepped right beside the fire before jumping out to kick the embers at him. He lifted his arm to block against the spray, and I lashed with the dagger, catching him below his breastbone. He grabbed my arm in an attempt to pin me down, and I stabbed his shoulder.

He threw me against the wall with a roar. I slammed against the frail bamboo and rolled to the side as he struck with his sword. The blade smashed into the window and was caught between the splinters. It left his neck wide open, but just as I lunged for him, he wrenched his sword free and swung at me.

I jumped back, trapped between the wall and an angry, bleeding man whose injuries only seemed to make him more furious. The door was behind him, and there was no way I could make a run for it. He could see me coming to that conclusion, because his face relaxed as he hefted the sword in his hand.

"You killed my friend," the man said in Jinan. "I'm going to make you regret that."

I didn't answer. Instead, I stared at the door and the wide field beyond it. For some reason, I half expected Khine to appear.

He didn't, of course. He was back in Anzhao, because after he had offered me nothing but kindness and friendship, I had thrown it all back into his face. I was alone; I had been for months. No wonder I had gotten so used to him. The mind seeks comfort where it can and sees only what it wants to see—I must have been convinced that all our run-ins meant something, the way I had once convinced myself Rayyel loved me. A sign, perhaps, that the gods hadn't given up on me—a sign that my struggles were acknowledged in the grand scheme of things. And yet it was nothing, after all. The man had his own damn reasons for helping people, and I grew attached to the idea because I had met so few friendly faces in that blasted empire. I could fight and kill and bleed like the rest of them, but deep inside, I remained the sort of foolish girl who still believed in fairy tales.

Was that what my hallucinations were trying to say? That I was doomed to be alone because I didn't want to be? It felt like the sort of rotten trick a swordsmaster would do to you—to smack you over the head for every instance you reached out for what you wanted, *because, child, have you forgotten who you are? To ask for more isn't allowed.* Why fight it? I couldn't separate myself from my duties, couldn't simply tear out the part of me that longed for more than the assurance that I was fulfilling my part in the world. Zhu Ong died for that same mistake.

No one was going to come and save me. I sidestepped as the assassin finally bore down on me, and stabbed him in the gut just as his sword came swinging down. The blade struck the bamboo wall again, and the man slumped to the ground, coughing blood. "They said you were harmless," he gasped. "They said you were just some woman from Dar Aso!"

I hesitated now. "You're from Anzhao?"

"You people don't fucking care what we have to do to survive," he roared as he tried to attack me again. His legs crumpled under him, and he fell face down instead. I drew the dagger from his belly and finished the job, now acutely aware I was killing my own countryman. To hire poor immigrants as assassins—Rayyel had stooped too low. Even in the empire, these were still our people. Did he really think it would work? That he could kill me by sending wave after wave of paid thugs? Maybe he thought someone was bound to get lucky, and he just didn't care how many people got killed in the attempt. Before, I wouldn't have believed Rayyel was capable of such cold ruthlessness, but then such naivety was what brought me here.

I found the assassin's horse tied in the yard, next to the skeletons. With a sigh, I heaved myself into the saddle and made my way down the road.

Find an official. Renounce Rayyel. Go to war. I repeated this to myself until the crossroads, where a group of travelling merchants pointed me to the nearest cities that weren't Anzhao. There was An Mozhi, to the south. Goleng, to the north. Both were a few days' ride away. In each city, I would be friendless; I would have to start again. People were already out to kill me, and others could be found wherever I went. Wasn't this what my father wanted? For me to use my head, not my heart? If he were in my place, what would he do? He wouldn't let anger cloud his judgment, for one thing. I swallowed. No—my father would find a way, even if it meant working with the enemy. I had to stop floundering. I had to live up to his name somehow.

I stared at the road leading to Anzhao. Anzhao, at the very least, was familiar to me. The certainty of the snakes hiding there also offered a damned sense of comfort. I might let my guard down elsewhere; in Anzhao, I knew at least whom *not* to trust. The others I could still work with. And there was at least one person back there who had not yet betrayed me, even after I had given him every reason to.

As my mind worked through these thoughts, I saw a mother place her son into the back of a horse-drawn wagon before jumping in herself. Her husband, in the driver's seat, said something, and she laughed and tickled her son, who giggled in return. The boy was younger than mine, but my heart trembled at the sound anyway. The man then whistled to the horses, which trotted off, carrying the family around the bend.

We see only what we want to see.

I took the Anzhao road.

I wrestled with two more assassins along the way.

One had been too obvious, a bumbling idiot who swiped at me with a curved dagger in the middle of a crowded inn in Nam Ghun. I didn't even have to do anything to save myself. The other patrons intervened on my behalf, calling him a drunken fool, a robber, a brigand. They beat him to the ground while he pointed a finger at me and called me a shameless slut, a whore who should've known better. I stepped on his outstretched hand and kicked him in the jaw before somebody finally dragged him to the guards.

The other one had been as subtle as the first. He arrived at the first inn near the Blue Rok Haize's territory and waited until I separated from the merchants I had travelled with from Nam Ghun. He thought he could surprise me on my way back to the inn from the outhouse, but a barking dog gave him away. Torn between carrying out his task and fleeing to try another time, he got my dagger in his back before he could decide. I hid his body in the outhouse, arranging it so it looked like he got stabbed while taking a shit.

Well over a week after Zorheng, I rode back to Anzhao on a clear morning, purse heavy with my own bounties, my heart filled with cold rage over the relentless assaults. Here, I went straight to the docks, where fishing vessels were making their way back in time for the market after days at sea. I could see barrels of small steel-grey fish being hauled from gangways for salting and red spotted groupers the size of my arm laid out right on the shore for picky buyers to peruse. Others had tables with shiny octopuses, squid, prawns, and blue crabs piled on top of each other. Some of the vendors were cooking their wares right on the street. The sharp tang of the fresh seafood in the air made my stomach grumble.

After a meal of rice and fish in black bean sauce from an open stall— delicious, if overly salted—I eventually found the courage to ask around for the harbour master's office and make my way to the street. But here, after days of near-death bravado, I faltered. I'm sure I would not be the first Jinsein trapped on these shores looking for a way home, and after the Ikessars' lax policies, it was actually fairly common for the Zarojo to skip across the sea and settle in Jin-Sayeng, but I couldn't help but suspect Yuebek would've already sent word of my escape.

I glanced at the people around me. The woman strolling with her children under that paper parasol, those fishermen, that man pulling a cart of pickled turnips and mangoes—were any of them paid to keep an eye out for a bedraggled Jinsein woman seeking passage to Jin-Sayeng waters? Were any of them assassins? A grey-haired crone eating grilled chicken feet on a stick stared at me a little too long, and I fought the urge to run her through with my knife.

The weariness bore down on me like a hangman's noose. I wanted nothing else except to wrap my arms around my son and cry into his hair, but I knew it would be a long time before I could do that again, if ever. Rayyel was still in Anzhao, and I had to take care of him first—whatever that meant.

Cold rage became dejection, became desperation.

Betrayal has a funny way of turning your world upside down. As familiar as I had already been with it by that point, it still amazed me how far I could stretch that moment of denial. The thought of what had been—of what could *yet* be—persisted. Perhaps it is not the same for most people. Perhaps, when you love less, it is easier not to let the emptiness become a cavern from which you can no longer see the sun.

Before I could realize what was happening, I found myself walking behind a pack of mangy dogs towards the dirty streets of Shang Azi.

I could hear my father's phantom voice screaming at me for returning to the filthy streets I had worked so hard to escape from. But there is no possible panacea for betrayal except to turn back time, and so you go to the next best thing: the solace of the familiar. And Shang Azi—dangerous, crowded, rundown Shang Azi—was the closest thing I could call home in those parts.

The roof of the covered marketplace dominated the skyline, marking my destination, and it was easy enough to find my way through the alleys towards it. If there was one good thing about my encounter with Prince Yuebek, it was that it had all but erased my fear of Lo Bahn.

Or perhaps I could not afford to be afraid. I still wasn't entirely sure what possessed me to stand at the edge of the street, watching the flurry of market-goers and vendors like a lost child seeking her parents. I only knew when I saw *him* appear, just as I thought he would, and how at the sight of me his face broke into a smile.

I came up to Khine, all words dying in my throat as I pressed my forehead against his chest. I felt his arms around me. It was the warmth of an embrace that held no expectations, my one shelter in the midst of the buzzing voices of people free to live their lives as they saw fit. Time seemed to stop. I pulled him closer, drinking in that same comfort I had first felt in that dark shed under the falling rain.

"At least this time, you can't accuse me of following you," he murmured over my ear.

"No," I said.

He drew me aside, looking into my face. I think he saw how thin I had become, the bruises, and the shadowed expression of someone who had been fighting for her life for weeks. The smile died on his face. "Zorheng was... not what you expected."

I couldn't even joke about it. I shook my head. "How long was I gone?"

"A little over three months," he said. "You never sent word, so I thought you'd found yourself in the company of friends at last. I didn't think you'd ever return. I thought for sure..." He trailed off, pressing his thumb over my chin thoughtfully before sliding it up to tuck a strand of hair over my ear. "There is something you should know," he whispered, at length.

I narrowed my eyes. "What did you do this time?"

He gave a quick grin. "Nothing yet."

"Does it have anything to do with Inzali? How is she?"

"Better than I had hoped," Khine said. "But no, this isn't about her. A few days ago, there was news from Jin-Sayeng. They are saying that there is unrest—that the warlords are riding for Oren-yaro to confront your advisers and decide who the next ruler of Jin-Sayeng should be."

"The hellspawn," I said through gritted teeth. "Useless, all of them."

I took a deep breath. "Gossip. It must just be gossip. The warlords wouldn't ride to Oren-yaro like that. They'd risk the wrath of the lords of the foothills, of all the Orenar bannermen."

"Perhaps," Khine murmured. "But from the sound of it, the Oren-yaro aren't doing a single thing to defend or assist you. It is said that Jin-Sayeng believes you've abandoned your duties and there is talk of having you deposed."

"Just like those bastards to squabble over my remains. They're not even sure I'm dead yet." The words rang in my ears. "What do you mean by *deposed*?"

"Don't shoot the messenger," he grumbled. "The news spoke of how you just disappeared from Oren-yaro. Didn't anyone know where you were going?"

I took a deep breath. "Not officially," I said. "The council wouldn't have allowed it. My advisers were vehemently opposed to the idea. You can only imagine how the Oren-yaro lords would've reacted. We left in secret before there could ever really be a decision, and we didn't exactly give out *details*. They didn't know I was meeting Rayyel, only that it had something to do with people he was involved with. I thought if I went quickly and then brought him back without a fuss, everything would work out."

He pressed his lips together.

"Clearly I was wrong," I quickly added before he could say anything else. "I didn't think this would happen. I had no reason to doubt Rayyel, and my son..." My voice choked.

"It's all right," Khine said. "You had good intentions."

"They want me *deposed*?"

He craned his head back. "Come. I'll buy you a drink, and you can learn all of this for yourself."

Numbly, I nodded.

I shouldn't have been so surprised.

I have heard someone once liken the balance of power in Jin-Sayeng to an egg on sword-point. A single whisper could topple it, yet even absolutely nothing could still cause it to crack. Even the Ikessars' reign had been tumultuous, and it was the one time in Jin-Sayeng history when long years of peace had been common. I had been hoping to beat the longest, which had lasted thirty years.

Such a thing seemed unlikely now. I sat with Khine in a tavern in the neighbourhood of Dar Aso, the immigrants' quarter, listening to conversations from Jinsein natives while nursing a cold mug of what may have been the palest, weakest beer I've ever had in my life. A fishing vessel from Akki had brought the news, and what had started as a private discussion between friends had exploded overnight.

"I have family in Bara," a man was saying, slamming his drink on the table. "How am I supposed to get them out of there? If war breaks out, Lushai will lock the city, everyone in it honour-bound to serve his cause. When did the royals ever think about the common people? I'm not rich. I can't afford to hire a ship."

"You won't have to, because there won't be a war," another said. "You're overreacting."

"The queen—why would she disappear? Just like her husband before her..."

"I bet she's off somewhere, getting her cunt pounded by some rich fucker."

"Or a guardsman."

"For all their talk, those royals wouldn't know duty if it bit them in the ass."

There was more beer-sloshing and sounds of agreement. I saw Khine give me a look before he turned to the table behind him. "How sure are you folk of these tidings?" he asked. I opened my mouth, astonished at how well he spoke Jinan. The Zarojo accent was strong but not distracting. "I can understand the warlords becoming concerned if the queen hasn't returned, but overthrowing her sounds pretty harsh."

"*Concerned?*" a man asked, snorting. "You may have been drinking the swill here for years, Lamang, but that doesn't make you Jinsein. Get this into your thick skull: the warlords don't get *concerned* about each other. Jinseins worry about their provinces before the nation, and the warlords are only concerned with their cities and their bannermen."

"Queen Talyien's claim has been shaky for years," another from the same table offered. "Dragonlord Rayyel's disappearance only cemented that. It's not a secret that the warlords think that the Oren-yaro had something to do with that—that they pulled a trick on all of Jin-Sayeng to put one of their own on the Dragonthrone."

My fingers curled against the table. In the past, I had the luxury of soldiers who would knock the teeth out of any who would dare speak such words in my presence. Now, I could do nothing, and admitting who I was in front of all these people—these people who were supposedly my *subjects*—didn't seem like the wisest choice.

"She has a son..." Khine began.

"A boy of seven," the man huffed. "Can he rally his mother's army to his cause? His father was an *Ikessar*. Do the Oren-yaro see him as the Orenar heir, or the Ikessar heir?"

"There is talk that even *that* isn't true," his friend added.

"Who knows? Warlord Lushai will say anything. He's been eyeing the Dragonthrone for decades. If he manages to plant his plump rump on it right before he dies with an arrow in his heart, I think he'll consider it a life well lived. Doesn't stop people from believing it, though. Anything happens, that kid will be dead before sundown."

"I think the Oren-yaro army will hold out for the queen's sake," someone from the table next to us called out. "But without a true leader, the others will tear them apart. Who are their generals now? Untried youngsters from the major clans? The Nee family can't even decide which of the old Lord Hega's daughters should lead their soldiers. The sons are all useless."

"They have Lord Tasho still. Lord General Ozo aren dar Tasho, the old wolf. Forget the queen—everyone knows he's been the true leader of the Oren-yaro since Warlord Yeshin's death. He..."

The talk turned to nonsense. I continued drinking.

"Who's your friend, Khine?" I heard someone call out. "We've never seen her here before."

"Right," Khine said, smiling at no one in particular. "I think we should go."

"Hold on a second, you Xiaran dog." This, coming from the table next to us. "It's been years since I've seen you with a woman. The baker's daughter—what was her name? Have you finally forgotten her?"

"Not likely. That's why he's been coming here all this time," the man nearest to me said, cranking out a grin that smelled of wine and gin. "Memories. Who are you and where are you from, girl?" It was a common Jinsein greeting, along with *Who is your family and whom do you worship?*

"Kora, from Akki," I said quickly.

"You don't sound Akkian," the man said. He frowned.

"I grew up in Sutan."

"You sound Oren-yaro. I can tell that accent from a mile away."

"You're mistaken."

There was a tense moment. And then the man started laughing. Half the tavern followed suit.

Khine gave a painful smile. "And that's our cue to leave. Thank you as always for the hospitality, my dear friends." He pushed himself away from the table, grabbed my wrist, and all but dragged me out of there.

He only released his grip when we were out on the path outside the tavern. "I'm sorry," he said. "I didn't realize they would be so uncivilized."

"I'm not really concerned about that," I replied. I took a deep breath.

"You were right about the rumours, at least. I didn't think…" I paused, struggling to find the right words. I had always known that the people doubted me, that they bore no love for my father, who they believed wrestled his way onto their beloved Ikessars' throne. None seemed to care that without my father's war, Rayyel would have never even been acknowledged as the Ikessar heir in the first place. In those days, a regent had ruled in the Dragonlord's stead because Rayyel's uncle Rysaran had disappeared with his mad dragon, the one that would later raze Old Oren-yaro to the ground.

What was new to me was that they doubted Thanh. Perhaps all mothers find it hard to believe that others do not see their children the way they do. But he was not just my child—he was as much Ikessar as Oren-yaro. If my birth had signalled peace, a momentary cessation of those tired old wars, his had promised a new beginning. The people could hate me all they wanted, but after his father, the child was heir to the longest line of Dragonlords the nation had known. Even if I wasn't around, his father's family still was; *his* family, too, by all rights. Of all the clans, only the Ikessars could hold rule without a massive army. They made the perfect prop.

I stopped as I remembered Saka's words. *They'll kill your boy.* My son was guarded night and day by the Ikessars, but he had never been presented in their ancestral lands, never seen his elders in the clan. His own grandmother, Princess Ryia, had never laid eyes on him, not even after his father had left. Were they trying to discredit him?

I balled my hands into fists. Family was sacred. But perhaps the Ikessars no longer saw my son as family. Perhaps there was too much of me in him. Too much of my father.

"I'm out of my element," Khine chuckled, breaking my thoughts. "If this was a situation I could solve with a ruse, I'd have figured something out by now."

"Thank you," I said. "But it isn't your problem to solve." I stopped myself before I could say anything else—that legendary bluntness rising to the surface. I meant nothing by it, but it was starting to occur to me that I cared about how I made Khine feel. "Back in the tavern," I said, trying to change the conversation. "They mentioned a woman."

He scratched his head sheepishly. "Drunk talk."

"You spoke of her when we parted before Zorheng." I lengthened my stride to match his. "Talk. I think you owe it to me."

"Why? We're not friends, remember?"

I wasn't sure if he was serious or not until I saw the light in his eyes. "All right," I said with a chuckle. "Perhaps not yet. But friends start by trading secrets, and I've already given you some of mine."

"Your fault."

"Khine…"

"I don't…" He paused, snorting. "I guess one of my sisters will talk in time, anyway. This was back when I was still a student. A Jinsein, like I told you."

We walked in silence for several moments while he thought things through, wondering, no doubt, about what he felt he could or couldn't say to me. I was so focused on waiting to see what he had to say that I almost didn't notice the shuffle of a shadow in the alley beside us. I glanced sharply to the left, but whatever it had been was gone.

I stared at the empty alley, my hand dropping to the hilt of my dagger. All the assassination attempts from the last few months had done wonders for my reflexes. I wished it had been a sword, but the one I had stolen from Lo Bahn's man was back in Zorheng, and I hadn't been able to find another along the way. Thinking of confronting yet another assassin with only a dagger for protection kept me on edge. I glanced behind me, eyes scanning the gutters overflowing with congealed sewage, the rooftops, and the curtained windows of the narrow houses for anything amiss.

"She was from Kai, she told me," Khine continued, oblivious. "I know how you Jinseins like to know those sorts of things."

I didn't want to alert him, which would inadvertently alert whoever was trailing us. I didn't want them to try again when I had dropped my guard. I leaned closer to Khine, wrapping myself around his arm. He gave a surprised grunt. "Keep talking," I said, glancing back at him with all the sweetness I could muster.

"I'm not sure what else there is. We argued after I failed that year's examinations the first time. I said things I didn't mean. She may have taken them the wrong way." His fingers twitched. "That was a long time ago. I was a different man, then...one full of anger and regrets. Now, only the regrets remain."

"Yet you still go to that tavern."

"That tavern. This whole district. I find myself wandering our old haunts in Shang Azi. It's a bad habit. I've been trying to break out of it."

"For how long?"

He gave me a knowing smile. "Years," he said. "It's... not easy."

"Are you still hoping to see her?"

"I think for a while, perhaps... I was hoping I could run into her and beg for her forgiveness. I ruined her, you see. Our time together brought her nothing but pain. But I—" He stopped and shook his head. "She's not even here anymore. She joined a group looking to settle in Kyan Jang and left with her family, whatever shambles of her life there were that remained. By then, I had grown accustomed to the company and that beer."

"Really? *That* beer?"

"What can I say, my queen? Love is blind, something you know all too well."

"I should've never trusted you with my secrets."

"Too late. I plan to sell them to the highest bidder as soon as I can make you let go of my arm."

"Are you giving me an incentive to clutch on to you like a monkey for life?"

"You are a dangerous woman."

"At least you know." I smiled up at him, drew my dagger, and threw myself at the man behind us.

The houses were very close together in Dar Aso, even more so than in Shang Azi. I think the tight alleyway had confused my would-be assassin. Between the shadows, I saw the figure lumber to the side. He was a large man, and he moved like someone who had not been expecting me to fight back. I shifted my feet, preparing to draw the dagger across his chest, when I saw the movement he used to block my attack: one arm held up, hand in a fist, the other—the dirty hand, where you could conceal a knife or throw an unexpected punch—trailing behind.

It was a movement they taught in the Oren-yaro military. But none of my guards were this size. I allowed the blade to skim over his garments, nicking him, before I stepped back into the sunlight. "Show your face!" I cried.

The man didn't even hesitate, striding after me and pulling his mask and cape off. I dropped the dagger in shock. Panting, I watched him drop to one knee. "My queen," the man said. It was Agos's voice, underneath a heavy black beard and hair so much longer than he used to wear it. Agos, my oldest friend, whom I had last seen the day Rayyel disappeared.

I dropped to the ground with him and hid my face in his shoulder. I don't remember if I cried or not. If I did, neither he nor Khine ever spoke about it.

CHAPTER TWENTY-THREE

THE QUEEN'S GUARD

ᔑ ᔿ ᔍ ᐳ

Agos was the son of the head cook at Oka Shto. Rumours said he had an unnamed blacksmith father from Shirrokaru, a man who I assumed was either dead or missing. Before I was born, he had been the only young child in the newly built castle at Oka Shto, which caused the staff to dote on him. I've been told that even my own father would occasionally steal him from his nursemaids to ply him with sweets. The laughter of one single child had been enough to fill those empty halls. Oka Shto, which began as a memorial for the dead we lost to Rysaran's dragon and the Ikessars' attacks during the war, began to look more like a proper warlord's place.

It was such a simple thing, one difficult to understand unless you had been there and felt loss after loss the way the Oren-yaro did in those years. Even when my mother died in childbirth, so young and frail that it was common knowledge a man of Yeshin's age should have never married her, the shroud of mourning did not last long. My nursemaid had told me that the sight of me and Agos toddling after each other through the grounds was like a beacon of light, a sign from Akaterru that my father's sins could be forgiven.

Growing up, I didn't really understand much of what that all meant. I knew that both Agos and I got away with so much; he occasionally got whipped for troubles *I* created, but I always felt that the staff did this half-heartedly, if only so they would have something to tell my father afterwards. He never got more than a welt or two, or a pinched ear most of the time. Later, other children arrived—mostly the servants', although there was the occasional son or daughter a councillor would bring to visit—but we were always *the* children. If the kitchen staff asked if *the* children ate yet, or if *the* children were responsible for letting all the dogs loose in the garden right before Warlord Graiyo's arrival, they meant Agos and me.

Perhaps that was why I had always taken Agos's constant presence for granted. Even as I grew older and started spending more time with my studies, I always knew he would be there whenever I needed it. The last few years would've gone a lot better had he been around. Even the whole damned trip to Ziri-nar-Orxiaro wouldn't have taken the turns it did if he had still been the captain of the guard instead of Nor; one swipe from his blade would've finished off both assassins at the Silver Goose and maybe Zheshan, too. He could've dragged Rai by the collar, and we would all be home by now.

I knew it was all wishful thinking—an echo of guilt, a tinge of regret, in the way I examined what his absence had caused in my life. I knew, too, that if it had been up to him, he would've never left. Faithful to the end, he had followed my order to *disappear* as simply as if I'd asked him to fetch my horse.

To see him here, in Ziri-nar-Orxiaro after all these years, was more than unexpected—it felt like something out of a dream. "How did you get here?" I found myself asking after I had gotten back to my feet.

"I heard the rumours about your disappearance," Agos said. "I just had to find out for myself. I learned you were here, that they were saying that Magister Arro had been killed and you and your entire personal guard had disappeared, *and no one was doing a damn thing about it*. I couldn't believe it." He was a young man the last time I had seen him.

He still was, I suppose, but there was a presence and weight to him that hadn't been there before. Time had taken those children and left behind these aging vessels, doomed to continue down the path of yesterday's mistakes. His eyes flicked towards Khine.

"It's all right," I said. "He's a friend."

"*Now* he's a friend," Khine remarked.

Agos didn't look too happy. "He's Xiaran."

"Zarojo. Let's not insult what few friends we have... unless you have some of my soldiers with you, by any chance?"

Agos shook his head. "I left the army, and I haven't talked to any of my soldiers since... since that day. Like you told me to."

"You spoke with Saka."

His face flickered. "Where is he?"

"The city watch killed him."

Agos swore under his breath. "The bastards. This city's officials are fouler than sewage water."

"He said you sent him to watch over me."

"I asked him to take care of Prince Thanh," he said. "But that was before I left. We haven't spoken. You ordered me to stay silent."

"I don't remember saying that."

He sniffed. "Don't you?" He was still staring at Khine. I remembered the way we had walked, when I thought I had been trying to draw the assassin out, and inadvertently felt my cheeks burn.

"We can trust him, Agos. He knows everything."

"*Everything?*"

"He knows enough. He hasn't betrayed me yet. I don't think he means to."

"How can you be sure? Have you tried knocking his teeth in?"

To hear Agos question my decision three times in the last few minutes was a little disconcerting. The last five years had changed him, but I couldn't quite pinpoint how or why. "We shouldn't talk here," I finally said.

"I have a room in an inn nearby," Agos said.

"You can also go back to my home," Khine offered. "Lo Bahn's men have been busy with other things lately. I'm sure…"

Agos's lips curled into a half snarl, causing Khine to fall silent abruptly.

"I think…that I need to speak with Agos alone," I murmured, touching Khine's shoulder. "I have not forgotten what you and your family have done for me. I will pay you a visit later."

Khine didn't protest, though he looked torn about leaving me alone with Agos. I couldn't blame him. To the naked eye, Agos looked like any other scoundrel skulking through Shang Azi's streets, far from the decorated member of the Oren-yaro Royal Guard that he had been. But of course, Khine wasn't one to say such a thing out loud, and even if he did, it only meant that Agos was in good company.

We parted at the next street. I followed Agos, who puffed up his chest as soon as Khine was out of earshot. "Nor was your captain," he said. He made the statement sound like an accusation.

"I see you've been asking around."

"It was the first thing I learned. That you took your personal guard and Magister Arro off to some secret meeting in Anzhao City and that no one could agree exactly what for. *Captain* Nor. Who promoted her? As far as I'm concerned, this is her mess."

"Lord General Ozo did."

"There's at least five other better candidates, and he knows that. Was it just because of her name? Because she's an Orenar?"

"Do you know where she is?" I asked.

"No," he said. "But she was the first person I looked for when I arrived a few days ago. A captain of the guard doesn't just *lose* her queen, especially not after Magister Arro's body turned up and hers didn't. I've heard of someone fitting her description walking around town and was on my way to make arrangements to meet her when I saw you leave the tavern with that man. Luck," he said grimly, "is a fickle mistress."

"So she is," I murmured. "You think Nor has anything to do with what happened?"

"Finding you was my only concern," Agos said. "I didn't really think that far ahead. And now that you're here..."

"Yes, alone and abandoned by my personal guard, with a nation that doesn't seem like it wants to send help for its queen any time soon, *all* while being hunted by assassins from an unknown source." I didn't want to talk about Rayyel's involvement in the whole thing, not to Agos. If he found out about the assassins, nothing would stop him from killing my husband. "I think I need to get to the bottom of this."

"I've heard," Agos grumbled, "that the Oren-yaro lords knew exactly where you were."

I didn't answer him. Who knew what my bannermen did or didn't know? My advisers were asked to keep quiet, but clearly some hadn't.

"I've also heard," Agos continued, "that even though they all know, they refuse to send aid. I rode up there when news of your disappearance broke out, you understand. Found Lord General Ozo first. Demanded to know why he wasn't sending out soldiers, why your lords weren't doing a damn thing. He told me, 'Dropping soldiers on lands already hostile to us—do you want war on our doorstep, boy?' I begged him for men, that I would come find you myself and keep discreet, but he said he didn't want to risk the other warlords learning he had done so under their noses, and what was I doing there anyway, what did I care? I gave up my position to Nor."

"You're still angry about that," I said.

He shrugged. "You're my queen. You can do whatever you want with me."

I didn't want the conversation to go down that way, not so soon after our reunion, but it seemed like I wouldn't have a choice in the matter. "Good for you to remember. I wonder if Nor does. Make those arrangements."

Agos opened his mouth to argue. I turned to face him.

"Did you come here for your queen, Agos? Or was there something else?"

He hesitated. He probably didn't know it, but it was the most dangerous hesitation he had ever made in his whole life. I was on the edge—I really didn't know whom to trust anymore—and his sudden appearance was more than I knew how to deal with. But before my thoughts could take me any further, he dropped his head and thumped his chest with his fist.

"My queen," he said. A simple phrase. My insides unbuckled. Relief, but also grief, flooded me. I wondered if I could ever hear Agos's voice again without those two emotions intertwining.

The arrangements Agos spoke of involved an herb and tea shop, which a woman fitting Nor's description was said to frequent, and a letter indicating that I would wait for her in the inn Agos was staying at.

I questioned the sanity of such a bold move. What gain would there be in showing a potential enemy my hand far too soon? Agos's response was the clink of the sword he carried on his belt. I leaned back on my chair and watched the motion with concern. This Agos, seething with barely contained fury, was not the Agos I had known in my youth. I watched him pace in front of the door like a caged beast, breathing through his mouth.

"We don't even know if she'll come," I said.

"She will," Agos grumbled, casting a quick glance at me. "Old bitch's been looking for you, too."

"And you didn't think to mention that?"

He crossed the room to stand in front of me. "She lost you," he said in a low voice. "As far as I'm concerned, the only thing left for her to do after she shows up is to kill herself in the most horrific manner in the courtyard in Oka Shto in front of *all* your guard to make them think twice about ever failing you again." He paused long enough to let out a huff of air through his nostrils.

"Please do not hurt her," I said. "Not until I've talked to her, at least."

"I can't promise that."

"Agos—"

He placed his hands on my shoulders. "You are too gullible," he said. "For all that you are the most intelligent woman I know."

"Thank you for that observation," I said, irritated. "Now, if we're done criticizing me..." I tried to push him away.

"An entire guard, and you never thought to question any of them?"

"Captain Nor and Magister Arro were there. I thought that was enough. When I learned Rayyel was—" I realized my mistake and closed my mouth, but it was too late. Agos's eyes widened.

"Rayyel," he said, speaking the name like it was cursed. "He was here?"

"You must have heard that this journey had something to do with him," I said, glancing away.

"Of course," he grumbled. "It's always been about him."

"Don't give me that. He sent me a message. It was *my* responsibility to see it through."

"Tali..."

"*Queen* Talyien."

"My queen," he snarled. "There is a difference between trying to find information on a slippery eel and actually speaking with the cursed creature. *Was* he here? Did you actually see and speak with him? After everything he's done to you?"

I didn't answer. I heard him groan. "You were ever the fool when it came to that man."

"Dragonlord or not, he is still your lord. I should have your head for this insolence."

"But you won't."

"Do not test me, Agos."

He pressed his face close to mine. I thought he would kiss me.

I heard three sharp knocks on the door and quickly turned my head. He pulled away, placing his hand on the hilt of his sword. I caught myself and got up to follow him. "Come in," he said in a low voice.

The door slid open. Captain Nor was there, as we expected—a thinner, paler version of her former self. But what struck me dumb was the woman behind her, one whom I had last seen bellowing out orders for her men to capture me: Anya Kaz, wife of the leader of the Blue Rok Haize bandits.

I went for my dagger. Agos, seeing the movement, drew his sword.

Nor stumbled into the room and fell at my feet.

I glanced at Anya. She hadn't moved a muscle the entire time. I turned back to Nor. "My queen," she said without looking up. "Oh, my queen. I had given you up for dead."

"She almost didn't believe she'd see you again," Anya Kaz piped up.

"Be silent, worm!" Nor cried out. She crawled forward, close enough to lay her forehead on my boot.

"Get up," I said, pulling her to her feet. "Cousin. There's no need for this."

She rose, swaying slightly. Her eyes were red. She grabbed both of my hands, pressing them on her forehead. "I failed you, Beloved Queen. I promised Magister Arro I wouldn't lose you again and yet..." Her face tightened. "You may have my life, only allow me to get you back home first. You can do what you want with me after."

"I was just suggesting the same thing," Agos said. "A public suicide hasn't been seen in Oren-yaro since Warlord Yeshin's time."

She turned, noticing him for the first time. "Agos," she growled. "What are you doing here?"

"I had to fix what you fucked up. Don't tell me you have it under control. Look around you."

I expected Nor to argue. She was still a royal; he wasn't. Instead, she dropped her head in resignation. "I... don't. I can admit that. I was looking for enemies in all the wrong places. My queen," she said, giving me another bow. "We were betrayed. Half my men killed the others while you were in the Silver Goose. It happened so quickly. I was surrounded before I knew it."

"You hand-picked these men?" Agos asked.

"I did," Nor replied. "I had no reason to suspect any of them."

"None loyal to Rayyel? To Lushai?"

"They were all Oren-yaro," Nor said. "Veterans who had served for years. Saka was one of them. He was one of Captain Agos's, if I recall."

"Before the city watch killed him, Saka told me he had warned you some of the guards were acting strangely."

"Saka was being argumentative the whole trip through. I suspected he was simply trying to undermine order. Order is important. Without discipline, our morals falter. We... we're Oren-yaro." When she would once say these things with certainty and pride, there was now a hint of desperation in her voice, as if she was trying to convince herself instead of me. Oren-yaro, indeed. The word that united our province, the tenets behind it, was starting to lose all meaning. Our own had betrayed us.

"I think I need to sit down," I murmured. But I didn't trust my own feet to take me all the way back to the chair. I didn't think I'd ever see the day I would hear of Oren-yaro turning against their oaths and killing their brothers in cold blood. And for what? Money? How much money could buy honour? My father's men *died* for him, even when the Ikessars were burning their homes and slaughtering their families in secret. Was it me? Did I inspire so little confidence from my people that they were willing to forget their vows and abandon their duties?

We are swords first. Servants first.

I glanced at Agos.

For all their talk, those royals wouldn't know duty if it bit them in the ass.

"As heart-warming as this reunion seems to be, I find I must intervene," Anya Kaz said. "This woman promised me a reward for helping her locate you."

"I promised you your head for helping," Nor replied. "I said you could be rewarded once the queen is back home, sitting on the throne where she belongs."

"You didn't exactly phrase it that way."

Nor turned, her hand on her sword.

Anya held out her hands. "I was just reminding you..."

"We need to get home. You will help us find passage back. Weren't you just telling me about some big thing happening at the docks right now? How about you go over there to take a look?"

Anya pursed her lips, but after a moment, she stepped out and closed the door behind her. I heard Nor give a sigh of relief.

"I hope this one is more trustworthy than your hand-picked men," Agos drawled.

"She's a bandit," I answered for Nor.

Agos was dumbfounded for a moment. And then he broke out in laughter. "You've a gift, Nor!" he declared.

I could see Nor's face turning red. "We've met before," I spoke up for her. "If Nor promised her a reward, we can at least be reasonably sure she's working for personal gain and not for our enemy."

"Who *is* the enemy?" Agos asked.

I licked my lips. "I don't know," I said. I turned to Nor. "Do you?"

Nor shook her head. "During the attack, I escaped over the wall in the alley. After I was able to shake off my pursuers, I went straight to the city watch. The bastards laughed in my face before putting me behind bars for spreading *false rumours* about the Silver Goose."

"Was that during that same night?"

"It was the morning after."

"After they killed Saka. I'm surprised they didn't kill you, too."

"I half expected them to. I was there for a few weeks before they let me go. I made my way here to Dar Aso, where I learned Magister Arro had been killed in the Silver Goose and that news of your disappearance has spread to Jin-Sayeng. Someone was bragging about having seen you heading north, and I tracked the information down to this woman, Anya Kaz. I was able to ... coerce her ... into my service, but we couldn't find any info on you. The last man who claimed to have any knowledge was this businessman over at Shang Azi, Han Lo Bahn. But he didn't believe you were the queen. He called you ..." Her eyes flicked over to Agos. "Well, it doesn't matter."

"What the hell did he call her?" Agos asked.

"I said it doesn't matter."

"Everything matters, you crone. This is how shit like *half your men killed each other* happens."

"Are you saying you would have done a better job, Agos?" Nor asked. I had heard her yell at her men before, but not like this. "Because the last time I recalled, you were the one who voluntarily left your post. I didn't make you do it."

"If I had known she would be left in hands as incompetent as yours ..."

"It was not," I broke in, "your decision, Agos. Enough with this argument."

"I don't know if we should trust her," Agos insisted.

"And I don't know if we can trust *you*," Nor replied. "You left the queen once. What's to stop you from doing it again?"

"I said enough!" If they were dogs, I would've thrown a bucket of water at them by now. I grabbed Agos's thick arm to try to pull him out of the way. "Maybe if you're that concerned, you can help the bandit with our travel arrangements."

"Like hell if you think I'm leaving you with *her*."

I held my breath and turned to Nor, who looked like she wanted to stick her sword in him. "Agos," I said. "Out."

"But—"

"Now!"

That last command came down like a headsman's axe. He stepped away, slamming the door so hard I thought it would bounce back. I found myself sinking into the chair now, my hand on my head.

Nor heaved a soft sigh of relief. "What happened to him?" she asked. "He was always a hard-ass, but not like this, and never in front of *you*." She stopped, as if suddenly aware she was, in fact, speaking to *me*. "My apologies, my queen. I did not mean…"

"It's all right," I said in a low voice. "I think after everything, we can at least talk more openly, can't we?"

She stared at me.

"Well, maybe not," I said with a sigh. "But do me a favour and be patient with him. I'm sure the last few years have been rough."

"I…" She stopped herself.

"Speak freely, Captain Nor."

"Some of us thought he had followed Lord Rayyel into his self-imposed exile," Nor said.

I smiled. "You don't have to lie for my sake, Nor. I know you've heard the rumours. Don't even pretend you haven't. From the highest-ranking lords of Oren-yaro right down to the kitchen maids…we all know about the queen's *debased* activities. As if Agos would ever *follow* Rayyel on purpose. No—you know I sent him away to protect him."

"There are always rumours, my queen. Shall I tell you of the ones about Lord Rayyel and the monkey?"

My lips quirked into a smile. "Maybe another time." I glanced out the window, but my thoughts had barely had time to wander when I heard stomping out from the hall. The door slid open, and Agos walked back in, a scowl on his bearded face.

"We have a problem," he said.

"We have lots of problems," Nor grumbled. "What's another one?"

"Spare me your attempts at humour, *captain*," he hissed. He turned to me. "The innkeeper told me on my way out. There was an announcement just now, straight from the docks. There's an embargo. No ship, chartered or otherwise, is allowed to sail to Jin-Sayeng on pain of death."

CHAPTER TWENTY-FOUR

THE LORD OF SHANG AZI, REPRISED

ᛏᛁᛗ

After a moment of silence, I uttered a sigh. "Well, of course. The gods rain shit and fire on mere mortals."

Agos looked at me, a line of irritation on his face. I think he must've expected a better reaction from me—perhaps one befitting a queen. But I was too exhausted to care what he thought.

"On *pain of death* sounds excessive," Nor said. "Even when we were at war with the empire, they never prohibited ships going to Jin-Sayeng. Even when Dragonlord Reshiro put a stop to *our* ships going here, they didn't seem rankled. Why now?"

"Isn't it obvious?" I asked. "*I* happened."

"They want to stop you from going home," Nor said.

"You don't even know who *they* is," Agos said. "Neither of you. And you wouldn't have had to if you had been wise enough to stay at home."

"It's a little too late for blame," I mumbled.

Nor stepped towards him. "I would advise you to watch your tone when speaking with the queen."

Agos snorted. "This tone…"

"Agos," I said. "Leave it be."

Nor turned to me and bowed. "I'm going to find Anya. Perhaps we'll get to the bottom of this."

I got up as soon as she and Anya disappeared around the hall. "We should follow them," I said. "I hate just sitting around, something which probably isn't the wisest thing to do, anyway. I'm really not in the mood to deal with assassins right now."

Agos blocked me with his arm. "How long since you've last slept?"

"I can still stand. I think I'll be all right."

"I can smell wine on your breath."

"Hardly your concern. And it's beer, if you must really know. Move aside, Agos."

He didn't. "Five years ago..."

I didn't meet his eyes. "It is all over. Let us not speak of it again."

"And Thanh?"

"What about your prince?" I kept my voice nonchalant and placed my hands on his arm. He drew a deep breath.

"My prince? Is he, really?" A question for a question. He lifted my chin with his other hand. *Now* he kissed me, hard, his tongue grazing my teeth as he drew me deeper into his arms. My knees buckled before I had the sense to push him away.

He stared back at me, eyes defiant. I wiped my lips. "To the docks," I hissed.

"As my queen commands."

We walked in silence all the way to the docks.

Agos had served as captain of the guard for only two years, promoted by Lord General Ozo himself not long before my son was born. Who else to better protect the soon-to-be queen, Lord Ozo had exclaimed, than the man who had been at her side since birth? The old lord's fondness for Agos ever since he had gone to his keep to train with the Orenyaro military was no secret... Lord Ozo had been so disappointed, and so angry with me, when I sent Agos away.

I could not blame him. He was right about Agos—never was there a man more dutiful, and in his service to me I had never once questioned his loyalty. But I was starting to realize, with a sinking feeling, that the world did not turn on loyalty alone. That even a man who would never betray me had his own definition of what it meant. *Stay away*, I clearly remember telling him, and yet here he was. And I would send him away again, only I was at a point where I could count the number of my friends with one hand. I didn't want to end up with a closed fist.

We reached the fisherman's wharf, where I spotted Anya waiting outside the harbour master's office. Her arms were crossed, and there was a smug look on her face. "Maybe you should tell your captain that arguing with officials in Anzhao City is the fastest way to get noticed," she said. "And I don't mean in a good way."

"Nor knows what she's doing," I said.

Agos opened his mouth.

"I *know*," I told him quickly. "Just leave it." I turned back to Anya. "Is it true, though? An embargo on Jin-Sayeng?"

"That's what I was told," Anya said. "Looks like you're stuck here."

"Which means you're not going to get paid any time soon."

She shrugged. "I could always sell you to Lo Bahn. I hear he's still looking for you, and he's pretty generous under the right circumstances."

"Don't be an idiot. Han Lo Bahn will pay you a whore's ransom, not a queen's," I said. "And that's also supposing I'll let you walk away with your head intact."

Anya rolled her eyes. "You people are so humourless. I'm jesting. Believe me, I know what you're worth—your Captain Nor made sure I know that much. Still, that embargo isn't going away any time soon. I'd suggest taking a different boat to An Mozhi City by the Ruby Grove lands, if you can get there before word of this gets out. Maybe there you'll find some clueless fisherman willing to risk it all."

"What do you mean?" I asked. "This order came from Anzhao?"

"Requested and signed by Governor Gon Zheshan himself," Anya said. "A messenger carrying Emperor Yunan's approval arrived this morning."

I felt light-headed. "He's trying to flush me out."

"Gon Zheshan?" Anya asked. She whistled. "You've got enemies in high places, I can tell you that. But you can see why I'd rather help *you* instead. Those bastards would all see me and my husband hanged if they had their way."

"I think I understand what's happening," I said, looking up just as Nor joined us, a dejected look on her face. I switched to Jinan. "Kora told me that Governor Zheshan has Rayyel in his custody. It was why I went all the way to Zorheng to try to get Governor Ong's assistance on the matter. I learned there that Ong was nothing more than a puppet to Prince Yuebek, Emperor Yunan's Fifth Son. Yuebek wanted to force my hand in marriage. A play for power. I barely escaped from there with my life."

Nor absorbed this information without a flicker on her face. "If Zheshan still has Lord Rayyel, we have to save him," she said.

"*What for?*" Agos broke in. "After what that man did to you, you would come crawling after him like a bitch in heat?"

"Agos, I'm warning you..." Nor started.

"My respects, yes, I know. But perhaps *the queen* needs some sense knocked into her!" Agos roared. "Take my head for it if you want to. He left you. He left Thanh. Have you heard from him at all in five years? Where was he when you were at death's door with the moon-fever? Or when Darusu was accosted by rebels yet again and you had to ride out there half-dead from your illness? Did he send you a letter when Thanh broke his leg from falling off his horse?"

I didn't know he had been keeping track of these things. Hearing them from his lips made me feel ill. "Are you done?" I asked in a level voice.

He flushed, as if suddenly ashamed. "I've been waiting to say that for years. I…"

"Did you only come here to lecture me?"

"I came here to save you," he breathed.

"Like a hero, come to rescue the maiden? Is that why you decided to break my command? You wanted to rush into my first stumble. Which meant you've been watching me, like the rest of Jin-Sayeng, waiting for me to fail."

"Think whatever you want. You know it's not true. And you need me—that much is plain."

I laughed. "I am grateful to have your company, Agos, believe me, but I will not have this argument. Not with *you*. I've had it more times with more pompous fools in the land than I care to remember." I took several deep breaths in quick succession, trying to control my rage the way Arro taught me once after I had thrown a potted plant near his face. I turned to Anya and spoke in Zirano once more. "Walk with me to Shang Azi. You two," I said, pointing at Agos and Nor. "Stay here and learn what you can about this whole thing."

"My queen," they both barked at the same time.

"And learn to get along, while you're at it. If I had dogs who snapped at each other as much as you did, I'd have them castrated."

"Why would you want to go to Shang Azi?" Anya asked.

"I'm tired of having to explain myself," I said. "Either obey, or find a new employer." I paused, waiting for her, for any of them, to protest. "Nothing? *Good.* Then let's go." I started walking.

———

"You have interesting guards," Anya said, catching up to me.

"They're stubborn. It is, unfortunately, a trait of our people."

"I can believe it," Anya said. "The things I've heard them say you did…"

"What *have* you heard?"

Anya's face crinkled as she smiled. "Oh, little things. Escaping Lo Bahn's men not once, but twice. Tricking him into getting you out of Ziori's. A fine job, by the way, but you should have made it so that she lost money during the whole deal. And of course, we can't overlook our favourite physician's infatuation with you. This street leads to his house. But you already know that, don't you?"

"He's not a physician," I said.

Anya laughed. "He doesn't charge us anything, which makes him a damn better doctor than some of the others in the city. And he doesn't turn us in to the city watch, which makes him the best, guild or no guild. Ah, speak of the devil. Lamang!"

Khine was outside, sweeping the street in front of his house. At the sight of us, he stopped, and I saw his fingers clench tightly around the broom. "Anya Kaz," he said. "What is this?"

"Not what it looks like," Anya replied. "For once, anyway." She seemed to find this amusing.

"It's a long story," I added. "She works for me now." I craned my head at his front door. "Is there anyone at home?"

"No."

"May I come in? I'd like to talk. Alone." I gave Anya a look.

Anya grinned at me. "I'll hang out here, whistle if I see Lo Bahn's men." She started down the street to where a group of men were huddled around a table for a card game of some sort. They cheered when she arrived, clearly recognizing her. One even offered her a bowl of his own drink, which she politely declined. That sort of comradery and respect was foreign to me.

I turned my attention away from them and followed Khine indoors. As soon as the door closed behind me, I was hit with a rush of relief, as if I had entered a world where my title and my responsibilities were no longer weighing me down. I had not realized how much I had been holding in until that moment. I meticulously removed my shoes and went upstairs, lingering by the top landing. It was the sensation of having come home even though I was still so very far from it.

"How much would you trust Anya Kaz?" I asked, as a way to distract myself from the myriad of confusing thoughts.

"Depends on the circumstances," Khine said. "*Her* own interests, along with Jiro's, come first, and if yours align with that, then I don't see a problem. They're not idiots. But why are you with her? What happened to your, uh—companion?" He hesitated at the last word.

"He was a former guard." I glanced around. The cramped common room still looked exactly as when I had left it, and even the book I had been reading on that last morning was laid flat on top of the shelf, as if someone had placed it there after the events and forgotten about it. I also recognized the same blankets and pillows with the red floral embroidery that he had lent to me during my stay, folded in the exact same corner. And yet everything that had happened before Yuebek's palace felt like a lifetime ago.

"Former *guard*?" Khine asked, quirking an eyebrow.

A foolish smile crept up my face, like a dog seeking appeasement. "Guard," I repeated. "We were also childhood friends. I suppose that makes a difference." I took a deep breath and spotted Olliver near the kitchen. I called for him. He darted towards me, his tail a straight line, and got up to put his paws on my knee. He rubbed his face on my outstretched fingers, filling the room with his purring.

"Don't get too flattered," Khine snorted. "He acts like everyone is a long-lost friend." He picked the cat up and draped him over his shoulder. "I have to admit—I'm impressed that you could get Anya Kaz to listen to you like that. She wasn't very happy when I gave her the slip back at that inn."

"She has incentive," I said. "She's been promised a hefty reward when I get home. *If* I get home."

"Remind her exactly how hefty, and you have her loyalty for life. The Blue Rok Haize haven't exactly been doing well these days, what with merchants hiring expensive guards to get them through the roads and the scouts getting dangerously close to sniffing out her village. I haven't seen Jiro Kaz since we met him out on the road." Olliver made a soft grumble, and Khine set him down again. The cat rushed back to my leg.

Khine laughed. "What do you know? Maybe he does like you better."

"I may have overfed him when I was staying here." I sat against the wall, and Olliver immediately took the opportunity to curl up on my lap. I sank my fingers into his rough coat.

I felt Khine's eyes on me. "Why are you here, Tali?" he asked.

I smiled. Not *Queen Talyien*. I liked how he pretended to forget. I didn't think I would've tolerated that sort of brazen informality from anyone else I had known for as short an amount of time. "I told you I'd come by."

"So you did."

"And my guards were getting on my nerves."

"Oh, so they've multiplied?"

"They tend to. Queens, you know. Can't even feed ourselves without issue."

"I've seen you eat. I can almost agree with that."

"That's mean-spirited, Lamang."

"And the way you try to wash dishes..."

I threw a spare cushion at him. Olliver, finding much to be amused by in this, dug his claws into my pants and purred a little louder.

Khine laughed. I had forgotten how much I missed his voice. The pressure from my arguments with Agos and Nor dissipated almost instantly. *I could*, I thought, *listen to this voice forever.*

I petted Olliver. "Right after we parted this morning," I said, returning to a more sombre tone, "word got out from the docks. There's an embargo on ships leaving for Jin-Sayeng."

From the look on his face, it was the first time he had heard the news. "Governor Zheshan's orders?" he asked, taking the cushion to sit next to me.

I nodded. "My guards are trying to get to the bottom of things."

"I highly doubt an embargo would stop the Jin-Sayeng fishermen from trying to get home." He took a deep breath. "But this isn't about trying to find a way home, is it?"

"Since when did you learn how to read me?"

"Since the day I first met you," he said.

"That's disconcerting."

"Oh, I've been told that before. Disconcerting. Unsettling. Creepy." He started petting Olliver. "So tell me what's on your mind."

"Governor Gon Zheshan gave this order," I said. "So it's reasonable to suggest that he could rescind it, right?"

"I can't really say. I don't know much about politics."

"What do you know about relations between Anzhao City and Zorheng City?"

He tightened his face. "What relations? There are none."

"I'm not surprised." I fell silent for a few moments, and then I turned to him and found myself telling him about Zorheng City—Yuebek, Zhu's death, and my escape. I left the part out about the ghosts; I didn't want him thinking I had gone mad. But I told him about the assassins, about finding that note and how I knew it was my husband's handwriting even though it wasn't signed. Khine never said a word during my story, even when I found myself choking through parts of it. When I finally stopped, he set the cat aside and took my hand.

"Come with me," he said.

I stared down. It felt wrong to allow myself to take so much comfort from him, but I couldn't help it. And anyway, I wasn't sure if he would be offended or not if I pulled away immediately. I found myself nodding.

I followed him up to the loft. Here, Khine let go of my hand in order to push the window open. "After you," he said, gesturing at the roof-top ledge. I remembered clambering down that same ledge to escape Lo Bahn's men and smiled.

"You sure know how to treat a lady." I climbed out. The air was dry, with a slight chilling bite, unlike that cold, wet morning. Yellow sunlight bounced off the rooftops, making the layer of frost sparkle. To see beauty cast over what should have been a wretched place made me take a deep breath. I sank next to the window as Khine heaved himself after me.

"A speck of dirt compared to the riches you're used to," Khine said, clearing his throat. "If I had known you were a queen when you first came here..." He trailed off, scratching the stubble on his cheek.

"You suspected I was someone."

He smiled. "Not a queen."

"And yet..." I indicated his informal stance with a wave.

He flushed red. "Deep inside, we're just people."

"Are you telling me that? Or yourself? If you had known I was royalty, you would have never offered me hospitality," I pointed out.

"The things I've said before..." He was clearly embarrassed, but he didn't offer an apology.

"It's why I came back here," I said. "I've never known that kind of honesty in my life. I...I need it now, more than ever." I glanced away. My elders would have frowned over admitting weakness in front of a stranger. Or was he a friend now? I didn't even know my own husband— did it matter?

He sat next to me. After a moment's deliberation, he offered his hand again. I paused before accepting it. "You can't be sure it was him," he said.

I blinked back my tears. "Have you ever read someone's letters so often that you know his brushstrokes by heart?"

"His? No. Her?" He gave a sad smile.

"Then you know the sort of foolishness I'm talking about."

"I don't know if I want to call it foolishness."

"It is. He knew I loved him."

"And why shouldn't you love and trust this man, the one they've all wanted you to marry since birth? You said he had never lifted a hand against you. Has he always treated you fairly?"

"Why shouldn't he have? I would have never tolerated it otherwise. But no matter how you cover it up with words, our marriage is political, and politics—to our families—come first. He tricked me into going all the way out here and then tricked me into thinking Gon Zheshan had him imprisoned when it's clear that he's *willingly* working with him. Because he wants me dead. And I, like a fool..." I finally slid my hand from his and folded my arms over my knees. "I can't even tell my guards. If word of this gets out, there will be civil war. The warlords will feel like they have to pick a side. Some will feign insult. It will be a bloodbath. Always at the edge of a bloodbath, the damned fools..." I closed my eyes. "I will not revive my father's legacy. I cannot."

"I think," Khine said gently, "that it's no longer up to you. You can't honestly think you can control everything your warlords and their lords do. Even now, it's clear that they're moving on their own, queen's approval be damned. The fate of your nation is out of your hands."

"Such comfort," I drawled.

He smirked. "The truth, nothing more. You make it seem as if this whole thing hinged on you maintaining this marriage. You never considered the snakes around you? That perhaps you actually succeeded against all odds? How many betrothals fall apart within the year? Yet as much as your clans hated each other, you tried to make it work. You fulfilled your duties. You bore them an heir. Twenty-six years, you kept this thing at bay. Now that the inevitable unrest has arrived, why should you blame only yourself? What about the man who was supposed to shoulder half this burden?"

I stared at the floor and didn't reply.

"I don't know if you want a con artist's opinion," he said.

"I'm not sure I can stop you from giving it."

"You know me too well." He paused, as if mulling over his words. "The last time you spoke with Rayyel, you were set up. Regardless of who orchestrated the plans, the fact is, *you* were the mark and you were walking straight into a trap. You said you were supposed to meet elsewhere, and then things changed at the last minute, which led you to the Silver Goose, where your men were neatly disposed of with you none the wiser. In the meantime, you were at a meeting where the talk was going nowhere because it wasn't supposed to—it was supposed to be a distraction until the assassins arrived, probably at a time when there were no other patrons in the restaurant.

"So at no point were you in a position where you could discuss—*freely* discuss—things with Rayyel. You never found the opportunity to come to a resolution. In the Silver Goose, he was as much of a mark as you were. Perhaps he wants you dead. He didn't before, or he'd have already knifed you in bed back home, or sent assassins at least once over the last five years. So only a recent thing made him want to kill you, and if you want to find out what and how you could maybe change his mind back so you can work together long enough to get your nation out of this mess, then you need to go to Gon Zheshan and talk to your husband when he least expects it, when he's got no one else whispering in his ear."

I stared at Khine. "You think it's going to be that easy?"

"No," he said, finally looking up with a smile. "But it's a start. From what it sounds like, your lords already think you've abandoned your duties. I hardly think they'll *believe* you if you told them that *no*, here I am everyone, silly me, it turns out I just missed my ship!"

"I don't sound like that."

"So you're going to need Rayyel's support."

"And you think Gon Zheshan is just going to let me walk in there and entertain me?"

Khine smiled. "That's where the con artist bit comes in."

I saw the glint in his eyes. "You're suggesting a ruse."

"A grand one. They won't see it coming. You'll drop in on him unexpected. We don't even need to get him out—we can just have him sign a letter for your council, figure out how to get it to Jin-Sayeng after. There must be a way."

I digested his words in silence. "I suppose it's worth the risk. But... if we're going through all that trouble, a letter alone won't do it. You think my warlords like to *read*?"

"What do you mean?"

"We get Rai out." I chewed on my lip. "I don't think he'll want us to."

"You're suggesting we take him by force?"

"You said yourself I need to speak with him freely, as we are. That's not going to happen when he's surrounded by these people."

Khine scratched his cheek. "I suppose I can come up with something. Would be the first time I've had to make an entire man disappear, but I like challenges. Is he, ah... heavy? This husband of yours?"

"Agos can carry him," I said.

"Your guard didn't seem to like me."

"Believe me, he likes Rayyel even less." I folded my hands together and got up. "It's decided, then. A ruse. I haven't even asked what you're getting out of this."

"Helping a friend isn't an answer?"

I touched his cheek. The smirk on his face faded.

"You haven't lived in a world where that's enough, have you?" he asked.

I shook my head.

"Very well." Khine took my wrist away. "You're not going to like how this begins, anyway."

"What do you mean?"

"To get this ruse started, we need a reason to see Governor Zheshan. A reason that he can't possibly deny. And to do that, we need to speak with Han Lo Bahn."

Neither Ziori nor Tati, from the whorehouse, ever clarified exactly what being a lord of Shang Azi meant.

Khine explained to me that a city as large as Anzhao meant that inevitably, certain neighbourhoods fall through the cracks. With very little restrictions, houses were built on top of each other, causing the streets to become dark and narrow and allowing crime to become rampant. The city watch abhorred sending out guards to such places, as they saw it as a waste of time and money. As a "favour" to city officials, certain enterprises would hire their own men to keep the peace. What these businesses actually enforced depended on the city official they were involved with and any number of things such as bribes, marriage arrangements, partnerships, or family ties, most of which had nothing whatsoever to do with the law.

Such illicit activities were not unknown in Jin-Sayeng, especially in the west, but I think I had never expected that Anzhao City's officials would openly acknowledge such people. Yet it seemed that they did: I noticed uniformed members of the city watch lounging around the steps leading to Lo Bahn's house. The house itself was not as large as Deputy

Qun's mansion, but it seemed oddly out of place in that neighbourhood, sprouting up from between the cramped buildings and tight alleyways.

The sight of the city watch made Anya visibly uncomfortable, although she didn't say anything. Neither did Khine. I heard snippets of the men's conversation and gathered that they were trading winnings from the gambling halls, as well as talking about their favourite whores and the various positions in which they liked to take them. I turned to my guards, both of whom didn't try to hide the distaste on their faces.

"To let the queen sink so low..." Agos murmured, directing his ire towards Nor.

"We need to focus," I said.

"I don't know if I can," Agos grumbled. "Working with such men. I would've clouted my own soldiers for speaking like that around company. Perhaps I can understand if the others had to resort to it. The lords of the Sougen hire mercenaries. They do it in Kyo-orashi and Meiokara, too. But you are of the Oren-yaro. You have battle-honed soldiers willing and ready to fight for you at any moment, and loyal..."

"Remember," Nor broke in. "It was Oren-yaro who betrayed us, too."

"Whoever the hell those men were, *clearly* they were not true Oren-yaro. You don't just pick the queen's personal guard from a dung heap. You must've missed something."

Nor rolled her eyes. "And where were you, in all this? Oh, that's right..."

"Please," Khine broke in. "Most of these people probably can't understand you, but they can tell you're arguing, and that's just going to make our case even harder."

"Don't let me get started about this one," Agos hissed. "The scum you're surrounded with these days..."

"Should I ask the queen to leave you outside?" Khine asked sweetly.

"Maybe they can find bones for you to chew on," Nor added.

I struggled to keep a straight face and stepped ahead of them to greet what I thought had been a servant at first. It turned out to be Inzali. She bowed, her freckled face crumpling into a half smile. "Lo Bahn is expecting you," she said.

I took her hands in mine. "Inzali…" I began.

"We won't talk about this here," she said. "If my brother said anything, forget about it for now. He can be a bit—what's that word?"

"Stupid?" Khine offered.

"*Idiotic* also works." She cleared her throat as she led us into a large common room, where we were asked to remove our shoes. Servants came to whisk them away, and I found myself thinking that if *this* meeting went badly, I didn't want to escape through a window and land on the street in my socks. Another set of servants came for our weapons.

This time, I hesitated. "We don't want trouble," Inzali said. "And Lo Bahn has learned that you are more deadly with a blade than he has been led to believe."

"Do as they ask," Khine murmured. "He will not betray us."

I unstrapped the dagger and nodded at Nor and Agos, who bristled at the notion. "If worst comes to worst, you can always tear a leg off a table," I suggested.

Agos stared at me. He eventually took off his sword, nearly ripping it off his belt, and threw it across the floor so that a servant had to chase after it.

We were led to the middle of the room. Cushions had already been set out, and trays of fruit: mangoes, rambutans, plums, lychees, sapodillas. More servants arrived, this time to pour wine. My guards refused them, but I drank enough for three. My nerves were beginning to fray.

"You're under Lo Bahn's employ," I observed as Inzali dismissed the servants.

She nodded. "For less pay than what he would have hired me for, but then he wouldn't have known my value otherwise. I also tutor his children. Why? Did my brother make you think he took me in as his whore?"

"Clearly, your brother has problems in articulation," Khine offered. He smiled at me. "It was, ah—a confusing time. Inzali took care of everything. She always does."

"Not everything," Inzali murmured.

"What do you mean by that?"

Her face flickered. "Our family's troubles aren't yours to solve, Queen Talyien. Don't you have a kingdom to rule?"

A bell rang. I turned to see Lo Bahn descend from the staircase. The entire chamber fell silent.

For all his bulk, Lo Bahn walked deliberately. This was a man who knew he wielded power and didn't have to make any efforts to show it. I remembered Prince Yuebek, in comparison—hurling himself at his servants, demanding they do more, *be* more, to make his authority clear. Lo Bahn didn't have to do any of these things. A cabinetmaker's son, Khine had told me, not an emperor's, yet he carried himself with more pride than Yuebek ever did. I had spent weeks in utter fear of the man, but seeing him now, I was more in awe than anything else. How could I be the one falling silent when *he* was the one entertaining a queen?

"We meet again, Kora," Lo Bahn said, his voice filling the room. Even his choice of words was deliberate. "Or shall I call you Queen Talyien, now? I can never really tell. Are you here to tell me to whisk you away to safety so you could lie to my face about my performance afterwards?"

"A necessary deceit at the time," I answered.

"I should have you punished," he said. "A woman just doesn't take Han Lo Bahn for a fool like that."

"All due respect, my lord, but she did." I flashed him a smile.

He snorted, but a moment later, as if just remembering his manners, he bowed. "Perhaps I *should* be glad I was outwitted. I believe you would have my head now otherwise."

"Believe me, I am just as glad that you let yourself be fooled. Decapitations can be so inconvenient."

His nostrils flared. "What brings you to my humble abode, carrying garbage?" His eyes fell on Anya Kaz, who laughed.

"Let's put our differences aside for now, Lo Bahn," Anya said. "It's not every day we have a queen in our midst. It will be something to talk about for years to come."

"A truce, for now," Lo Bahn agreed. He turned back to me. "Lamang tells me you have a proposition."

"I do." I glanced around the room. "But I'm not sure if you are, after all, our best option."

"You have others?" Lo Bahn sounded amused.

"Khine mentioned you may be interested in helping out, but I must confess, Lord Han, that it would look very badly for someone of my position to be seen with people like you. Some would accuse me of having sunk too low, of being so weak that I have no other choice but to seek *your* help." Sometimes the best lies come close to the truth.

Lo Bahn's face twisted into a sneer. "Now you insult me."

"Not an insult but a fact, Lord Han. That, and considering our very... tense first meeting, I'm not sure if this was a wise idea after all." I turned to Khine, whose lips quirked upwards ever so slightly. "Lamang, you assured me he would be *begging* to make amends. I'm not comfortable with having to convince someone of his stature—respectable as I'm sure it is around these parts—to help *my* cause."

"I don't think I used the word *begging*, to be exact..." Khine said.

"Regardless," I insisted, "Lord Han did force me into a precarious situation—several precarious situations, to be honest. Had things turned out differently, he would have done more than simply allow me to *outwit* him. Do we normally let these things pass back in Jin-Sayeng, Captain Nor?"

"No, my queen," Nor said.

"You are not in Jin-Sayeng," Lo Bahn pointed out, his voice rising. "If you think you can threaten me to servitude, you are a poorer judge of character than I thought. Your authority holds no weight here."

"Believe me, Lord Han, you would know if I threatened you," I said. "But there are a number of other lords in this neighbourhood—your rivals, I assume?—who would find more to gain out of helping the queen of Jin-Sayeng than trading insults with her. If this is the hospitality I can expect for the duration of this meeting, then perhaps it's best if we cut it short. Good day, sir." I got up. Almost at once, Nor and Agos turned to follow.

"Queen Talyien," Khine said.

I paused. I heard Lo Bahn cough.

"For the third time, you try to walk away from me." Lo Bahn's voice was curiously low. "I think we need to stop meeting like this." I heard an added *woman* in there, unsaid. This was not a man used to ceding power, even to a queen.

"I'm listening," I said. "Make it quick."

I heard him take a gulping breath, like a drowning man coming up for air. "Tell me what you want. If it is within my authority, I will grant it."

"Now you change your mind. Is this the kind of instability I should expect from you?"

"I never said I wouldn't help you in the first place, wo—my lady." His face twitched.

"Beloved Queen, I think, is how they say it," Khine said helpfully.

"Silence, dog!" Lo Bahn hissed.

I returned to my seat, but not without making it seem like it took some effort. "I need you to speak with Governor Gon Zheshan about sending a request to lift this ridiculous embargo that is preventing me from going back home," I said.

"And what makes you think a man like him will listen to a man like me?"

"Am I mistaken? You do not have Governor Zheshan in your pocket? I had thought you had that much power, at least."

Lo Bahn licked his lips. "He may... grant me audience, if I give him a good enough reason."

"I can think of one. A ship, the *Singing Sainsa*, was found shipwrecked south of Sutan in Jin-Sayeng with an entire season of *your* cargo pilfered from one of your own ships. The dock authorities should've had the sense to inspect the ship before it sailed, yet they never did. He bears responsibility in helping you get back that lost cargo. Of course, to do that, you'd need to travel to Jin-Sayeng in the first place."

"Supposing I did manage to convince him that I'd lost cargo without reporting it," Lo Bahn said, "he wouldn't be at fault. That ship left without proper authorization. Near smashed the docks into smithereens."

"You didn't report it because you didn't think it was stolen. Because one of your ships got all the way south before the crew realized the cargo was missing, and they didn't know *who* to blame until you received word of the shipwreck. As for the governor not being at fault..." I smiled. "I'm sure you can think of a way to put the blame on him. It happens often enough, doesn't it? You just want a quick expedition west. If he will not help lift this embargo that *he* called for, perhaps you can convince him to make an exception."

"And what do I gain, from all of this?"

"I thought keeping your head was clear enough," Agos grumbled under his breath.

I tapped him on the arm, and he closed his mouth. "I have been meaning to return trade with the Zarojo for years," I said, keeping my eyes on Lo Bahn. "And I believe, if we can somehow get me home with at least my dignity intact, I can still bring those plans to fruition a year or two from now. I can send you information that will give you years ahead of your rivals when that occurs. I can also recommend your name to some of the largest merchant companies in Jin-Sayeng. The word of a queen should do a lot to sway things to your favour, shouldn't it?"

I saw his face flicker. The promise of personal gain had been enough. I had him.

"What is the Jinsein way to seal a deal?" he asked.

"We cut ourselves and drink our blood from a cup," I replied. "But for the Oren-yaro, your word is enough."

"To the beginning of a profitable friendship," he said, lifting his wine glass.

I smiled and did the same.

CHAPTER TWENTY-FIVE

THE LAST RUSE

I found myself drinking and feasting with Han Lo Bahn long into the night, pretending to listen to him talk about business and trade and his wife, who was visiting family in Kyan Jang at that moment and was likely to run him into the ground with her spending habits before long. The events from four months ago seemed nothing more than a dream, now. This—the push and play of power, the facade of people acting nothing like they were behind closed doors—was my life. Had always been my life. That woman running for her life in the rain, stripped of her name and title, was a stranger.

It felt unsettling, like having blinders returned right after you had seen the world. I wasn't sure which I preferred. I turned to Khine, who was nodding along, half-asleep, and had the inkling that perhaps I did, only...

We are swords first. Servants first.

"I must confess that it's been a very long day, Lord Han," I said. "We must return to our inn soon, or else we might have to roll my guards out of here."

"You are welcome to stay here," Lo Bahn replied. "I have guest rooms, and my servants are yours to command."

"I believe that after the...awkwardness...of our first meeting, I'd best not," I said. I was really thinking about Yuebek, and all the mistakes I was not eager to make again any time soon. "I did deceive you, Lord Han. Several times over. I would not want to impose after we've had such cordial talk."

"You may have injured my pride a little," Lo Bahn said with a snort. "But all of that belongs to yesterday. In any case, your debts are being repaid."

"Perhaps another time."

He bowed as I left. Inzali appeared by the doorway to return our belongings and accompany us out on the street.

"What does he mean my debts are being repaid?" I asked. "What else happened after I left?"

Inzali simply looked at Khine. "This is *your* mess," she said before she withdrew.

I waited. I realized Khine wasn't talking because Agos and Nor were standing right there, two constant reminders of who I really was and will always be. Since when were other people's concerns my own?

"Go back to the inn," I told my guards. "I just want to take a walk."

They stared at me incredulously.

"With all due respect—" Nor began. "At this hour?"

"It's dark," Agos added. "These streets aren't safe."

"Safe enough for me," I heard Anya say.

"Maybe for a bandit," Agos growled. "Not a queen."

"I've survived it before," I said. "I'll survive it again." I turned to Anya. "We need to make preparations for tomorrow, anyway. You remember what you have to do?"

She smiled. "It'll be glorious."

"Let's not get ahead of ourselves." My guards weren't moving, so I clapped my hands. Only then did they lumber away from me, though I still caught Agos sneaking one last sideways glance.

As soon as they disappeared, I gave a sigh.

Khine appeared near my elbow. "What does it feel like to have other people be so sure of who you are and what you have to do?"

"Horrible," I grumbled. "And you have to stop doing that."

"Doing what?" he asked innocently.

"That thing you do. Just stop." I folded my arms. "You owe me an explanation, I believe."

He gave a small huff. "It's nothing. I came back, and Lo Bahn was still furious. Not entirely unexpected. Inzali's services weren't enough. So I offered mine. I've been his right-hand man the past two months, now."

"So this was what she meant. For until how long?"

"Until he tires of my work? Until he thinks his expenses with Ziori have been sufficiently justified?"

"You should have told me. I mean to pay him back once I've returned."

"It's not about you, Tali," he said. "I lied to him. Caused trouble for his men and went under his nose, after he had been so generous with my family and Cho's debts. He could've had him killed, you know. He's done it to others before."

"Is he even paying you?"

"Once I've made back what he paid Ziori in wages, he says he will."

"So *no*. Gods, Khine…" I shook my head. "You can't do this. Not you or Inzali. Do you mean to waste your talents among lowlifes until the day you die? People like you don't belong here."

"You say that." He shrugged. "Yet here we are."

"You'll never get back to your studies at this rate."

"I've given up on that dream," Khine murmured.

"Why?"

"Why not? The things my mother had to do to afford to send me to Kayingshe Academy in the first place…and where did I end up? Stitching up bandits for a week's supply of eggs or whatever they can offer, just so they can go and cut each other again. And my sisters working their fingers to the bone while Cho's debt grows larger…" His face tightened. "How many tricks can I pull off until the city watch catches me? I wouldn't get far enough to repay Cho's debt, let alone save up for that last year's tuition. What good would I be to my family then? At least as Lo Bahn's man I can earn decent wages at some point. He is generous, in his way. My family's needs come first."

"You'd have to do whatever Lo Bahn asked. Good *or* bad."

"How is that any different from the scams I've pulled?"

"You chose your marks. You had morals."

He smiled. "Big talk from a small man."

"Being chained to Lo Bahn was never your dream."

"What would you know of my dreams? I trampled the little I had to the dust." He caught himself as soon as he spoke, and lowered his head. "I apologize," he mumbled. "I sometimes forget…"

"That I'm a queen? That's exactly why I still talk to you."

We fell quiet and found ourselves walking all the way to the edge of the canal. My eyes wandered down the street, to where I knew the Silver Goose stood. I thought about what tomorrow would bring, about seeing Rai again. Despite everything, that familiar excitement was still there. I had a treacherous heart.

"Have you never asked yourself all these years if duty is all you are?" Khine asked, breaking my thoughts.

"What do you mean?"

"Does what you want ever truly matter?"

I watched the glint of moonlight on the clear water before looking up at him. "I think you can answer that question yourself."

He shook his head. "You are, unfortunately, the expert on such things."

"I was born with that sword in my hands," I said. "How could I walk away? What else is there for me? I want…" I gave a wistful smile. "I want Rai to give up this crusade and come to his senses. To remember all the things that truly matter—our life, our son, everything we once had, for the short amount of time we had it. To…love me, like I loved him."

"And so the prince and the princess together build a lasting peace to the end of their days."

"It was too much to ask for, I suppose," I murmured.

"It was," Khine agreed.

"And you?"

"What about me?"

"Your take on all of this? On duty? Love?"

"I am not Oren-yaro," he said with a smile. "Everything I do is for love."

A boat drifted past us. There was a man there, singing his heart out.

"Your woman missed out when she let you go."

"Do me a favour: if you ever meet her, tell her that."

"Would it change her mind?"

He laughed. "No. Gods, no. She would probably sooner kill herself. Or, no...she'd sooner kill me and then be done with it. What is it with me and stubborn women?"

"Tell me about her."

"I already did."

"No, you were just starting to, before Agos oh-so-gracefully interrupted us."

"Why do you want to know?"

I leaned on the railing so I didn't have to look at him while I spoke. "You said you loved her. I want to know what it sounds like to hear a man talk about the woman he loves."

For a time, he didn't answer, and I was almost afraid I had asked for too much. But then I heard him drift close to me, his mouth by my shoulder. "I met her right here on this street. She had fallen into the canal and was chastising the man who had accidentally knocked her in. I had to see if she was all right, but she was more angry than hurt. Kitten-angry, Inzali liked to call it—more hissing than venom, and she was new to the language, so she was using all the wrong words. I ended up laughing more than I should have, and she left in embarrassment. Wanted nothing to do with me."

"I don't blame her."

"Me neither. I had to find her later, to offer my apologies. I knew she was Jinsein, so I took some time after my classes to ask around in Dar Aso. I was told that she fit the description of a baker's daughter who had just set up shop around the corner, so I went there. She didn't recognize me at first and was politely showing me their freshest loaves, but then I said something that gave me away. She, ah—didn't have the best sense of humour. Screamed and hid in the back and wouldn't come out for hours. I had to buy half their wares that day just to convince her father I hadn't done something despicable to his daughter, and gave all the loaves away to my classmates in Kayingshe the next day."

"An expensive woman."

"Not always. Just that day." He was scratching the railing with his fingers. "She found me herself afterwards. Apologized for her behaviour. Said it was not right for her to act the way she did, especially not after I had acted so honourably. Her words, not mine."

"The Kaitans are very strict about their honour. Almost as strict as the Oren-yaro with our duty. What was her name?"

Khine hesitated. "Jia asor arak Heiro."

"Soldier caste," I said. "But her father, baking bread?"

"I believe he wanted a better life, away from the warlords' meddling."

"He could have gone to the west. You can be whatever what you want in the west, regardless of your name. They wouldn't hold it against you."

"I clearly remember he wasn't fond of the idea of *mad dragons* in your west."

"I can see how those could be detrimental to a thriving bakery business. So Jia…"

"Jia," Khine repeated, and there was a crack in his normally calm voice, a hint of boyish excitement, or at least the faded echo of one. "She started visiting more often. She didn't have many friends—they'd only just arrived, you see. I taught her how to speak better Zirano, and she taught me Jinan. And it...grew from there. Her father did not approve. He liked me well enough, but he wanted to see I was capable of providing for her. An aspiring student is very different from a proper physician, after all."

"You wanted to marry her," I said. I didn't know why that came as a surprise.

He blinked. "Of course. We were talking about it. I wanted to take her back to Phurywa to see my mother, and I thought perhaps the trip could convince her we could live there someday. If I set up shop there..." He fell silent. I saw the struggle in his face, how difficult it must be to be speaking of broken dreams. *Trampled to the dust*, he had said. I wondered exactly what he had meant by saving her life and then ruining it, and then decided it wasn't my place to ask.

"I'm sorry. I shouldn't have made you speak."

"It's all right," Khine said. "I want to speak. The loss does not... diminish the love. And now that the memories are all I have, I still find myself wanting to wander back down that road. Would you believe we were happy for a time? I didn't have much money then—"

"You still don't."

"I had even less. Sometimes I would wake up at the crack of dawn, an hour or so before my classes began, and I would just stare at her face, just drink in all the details of it." He looked at me. "I would imagine how it would change as we grew old, and found myself oddly looking forward to how much more I could love her then. I would think—even if her ears begin to droop or her eyes become crested with wrinkles, I wouldn't mind one bit. And then I would pray to the spirits to stretch the moments a little longer, another second, and then another, as if the flow of time was a thing you could stop somehow. I didn't want to go to Kayingshe—I just wanted her in my arms. The rooster would crow and

I would, eventually, have to leave, but it didn't stop me from thinking about her until I saw her again."

"And you told her these things?" I asked, echoing his words to me back to him.

"Every day," he breathed.

My heart skipped a beat. I turned away from his gaze and stared back at the water.

"It's funny, isn't it?" I heard him continue. "How I would be the one to fuck it all up?"

"So you were wrong. Speaking of love…it wouldn't have changed a thing. You loved each other, and it ended, anyway."

Khine smiled. "Maybe. I don't know. It did make a difference to me. I knew what I was throwing away. But fool that I was…I let myself forget for a moment. It was enough. Enough for her to leave me."

The image of Rayyel walking away that night returned to me. I knew what he meant. "Remind me," I murmured, "why a single moment is enough to outweigh the rest. Why fickle tempers rule over steadfast hearts."

"We listen only to what we want to hear," Khine said. "And see only…"

"What we want to see," I finished for him. I gave a sad smile. "I suppose I do know."

"We all lie to ourselves."

I was the one who had wanted to hear him speak like this, but the emotion in his voice was suddenly unbearable. Old wounds, girlish pride—the hope of ever knowing love like that had long left me. It was enough to have caught a glimpse of it through his eyes. I stood on tiptoe to kiss him on the cheek. Startled, he reached up to touch the spot where my lips had been. It was a thank you and a goodbye.

Agos was waiting for me outside the inn when we returned to those streets. He and Khine exchanged glances. Agos's shoulders rose and fell, a man as much on the cusp of desperation as I was. I was not such a fool that I didn't understand what he was implying, but I didn't have the energy to stop him. It didn't matter. None of it mattered. Only Rayyel mattered, and Thanh, and Jin-Sayeng, and I was going to give it one last try even if it killed me.

＊

Morning arrived like a forlorn lover, bringing gifts of light and clear sky only to find that it was not needed to start the day after all. We were already up, and had been for hours, having broken into a wine seller's warehouse and hidden ourselves between the barrels of his next shipment inside a covered cart. We were right there when we heard a messenger from Governor Zheshan's office arrive, claiming that all their wine had been spoiled overnight. Could they not spare a few barrels? The governor was having an important meeting, and his guest, Han Lo Bahn, could not abide poor wine.

They could, the wine merchant said. An entire cartload, in fact, his secretary—who also happened to be Anya Kaz's niece—added. She was the one who had mysteriously forgotten to lock the warehouse overnight, and was responsible for making sure our cart was picked. The wine merchant's men came to hitch the cart up to their horses, and we felt ourselves being rolled along the street.

I glanced at the sky. Lo Bahn, Khine, and Inzali would've arrived in Governor Zheshan's office by now. I drew a deep breath and checked that I was sufficiently armed. Sword. Dagger. An extra knife, small enough to fit in my boot. I tried not to think about having to use them, whom I might have to stick a blade into. Rayyel wasn't stupid. He was a lot of things, but he wasn't stupid.

We rolled to a stop. I heard gates open and then close. We were inside Zheshan's office. I turned to Nor, who bade me to wait.

Sweat rolled down my nose and trickled past my lip.

I heard it then—fireworks. The explosions were so loud that my ears started ringing. I saw Agos peer through the canvas flap before he grabbed my arm and pulled me from the wagon. We made our way to the bushes of the courtyard while everyone clustered around the open gate, laughing and pointing.

The fireworks were still going off, filling the sky with bright light and grey smoke. I hoped Anya wasn't hurt. The plan had been to pretend that she was transporting a crate of fireworks and then to feign an accident of some sort along the way. Khine had been able to procure the fireworks from one of Cho's friends, but we couldn't find a horse that would help Anya make a quick escape. She had promised she would improvise.

"You shouldn't worry about her," I heard Agos grumble beside me. "Focus on the task at hand."

I hated that he knew me too well. I hated even more that I had to bring him. I pushed the thought as far away as I could and followed him into Zheshan's storeroom. Anya's niece had been in the keep before and had told us exactly how there was a door there that allowed us to get in, what turns to make, and that there was an unused closet at the far end. There, we could hide until things had calmed down and we could go out and pretend to be her master's men, returning to check on the quality of the wine. A spoiled batch, among the barrels; you don't want Gon Zheshan serving it to his guests.

I didn't ask why she would know about the closet. We are all allowed our secrets, even from a queen.

I focused just as I was advised, ignoring the sound of Agos's breathing, of the uncomfortable silence in the darkness, marred only by our heartbeats. *We are swords first. Servants first.*

It didn't help that I knew Agos would die for me. It didn't occur to me to question why things would be different now than they were five years ago.

Five years ago…

Agos's hand drifted to mine, a brief touch to remind me it was time. I quickly pulled away. We returned to the hall, hiding our weapons under our cloaks. "We'd be somewhere in the servants' quarters now," Nor said, looking around.

"She said the guest rooms are upstairs from here." I spotted a wide staircase decorated with long, laced tapestries. The stair balusters were carved with lionbeasts on every turn. "Agos," I said. "Keep an eye out for us. Stay here."

His face darkened. "Why?"

"Because I'm about to see Rayyel. Don't be an idiot."

"He'll be surrounded by this Governor Zheshan's guards," Agos said. "Idiocy will be to face them alone."

"I think…he'll be unguarded," I said. "Please, Agos. Consider it a request."

I heard Nor utter a soft sound.

Agos turned his head. I took that as an agreement and began to climb the steps. Nor followed me.

"You want to ask, don't you?" I said when we reached the next level.

"My queen," she said. "It is not my place." But I could see the question dancing in her eyes.

"I will tell you this," I said as we turned into the first corridor. "Rayyel might not be willing to go with us."

"I don't understand. You said he was Governor Zheshan's prisoner."

"I was told that, at first. But it has come to my attention that he may not be as much of a prisoner as he is possibly working…with Governor Zheshan…to get rid of me."

Nor slowed down. "Lord Rayyel wants you dead?"

"I think so."

"Why?"

"I don't know. That's what I've come here to learn."

"My queen…"

Her voice had turned; there was a note to it that made the hair on the back of my arms stand on end. It was a broken sound, and we were alone. "What is it, Captain?"

"My men died," she said. "I still don't know why."

"We were betrayed."

"But *why*?" Her voice was rising. "What did you do to make Oren-yaro lose faith in you like that?"

"I thought we came to the conclusion that they were bribed."

"We knew how, but not the reason behind it. My queen, my men were Oren-yaro. For them to *kill* their brothers in cold blood would take more than the promise of money."

I turned to face her. "What are you saying, Nor? You know the rumours. You told me yourself that there will always be rumours."

"Yet if Lord Rayyel would see you dead for them…"

I saw her fingering the hilt of her sword. "You would do this now, Captain?"

"I don't know," Nor said. "Tell me that what they say about you isn't true. That my men died because their brothers erred and not because *you* betrayed us."

I hesitated. She didn't notice, though, because we saw Agos appear at the stairway, panting. "I thought I heard—" he started. He saw Nor's stance and snarled, drawing his sword before I could stop him.

Nor backed away. "Stay out of this, Agos."

"Make me."

"She needs to answer my question."

"She is your liege lord. She doesn't."

Nor laughed. "You'd think that. But I am part of the clan she represents, and she owes me an answer. Oh, dear Agos, she is in a hole, and you are making it deeper. I know you enough not to hold it against you. But the queen…" She turned to me. "Half the Queen's Guard. The

Singing Sainsa's crew. They all willingly sank that knife into your back. And now you are telling me that Lord Rayyel would've joined them without second thought."

"You can't blame me for what they did."

"My queen, do you think we are all like him?" She pointed at Agos. "Did you think you could do whatever you wanted and still expect blind loyalty? We gave it to your father easily enough because we believed in his ideals—we knew the Ikessars were bringing death and ruin to the land, and rising against them was the only way to preserve ourselves. You, on the other hand, have done nothing but drag us back to the brink of disaster. And for what?"

"Nor..."

"My queen!" The desperation was thick in her voice. "Tell me I am wrong, and I will take my own life when this is all over. Assure me my men died for nothing. Tell me—what happened five years ago? When we took this godsforsaken trip, was it to confront Rayyel for abandoning his duties, or so that you could beg his forgiveness because you abandoned yours?"

I could hear her stark breathing in the following silence. I think she must've understood that no matter what I said, she couldn't take another step without Agos's blade swinging down on her neck. And that in a straight fight, she was no match for his size and strength. I didn't want it to come to that. We had already lost too many people on this trip, and I didn't want to add my cousin to the toll.

It seemed that my father's efforts to surround me with loyal followers had been all for nothing. I think I suddenly understood that moment of panic in his face when he was dying. I had thought that it had been for himself, even though he had assured me so often that he wasn't afraid to die. A moment of panic, followed by thoughtfulness as he stared at me, an old man regarding the young daughter he was too old, really, to have fathered. Yet all we had was each other; he was leaving me alone for all of this, and I had not been ready.

Fifteen years later, I still wasn't.

I heard footsteps and touched my sword, preparing to throw it all to hell and fight my way to Rayyel. But it was only Khine. "Are you arguing amongst yourselves?" he asked, slowing down as he came up to us. "Right after we all risked our lives to get you this far?"

"How's your end coming along?" I asked.

"Well enough," he said. "I didn't have to do much. Inzali made a curious point back in the meeting about how Governor Zheshan should've consulted with the people before requesting such an embargo, and they started arguing. I excused myself and don't think they even noticed me leave. What the hell is happening between you all? I could hear you from down the hall."

"Nothing," I said. "Let's find Rayyel."

"Stand down, Captain Nor," Agos said.

"You're the one with the fucking blade drawn on me," she hissed.

"I understand you're all in a tense situation here," Khine said, walking towards them. "But it can wait until you all get home."

"You hear that, Nor?" Agos said. "Or I can kill you right now. It's all the same to me. Either you are loyal to Queen Talyien, or you're not."

"Because you are the epitome of loyalty, I suppose," she snorted. But she dropped her hands to her sides. "I can at least admit defeat when I see it. I'm outnumbered. What is your judgment, my queen?"

"What?"

"Will you leave me alive only so I can question you later? Or will you kill me now and be done with it?"

I started to ask what sort of person she thought I was, and then realized I already knew the answer to it. I turned away and made my way to the first door, all but kicking it open. It was empty. I went down the hall to the next.

Behind me, I heard them move to follow. My people: a doubtful captain of the guard, an ex-guard with boundary issues, and a con artist. No wonder my father was haunting me.

I pulled at the next door. Empty.

On the third, I caught sight of Biala Chaen's pale, painted face. She was sitting on an exquisite wooden stool beside a round table in the middle of a large, ornate room decorated with paper lanterns. As surprised as I was to see her, her expression barely changed. I think she had been expecting me. She smiled. "Queen Talyien," she said, giving a mock bow. "We meet again. He was so convinced you would come. Come, take a seat. Have some tea." She gestured at the porcelain cups on the tray beside her.

"No, thank you. It's probably poisoned. I knew you were a snake the moment I laid eyes on you," I said in a low voice.

"Did you? How interesting." She fanned herself. "And what, pray, have I done to earn such a verdict from a queen? Me, a mere architect's daughter? I've moved up in the world."

"Spare me your prattle. Where is my husband?"

"What makes you think I know?"

"You and your husband fooled us the moment we entered your doors," I said. "Kora said Governor Zheshan has him in his custody. She told me *you* told her."

"Kora," Biala said. She looked confused for a moment before breaking out into a smile. "Right. Kora!" She clapped her hands.

My handmaid appeared from one of the adjoining rooms, looking frailer than she had when I had last seen her. She shuffled past the giant clay vases and kept her eyes on the floor the whole time. *Kora aset gar Angjar. Priest caste.* Nor had said that, a lifetime ago.

"Did I really say such a thing, Kora? Did I tell you to tell the queen that her husband is here, in this very keep?"

Kora's face was blank. "My lady," she said.

Biala struck her. "Tell your queen the truth."

"The truth?"

She struck her again. I wrapped my fingers around the hilt of my sword, but Nor stepped in front of me before I could do anything else.

"Poor idiot thing," Biala said. "You gave the queen the letter from her husband, didn't you?"

Kora turned helplessly to Nor.

"She gave it to me," Nor said. "She said a courier had slipped it to her through the gates."

"How long have you been in the queen's service, *Kora*?" Biala asked.

"F-five years," Kora stammered.

"Long enough," Biala said. "You kept quiet. Kept behind the scenes. No one could've ever suspected you. Smart, for such an idiot girl. Who hired you?"

Kora turned to me. "One of the queen's councillors."

"Who?"

"I don't know his name."

Biala slapped her.

"Leave her alone!" I roared.

"Who?"

"Dragonlord Rayyel!" Kora cried.

My head pounded. A rush of blood, dizziness. The girl was looking at me now, tears falling across her thin cheeks. Biala's face broke into a triumphant grin. I stared at one, and then the other.

"You're lying," I said.

A shadow crossed Kora's face. "No, my queen," she murmured. "That last part...is the truth. He hired me five years ago to keep an eye on you. I've been sending him letters...reports..."

"Your fucking handiwork," Agos hissed at Nor.

"But it's not what you think," Kora quickly added. "It's not what she's trying to make it sound like!"

"Me?" Biala asked. She laughed. "What do I have to do with this?"

"You want the queen to think I've betrayed her. I haven't! I just—"

"You've been conspiring against the true crowned ruler of Jin-Sayeng.

You don't think that's betrayal?" Biala knew she had the knife in; now she was just twisting it.

I had never seen anyone look so frightened as Kora did in that moment. Her voice dropped to a whisper. "He wanted to know about you and the prince. The things you did. The people you saw. Harmless things."

"Harmless things, but *everything*. You gave him enough information while he was biding his time, waiting to make a move. You made this possible," Biala said, holding out her hands and gesturing around the room.

"No!" Kora cried. "He just wanted to know! And the letter—it *was* handed over the fence. I didn't know it was from Dragonlord Rayyel! I didn't open it!"

"Foolish girl. You think every intention is innocent?"

"Not yours! You told me to tell them that Lord Rayyel was with Governor Zheshan, or else you'd tell the queen what I've done..." She turned to me and dropped to the ground. "My queen. My queen!"

"I trusted you," I said in a low voice. "When you entered the service of the Oren-yaro, you were supposed to know where your loyalties lay."

Her face had gone completely white. "Please..."

"Agos," I murmured. "Off with her head."

Treachery was unforgivable. They had been warned. Agos killed her on the spot. Her body toppled next to a vase, one that held a purple flower.

I turned to Biala Chaen, who was suddenly deathly still. I think she hadn't expected me to make a decision so quickly. "Let's talk about you," I said. I pulled myself onto a stool beside her and crossed my legs. I placed my elbows on the table.

She licked her lips. "There is nothing to say. *I* never betrayed you."

"Do you think I'm an idiot? Kora herself said you *made* her say things.

And what's this about *him* being so convinced I would come? Where is Rayyel?"

"I don't know," Biala said. "He told me to show you what you are: only a woman, trying to play queen. I mean, look at you! Is this what a queen is supposed to look like? Who of your followers are loyal to you—truly *you*, and not just the idea you represent?"

"Thank you," I replied. "Is that everything?"

"*Ideas* do not create rulers, Queen Talyien. Only power does. You have no power."

I smiled. "Unfortunately for you, in this room, I do." I drew my sword and struck her across the belly. She gave a small, disbelieving yelp, and then a groan as I did it a second time, across her throat. I watched her body twitch on the floor, the blood mingling with Kora's. Her eyes met mine, opening and closing as her life ebbed away. I stared right back.

"Queen Talyien," Khine croaked out.

I pulled away from Biala's dying gaze to turn to him. "Yes?" My own voice sounded like a stranger's.

He cleared his throat. "There is another guest wing. I saw armed guards along the way. I'm sure they're protecting his room."

"Can we take on armed guards?"

"Before you killed them, I would've said no," Khine said, looking at the mess. He scratched his head. "Now, though, I would think it's a little too late to do anything else. No point in continuing your disguises, anyway."

"Let's go say hi to the bastard," I murmured, stepping over the bodies. Agos shut the door behind us.

CHAPTER TWENTY-SIX

THE IKESSAR HEIR, REPRISED

ᛏᚢᛰ

I had expected to grow old with Rayyel.

Foolish, romantic notions. I was not a child anymore, but I still remembered being the young girl who had let herself fall so deeply in love, thinking it was safe. *Ordained by the gods*, the priests had said.

Even after discovering that Rai had a lover, I had tried my hardest to believe I could still turn things around. I returned to Oren-yaro and continued with our wedding preparations as if nothing had happened. The warlords' gifts poured in: gold, silk, hand-carved furniture, and high-stepping horses so beautiful the sight of them alone could make you weep. Courtiers from all across the nation came to offer me their congratulations. The women spoke to me behind fans, coyly suggesting how lucky I was that I could at least look forward to my wedding night. A jibe at my father, I think...I didn't need someone else reminding me that my mother was forced to marry an ailing man five times her age while I "only" got Rayyel, who was young and handsome. Whatever problems I had with my betrothed could have been locked away, buried, forgotten like our dead.

I officially saw him again on the day of our wedding, in the Kibouri temple in Shirrokaru. We knelt before the statue of his ancestors' Nameless Maker and swore to love each other to the end of our days. He took my hand while ignoring my shaking fingers and presented me to the people with a bow, like I was this most precious thing.

We didn't talk to each other throughout the whole celebration. We greeted everyone who came to congratulate us, sometimes hand in hand, but to each other, we were quiet, subdued. Not a single word passed between us, not even the most furtive of glances. Which was normal for him, but I had wondered if he noticed how strange it was for me. The rest of the evening flashed by. We soon found ourselves alone in a room, the same room where I had found him with that other woman. My first thought was a fervent hope that they would at least have changed the sheets.

"I will be gentle," he said, his lips grazing my neck. I barely heard him. Every part of my body was recoiling from his touch, even as I tried to shut out the image of him being ridden naked by that bitch from my mind.

Duty? Don't tell me I don't know duty. I know it like the back of my hand, like the breath of air from my lungs. I know it better than my own mother, and in the thick uncertainty of that dark room, I held on to it like a sharpened blade. The blood running through my fingers? Inconsequential.

He took my shaking as virginal nerves. If I hadn't known any better, I could've taken his awkwardness for the same. The ordained, lying to each other. He took my clothes off, drew a quick breath, and marvelled out loud at my beauty in the moonlight. Me, with my thick bones and angles and the muscles on my frame, when he had tasted supple breasts and soft skin.

Forced smiles. Lying on the bed, pretending to respond to his touch. Duty? Another would have forced their eyes shut and urged him to get on and be done with it. I pulled at his robes, running my hands over his smooth scholar's body. Not a flaw or mark on it—no deformities, no battle scars. My own sunburnt skin, with its many bumps and bruises, looked rougher in comparison. I had nothing to complain about.

"I am sorry," he said.

"My lord?"

Rayyel kissed me, his beard tickling my chin while his fingers curled over my shoulders. He had not lied about being gentle, at least. "We are going to usher in a new era," he whispered. "One our ancestors could have only dreamed of. I did not always believe we could make it work, but I think…having known you all these years…I can believe your heart is in the right place. Forgive me."

I shut my eyes then, forcing back the tears. I didn't want to ask *what for*. I didn't want to hear his explanations. I allowed myself to listen to his words, to absorb the weight of them. "We will put everything behind us," I heard myself saying. "There is nothing to forgive, my lord."

That marked the last conversation of our first night together. He entered me, finding no barrier. He wasn't surprised. I had ridden horses all my life. He knew that, at least, or else simply didn't know any better. I was young and took no pleasure in the act, but after he was done, I held his sleeping form in my arms and stared at his face for the longest time.

Duty? Love? It was one and the same, and it left the sensation of my heart wanting to leap from my chest and strangle the living daylights out of me. But I still remember how tightly I held him that night, how I left no space between us. You would've had to rip me away.

In my years as queen, I think I had done a remarkable job of pretending that Rayyel's absence did not affect my ability to rule. When he left, I did not spend the days curled up in a ball, sobbing my sorrows away. After my coronation, we went on with the celebrations, and I proceeded to rule Jin-Sayeng from Oren-yaro, appointing Thanh officially as the heir. The nation watched with unblinking eyes while the warlords wandered back to their provinces. If they had been expecting me to declare war on the Ikessars or create an uproar of any sort, they were sorely disappointed.

It made me wonder if my reactions—or lack thereof—made a difference to Kora's reports over the past few years. What did he want to know, anyway? The policies I had signed? If I had chosen to take lovers after he left? What I ate for breakfast each day? If he had learned I cried myself to sleep each night, would it have changed a thing?

It made sense that he would want to place someone close to me in order to learn what he could. I might have done the same thing. But the implication of it stung. Despite everything I had learned, that stubborn part of me still clung to the belief that he wasn't capable of taking things this far. That we had shared something meaningful, at least, in those three years of marriage. All he had to do was *ask*, and I would have told him everything. *Everything.*

We reached the hallway with the guards. There were only two. Agos and Nor rushed forward, swords drawn. I moved to join them, but Khine dragged me by the wrist.

"Quick," he said. "While they're distracted."

I followed him up the corridor. There was a single door at the end, unguarded. I pulled it open and walked in. There was a man with his back to the window.

"Rayyel!" I called out.

The man turned.

Panic rushed into me. *Rayyel*, my mind begged. *I need to talk to Rayyel. We got this far. Please. I need to know—*

Yuebek must've seen my expression. He broke into laughter.

"I got you!" he said when he caught his breath at last. "I got you, didn't I? Queen Talyien!" Yuebek crossed the room and caught my arm. I was so stunned that I didn't even try to move away. "You escaped my trap, my little dove, only to find yourself in another one. How wonderful! Beautiful! And you, Queen Talyien, none the wiser!"

"I take it that's not Rayyel," Khine commented.

Yuebek turned to him. "Who are you, fly? Where are my guards?"

I shook myself from his grasp. "You've gone too far, Yuebek."

"Oh no, no, my lovely queen. I think I went *just* the right amount. You *are* here, after all." He laughed again, this time a high-pitched, wheezing sound. I stepped back.

"I came here for Rayyel," I said.

Yuebek's face fell. "That man, still?"

"He's my husband."

"After everything he has done to you? The betrayals, the schemes?" He grabbed my shoulders and shook me. "I wouldn't do such things. I would be loyal to you. Ask Zhu."

"Zhu's dead. I believe I remember you killing her."

"I did," Yuebek said. "She betrayed me. A traitor deserves nothing less. But if she could, she would tell you that I never touched another woman, not while we were married. Oho! I saw the look on your face. So the rumours are true, then?"

"I don't know what you could possibly be talking about."

"That he left you for another. That he was fucking his way through the royal clans. Tell me I'm wrong."

"You're wrong."

He smiled, my words nothing but air to him. "And you knew. You knew, and you ignored it. Swept it under the rugs. A travesty. Do you wonder why they talk about you, why you've lost the support of so many of your lords and royal clans? Marry me, and we can help you gain your dignity back."

"I can't believe you're not done with this," I hissed.

"I can't believe you can't see reason," he retorted. "I was told Queen Talyien was intelligent. Perhaps they were wrong. Surely an intelligent woman will know when she's been beaten, when she is powerless…"

"Biala was your creature, wasn't she? She was talking about *you*."

He continued to smile. I heard the door open and saw Nor and Agos arrive. Nor was holding an injured arm. Their appearance did not seem to concern Yuebek one bit.

"There's four of us and one of you," I said. "Talk."

Yuebek lifted his chin. "I think you're confused, Queen Talyien. Why do you think you have the upper hand? Here, or at all? I am Emperor Yunan's Fifth Son. Who are you but the youngest daughter of a rebel and some nameless whore he picked for her warm cunt and lack of sense?"

"I escaped your prison once, Yuebek. You don't frighten me."

"Did you think you escaped because of your own skill? Or because I *let* you?"

I saw Agos lifting his blade. I held out my hand. "Stop," I said. "He knows where Rayyel is." I turned back to Yuebek, whose face had assumed an expression of bright-eyed wonder, like a child watching a play unfold in front of him. "You used Biala Chaen to feed me that line about Rayyel being here. She said *you* were expecting me. I don't understand why you went through all that trouble."

"It's brilliant, isn't it? You learned he was here, so you went all the way to Zorheng, *to me*, to get help for him."

"That's it? You orchestrated this just so I would go to you for help?"

He clapped his hands.

"Tali," Khine said. "I don't think he's got your Dragonlord. This man is clearly mad."

His words filled me with a sense of dread. If Rayyel wasn't here, where was he? *Dead, in a gutter somewhere…* "No," I said, shaking my head. "No! Yuebek will talk."

"*Prince* Yuebek," he corrected. "*My darling* also works—I'm fond of affections. When we're married, you'll have to address me properly. This lack of respect won't do. We can't let the people know that their new monarchs don't get along." He shuffled over to a table and picked up a jar of ink. "After I write to my priest in Zorheng...we can get married before the moon turns. And then I'll have my father lift this embargo, and I'll take you home myself. Do you think—will the people embrace me as the new king?"

Revulsion stirred in my stomach. "Stop."

Yuebek did, but only to turn his head slightly. "I know you don't love me right now," he said. "But you will learn. You loved that despicable man, didn't you? Even after he sent an assassin for you in my dungeons. And then another, and then another..."

"How did you know about that?" I asked.

His face tightened, the look of someone who had realized he had slipped.

I drew my sword. "You sent those assassins."

The smile broke from his face. "Only to show you what your husband was capable of!" he cried. "Only to show you what he was going to do, anyway! I have it on best authority that the man has been conspiring with Zheshan! And I asked them not to hurt you—"

"You son of a bitch. They tried to *kill* me."

"I said, *make sure they don't hurt her*, and I made sure I didn't hire real assassins like the first time..."

My head was swimming. "What do you mean the first time?"

Another slip. Yuebek jerked away from the desk, spilling the jar of ink all over his robes. "He was conspiring with Zheshan," Yuebek said, his voice dropping to a whisper. "Your husband is evil, Talyien. Can't you see? You don't deserve him. He's a pauper, a nobody. If you rule with me, you can have everything. You've seen what I can do, what I'm capable of. Imagine what will happen if you let me lead you and Jin-Sayeng to glory."

"The Silver Goose, the guards...the *Singing Sainsa*...you did all of those?"

"Yes."

"And the letters—those were you, too?"

He nodded eagerly.

"How did you copy his handwriting?"

"I've been studying both of you," he said, "for years."

I felt a prickle in the back of my neck.

In my blindness, my naivety, I had imagined that the world revolved only around Rayyel and me. That if we were together, everything would fall neatly into place, just as our parents had promised our people. I thought it had been like a game of *Hanza*: two players on the board, limited moves, one resolution.

Perhaps he had been right about how I had only been playing at being queen. Why didn't I notice the other players? When did Yuebek arrive in the picture? *Years ago?* Who had been feeding him information? Who else had betrayed me? Arro?

No. Not Arro. Everyone else I could doubt, but not the man who had been there for me since my father died, a man my own foolishness had killed. But if Yuebek knew enough to copy Rayyel's handwriting and knew the subtlety with which I would recognize it, then he knew other things as well. Dangerous things.

"I know everything," Yuebek said, as if reading my mind. "The colour of the drapes in your room. Your preferred soaps and breakfasts, and the names of your favourite dogs and horses. I know you like dresses *and* swords, how fond you are of the strange colourful fish in your gardens, and that yes, you worshipped the ground this Rayyel walked on, even when you didn't have to. That you know the names of his relatives, living or dead, and still send flowers to his father's grave every year. That you read most of his books and know them by heart, even though they bored you half to death, just so you could have something to talk about. And I know about Thanh, your son."

"Don't go there," I hissed. His words had turned panic into dread.

"Of course, when we are married, I could not allow a bastard to be my heir. He would have to be disposed of. The poor boy, but unfortunately..."

I didn't let him finish. I struck him with my sword.

The blade bent before it could touch him.

He looked down, seeming surprised, and moved his ink-splattered fingers into a circle. The sword began to crumple and started to spread heat along the hilt and up my hand. I dropped it.

"Oh, that's right," Yuebek said, looking up at me. "You don't know much about mages, do you? Another thing to rectify in your backward nation. But I can already see that I can't make you change your mind now, not with words. I think we have to get rid of distractions first."

He drew a dagger. I thought he was going for me and pulled out a chair to block the attack.

Instead, the dagger slid out of his hands and flew back, as if held by something unseen, and struck Khine in the gut.

I leaped forward, screaming. Khine pulled the dagger out and tried to swing at him—the idiot didn't bring his own sword—but Yuebek simply walked past him and scampered for the window.

"He can't be allowed to leave alive!" I cried. Agos rushed after him.

I reached Khine, who had managed to drag himself to the corner, and helped him to the ground. His skin had the pallor of chalk, and his eyes were flickering. He grabbed my arm, groaning from a spasm of pain.

Outside, Agos roared. I heard a loud crash.

"Your sword!" I called to Nor.

She unstrapped her belt and threw the sheathed sword at me. I caught it in mid-air. "Take care of Khine," I said before hurling myself out of the window and onto the rooftop.

Agos was nowhere in sight. I saw Yuebek scampering in the distance. I drew the sword, dropping the scabbard on the ground, and raced after him.

He was a slow runner. I struck down, cutting him across the leg a few paces in. But I barely nicked him. He spun around to face me, that damnable smile still on his face. "Look at you," he said. "It's touching how you can't let me out of your sight. We have a connection after all. I really think you could learn to love me more than Rayyel. I could be so good to you."

"You don't see it, but I'm trying very hard not to vomit in my mouth."

"Such harsh words. And yet I can tell—you're curious about what I can do for Jin-Sayeng, your once-glorious nation. Do you not want to know what it can look like again, as in the days when you ran on dragon-fire and you actually had things the empire wanted? Not the disarray you've inherited...the squabbling warlords...the crumbling dragon-towers..."

I lifted my sword. "Your sense of perception is extremely dull."

He held out his hands. "Queen Talyien. I am giving you a chance to show your true worth as a leader. You have seen what I've done with Zorheng City."

"I have. I'm not particularly impressed."

His cheeks dimpled, as if he had been expecting that. "Yet you have not seen what it *was* before I arrived. The people complain now, but before my work, there had been nothing in it worth saving. Zorheng was an outhouse in the far corner of the empire. Now it is a fortress, impenetrable, sturdy. Imagine what I could do with a better canvas, better paint…" He lifted his fingers again. A sharp wind struck me, scraping across my robes like a rough caress.

I jabbed my elbow into his chest, stopping him from doing whatever it was he had been attempting. An equally forceful blow slid past my shoulder, although Yuebek never lifted a finger. I grabbed his throat in my hands.

"Don't you want to prove yourself?" Yuebek asked, giggling. "You're letting your anger get in the way of good sense."

"I don't care," I hissed.

He clutched at my fingers. "You should. This is your chance to show the world that you are a wise and sensible ruler, instead of this…heart-broken woman." He spat the last two words out.

I dropped him. He crawled back, his hand on his neck, before he got up to face me once more. "You realize what I can do to your Rayyel?" he snarled. "And your son? Your precious son?"

"I won't know," I said. "I don't have to. I'm not going to let you leave alive." I struck him again, a long line across the chest. The blade tore through the silk robes like butter. Yuebek looked at the gash, at the blood beginning to seep through his thin chest, as if he couldn't quite believe it was there. He held up his ink-stained hands.

"Two things." He showed me his fingers. "One, I die, and you don't find out where Rayyel is."

"One of your men will talk," I said.

He ignored me. "Two. I die, and word about your son gets out."

"I don't know what you mean," I said. I moved to stab him.

Yuebek grabbed the blade before it could sink into his body. I saw the blue glow appear around his bleeding hands and didn't wait for it to break my sword this time—I kicked out his legs from under him. He stumbled back, yanking the sword out of my hands. It clattered just out of reach. Before I could grab it, his hands wrapped around my shirt collar. He gave the deranged grin of a predator who had finally caught his prey.

We fell from the rooftop and crashed onto another below.

———◆———

Dust coated the back of my throat, and my senses were swimming. The roof we landed on had caved from the impact, dragging us into a room with a pile of debris. I coughed and reached for something to steady myself in the darkness. My hand found the wall, and I pushed myself up.

A cold hand wrapped itself around my wrist. The shadows receded, revealing Yuebek's face, glowing a faint blue. The grin was still on his face, ear-to-ear, and I had the sense that it never went away.

I struck him. At least, I tried to. My fist slammed into an invisible barrier, which sent a shock from the tips of my finger bones all the way to my toes. I fell to my knees. Yuebek opened his mouth and laughed like this was the most amusing thing he had seen in his whole life.

"I almost had you, you know," he said, his eyebrows rising. "I was going to take you on that street, in front of the whole city. Find out what that famous cunt actually feels like. But Ong, poor, babbling Ong, stopped me. I suppose we both have him to thank for that—we can do it properly, as man and wife. I *do* like them awake."

I spat at him. "You are the most presumptuous bastard I've ever met in my life."

Yuebek smiled. "Am I?" He stepped back, robes fluttering against the splintered wood and pieces of tile. He placed his hand around a torch on the wall. It lit up. He dropped my wrist and began to walk through the room, lighting the rest of the torches this way. In the light, I saw that we had fallen into the servants' quarters, empty at that time of the day.

"I could also take you now," Yuebek said, returning to me. The unsettling grin was still on his face. "You wouldn't be able to resist once I start."

I struggled to get up. I realized my entire body was frozen on the spot. I couldn't even reach for the dagger on my belt. Somehow, he had cast another spell, and it was keeping me from moving. A heavy weight pressed against my chest and over my back, squeezing against my every breath, as if I was being buried alive.

"Presumptuous, you said?" he continued. "But that would imply that I'm overstepping my boundaries. I don't believe I am. In fact, I think that after years of being patient, I've simply been inching my way back to where I truly belonged."

"What the hell do you mean by that?" I snapped. I was a little surprised that my mouth still worked.

He stepped back with a flourish, revealing a piece of parchment in his hand. It was very old, almost grey. I caught sight of a red seal at the edge. "I didn't want to tell you, not like this. It would have been nice if you had fallen in love with me in your own time. All those assassins...I had thought they would help drive you into my arms. That you would admit your own weaknesses and we could be together without having to resort to all of...this." He made a dismissive gesture.

"You're delusional."

His eyes flashed. "Ambitious. There's a difference. You continue to insult me, yet even now, I am thinking *only* of your comfort. A thoughtful husband, Queen Talyien—even without everything else I am offering, it's a step up from what you had." He waved the letter at me. "Should I read it to you? Or do you want to read it for yourself?"

I stared at him.

"I'm a gentleman. I'll read it for you." Yuebek cleared his throat and flicked the paper in the air. "*Esteemed Fourth Consort*—that's my mother," he said, glancing at me for a second. "*I am honoured that you have not only acknowledged my proposal, but that you can see the good this will do for both of our nations. I have no doubt that your assistance will ensure my victory in this war. However, an unfortunate predicament has come up. Ikessar agents have infiltrated three of my towns, and Princess Ryia aren dar Ikessar is threatening mass slaughter of the common folk if we do not find a way to end this war. She is asking for the exact same thing I have offered you: if the child is a girl, as the healers have predicted it would be, she is willing to allow her to marry her son Rayyel.*

"I find myself in the curious position of having to ask an Emperor's Consort to be patient. It is not my intention to turn against my word, but understand that the lives of many hinge on how I react to Princess Ryia's offer. She is, in essence, conceding to me in this war—my blood will sit on the Dragonthrone, and our clans need not be divided any longer... provided, of course, that the child is a girl."

"Lies," I said. "Everyone knows—"

Yuebek held out a finger and continued reading. *"I do not, of course, believe that things are as simple as Princess Ryia makes them out to be. The Ikessars do not give up this easily. She will have a trick or two up her sleeve, one that will see to my downfall and my clan's eradication from this world. I will not have my nation ripped apart because of some foolish woman's pride.*

"Give me time. Our alliance is still my priority—I know full well that my army alone cannot hold my nation against those fools. But together? Only the gods can speak of the power that will come from this union. When the boy Rayyel is dead, your son Yuebek is free to marry my daughter. Let me worry about the details. I will find a way to honour our agreement. In time, you will see yourself be mother to a Dragonlord of Jin-Sayeng.

"If, contrary to the healers' predictions, the child turns out to be a boy, then there are other avenues we can pursue..."

"Lies," I repeated. "My father would have never sent such incriminating letters. He would have told me if he had. Did you really think you could hurt me this way? To use my own dead father against me? You're lying. *Again.*"

Yuebek began to hum.

My skin prickled. It was the same tune the woman in Deputy Wan-he's home had been humming, the same tune my brother was playing in my hallucinations, and it suddenly struck me where I knew it from: my father. It was his voice that sang that lullaby, on the nights he took the time to tuck me into bed.

Sleep, my little darling, father went off to find a deer, soon he'll be back...
Soon he'll be back...
Soon.

I screamed.

The spell around me broke—I could hear it shatter even when I couldn't see a thing. I drew my dagger and lunged at Yuebek. Laughing, he stepped out of reach, and I realized that even without his spells the man had the grace of a swordsman. He was still toying with me.

I doubled my efforts, trying to corner him. He didn't have a weapon, just the damn letter in his hands. All I had to do was strike a killing blow. Yet the man looked like he wasn't breaking a sweat. He didn't look worried.

"Give up, Yuebek," I gasped as he found himself backed up against the lanterns. "You've got nothing. Give up now, and I'll let you walk away with your life."

"You really *are* a queen," he said. "Even when you're losing, you act as if the world is still yours. Imagine if you were empress. Together, we can make that happen. But if you're going to continue to be stubborn, perhaps a little lesson is in order." He smiled and toppled the lanterns. I watched in horror as the floor caught on fire.

"This letter," he continued, holding it up, oblivious to the crawling flames. "Your duties, your real duties, are in this letter. Why resist your destiny, my queen?"

I coughed, smoke stinging my eyes as I grabbed his wrist. He let me briefly, long enough for me to catch a flash of the words on the letter. It *was* in my father's handwriting. I pushed the thought out of the way as I stabbed him in the arm with the dagger. Unfazed, he yanked the dagger out of my hands. In that same instant, the letter fell from his fingers and into the fire.

He threw the dagger across the end of the room before striking me with the back of his hand. His strength caught me off guard—I stumbled to the floor, coughing. "You think that would do anything?" he laughed as he flicked blood from his sleeve. "There are others. Your father spent some time here, planning this elaborate scheme that would've seen your Rayyel dead before you ever laid eyes on him. Such a sharp mind, for his age. I think he had been expecting to live forever."

I got back to my feet. The flames were curling along the curtains, and I didn't know how much time I had before we were engulfed. If I stayed awake long enough to see that. The heat was stinging my eyes, crawling into my lungs. "You don't have to believe me if you don't want to," Yuebek continued, oblivious of our impending death. "Everything is set in place. His death didn't change that, although *you* made it all doubly difficult by marrying the blasted man anyway and then making him disappear. How else did you think I was able to learn so much about you? Or make your guards turn against their brothers?"

"You bribed them," I hissed.

"Incorruptible, the Oren-yaro," Yuebek said. "Or so they claim. I didn't have to try, not this time. Those men were loyal to your father. Loyal to *his* last wishes."

"So what if they were," I said. "We're going to die here." The flames were up to the ceiling now. Soon the rest of the rafters would come down on us.

"*I* won't." Yuebek snapped his fingers. Another barrier appeared around him. I could see this one now—it glowed a bright blue. "*You* could," he continued. "If you insist on staying out there, you will burn to a crisp right in front of me. Would you want that, my dear? How will your poor boy fare without you? Who else will fend off the wolves when they come for him?"

The door on the other side of the room opened, and I caught a glimpse of Agos's face. Yuebek sent a spell upward, crashing a beam and blocking the way.

While he was distracted, I took the opportunity and pulled out the knife from my boot. I knew by now the source of the spell was concentrated around Yuebek's hands, and aimed for his ankles. The knife went through and drew blood. His shield disappeared. We fell to the floor, grappling for the knife.

From behind the door, I heard Agos yelling as he hacked away at the beam.

"I don't mind a disfigured queen," Yuebek laughed. "I can make you wish you were dead—all I have to do is put you back together. You can wake up my bride. Maybe by then my seed will have sprouted in your belly."

"Tali!" Agos roared as he finally broke through.

I let go of the knife, allowing Yuebek to stab me in the ribs as I screamed for Agos to throw his sword. He hurled it. I rolled over as Yuebek moved to stab me a second time, and I managed to grab the hilt of the sword.

I stabbed him first.

I saw Yuebek's face turn pale as a spray of blood appeared on his robes. They disappeared when I kicked him off me and he stumbled straight into the fire. He opened his mouth, but no sound came out.

Agos arrived to shove him further away. A moment later, Yuebek finally screamed. Dying screams. His burning body crashed to the other end of the room, into the sea of flame.

"Are you all right?" Agos said over my shoulder as the fire continued to crackle around us.

I placed a hand on my side. The blade had nicked the bone but hadn't gone through all the way. "A scratch," I said. "I'll live."

"Then let's get out of here."

Outside in the hall, Nor was bent over Khine's body, her hands on his belly. "Keep pressing," he was telling her, which was not easy because her own arm was in shreds. He waved at me. "Glad to see you're in one piece. Not easy, having all of us limp after you. Did you take care of him?"

I nodded. "Tell us what you need."

"More cloth," Khine grumbled. "Stop the bleeding. Wine. Lots of wine. Some for the wound. Mostly for me."

"Does a sense of humour signify survivability?"

"Not sure yet. Have to . . . observe."

"He won't be walking out of here any time soon," Agos said. "Leave him. There's a commotion outside. The way it all sounds, he might as well be dead. How do you propose we walk him through those gates while Zheshan's men wait to slaughter us?"

"An oversight," Khine said. "This *was* supposed to be a silent operation, after all."

We heard footsteps. I braced myself, pulling my sword closer to me.

Lo Bahn appeared at the end of the hallway. "What in the blazing hells is happening here?" he thundered. "First Lamang disappears, and then I hear Zheshan's men say something about an attack, and now I see *you* here . . ." He looked at us and his face tightened.

I heard the beginning of chaos out in the grounds below. "What's going on outside?" I asked.

"Inzali had convinced me that Zheshan would double-cross me, so I thought I'd have my men ready. Their guards came in, calling about an attack, and came after us before we knew what was going on. Of course we had to fight back. I didn't know it was *you* who would be using me. *Yet again.*" He snorted.

"I'm sorry," I said. "I'll explain later. Can you help us get out of here?"

"No, leave me," Khine said. "If I die here, I won't have to repay him."

"To hell with that," Lo Bahn snapped. He grabbed Khine and hoisted him over his shoulders. "Is there anything else?"

We left through the back gate, amidst an explosion of smoke and clashing swords.

CHAPTER TWENTY-SEVEN
THE AFTERMATH

ᛁᛏᚬᚢ

Khine bled like a stuck pig all through the streets. At least once or twice, his entire body slackened and he closed his eyes, and I was almost sure we'd lost him. I stayed as close to him as possible, talking to him and trying to make him laugh, which was not easy with Lo Bahn's sour expression in the way.

It was a long way back to Shang Azi, but we finally made it to Lo Bahn's mansion. Anya was there, looking as fresh as if she had just walked out of a dress shop, and Inzali, who must have escaped the governor's building before the carnage began. She barked for the servants to call for a physician before taking Khine upstairs, along with Nor and Agos. I wanted to follow them, but Lo Bahn cleared his throat and stepped between us.

"Explain everything," he said, a dangerous glint in his eyes.

"I don't know if I could."

"I just lost half my men in that skirmish. More, with my luck." He sat down, Khine's blood all over his robes, and pointed at me. "And by tomorrow, I'm probably going to learn that all my businesses have been shut down because I was fool enough to *attack* a governor's office. Everything I worked hard for, my whole life. Gone in an instant."

I closed my eyes for a moment and took a deep breath. When I opened them again, Lo Bahn was still staring at me. "I am at war," I said.

"No shit," Lo Bahn hissed.

"I won't beg you for help," I continued. "You're a smart man. You know the depth of my need. I will say this: they know you're helping me. Even if you throw me out on the streets and pretend you've never met me, they will come for you, anyway."

"Who are *they*?"

"I don't know," I said. "Officials from your empire. My own people. My husband. Until I find myself back home and learn who my enemies exactly are, my options are limited. But I can guarantee you that those bastards are less generous than I am. Sell me out, and I can't say whether they'll want to take your head for getting me this far. I am your sure ticket out of this mess, Lord Han."

"You're the bitch who got me in it in the first place," he said.

I shrugged. "It is what it is."

"I should have you flogged. Stripped naked and left for the scum of Shang Azi."

I stared him down. "But you won't."

"Woman."

"*Queen.*"

A servant came scurrying towards us. He gave me an awkward bow first, before dropping in front of Lo Bahn. "Someone outside wants to see you, my lord," he whispered.

Lo Bahn nodded. The servant pulled open the main door and gestured.

Gon Zheshan limped in, his robes in tattered shreds. There was mud and blood all over him.

"Have you come to chastise me for that little mishap?" Lo Bahn asked. "Because I'm going to tell you right now, Gon, that if you think you can pin that whole thing on me, you're going to have a fight on your hands."

Zheshan ignored him. He placed his hand on my knee and all but collapsed at my feet.

"Prince Yuebek got to me," he gasped.

"What do you mean?"

He opened and closed his mouth, like a dying fish, before he reached into his robes and pulled out a sealed letter. I took it.

"I didn't know, I swear, until it was too late. When Lord Rayyel approached me, I was only too happy to offer my assistance. An honourable man like that, a true *nobleman*—how could I say no? Then the assassins came, and frightened as I had been, I was ecstatic to think that I was useful to a true king, a Dragonlord of Jin-Sayeng. Me, a lowly governor of such a vast kingdom…" Zheshan swallowed. "My soldiers got us out of the Silver Goose alive, but afterwards, I received orders to have Lord Rayyel killed while he was under my care. *In service of the empire*, it said. It seemed that Lord Rayyel was the target of the assassination in the restaurant in the first place."

I stared at him, unsure if I wanted to believe him or not. The man was chattering like a nervous wreck.

"Go on," I said.

"I thought it was a trick, that Lord Rayyel's enemies were trying to use me. What gain would the Empire of Ziri-nar-Orxiaro get from killing Jin-Sayeng's wayward monarch? They know it wouldn't do anything. I told Lord Rayyel as much, bade him to stay away. And then a few weeks ago, Prince Yuebek arrived. He told me everything. About his plan to fulfill this bargain your father struck with his mother years ago. About Warlord Yeshin's loyalists, who have been working with him since the beginning, who will do whatever it takes to carry out your father's last wishes—they would see Lord Rayyel and Prince Thanh dead before your eyes, and you married to Prince Yuebek while you are yet young enough to bear *him* children. None of this is sanctioned by the Esteemed Emperor, but Prince Yuebek made me understand what was at stake if I refused to work with him. Between my honour as a man and my responsibilities as a servant of the empire...my promise to your husband and my duties to my family...I could not refuse the prince, I could not betray him to his father, and yet..." Shaking, he pulled away from me.

"It's all right, Governor Zheshan," I said. "None of this will happen. Prince Yuebek is dead. We will make it right again. You have no need to be frightened."

His eyes widened. "No. You don't understand. Prince Yuebek...the *agan*..."

Lo Bahn frowned. "Now, Gon, perhaps we—"

Before Lo Bahn could finish talking, Zheshan pulled out a sword and slid it into his own belly. I watched in horror as he collapsed on his knees.

"Shit," Lo Bahn finished.

I looked down at the letter he had handed to me. After a moment, I tore the seal away.

It was Rayyel's handwriting again.

Come see me.
—Rai

There was an address.

I stared at it for a heartbeat.

"What's that?" I heard Lo Bahn ask. He peered over my shoulder. "That's an inn," he said. "North of the docks. What the hell does it mean?"

"I think my husband wrote it." I remembered Yuebek. How many others had studied us so closely that they could mimic my husband's letters?

"You *think*?" Lo Bahn snorted.

"I don't know anymore." I folded the paper and looked at Gon Zheshan's dead body. "Why would he kill himself?"

"He was never one to do things that made sense. I've told him more than once."

"I'm serious."

"I was, too. But I'll humour you. He must've felt like he had betrayed his lord."

"Wouldn't that be your Esteemed Emperor?"

"Kyan Jang is nearly two months' travel from here," Lo Bahn said. "I don't think Zheshan had ever met him in his life. Whoever had his loyalty, it was someone a lot closer to home."

I looked at the letter again, at the neat handwriting and downward brushstrokes.

Come see me.

I went up to check on Khine sometime during the evening. Inzali had called a physician—a certain Tashi Jhao, who didn't at all seem to recognize me. He told me to let Khine rest and to feed him warm broth every two days so that his muscles didn't waste away.

"That man," Khine said as soon as Jhao had left, "is a fraud."

"As opposed to the fraud in front of me?"

"That's the thing about frauds. You could let them take as many examinations as you want, let them pass all of it, and they'd *still* be frauds."

"You're talking nonsense."

"The fraud slipped half a bottle of snake-bile tonic steeped in gin inside me. It'd be a miracle if I don't start reciting poetry by nightfall." He cocked his head. "Are you all right?"

I hesitated for a moment before showing him the letter. "Gon Zheshan had it all along," I said. "Did Yuebek write it? If I went there now, would I just fall into another trap? Zheshan spoke of plots and traps and things

I don't even know how to begin to explain to you. You're all drugged up—I'm not even going to try."

"It would be wise not to go," he agreed. "Also very wise, the not explaining. I don't think I could tell the difference between a lion and a dog right now, to be perfectly honest."

I nodded. "And after everything that had happened, after everything I had learned..."

"Besides, I don't think your guards would let you."

"No," I said. "At this point, they'd probably rather kill me first before bemoaning their misfortune at having been born in the wrong province. Warlord San of Kyo-orashi—now *there's* someone who knows how to have fun." I sat on the edge of the bed, and Khine slid across the mattress to make more room for me. I patted his hand. His skin felt a lot warmer than earlier.

"The folly of love—" he began.

"Enter the poet," I mused.

He laughed. "You don't say."

I glanced out the window. "You're on the right track, anyway. I think I could've done a lot better to foresee events. Yuebek was using our troubles to fuel his own ambitions. And in the meantime, I don't know what's happening back home. My nation may be going up in flames as we speak."

I turned back to Khine. He had pushed himself up into a sitting position, his elbows on his knees, so that he could look into my face. "The snake bile will have run its course by morning," he murmured.

"An absurd thought. After all that happened, it would be foolish," I repeated. "Irrational. Selfish."

"True," he said. "But you should go, anyway. You can make a decision this time: if it is a trap, then you know he is truly your enemy, and you can put all of this doubt behind you."

I swallowed. "And if it is not?"

"If it is not," Khine continued. "If he still loves you, then you owe it to him to try again."

I smiled. "That's the biggest *if* I have ever heard in my life. I don't believe the man ever loved me."

"Because he never told you."

I nodded.

"Foolish girl," he said. "Didn't you tell me you've made the same mistake? Somewhere along the line, your parents messed up, forgot to tell you the basics of life and living between your lessons on how to maintain a stable economy or whatever it is you princesses have to learn."

"Not all princesses," I said. "And don't call me *girl*. I'm older than you are."

"*Girl.* That's a girl's heart you've got, sitting there holding on to that letter like your life depended on it. We grow up, and some of us think we learn, but the truth is we would rather listen to our own lies for as long as there is a sliver of hope that they would turn out correct after all. There is nothing wrong with it. Will the world run on cynicism? What would happen if we all started hating each other every chance we got?"

"I envy how simply you see it."

"I'm lucky. I don't have the burden of an entire nation resting on my decisions," he said. He touched my hand. "There are never any easy answers."

"No," I agreed. "Go to sleep, Khine. Your head is in the clouds. Tomorrow..."

"Yes," he said. "Tomorrow." I helped him lean back against the pillows and watched him close his eyes.

Tomorrow, I repeated to myself. It was a loaded word. But I had come this far, on the backs of a dead adviser and guardsmen and a handmaiden whose name I should have learned a long time ago. I had to see it through.

CHAPTER TWENTY-EIGHT

THE LEGACY OF WARLORD TAL, REPRISED

ıзῶ̃ῦ̃ᴦᴣ̃ᴦ

I woke before daybreak to get ready.

I pulled my sore body into fresh clothes and my boots, and went through my weapons, which included a new sword. Lo Bahn had been generous in that regard, at least. I sneaked past my guards—still sleeping soundly, no doubt due to the fraud physician's intervention—and made my way downstairs.

Khine was sitting on the bottom step. "I'm not letting you go alone," he said before I could speak.

"You've indicated as much. Are you sure you can take a step without your guts spilling out?"

"Let's find out."

He struggled to get up. I had to help him, but after a few steps, he seemed to gain momentum and could walk without support. We slowly made our way through Lo Bahn's courtyard and to the gate, which was manned by a single guard. I recognized Ning; I don't think he remembered me, or at least, he was doing a good job of pretending he didn't.

"Any word from the governor's keep?" Khine asked.

"Governor Zheshan is still missing," Ning said. "That's all we know. They're keeping things very quiet over there. Haven't even blamed us for anything."

"Remember, Lo Bahn wants everyone to shut their mouths. If officials come sniffing around, tell them he'll set up an appointment."

"I know. Are *you* allowed to walk? You were at death's door yesterday."

Khine patted Ning's shoulder for an answer before we headed out on the street.

We walked very slowly. It was probably good that the sun wasn't up, because we would've attracted too much attention in daylight.

I made the mistake of thinking of other long early mornings. Like when I would throw open the windows to my room while rocking Thanh back to sleep, and my eyes would drift over to Rayyel's still form in bed. Such memories were dangerous, especially in the dark. They made you question what was real, made you wonder if *right now* was a dream and you could wake up and find yourself back in that space in time: holding your son, a little annoyed that your husband could sleep so soundly while the baby was crying, but also content that you were together, that you had what you had. Content enough to forget everything else, *these lies we tell ourselves*, or so I think Khine would've phrased it if I had brought it up and he had still been under the influence of Tashi Jhao's vile medicine.

I didn't. I had told him a lot of things, but there were others I dared not speak of to anyone but Rayyel, memories in the dark, traces of moments I was never really sure belonged to me. And I was setting them free. I had to. I was not so foolish as to believe that I could still bring back yesterday.

Almost as if to cement that thought, I heard Agos's booming voice and stopped in my tracks.

He appeared at the end of the street with a torch. The sky was turning a deep grey by now, but the dancing flames cast long shadows on his face. "It's not worth it, you know," he said. "What are you hoping to gain out of this? Why bother giving him a second chance? You have enough dirt on the man to get the council to investigate him formally. Throw doubt on him, the way they're throwing doubt on you. Show them the Ikessars are as foul-smelling as the rest of us."

"And let all hell break loose," I said. "It isn't about chances, Agos. It's about taking responsibility."

Agos drew closer. "Then we should both go."

"No." I stared at the building ahead of us. We had reached the spot marked by the address. "Stay out here."

Agos's face hardened. "You said this was about *responsibility*," he said. "This isn't just your doing. Yet instead you tell me to stay. Stay. Go away. Bark. *Fetch*. Am I just a dog to you? To call when you need me, and throw out when you're done?"

"I'm your queen," I reminded him.

"Friend—" Khine started.

"But him. You'd trust him, over me," Agos said, jerking a thumb towards Khine. "This nobody."

I didn't reply. I had nothing to say to him—nothing, at least, that he could understand. Five years ago, I had tried. Had cornered him in the stables and bade him to take the fastest horse and go west, where eastern traditions were not as strong and he could find a better life for himself. Back then, he was not the sort of man who questioned my orders. He took the bag of supplies I gave him, picked the horse, and swung into the saddle.

"When do I come back?" he asked.

I threw open the doors and looked him in the face. "Never," I remember saying.

His expression changed, but he didn't protest as he rode out into the rain. I, on the other hand, had walked back to the castle exactly as I walked back to my husband now: like someone on their way to a funeral.

The address pointed to a number of a rental flat, a little wider than

Khine's house. I knocked on the door. And then I waited, long enough that doubt began to seep in again, and I seriously considered turning around and returning to Agos and Khine.

And then the door opened, and there was Rayyel, unharmed, unarmed. There was a flicker of surprise at the sight of me, but his calm expression returned almost at once. He stepped aside to let me in and closed the door behind us.

I could feel my heart racing. He still hadn't said a word. Instead, he crossed the room, drawing open the curtains to let in what little light he could. I saw a table, bookshelves. Books strewn on both and all over the floor, Zarojo script on all the titles. There were scrolls and ink.

I forced my eyes back on him. He was wearing loose robes. His hair was unbound and in disarray, falling all the way past his hips, and he had neglected to tie his beard as well. He didn't look like a prisoner. He looked the way he had always been in all the years I had known him.

"You got my letter," Rai finally said.

Numbly, I nodded.

"I had heard that you were back in town a few days ago. I asked Governor Zheshan to send word as soon as he was able. Where did you go?"

I swallowed. "Zorheng." How could we be talking so quietly, so *normally*, after everything? Arro was dead, and Kora, and half my guards, and here he was discussing things as if I had simply been an ungrateful wife who neglected to tell her husband about some vacation.

He noticed my distress. "Would you like some tea?" he asked. Or maybe he was being polite. Or maybe he was trying to make me drop my guard—I would not be the first royal poisoned by a cup of tea. I shook my head.

"I am sorry about Magister Arro," he continued. "I heard they claimed him from the mortuary and buried him. I would've asked for a proper funeral pyre myself, as befitting one who had served as loyally as him, but that night I was too busy trying to avoid getting killed and I didn't hear about it until much later."

"So was I," I murmured.

He looked a little embarrassed. "Yes, I clearly remember."

"How did you escape?"

"Not gracefully. Zheshan cracked a vase over the head of the assassin, and then, thinking there might be more waiting for us in the hall, we tried to get out through the window like you did. The assassin came to while we were halfway down, and tried to chase after us. I stuck him with my sword at the first opportunity."

"The blood on the street…"

"What do you mean?"

"Nothing. So what happened?"

"We tried to find you, of course. But you and all your guards seemed to have disappeared into thin air. And then a few months ago, I received a letter from Prince Yuebek, Emperor Yunan's Fifth Son. He said he had you in his dungeons and that he required my cooperation if I would ever see you alive again. I didn't believe him—Zheshan hinted as much that I shouldn't. I see I was right not to."

"I *was*, though," I managed to say.

He blinked.

"In his dungeons," I explained. "But I think he was just trying to wear me down. He wanted me to marry him."

"I see." He flexed his jaw, an old habit of his when he was thinking things through and didn't want to make a decision just yet.

"I was able to escape." It felt odd to reduce those struggles to a few words. I tried to keep calm. I wasn't afraid of having to fight Rayyel if he was going to turn on me. My nerves were the result of something else, of the knowledge of how the sound of his voice could make me throw everything away. I tried to recall my father's sneering words. *You fell in love with the brat.*

"Well, at least I don't have to tell you that he isn't someone to be trusted. I heard there was trouble up at Governor Zheshan's office yesterday."

"Gon Zheshan is dead," I said.

His face flickered with that same, unreadable expression.

"By his own hand," I continued. "You have nothing to fear. I think he didn't want to betray you. Prince Yuebek had been there, trying to bait me. Kora was there, too. Did you know they had her in their clutches? That they were trying to use her against me?"

He didn't reply.

I turned away from him, glancing at the walls. "You've been here all this time," I said. "I'm willing to wager longer than the four months since I landed here."

He took a deep breath. "I wanted to speak to you about that."

"Please do," I said. "Better yet, though, start with Kora. She told me a lot of interesting things before she died. Sorry—before I killed her. For treason." I turned back to him. "Start with Kora, Rayyel." The venom was crawling into my voice, turning around, making a bed there. It wasn't going to leave any time soon.

He moved towards me. My right hand dropped to my dagger, but I didn't have time to draw before he had my back to the wall. His lips met mine. In the haze of confusion, I tasted hunger and desire, the sort of things a man like Rayyel couldn't fake, not even in my wildest dreams.

I felt like crying. But before I could respond, before my hands could even come up so I could bring him closer to me, he tore himself away. "I can't do this," he said, nearly spitting the words out. If my voice had been venom, his was the cold sharpness of steel. "No. It would be a lot easier if you would just leave, Talyien. Spare me all of this."

"I don't understand."

"Isn't it clear? I hired her to see what a woman like you would do if left to herself."

"You were *testing* me?" I found myself wanting to laugh at the notion. "And what *did* you find out, Lord Rayyel? Tell me."

"You took no lovers," he grudgingly admitted. "So I had hoped...I had hoped that I would be able to speak with you when we met again. To reconcile."

My mind was running backwards, back to that ill-fated meeting in the Silver Goose and the long hours spent arguing over a piece of map and brushstrokes. "You wanted to split Jin-Sayeng in half," I said. "You never mentioned *reconciliation*."

"We had to start somewhere!" I had never heard Rayyel raise his voice before. "Gon Zheshan had suggested that if we could make such a thing work..."

"Oh, Rayyel," I said. "If that was all you wanted, all you had to do was *ask*."

"That wasn't *all* I wanted. There were other things, too—a way to mitigate the warlords' aggression, help us find common ground between some of the factions..." He threw his hand across the air. "But none of that matters anymore! I cannot trust you. After all these years, halfway across the world, and what do I find out? That you're with *him*, still."

It took a moment for his words to sink in. "No," I found myself replying. "I never asked him to be here. Agos followed me. I wouldn't even have known he was alive until two days ago!"

"And you didn't think of sending him away?"

"I have no one else to depend on, Rai. If you think I'm that much of a fool—"

"Talyien," he roared. "This is exactly the kind of thinking that got us here!"

He didn't punch the wall, but I could tell he wanted to. He looked at his hands and then helplessly turned to me with a sunken expression. Not unreadable now, no. It spoke of pain, of years of uncertainty, as if someone had taken those precious early-morning memories, placed them inside a crystal ball, and smashed it to pieces. If you had asked me, I would have told you that he had done that himself five years ago when he walked out on us.

And yet it was clear that he thought he was walking away from the woman who did the same.

"I loved you," Rayyel said under his breath. Words I had wanted to hear in all the time I knew him. I had never dreamed he would say them in a voice seething with hate.

I remembered the man I had killed, the poor ambitious innkeeper who thought he could blackmail both of us in my own father's garden. I thought of his blubbering face when he realized I was having none of it, pockmarked cheeks pale with fright, eyes like pinpricks in the dark. One tearing slice across the gut, a messy wound that a skilled warrior could've easily avoided. Not this one. He was at my mercy the moment he showed his face, dead the moment he told my husband of my affair with Agos before our wedding. The choices that led me to that road to Shirrokaru and then out, that had me inviting Agos into my room on that roadside inn after (heart beating loud enough for me to hear, he had obeyed, would've thrown himself off a bridge if I had asked him to)—up until then, I had been content to pretend it had all been a dream. But we make mistakes and we hide them with more mistakes, and so life goes on like a broken marionette finishing a play, like a lame horse trying to win a race, like the melody from a lute with missing strings.

I also remembered Rayyel's face when he heard. Blank. Silent. As if he was considering nothing more than the morning news from a messenger. His expression was very different now, as if five years of thinking it over had unhinged those feelings at last.

"I said the last time we saw each other that you didn't let me explain," I said.

"Why does it matter?" he asked. "Could it change the past? Will it undo the truth?"

"It happened once before our wedding. I was faithful to you through-out our entire marriage, Rai."

His face flickered. Was he thinking of his own mistakes? *Did* he know I knew? "Regardless of the circumstances, we were already betrothed. What you did...you neglected to think of the repercussions. As it hap-pened, I paid attention to the innkeeper's story. You were with him before our wedding night: three days before our wedding night, to be precise. The same wedding night when we supposedly conceived our son."

My stomach turned at his words. "Thanh is yours," I managed to gasp out. I had never once considered this angle, that Rayyel would question the son he had been so proud of, the son he had adored in the two years we were a family together. How was I supposed to know? He had given me *nothing* to go on, nothing except...

I remembered the letter, the one I had stuffed in my desk back home, half-unread. He must've asked me then. He must've asked me. I hadn't answered. And then the years flew by...

"How sure are you?" he asked.

"He's yours," I stammered. "If you see him..."

"I've heard the reports. He looks more and more like you as he grows up. A spitting image of Yeshin, others say. Who is his father, Talyien? You *want* it to be me, that much is plain. Forgive me if I can't just take your word for it. I have spent the last five years trying to find a way to learn. I've travelled through the Kag and as far as Dageis. Only in Ziri-nar-Orxiaro did I finally learn of a way they will know who sired him."

"All these years...this is what you've been doing? You've been trying to find a reason to cast him aside?"

"Call it what you will," Rai said. "I had to. For as long as there is doubt, I cannot knowingly proclaim him my heir. What would you rather I do, Talyien? Pretend it never happened? I have a duty to our people. You did, too, or so I once thought. I cannot say what your priori-ties are anymore."

He walked towards his desk and gestured at the pile of papers. "I've been researching how the Zarojo work with the *agan*. There is an academy of mages to the south. I am told they can provide me answers, perhaps lend me someone I can bring back to Jin-Sayeng. I intend to travel there. Governor Zheshan had made arrangements and lent me a portion of his guard for protection. My ship leaves this morning."

"I thought you wanted to speak with me first."

"That was before I had learned you were with that buffoon again." He began to straighten the papers before picking up a scroll with a golden seal around it. He stuffed it into his robe.

"And if they say otherwise?"

He stared at me.

"Thanh is yours," I said. "From the moment he was born, he was yours."

"Just like you were once mine?" he asked dryly.

I ignored the insult. "These people will tell you anything. They are using us to throw a rift as wide as an ocean in our own nation. Surely you've heard of the reports back home. By all the gods, Rayyel—set aside this ridiculous tantrum. It's been five years. Come home with me. See the boy for yourself. You will know the moment you lay your eyes on him. He is just like you, Rayyel. The way he talks, the way he moves, the way he shuts himself in his room to read instead of riding with me, the way he holds a sword. The gods be damned—listen to me, Rai!"

The door opened. I stiffened, thinking it was Agos, but it was only Khine. "We spotted men on their way here," he said. "I think they're from the governor's office." His eyes flickered towards my husband. "Is everything all right?"

"Out of respect for what we once had, I will let you walk out of here alive," Rai said. "What you do from here on out is your business. Zheshan, at least, knew what *loyalty* meant."

"They would lie to you," I said. "These Zarojo, these mages. You didn't see Yuebek, the things he said, the lies."

His eyes hardened. "I have to believe *someone*."

"Let's suppose the warlords somehow overlook the fact that you're going to bring Zarojo witchcraft, or whatever they call it here, into court. You can't even talk about the *agan* back home without people making signs of every deity they can think of! These people are using you, Rayyel. Did you know the extent of Yuebek's attempt to force my hand in marriage? He copied your handwriting, he hired assassins to concoct this elaborate scheme...he killed his own wife! You cannot trust them! And what do you think they'll do if they find out about this back home? They will kill Thanh and seize control before we can prove anything. They already *think* it, Rai. Our son is surrounded by snakes."

"Do not refer to him as *our* son. Not until I'm sure." He straightened his sleeves. "You know I'm doing the right thing. If you truly believed that the land came first, you would agree with me. Think of the war we could be averting. "

"We are not *averting* anything. We are creating war as we speak, Rayyel!"

"I will not have it said that the Ikessars entertained a farce that would ruin the land."

"What would you know?" I asked. "You weren't around the last five years to raise him."

"That," he said, "is on you."

"I didn't force your hand!"

"You might as well have and you know it. If you had prepared me beforehand—"

"How in heavens was I supposed to do that? Was it a conversation you would have appreciated having, *ever*?"

"As political figures—"

"Ah, I see. I had no idea being political figures gives us the permission to dredge up the past and ruin our lives. You could have returned. Once your temper cooled, you could have come back, and we could've discussed this like adults. Your letter—" I laughed. "I didn't read it. I would have let Ozo have his war if I had known your reasoning was this petty."

"You didn't read it. I see. I said nothing that would compromise our position, but you see why..." He gave a grim smile. "My temper isn't the problem here, Talyien."

"You stayed away for five years because you're afraid I am Oren-yaro and you wanted to see what I would do first. You coward. I shouldn't have expected more from an Ikessar."

"Is that what you want to bring this down to?"

"You did it first. I'm a wolf before I am your wife. To you, I will *always* be a wolf." I pointed at him. "And if they say he isn't yours? What do you intend to do then?"

"I will do what I should have done a long time ago," he said. "I'll kill him myself."

And with those words, he walked out, just like he did before.

I heard Khine say something to me, heard someone calling for Rai—Agos's voice, the damned man in whose arms I sought comfort from my husband's own betrayal. Did Rai think I enjoyed it, the way he enjoyed his Baraji whore? I heard the sound of squawking seagulls and crows, and the marching of Zheshan's soldiers as they came to fetch him. Nothing stuck. I found myself rising from the chair and drawing my sword and racing to the doorway like my feet were on fire. Rayyel was three, four paces away. One leap could do it. I could knock him to the ground, slide the blade through his throat before his guards could get me.

The thought of killing Rayyel filled me with more grief than I had ever dreamed possible. But a part of me screamed that I had to do it for my son. If this secret died with us, there was a chance the warlords would ride in his defense against those who sought the throne for themselves, even if—*especially* if—they were men who claimed to work for my dead father. They had done more for Rayyel as an infant. Thanh as the Ikessar heir could still be Dragonlord.

I hesitated, just as Ozo said I would.

The opportunity passed. Rayyel was gone, a dozen of Zheshan's guards at his flank.

"He is going to get Thanh killed," I breathed. "He doesn't understand what he's walking into, what he's dragging all of us into. We have to stop him."

"We will," Agos promised. "But not as we are now. You need allies, and an army to fight for you. You need power worthy of the queen of Jin-Sayeng."

But his words faded in the background. The breath bubbled in my throat as I thought of my son, alone in the castle while our enemies rose from the shadows. I had done that. I had pushed him into the fires myself. Even if he forgave me, the gods never will.

"I want to go home," I whispered.

A century ago, Warlord Tal was the last to die on that battlefield.

The history books speak of how bravely the Oren-yaro fought until the Ikessar lord came to take back Shirrokaru. They speak of the immeasurable courage of this lord, who would choose to ride against the enemy with only a hundred men at his behest and somehow—against all odds—win.

We Oren-yaro know better. But we do not speak of the wrongs that were done to us. We do not count the ways we have done more, the battles we were forced to fight, or the sacrifices we had to make. My father's last wishes could only be a lie. That he would want both my husband and my son dead so I could be sold off to another, a foreigner who would claim the Dragonthrone? That there would be people loyal to him, and not his daughter? The Oren-yaro had been fending off suspicions about our ambition and our greed for centuries; one whiff of this madness and the others would latch on like vultures. The rumours alone would ignite civil war.

Yeshin wouldn't. My father did everything for the good of the land—he had told me himself that he had been winning the war, but when they offered him a chance for peace, he took it. After years of trying to kill them, he welcomed Rayyel and his mother into Oka Shto with open arms and, with the hope that he was doing what was best for us all, placed the boy's closed fist on my infant chest.

No matter the truth, that promise was long gone. But I am a wolf of Oren-yaro, and my tenet dictates that I swim against the tide if I must. So we buried Warlord Tal in silence while the rest of the nation celebrated the Dragonlord's ascent. Let them bury me in scandal; let them carry the sound of my name with distaste. Let them speak ill of the Bitch Queen who brought ruin to the land with the same gilded tongue they praised the uncrowned king who was just as responsible.

None of it mattered. My duties were far from over. A wolf of Oren-yaro fights to make it right, down to the last breath. A wolf of Oren-yaro does not beg. A wolf of Oren-yaro suffers in silence.

THE STORY CONTINUES IN...

THE IKESSAR FALCON

CHRONICLES OF THE BITCH
QUEEN: BOOK TWO

ACKNOWLEDGMENTS

My husband came home the day I told him my book was going to get traditionally published, looked me in the eye, and said, "You were always going to make it. It was only a matter of time."

We don't get far without others, and I'm fortunate in the sense that my book found its people. To get even this far, I owe a huge debt of gratitude to my editor, Bradley Englert, who took a chance on this series and has been an ardent champion of it since. I also want to thank my fantastic agent, Hannah Bowman, and her protective momma-bear shadow that makes me worry a lot less (and that's saying a lot). It's amazing enough to be here; to be working with people whose work I've admired before they took me on is surreal. I couldn't have asked for a better team.

I want to thank my crew of authors who have been there since Day One: Quenby Olson, A. S. Bohannan, Julie Midnight, Bo, Cheyanne, Sheena, and the rest of the gang from way back. My writing group, my stroke of good luck, my bestest friends—I wouldn't be the writer I am today without you.

I am deeply grateful for the support of so many authors. There are too many of you to name here, but I want to give an added shout-out to those who've offered their mentorship, support, or just general positivity when I was new to all of this: Michael J. Sullivan, Krista D. Ball, Courtney

Schafer, Dyrk Ashton, Steve Thomas, Benedict Patrick, J. C. Kang, and everyone else from the Terrible Ten writing group. I also want to especially thank Phil Tucker, who is incredibly generous with his guidance and wisdom, and who is a wizard with those fight scenes.

Last but not least: Josiah Bancroft is a wonderful colleague whose kindness and wit always gladden my heart. He has also been an inspiration since I first read his self-published book in the fall of 2016 and realized I was wasting my time chasing after things that didn't mean the world to me. I walked out of class that day with the intention of going after my dreams with everything I've got left, and here we are. Thank you, Josiah.

There are many, many people from the fantasy reading, writing, and review communities who have been instrumental in this journey, but I especially want to thank Esme from the Weatherwax Report, patron saint of indie novels; Kristen; and Para. I am also indebted to the crew over at the Fantasy Inn: Hiu, Jenia, Travis, Sara, Kop, and Tam, but most of all, Wol, who was one of my first readers, who listened to my bellyaching before any of this happened, who told me there was something worth reading in my garbage, who believed in me. Without all your endorsements, your sneaky promotion tactics, and the laughter that's kept me afloat through the worst of days, none of this would have been possible.

Thank you to the rest of the Orbit team (including its crew of lovely and ever supportive editors—God bless you for encouraging my weirdness), Simon Goinard for the fantastic cover art, and everyone helping bring this book into the world. You are rock stars.

Finally, for their endless tolerance for this life I chose, my family and friends, Filipino style: Mom, Dad, my mother-in-law, my father-in-law, Paolo, the Velasco clan, the Solano clan, the Reynoso clan, the Villoso clan, Raymond, Cristina, Jury, Annlyn, Erica, Santos, Jury and Santos's bandmates, Janet, my kids, dear God, I hope I didn't forget anyone . . .

My husband's words were the culmination of watching my flailing attempts for eighteen years and counting. I don't know how much of our struggles are seen by others—we aren't owed anything just because we have them, after all. But difficult journeys are better when you're with the right people, and I've had at least one from the very start: Mikhail, first reader, biggest fan, and forever my rock—you have made every moment worth it. Let's go even further.

extras

orbit

meet the author

Photo Credit: Mikhail Villoso

K. S. VILLOSO began writing while growing up in the slums of Manila amongst tales of bloodthirsty ghouls, ethereal spirits, and mysteries under the shadows of the banyan trees—a world where fantasy meets the soiled reality of everyday. She immigrated to Canada in her teens and was briefly distracted working with civil and municipal infrastructure. When she isn't writing, she is off dragging her husband, dogs, kids, and anyone insane enough to say "Sure, let's go hiking—what could go wrong?" through the Canadian wilderness. She lives in Anmore, BC.

interview

When did you first start writing?

I was six or seven years old. I had always loved books, but writing was a very deliberate decision. We went to the mall, where they were announcing the winners for a young-writers' contest. The winner was titled "Ang Prinsesa" (The Princess), and it occurred to me that I loved stories so much I should be writing, too. I went home and wrote my first story that very same day.

I never stopped.

Can you tell us a bit about your writing process?

My writing starts out like a memory. There's an idea and characters that embed themselves into my subconscious, and I let them sit there for a few years until I feel strongly enough to write about them. I also need to know the project's themes, character arcs, and major relationships before I can begin. I don't necessarily know how all of these will tie together—I just have to *want* to learn this story. I need to care deeply about these characters and look forward to exploring their world with them.

From there on, I juggle a very structured outline with discovery writing, and finding this balance is a unique experience with every project I write. I need that storytelling symmetry; I need every scene to have a purpose...but I also need for it to feel organic, for the characters to whole-heartedly believe what they are doing. I need to know what's going to happen, but I also need to surprise myself. This contradiction has resulted in a "throwing a ball and then running across the field in order to catch it" element to my process. I never know for sure how a project will turn out until I'm close to the end, which means with every book I write, I pray to the writing gods and sacrifice a bit of my soul...

Where did the idea for *The Wolf of Oren-Yaro* come from, and how did the story begin to take shape in your mind?
Around 2013, I wanted to do my own take on a couple of archetypes: the Strong Female Character and the Chosen One. I wanted to combine the two and see how having a woman as a main character in this position would change the story (particularly, say, if a Chosen One is learned to have sired a bastard—how would it look from the other side?). Then I had the idea of making her relationship with her husband the central conflict. I enjoy character studies and deconstructions, and I kept all these in the back of my mind, as I was writing a different book at this time.

In 2014, I was writing the sequel to that other book. A few chapters into the beginning, the main characters travel to Oren-yaro. Here, they meet the secondary antagonist, Warlord Yeshin: an aging warlord with a fiery temperament, whose second wife has just left him. Later, Yeshin's power play moves the story forward; as I was exploring his character as a broken man, reeling from the loss of his sons, I suddenly realized this was going to be central to the other story, too. *This* was going to be Talyien's beginning. She is going to be born to a world where she is the bad guy, where her family has done all these terrible things, and somehow, she's going to have to make it work. By that point I knew I needed to tell this story, one way or another.

I formed her husband Rayyel's story the same way. In those other books, his family is on the protagonists' side, his mother a reluctant leader thrust into the spotlight because of Yeshin's treachery.

I threw Talyien and Rayyel straight into the heart of this mess. Because their relationship is so crucial to the story, the rest just fell into place.

The world of the novel feels lived in and real. Were there any challenges in creating the history of the world and the vivid settings?

I've been writing in this world for a good fifteen or sixteen years now. Originally, it was made for a video game I was designing with RPG Maker 2000 in high school. Although I managed to get only a world map, two towns, and an amazingly melodramatic intro cutscene done, I got bit by the worldbuilding bug and started expanding it from there.

A lot of the challenges lay with creating a fantasy world using Filipino culture and myths as a base while trying to do away with the Philippines' colonial history. In the case of Jin-Sayeng, I wanted a nation that took influence only from other Asian nations, the way we might have if the Spaniards never came (while viewing the "European" influence to the west as an equal). This meant mimicking certain structures that most of my readers would be more familiar with—that is, East Asian and other Southeast Asian influences. I've heard people wonder, for example, if it's based on feudal Japan, when it isn't—it's all completely Filipino in my head, from the family structures to the interactions. But I use words to trick people into *thinking* it if they're struggling to place themselves, a challenge that wouldn't exist when writing for a culture that already has a template for it.

So a lot of the worldbuilding is an exercise in what-if... in borrowing and restructuring and pretending to make up for what we've lost. I like to say that my worldbuilding is a love letter to the Philippines, which is to say most of it is designed in a way to explore my feelings about my own culture, history, and identity. It's especially clear when you look at the various nations' themes. With Jin-Sayeng, we have a nation mourning lost glories, trying to survive while dealing with internal strife and politics, and all while more-powerful nations look down on it.

Every nation has a struggle, every city is a character, and most of it is a medium for expressing whatever is needed for the story. The seedy underbelly of Anzhao City, for example, was meant to turn Talyien's world upside down; the oppressive, fortress-like Zorheng was designed to reflect Tali's own internal prison. I then draw on my own experiences to colour these environments—every scent, sight, and sound I've known. I "see" it all in my head and do my best to relay it as the story demands.

Talyien has such an immediate and endearing voice. How did you tackle her narration? What excited you about writing from her perspective? What was the most difficult aspect of writing her character?

I rarely write in first person, and I've noticed that when I do, the main characters always have very strong, vibrant personalities. Talyien came fully formed: the biting sarcasm, the wit, the fierce nature combined with her unbelievable naivety. These sorts of characters are a joy to wade through. Such an active character makes my job as a writer really easy—she has a tendency to jump into things first and asks questions later, which means almost every scene she barges into is rife with conflict. I love how she has a ready response to insults, how she has protected her vulnerability with thorns, how she's always right at the edge without fully tipping over.

But all of this intensity made writing her insanely difficult as well. She has a certain way of thinking about things, so I'm struggling to keep up at times—using metaphors only she would use, for instance, or trying to remember how she was raised, because certain aspects of her personality are extremely rigid. At other times, she's wild and unpredictable. I'll say, "The plot demands we have to do Point A and then B, Tali, okay?" and she's bypassed Point B and is already at Point E, with Points C and D somehow in flames. I wouldn't have it any other way, of course, but it's made for some emotionally draining moments...

Talyien goes through dramatic changes and shifts in her understanding of the world throughout the novel. How did you approach this development from feared queen to hiding-in-plain-sight commoner to a queen determined to be respected?

Everything starts and ends with character for me. The plot is the character; the character is the plot. So you have, in the beginning, this person who was raised a certain way, by a demanding father no less, which shaped her worldview. But she *isn't* her father; what she is inside is very different from what she presents outside. So as the story goes along and she learns more about the state of things and about herself, we peel back another layer, which forces her to make difficult choices. With every step, she can continue to hold on to what she was even as it all unravels before her very eyes, or she can jump into the abyss towards an unlikely salvation, risking everything that matters to her.

The side characters are so wonderfully drawn, and each one truly feels like their own individual person. Who is your favorite (or favorites)? Whom did you enjoy writing the most?

I'm honestly fond of all of them in some way, or at least try to view them compassionately. I like to say that in order to develop really strong characters, you have to find people fascinating. You have to see them as a puzzle—regardless of whether you personally agree with their behaviour or not. Getting into their heads is always interesting, occasionally disturbing (particularly in Yuebek's case—I cringed all the way through writing his scenes).

That said, Khine is by far the most enjoyable to write about, simply because of how he interacts with other characters. He's got his own issues, but his edges are calculated, and he keeps them hidden very well, which means I can put him in just about any situation. Plus he's the character I've written who's least likely to murder me in my sleep...

Will any characters return in the future books (no spoilers!)?

Almost everyone who doesn't die gets a chance to...try to avoid* death again.

*Not completely true, because some of them don't even see it coming.

If you could spend time with any of your characters, who would it be and why?

People are going to expect me to say Khine, but the truth is, it would be Rayyel, Talyien's husband. The walking-encyclopedia aspect of his personality would be entertaining (I'm assuming in this scenario the internet wouldn't exist). I can imagine it would also be fascinating to pick his brain— engage in debate and conjecture and all that fun stuff. And since *I'm* not married to him, I don't have to worry about the rest... Once he gets too irritating, I can always give him back to whoever still wants him. If they still want him.

Do you have a favorite scene in *The Wolf of Oren-Yaro*? If so, why?

Without even thinking about it, it's the scene in the shed with Khine, where he holds Talyien and they talk and she thinks about how much his presence reminds her of her horses and dogs (symbolically, the only ones who have been true to her).

There are a lot of really cool and powerful scenes in the book, but that scene where absolutely nothing happens captures Tali's whole nature in a single snapshot. She is restrained, guarded, and unwilling to trust because of everything that has been done to her, but she doesn't *want* to be like that. So she takes what little comfort she can, all while dreaming of what she thinks she wants, when she knows every single sign points to a doomed quest. Her true desires are very simple, very human, and incredibly difficult to achieve in a world where she is the Bitch Queen.

Who are some of your favorite writers, and how have they influenced your work?

I remember reading Robin Hobb's Farseer Trilogy well over a decade ago, and I was just overwhelmed by how much I loved the characters, how *honest* the story was. It was the first time I realized fantasy could be written with a tightly character-driven focus, no holds barred, and still make it work. This was always my preference, but the majority of fantasy I'd read before had a more distant, ethereal style, which I was struggling to imitate. Hobb taught me it's okay to write raw, straight from the heart. It probably helped that around the same time, I was also consuming a lot of Dostoevsky.

As well, I'm a big fan of Guy Gavriel Kay and Steven Brust, and of course Ursula K. Le Guin. Outside of the genre, I've also been influenced by Richard Adams (with plots that revel in trickery and deceit), Jack London (who taught me how to use environment to develop character), and José Rizal (whose love for the Philippines bled into every sentence he wrote).

When you're not writing, what do you like to do in your spare time?

I try to fit in as much hiking as humanly possible in my daily routine. We live next to some magnificent hiking trails, and I'm out nearly every day with a dog or two. Otherwise, I'm planning backpacking excursions into the mountains. I'm trying to wean myself off picking some random trail nobody has heard of with only GPS coordinates and previous hikers' anecdotes as a guide. Exploring is awesome; falling off a cliff, not so much. I also love camping, fishing, biking, canoeing...it's hard to live in BC and not be an outdoor nut.

Reading is a given, of course, but I enjoy stories in all shapes and forms. I love watching movies (particularly horror) and playing video games (I especially enjoy RPGs, RTS, and city builders).

extras

The Wolf of Oren-Yaro **is the first book in a trilogy. Without giving too much away, can you tell us what we can expect in the upcoming novels?**

Talyien's story continues on. Because what you saw at the end of *The Wolf of Oren-Yaro* is far from the end—it's *just* the beginning.

And since this series is all about breaking facades and stripping layers, that's what you're going to get. We were skimming the surface with *The Wolf of Oren-Yaro*...now we're going for a dive. We're going deeper, learning more about the major characters and watching their relationships develop and change, all while unearthing the foul secrets that lie beneath Queen Talyien's nation.

There will be adventures up the mountains and through the wilderness, with monsters, mad dragons, shape-shifters, and blood magic. There will be heists, fights, mages, and even a tournament battle. There will be agony and heartbreak. Cities will fall, armies will clash, and the story will unveil exactly why *the chosen lie on a bed of nails.*

Finally, we have to ask, if you had the choice to visit any of the cities, which would it be?

I'd like to go to Oren-yaro and take you with me. We could walk through the old dragon-towers and imagine the shadow of the dragons as they land on the platforms. We could take a walk along the riverbank or visit the ruins of Warlord Yeshin's keep to the south or go up the steps to the north all the way to the mountain where Talyien's castle stands. I've written about this city in many books, and so much has happened here that I feel like I know its history like the back of my hand. I can see its scars if I just close my eyes.

if you enjoyed
THE WOLF OF OREN-YARO

look out for

THE IKESSAR FALCON

Chronicles of the Bitch Queen:
Book Two

by

K. S. Villoso

The spiral to madness begins with a single push.

*After Queen Talyien is abandoned by her people, her
quest takes a turn for the worse as she stumbles upon a plot
deeper and more sinister than she could ever have imagined, one
that will displace her king and see her son dead. The road to
Jin-Sayeng beckons, strewn with a tangled web of deceit and
unimaginable horrors that unearth the nation's true*

troubles—creatures from the dark, mad dragons, and men with hearts hungry for power.

To save her land, Talyien must come face-to-face with the worst enemy of all: Warlord Yeshin's daughter, symbol of peace, warrior and queen, and everything she could never be. For the price of failure is steep, her friends are few, and a nation carved by a murderer can be destined only for war.

CHAPTER ONE

The Price of Innocence

A thousand hooves trampled the sky the night my father died.

No words can describe what it feels like to gaze at the man you looked up to—a man you respected, and loved, and feared—and realize that somewhere along the way, he had turned into a shadow of his former self. That he had, in fact, been fading for years, and was simply doing a remarkable job of pretending the world wasn't falling apart. Where there was once power, presence, and might, now there was only sickness and the stench of death—not yet the sweet stink of a rotting corpse, but a moldy, urine-tinged scent, one that seemed to crawl away from his stiffening body and up the walls to fill the entire room.

The storm started with his last breath. I found myself sinking back into the chair, frozen in terror as the lightning flashed over his shadowed face, revealing the hollows under his eyes, spidered with black veins. Deep green bruises, cracked lips, yellow-white skin, wrinkled as parchment. I had been instructed to inform Lord General Ozo first should my father succumb to his illness, but I couldn't even find the courage to stand, let alone look away from the withered image of the man who used to be strong enough to lift me on his shoulders. *You're alone now*, my thoughts whispered, a thin thread that sought to wrap itself around my heart. *You will no longer be able to depend on him. From now on, everything falls on you.*

The sobs stopped at my throat, settling inside my chest and wrenching the breath out of me. My eyes were burning, but I was forcing the tears not to fall. What if one of the soldiers walked in and saw Yeshin's heir red-faced and bawling away like a child? The other warlords would think us weak, that they all made a mistake when they bequeathed the Dragonthrone to an Orenar. To an Oren-yaro. Would I let it all turn to dust after everything my father had sacrificed?

I slowly let go of Yeshin's hand, curling mine into a fist, before I reached up to plant a kiss on his wrinkled forehead. It was still covered in a layer of cold sweat. I wanted to say something, to utter a prayer or words of farewell for a man whose name carried a weight that could break the world. But silence seemed to be the only fitting poetry for someone who had lived as Warlord Yeshin had. So instead, I swallowed and murmured an oath that I would do everything it took to make his dreams become a reality. A united land, prosperous in the way the Ikessars couldn't make it, with the discipline and the ideals that made the province and the people of Oren-yaro stand head and shoulders above the rest. And so even if it meant facing my fears, if it meant walking the road laid out for me... if it meant becoming someone I was not...

He was dead, and yet I still carried on in my head like he was listening. It started there; it never stopped. And there was never a time after that I didn't find myself carrying out my duties to the echo of his voice—to that sharp, lightning-like roar of it, the one that could crumple my very soul.

It was that same voice that reached deep into me and forced me to consider my failures the day I lost my husband. My quest for Rayyel was a twisted reflection of the turbulence around me, a lighthouse in a stormy sea. I was accused of blindness, of obsession, of allowing my love for a man to become the center around which my life spun. I hardened myself to it. Embraced it. Call me what you want—irrational, careless, an idiot, even—every name you can think of. I know. I've told them to myself for years. When you internalize such thinking, allowing it to settle into your bones so deeply you know your own weaknesses to be fact, it becomes a kind of foolhardy strength. Make of that what you will.

So when the bitter truth came—when my husband declared that he had loved me after all, when I had long convinced myself that I was the one holding our marriage together— my world came crashing down. For the longest time, to hear those words was all I ever wanted. He loved me, but because three days before my wedding, I had fled from his ancestral city straight into my friend Agos's arms, he could no longer be certain our son was his. There is nothing worse to wash down anger than the taste of your own mistakes.

A just reaction, so many others will say. Rayyel deserved it after what he had done—after his own betrayal, his own languid affair with another warlord's daughter. But they don't understand. They don't understand that it was the kind of emotional reaction my father used to warn me against, proof enough to remind me that I was not what my father needed me to be, that I did not deserve to be Warlord Yeshin's daughter. What strength I thought I had was laughable—I needed to be more than this. Jin-Sayeng needed me to be more than this. Thousands had lost their lives to get me to where I was. If I faltered, thousands more would follow.

It was as if I had taken a sharpened knife and stabbed my father's dreams over and over. The worst part was that I didn't do it to rebel. I didn't do it out of spite. I did it because I was frightened, for comfort, because Yeshin could've done better than to pin all his hopes on someone like me. My father had a brilliant mind, but he was wrong about the one thing he couldn't afford to be wrong about.

Ignorance—yes, that's the word. Only an ignorant woman would willingly swallow a vat of poison in the hopes of finding a cure. Maybe another would have been allowed the mistake, but I was lady of Oren-yaro, future queen of Jin-Sayeng. I was supposed to understand the significance of my every move. My father had drilled these things into me the moment I was old enough to know my name was Talyien aren dar Orenar. I was the Jewel of Jin-Sayeng, a symbol of peace, a double-edged sword. I wielded enough power to send men running for the door or falling at my feet—an army of ten thousand, my father's bloody legacy around me like a shawl.

But in those moments of my mistake, I had dropped all trappings and left behind a girl of eighteen. Old enough to know better, but still too young to understand the nature of the world, the pitfalls that could open up and trap you. I remember the rain, the lightning across the sky and the thunder that followed, pounding against the glass windows of the inn. The smell of mint and beeswax candles, the ringing of wind chimes spinning with the storm. The hollow sensation of loneliness, of broken illusions and dreams disappearing rapidly, like a bucket of water upturned into the sea.

I cranked the door open and called for Agos. In crowded inns, he usually slept in front of the doorway by the hall, refusing to get his own room. I had long stopped insisting. I heard him stir from the shadows at the sound of my voice.

"Princess," he said, stepping inside with the surety of a beast stalking through the night. "Do you need something?"

"I'm frightened of lightning," I blurted out, forgetting whatever excuse I had planned to give.

He looked at me, a puzzled expression on his face. "Lightning," he said evenly. "Not thunder?"

"Lightning," I repeated. "The flash, the crackle. Not the rumble."

"You." He didn't sound like he believed me.

Almost as an answer, another flash of lightning lit up the sky, and I cringed involuntarily. His eyes widened, as if he had only just realized I meant what I said. A few moments later, the crack of thunder broke through, and I felt the tight grip of fear loosen itself around me. I was able to breathe again.

"Do you want me to make it go away?" he asked, a hint of laughter behind his voice.

"Could you?"

He was still wondering if I was serious or not. "I could ask around for the nearest temple..." he started.

I sighed. "I didn't mean...I am joking, Agos. Partly." A third flash, another cringe.

Agos continued to stare at me. "I can't tell, sometimes."

"Really? After all these years?"

He nodded.

"Just sit with me. Talk." I placed my hand on the mattress.

Agos took the furthest edge. He looked uncomfortable, like he was about to fall off. He placed his hands on his knees and looked back at me. "Are you all right now?" he asked. "You didn't tell me why we left the Dragon Palace as quickly as we arrived."

"Tell me about training," I said, ignoring his question. "I've heard General Ozo is a bit of a hard-ass."

"A princess shouldn't speak like that."

"A princess hangs around long enough with soldiers like you, she's bound to pick up a few things. Come on, Agos. We haven't seen each other in years." I had been fifteen the last time he had visited Oka Shto. "Surely you have some amusing story to tell."

"I don't..." he began. He scratched his cheek. "Nothing I could repeat in polite company. Especially not in front of a lady."

I punched his arm. I used to do that often when we were younger. His reaction now was more subdued than I remembered.

"You've got to act like one, too," he murmured, rubbing his skin like I had actually hurt him. "You're going to be a wife soon. What would Prince Rayyel say?"

The smile I had pasted onto my face disappeared. Hearing my betrothed's name felt like a blow to the head. I dropped my gaze. "I don't want to talk about Rayyel."

The fourth flash of lightning, and then thunder almost immediately after. And then the rain, pouring so hard around us that I scarcely noticed I had thrown myself at him. I was afraid of lightning. It wasn't something Warlord Yeshin's daughter should readily admit. If my father had known when he was alive, he would've locked me in a shed during a storm to try to knock it out of me, or at least numb my senses to it.

"Princess Tali..." I heard Agos grumble.

My hands were wrapped around his shirt. "I'm sorry," I whispered, glancing down so that I didn't have to look at his face. "I'm..."

"What the hell did Prince Rayyel do to you, anyway?"

"Nothing," I quickly said. "He did nothing." He did nothing while letting that woman do whatever she wanted with him. Chiha, Warlord Lushai's daughter. I didn't see her face, but it had to be her. Her father had wanted to undo everything mine had worked so hard for while maintaining a pretense of friendship.

I let my hands fall to the side. "I'm sorry," I repeated. My own weakness disgusted me. I could almost feel my father shaking my shoulder, telling me to stand tall, to think clearly. I was better than this. I took a deep breath. "Please. You may go, if you want."

He quirked an eyebrow. "If I want?"

"I don't know anymore." I could hear his shallow breathing, and I caught sight of his flushed face, of the rise and fall of his broad chest. What had happened to my childhood friend, the older boy who didn't think twice about indulging my harebrained schemes? I was acutely aware that this was now a man beside me. I tried to shut the images of the last few hours from my mind, and the sound of Chiha moaning with her fingers wrapped around my betrothed's sheets.

"Would you stay with me tonight?" I asked. I could barely recognize my voice.

"If I want," he repeated. His own had dropped another octave.

I hesitated and then nodded. I noticed his hand had been on my elbow. He now slid it up my arm, testing my reaction. I didn't flinch, allowing him to touch my bare shoulder.

He started to kiss me, but I twisted my head away from him. I wasn't exactly sure what I wanted at that moment, but I knew what I didn't want. I didn't want that sort of intimacy—I didn't want to play at love. He took the hint and let his lips fall on my neck instead.

There was a clicking sound. I watched in horror as the door opened and the innkeeper barged in. "Dinner is—" he began. He saw us on the bed, and his face turned as white as his beard. "I'm sorry, my lady. I'm..." He walked out just as quickly, slamming the door behind him.

I cleared my throat. Agos got up. At the doorway, he turned to me. "Are you sure about this?"

I almost said no. Wasn't this the sort of thing I was supposed to iron out with my betrothed first? I knew in the back of my head that I could approach the council with evidence of Rayyel's wrongdoing, which would discredit him without the blame falling on me. It was the kind of thing that would strengthen my support among the warlords, too—in a land as idealistic as Jin-Sayeng, adultery was seen as a great affront. It was true we weren't married yet, but there was protocol about these things, small subtleties I could've taken advantage of.

But I didn't have a template on feelings. I was aware I was acting irrationally, but I didn't know how to handle it. And so I didn't stop Agos when he locked the door and returned to me. One hand on my knee, he paused long enough to take his shirt off. I had seen him naked before, but five years in the army had transformed his stocky body into something unrecognizable, one of hard muscle and scarred flesh. His skin, which had once been as pale as mine, had tanned considerably under the sun. I made myself touch him, half-curious at the sensation stirring within me, but also half wishing it was Rayyel there instead.

Agos moved like a man possessed, as if he was afraid I would change my mind at any moment. He untied my shirt, sliding it off my shoulders, and pushed me back onto the bed, rough fingers running over my skin like it was made of glass. Lips on my neck again, and then down on my breasts, one after the other, hot mouth hungry for my flesh. I lay still, unsure exactly what I was supposed to do, what was expected of me. No templates, like I said. I had them for everything but this.

I could feel his hardness on my leg. A slight attention to it was all it took, and now he was unbuckling his pants and spitting on his hand. He slid into me, hard enough to make me gasp in pain, and only then—only then—did it occur to him exactly what was happening. I could see it in his eyes, the horror on his face as the blood began to run down my thighs. This was not a thing I just did, a thing I had picked up for fun in the few years since we had last been friends together. He had just claimed my maidenhood.

"Gods help us both, Princess," he exhaled. "What are we doing?"

What, indeed?

But he wanted this; he wanted this more than he knew how to say. Even before I could answer, he drove deeper, wrenching his manhood into me like a knife. I questioned what pleasure women could derive from this act, but I didn't interrupt him. The smell of the candles, the surrounding rain, the salt of his sweat on my tongue—they worked together to create a heady atmosphere that wasn't entirely unpleasant. After a few minutes, the pain numbed down, no more than what I had to suffer through with my monthly bleeding. He bucked his hips against me—I felt the ache turn into something else momentarily, rising as he sped up, a hint of what this was supposed to feel like, but before I could think about it anymore, he stopped, spent.

Agos pulled out, his seed spilling onto the sheets. The numbness was spreading throughout my body, up my fingers and deep into my heart. I craned my head to look at him. He was on his back, his arm on his forehead.

"They will kill me for this," he grumbled. I didn't have to ask who they were. If word of this got out, the entire nation would be running to avenge the future queen's lost honour.

I pulled my knees up, covering my legs with my robes. I was sore and confused and, more than anything else, exhausted. Which was surprising, given I had done nothing at all. Was that it? All that trouble and fuss for something that was over in a few minutes? I still didn't know how I was supposed to feel, and wondered, perhaps, if I was the one at fault. Perhaps I had expected too much from everyone—from Rayyel, especially. "Then why go through with it?" I found myself asking, hoping the conversation would drive my restlessness away.

"You don't know much about men, do you?" He looked up at my face and frowned. "No, you don't. I shouldn't be surprised, after...that."

"I'm sorry." I had lost track of how many times I had uttered the phrase.

"Don't be. I'm not." Agos turned to me now with his dark eyes, his brow furrowed. "But you're marrying Prince Rayyel in three days. You know what this means, right?"

I had gleaned enough from hearing gossip from the maid-servants. Losing one's maidenhood was supposed to be a moment of great importance. Belatedly, I wondered how much blood there was on the sheets and if I would have to burn the damn bed before we went. This—none of this—was how I imagined things would turn out. "I don't think he'll notice."

"And the innkeeper?"

"Threaten him. Bribe him."

"Wiser if he was dead."

"I won't kill a man for that, Agos. He didn't do anything wrong." I shivered, pulling the sheets up to my chest. My insides felt bruised. There was comfort, at least, from the torrent of rain outside. I wanted it to keep falling. I wanted it to flood the whole town, to carry me away and drown me.

"Can I sleep?" Agos mumbled. "I can protect you right here."

"Go ahead," I replied. "We can deal with the innkeeper in the morning."

He stared at me, hesitating. I think he wanted to try to kiss me again. Instead, he sank back to the pillows and fell asleep almost immediately. I watched the lines on his face ease away and only then remembered that we had been riding since early that morning. I had taken for granted all the things I'd asked from him, and a pang of guilt took seed inside my heart. I had no name for whatever I felt for Agos, only that it was the first crack to the rigid mold my father had constructed for me. I liked his company well enough—I didn't love him. I should've never allowed it. I should've never allowed a lot of things. Now all I could think of was how a moment's error had cast a shadow over my son Thanh's very being. In an instant, I failed not just as a daughter, but as a mother to a child not yet born.

But I didn't know, I didn't know, I didn't know.

Ignorance can be the sweetest sin.

That is, of course, old news, enemies I would have been glad to stick with a hatchet and bury in the dust once and for all. I did my best to move past them. What more could I have done? I had no right to complain—not everyone gets the chance to live out a fairy-tale dream.

But mistakes beget mistakes, and fairy tales turn into nightmares. And what would've been challenging in more capable hands turned into a catastrophe in mine. Now I was dealing with the knowledge that I had been betrayed by the very people who were supposed to be serving me, all to lead me into the arms of a mad Zarojo prince. That it was my own father who might've conjured such a plot. And that my husband, between all of this, had every intention of killing Thanh if he learned he was not his after all.

I didn't even know what got me out of bed every morning. My love for my son. Responsibility. Habit. I was counting on the chance that preventing Rayyel from his wretched quest would somehow stop all the other bricks from falling, like damming a bursting embankment with your hands. What else was I supposed to do? I had to save my son.

"You have children, too, don't you, Nor?"

My captain of the guard paused in front of the doorway of Lo Bahn's mansion. Nor was a tall woman, a match for many of the soldiers back at Oren-yaro. She hesitated, as if unsure why I was asking her such a thing. "A daughter," she said, at length. "Beloved Queen. You were at her last nameday. You brought a wooden sword for her."

"Akaterru help me," I grumbled. I had no recollection of this. She was my cousin...her child was my niece. I fulfilled my duties to my clan well enough if the gift sword was any indication, but I couldn't put a face to her daughter. I couldn't even remember her name.

I chewed over this as we walked through the gardens, past metal arches thick with leafy vines and bloated seed pods. Lo Bahn kept an impressive orchard behind stone walls, with no fewer than twenty fruit trees arranged around stone benches and decorative stones. He claimed to like nature, that the smell of the fresh breeze—an uncommon occurrence in the crowded, dirty streets of Shang Azi—was good for a man's circulation. I looked back at Nor. "I apologize," I said.

Her firm face remained unyielding. "There is nothing to apologize for, Beloved Queen."

"You would be back home with your family if not for me."

"We're trapped here because of an embargo. My duty is to remain by your side. There is nothing to apologize for," she repeated.

I didn't have the courage to correct her. She had no knowledge of what transpired in that dockside inn between me and my husband, only a faint inkling of rumours best kept away from prying ears. She didn't even know I had gone to see him that day. As far as she was aware, we were still trying to find him, still trying to piece together information we could glean from his activities in Anzhao while we remained hopelessly stuck, unable to board a ship home. It had made for a very dismal three months. I wasn't sure how she would react to the truth. She was a wolf of Oren-yaro, too, one still reeling from the bitter taste of her men's betrayal. The silence from back home was unnerving. As far as she was concerned, it looked as if our people just went and abandoned us overnight. Where were Lord General Ozo and our army? What was stopping them from sending ships after us, Anzhao City politics be damned? Did they know about my mistakes, and had they all but abandoned me because of them?

No. Nor would kill me if I told her. That the rumours were true—I had faltered, I had sinned, and the heir to the throne was possibly illegitimate, a scandal waiting to explode. It felt ridiculous to even think about how I had let it come this far. I, foolish woman that I was, had never thought to question it. Thanh came out looking every inch like Rayyel and was growing up to follow in his footsteps, much to my dismay. A quiet, serious boy who liked books and had to be reminded to hold a sword the right way—how could he be Agos's son? Agos, who had once pretended to read in front of me with the damn pages upside down?

I opened my mouth to say something in an effort to drown out the silence, but it was overtaken by the sound of the gates opening. I saw Agos's tall form stride past Lo Bahn's guards, but it was the man behind him that my eyes settled on. Khine Lamang, Lo Bahn's right-hand man, of whom I hadn't seen hide nor hair for a good long while. I felt a lump in my throat.

"The hell are you doing here, Lamang?" I called out. I was hoping the familiar banter would ease the beating of my heart. The sight of him brought solace, which was immediately followed by shame—emotions my father would've frowned upon. I had already asked for too much from him.

"Your language has been improved by your time here," Khine said easily. His voice had that cool, polite detachment that he used with people like Lo Bahn—people he disagreed with but didn't want to confront. An easygoing tone, swathed in ice. He nodded towards Agos. "I heard who he was looking for. A Gasparian merchant by the name of Eridu. This time of the day, he'll be at the hawker's hub in Dar Aso."

"Why have you decided to help me now?"

He looked over me. "Captain Nor," he greeted her with a smile. "You're looking lovelier these days. I think the Shang Azi air is starting to agree with you."

"Are we just going to stand around here listening to this idiot, or do we have a merchant to find?" Agos barked.

"This idiot does know his way around the neighbourhood," Khine replied. "Let's go before he changes his mind."

"Stay here, Nor. No sense scaring the man if we can help it." I spoke as nonchalantly as possible, but I could see her regard me with a look of suspicion.

"My queen," she replied. "As captain of the guard, I insist on being at your side at all times."

"She doesn't need two captains," Agos broke in. "I did the job just fine before you, Nor."

I saw Khine's eyes flicker towards Agos when he spoke. *There*, I thought. Khine had heard everything my husband had said that day, and then some. He never spoke to me about it, but he had started making great efforts to avoid me ever since, as if he despised the thought of having anything to do with me again. I couldn't blame him. Khine was an idealistic man, and there was nothing idealistic about what I had done.

Nor steeled herself for what looked like another argument with Agos. I interceded before it began. "We'll be all right, Nor," I assured her. "Please."

I could see the protest in her eyes, but she stepped back with a bow.

Khine pretended I didn't exist as we left Lo Bahn's. I was at a loss for words, the first time I had ever felt that around him—a chasm of silence that grated at my nerves like rusty hinges. It put me at odds with everything that I was, that I knew I was meant to be. Since when did queens walk behind con artists or care what they thought? Yet ever since that day at the docks, nothing felt right anymore. My righteous anger at Rayyel had been a crutch...without it, I was crawling and I didn't know how to get up.

if you enjoyed
THE WOLF OF OREN-YARO

look out for

QUEEN OF THE CONQUERED

Islands of Blood and Storm: Book One

by

Kacen Callender

An ambitious young woman with the power to control minds seeks vengeance against the royals who murdered her family, in a Caribbean-inspired fantasy world embattled by colonial oppression.

extras

Sigourney Rose is the only surviving daughter of a noble lineage on the islands of Hans Lollik. When she was a child, her family was murdered by the islands' colonizers, who have massacred and enslaved generations of her people—and now, Sigourney is ready to exact her revenge.

When the childless king of the islands declares that he will choose his successor from amongst eligible noble families, Sigourney uses her ability to read and control minds to manipulate her way onto the royal island and into the ranks of the ruling colonizers. But when she arrives, prepared to fight for control of all the islands, Sigourney finds herself the target of a dangerous, unknown magic.

Someone is killing off the ruling families to clear a path to the throne. As the bodies pile up and all eyes regard her with suspicion, Sigourney must find allies among her prey and the murderer among her peers...lest she become the next victim.

CHAPTER ONE

The invitation is a plain piece of yellowing parchment, folded shut—thin enough that I can see the red of my fingers shining through, as though the paper is a layer of skin in my hands. The paper itself hasn't been perfumed with the scent of crushed flower petals, as most posts from the kongelig tend to be. Only the seal of white wax, with the sunburst insignia of Hans Lollik Helle, marks the letter in any way.

It's an invitation I've been waiting to receive for nearly ten years: a symbol of all I've worked for, and everything still to come. I hold it in my hands, staring at the seal, my heartbeat drumming through my veins. Now that the moment has finally arrived, I can't bring myself to read the words.

Marieke sweeps into my room with a woven basket of fresh sheets. She sees the letter in my hands, noting the tremble in my fingers before I have a chance to steady them.

"What's that?" she asks briskly, even though she knows exactly what it is. She strips the sheets from my bed, and when I don't answer she says, without sparing me another glance, "Aren't you going to open it?"

I place the invitation atop the stand beside my bed.

Marieke watches me as she straightens my new sheets. Marieke has always valued patience, so it's almost amusing when she sucks her teeth as she fluffs my pillows. She thinks I'm falling apart. She can't blame me, she knows—the pressure I've put on myself with this goal of mine would be enough to break anyone. I've whispered to her at night that this plan is the only reason I'm still alive. Marieke believed me when I told her, and she thought it was sad, too, that a child should ever say that they want to die, but Marieke has known many children who've felt life wasn't worth living.

There's been another slave uprising, this time on a sugarcane planation in the fields to the east, so I ride with my twelve personal guardsmen across Lund Helle, through the groves of tangled brush and branches and thorns, weaving beneath the blessed shade of coconut and palm trees, crossing the fields of guinea grass shimmering in the breeze. Lund is the flattest of its sister islands, so the grass stretches on for miles, without any relief from the sun, which seems to reflect against everything here—the white of my dress, the blue of the sea forever shining in the corner of my eye, even the air itself. The heat is a living thing. It burns the corners of my eyes and lips, already cracking from the salt that's carried from the ocean on the wind.

The ocean has always terrified me. It isn't meant for the living. The water, burning my eyes and nose and throat, can so easily fill my lungs; the power of the tide can pull me beneath its waves. Most frightening of all are the spirits. My sister Ellinor would whisper to me that they walk the ocean floor, waiting for their chance at vengeance against the living; that their hands will pull you into the depths, so that your body, like theirs, can turn to salt and sand, and you can join them in waiting for a chance at revenge.

She'd told me this when I was a girl child, so young I could barely walk anywhere on my own without clutching at my eldest sister's skirts. I'd wanted to know if what Ellinor said was true, so I walked into the water—walked until I could no longer feel the sand beneath my feet. I took a deep breath and let myself sink beneath the surface and opened my eyes, stinging in the salt. There were no spirits standing in the sand, waiting for their revenge. All I could see was the coral, the schools of fish flashing silver in the light, the seaweed swaying beneath the waves. I decided Ellinor was a liar and turned to swim back to shore, but the tide was strong that day. I was pulled away from the shore. I would have kicked my legs, just as I'd been taught, but it was like I'd become stationary, unable to move. I swam, swallowing saltwater, unable to cry for help, but I was only pulled farther and farther, until I began to wonder if my sister had been right after all and if the spirits had grasped me by my legs, even if I couldn't see them or feel their hands.

My limbs became weak and numb, and I sank, my lungs burning and my vision fading away. I should've drowned, but when I opened my eyes again, I was back on the sand, salt drying on my skin. No slaves were nearby to claim that they'd jumped into the water and rescued me; my family was still in the gardens, enjoying their tea. It was just me, alone on the shore. The spirits weren't ready to take me yet.

I know that the path we take is dangerous. It leaves us too vulnerable, too much in the open. We're practically inviting an ambush. This would've been a silly thought, once, on an island like Lund Helle. The island only has a few sugarcane plantations, with houses scattered in between, but there've been three slave uprisings in as many months. Before this, the last uprising was nearly twenty years ago, when Bernhand Lund was still alive and Herre of this island. All the masters of the plantation had been killed. Herre Lund ended the uprising swiftly. Every slave on the plantation, whether they claimed innocence or not—whether they were children or not—was executed, their bodies staked and hung from trees so that the other slaves of this island could see. No other islander has attempted an uprising since, not until now.

Friedrich rides beside me. "You didn't have to come," he says again for the second time this morning. "It's a simple group of slaves that have now decided to call themselves rebels."

"I'm capable of deciding where I need to be, Friedrich."

He looks away, scathed. I feel that there's regret in his gut, regret he hopes I won't see, though he knows any emotion he has, any thought of his, belongs to me. If I will it, I can hear his thoughts the way I might think to myself; his emotions become my own. It requires effort, yes—energy, to make my mind become one with another's—but after holding this kraft for so many years, it's a skill that comes with the ease of racing across the fields of Lund Helle, or holding my breath beneath the sea. I know that Friedrich doesn't want to kill his own people. Before these uprisings, Friedrich had never killed before, not once in his entire life. He'd been trained to—had learned how to stab and maim and disembowel straw-filled opponents, as have all fifty of the guards of Lund Helle—but he never expected to see his sword shining red. He was surprised how easy it was to take the life of another man. His sword had pressed against the skin of the slave rebel who had run at Friedrich with a machete, and then his sword sliced through that skin and into pink guts, and it stopped as though hitting a rock—the man's bones, Friedrich later realized—and the man was still alive as Friedrich pulled back his sword, yanking at it with effort. The man looked as surprised as Friedrich felt before he fell to the dirt.

Friedrich killed three more men that day and, when the fighting was done, walked into the brush so that no one could see him or hear him vomit the cold oats and the juices of the sugarcane he'd swiped from the kitchens that morning. He prayed to the gods of the masters, asking for forgiveness, even though the masters don't believe that taking the life of an islander is a sin, and so there would be nothing to forgive.

Friedrich had hoped he would never have to kill another man again. How disappointed he was to hear of another uprising. "The fight won't last long," he tells me. "They never do."

My horse jerks back and forth beneath me. There's a clopping of hooves against the rocks scattered across the dirt, kicking dust into the air, already heavy with heat. My cloak sticks to my skin, and my neck and shoulders ache beneath the blistering sun. It's always hot on this island of mine, but the dry season has lasted a little too long. The crops are failing now, the plantations earning this island less coin every year. Bernhand Lund was put into his grave four years before, and since the title of Elskerinde was passed on to me, there have been nothing but droughts and uprisings. Proof, according to the Fjern of this island, that I shouldn't have the power that I do.

Lund Helle has no cities, no towns, only isolated collections of houses, which form small plantations holding its slaves and are owned by the few Fjern who live here. An abandoned house we pass leans to its side, as though the wind blew a little too hard one night. A rotted body hangs from a lone mahogany tree, bones visible through the rags it still wears, flies like a layer of living skin. It's always difficult to tell in death what color a body had once been in life.

I see the smoke of the plantation's houses before we arrive. It gushes black into the bright blue sky and burns my eyes, even from such a distance. There are brown bodies of islanders in the green field, already swelling in the heat—but there's no way to tell if these men, women, and children fought alongside the slave rebels, or if they were innocents killed in the clash. I see fallen Fjernmen as well, with their pink skin turning purple and blue. The masters of the plantation. I shouldn't be so pleased, seeing their bodies on the ground.

I ride closer to the plantation houses, a circle of wooden shacks and lean-tos ablaze. Some bodies have already begun to attract flies. My horse snorts nervously as I throw a leg over and leap to the hard ground, Friedrich and my eleven other guardsmen following. It's silent—the only sound is the crackling of the fire as it burns each house, splitting wood and stone, making it impossible to get too close as the heat sears the air. I can feel the heat on my skin, my eyes. We stop before a smoldering house that is already crumbling to the ground in embers. A fine layer of sweat and dust and ash covers me.

"Be careful. Some might have kraft," says Malthe, the captain of my guard.

"You think everyone has kraft," Friedrich mutters, smirking at me to share his joke.

Malthe has heard. "What was that?"

Friedrich hesitates. "Nothing, sir."

"Do you think this is funny, Friedrich?"

Embarrassment, then resentment, pulses through Friedrich, but he hides his emotions well. "No, sir."

It'd only been a joke—a joke born in discomfort, I know. It's always uncomfortable, seeing the dead. The sight of corpses reminds people of the first time they witnessed death: for me, the guests of my mother's manor, throats and stomachs cut, painting the flowers with their blood as my mother and sisters and brother were forced to their knees. Friedrich's memory comes to him as well, I can see now: A child, a boy no older than Friedrich had been, hung upside down by his feet as the master of the plantation taught his son archery. Friedrich often thinks about how easily he could have been chosen instead as the living target. That boy haunts his dreams at night, sometimes even now. The child will watch Friedrich with the same empty stare, arrows riddling his body. What had been the difference between them? The boy wants to know.

Malthe orders the guards to search for survivors. I walk down the path of the desolated plantation. Bodies are sprawled across the floors and straw beds of the slaves' quarters. In the distance, the fields of sugarcane are alight. Burning fields, charred houses, slaughtered people. This is my legacy.

Movement in the corner of my eye, a flare of rage—I spin and shout a warning, but too late. A man with a drawn machete has cut a guardsman's neck, so deeply that his head nearly falls. The rebel, machete shining, swings at Friedrich, but I focus on the slave, his rage and fear of death, yes, he wants to live more than anything else, and his mind becomes my mind as he slices his own gut, mouth open in surprise. More islanders burst from behind blackened houses with yells and screams. Machetes and knives drawn, the rebels clash with the swords of my guards, but there aren't many of them, and they have to know that they'll die. I enter another rebel, overtaken for a moment by his hopelessness as I see myself through his eyes, the traitorous island woman in my dress of white, my eyes fluttering as my kraft works through my veins, and he turns on his friends, cutting his fellow rebels down. Each man falls dead to the ground until only the man I've used is left. He slices his own neck. Pain sears, blood flowing, weakness filling him as he falls. For a moment, I feel death—know what it is to die, just as I have felt a thousand times. The sudden jolt of a heart stopping in your chest, the shock as your own body betrays you. This is what my mother and sisters and brother must have felt.

Friedrich uses a handkerchief to wipe clean his sword before dropping the cloth to the dirt. He's now killed his sixth man. He's heard other guards, such as Malthe, say they'll always remember the face of each man they've killed, but the faces of these slave rebels are already starting to blend together for Friedrich: the anger twisting their mouths, the surprise and pain in their eyes. How easily these men could've been Friedrich's friends, family, Friedrich himself. They were driven to desperation, he thinks. He'd had a cruel master once. He knows what it's like to wonder whether it might be better to fight, knowing he'll likely die, if there's a chance he might find a better life.

I walk to the body of my fallen guardsman. I don't even know his name. He was young—probably no older than twenty. His neck is cut, showing the red muscle beneath, the white of bone. Though his body lies on its front, his head is twisted, eyes stuck open. Some would say this was a good way for the boy to die. He stares at the gods and so will know which direction to turn in death. The gods were brought to these islands by the Fjern many eras ago; gods to be worshipped instead of the spirits of our ancestors, as our people had done since the islands themselves rose from the waters. Islanders are no longer allowed to pray to the spirits. If we do, we are hung, and so we learned the way of the Fjern gods. My enslaved people are told that if they worship the gods, they will be granted freedom after death. Most would rather pray to the Fjern gods, hoping for freedom, than fight for their freedom in life. In a way, I admire the dead rebels at my feet.

"His mother and father are on Solberg Helle," Malthe tells me of the dead guard, "working for a Fjern merchant family." *Working.* This is easier than saying his parents are slaves.

My eyes are still on the boy's face and the blood seeping from his neck and into the weeds. "Have his body returned to them." I should simply have his body sent to the sea, I know; it's easier, less work for everyone involved, but I can't help but think that the boy's parents would like to bury him themselves.

Blood has sunk into the dirt. The smells of iron searing under the heat of the sun, of the smoking wood and the charred stone, overwhelm me. My guardsmen sheathe their blades and walk into whichever remaining homes are still untouched by the flames to check for survivors and conspirators, kicking over the fresh bodies that lie at their feet. I watch their work as I walk, Friedrich beside me. There've been rebellions before, but this has been a particularly devastating uprising; it seems nearly one hundred have died, and the damage to the property and crop won't please the regent of Hans Lollik Helle.

The Fjern of Lund Helle have used the slave rebellions as an excuse to call for me to step down as their Elskerinde. To them, the rebellions prove that I don't have the necessary intelligence to control my own people. I'm an islander, after all, who should be a slave along with my brown-skinned people—not ruling over them and this island. Flower-scented letters are sent to me with open threats: *Elskerinde Sigourney Lund might soon find her own throat cut one night.*

"You don't feel any guilt," Friedrich says as he bends over to check the pockets of one of the fallen rebels. There's no question in his voice, just as there isn't any question for the guilt he feels. Friedrich worked hard for his position in my guard—he wasn't handed his title—but this doesn't take away from the comforts he knows he has over the other slaves of Lund Helle and all his people in these islands. He lives in the barracks, which have beds, not the overcrowded slaves' quarters, where his people sleep on dirt floors. He receives a meal of oats and banana in the morning and goat stew at night. He's even allowed to drink guavaberry rum, when he isn't escorting me across the islands. He isn't beaten, except while in training with the other guards as they practice their skirmishes; he isn't whipped for his mistakes. The scars he bears are fine, thin lines in comparison to the thick scars that cover the backs of the slaves who work the fields. It isn't easy for him, knowing his people suffer while he lives in comfort—knowing it was simple luck that allowed him to be sold into training for the guard. He could just as easily be trapped in the fields, whipped and scarred; just as easily have been hung upside down by his feet while his master's son practiced archery.

Friedrich stands from the body, mouthing a quick prayer to the gods. The gods don't bring him peace. He knows that these are the gods of the Fjern, and that these gods only care for people whose skin is paler than his own. Still, he prays to them. This, like most of our people, is all he knows.

"Do you think I should feel guilt?" I ask.

He glances at me, my mouth, my neck. "It's not my place to tell you how to feel."

"That is true," I say, and though he'd suggested the fact himself, shame still flourishes in his chest. "But I still want to know what you think."

Friedrich doesn't answer, not at first, and so I sink my consciousness into his, feel the pulse of his veins in my own. A jungle of voices echo in my mind: He wonders if I'm using my kraft on him and hopes that I don't; he fears, as he always does, that I might decide I don't want or need him anymore—fears that, though I would have no reason to, I might take control of his body in the same way I've taken control of so many others and force him to stab his knife into his own stomach. He thinks that the stomach is always the slowest, most painful way to die. Death should always be quick and clean. Ever since the first man he killed, Friedrich is careful to give merciful deaths to the slave rebels he fights.

And still, even with his fear of me, I can feel the emotion in him rising as though it's my own: desire—for me, for my body, for my freedom, for my power. He thinks of me at night, dreams that he's inside of me again even now. He doesn't think the words, not consciously, but whenever he's in my bed, he's able to imagine for a moment that he's not my slave. I'm not surprised. I know what Friedrich has convinced himself he feels: that he believes he, a knight in a Fjern fairy tale, has fallen in love with his mistress, his Elskerinde.

Friedrich glances at me again and swallows thickly, knowing that I'm in his head. He pauses beside another body, this time a pale-skinned Fjern—a woman, her face twisted in fear, her stomach cut open and spilling onto the ground. "I don't think you should feel guilt." He lies to himself, even he's aware of this. "These men were rebels, murderers. They would've been executed eventually, even if they hadn't died today."

"Is that really what you think?"

It's a cruel question. I know he's too afraid to tell me the truth. The truth is traitorous, the words of rebels, punishable by beheading. But his feelings are clear: None of these men can be blamed for wanting, and fighting for, their freedom.

"They were driven to rebel and murder because they preferred to die rather than live as slaves to the Fjern," I say. "I'm an islander. These are my people. I haven't done enough to help them. At least, this is what those who hate me will say."

Friedrich looks at me with pity. He thinks he knows me: his poor, misunderstood mistress.

He checks this woman's pockets as well, then murmurs a prayer for her. Remarkable, watching a slave pray over the body of a slaver and to the very gods that oppress him. But I can't judge Friedrich too harshly. These are my gods, too. I was never taught how to pray to my ancestors. Any thought of our ancestors, the spirits, was supposed to have died generations ago. I wait until Friedrich is finished, and we walk quietly for some time.

Friedrich says, "Only people who envy your power will hate you. The poor hate the rich. The slaves hate the kongelig. It's only natural, isn't it?"

I want to ask Friedrich if his envy of my freedom, my power, means he actually hates me as well, but the corners of his lips twitch into a smile, and he remembers an image, hoping that memory will become my own—a memory of only a few nights before, sneaking into my chambers, into my bed, beneath my sheets. I should be disgusted with myself. Ashamed. The boy is technically my property. Property, like the goats fenced in and awaiting slaughter. That is what the laws of these islands decree: Friedrich, and all other islanders, are not human. The color of their skin, the blood in their veins, make them undeserving of life. And so they must give their lives for the Fjern.

There's nothing beautiful in this, I know. In the same way there was nothing beautiful in the fact that my mother technically belonged to my father, before she was given her freedom; in the same way there was nothing beautiful in the fact that my father's ancestors belonged to the Fjern, who took these islands. If I cared for Friedrich, I would give him his freedom, along with all the slaves of Lund Helle. I wouldn't take Friedrich into my bed, pretending my company is something he wants, something he chooses, when he has no choice in a life he doesn't own.

I refused him, at first. This is what I remind myself in consolation. I refused him and told him that he's a child for thinking he wants me. But though I own my life, it's not a good life I live, and Friedrich is a distraction I desperately need. He's young and foolish in his ambition, cocky in his thoughts of surpassing his peers to follow Malthe and become captain of the Lund guard—but still handsome, with his dark skin and sculpted muscles and his smile, a smile that isn't easy to find on these islands, and certainly not this island of mine. And even I can't ignore that my body has its own needs, its own desires.

I tell Friedrich I'd like to make a trip to Jannik Helle, and I can sense his impatience. It'll be my second trip this month alone. Still, he nods his understanding as he kneels beside the body of one of the slave rebels, machete still clenched in his hand where he fell. Checking the rebel's pockets, Friedrich pauses with a frown and withdraws his hand, staring into his palm.

"What is it?" I ask him, though I see a flicker of his vision.

He offers his hand to me. He holds a rusted red coin. I pick it up and turn it over. The coin has the crest of a crude zinnia flower, the symbol belonging to the Ludjivik family.

Friedrich stands, brushing off his knees. "Do you think they were behind this?"

"I wouldn't put it past them," I say. "An ill-fated attempt at supporting and supplying a slave rebellion against me."

"Unless they meant to lose. What if this was meant as a distraction, or they hope to make you feel secure before attacking again?" *They will take this island from you.*

I toss the coin into the dirt. "It isn't incriminating to find a coin. Maybe one of the slaves recently traveled to Ludjivik Helle and took it."

Friedrich doesn't look convinced. I don't need to enter his mind to know his thoughts: There are those in the islands of Hans Lollik who want to see me dead, and if I'm not careful, eventually one will succeed.

Friedrich and I start the walk to our horses. The rest of my guardsmen will stay, searching for clues and valuables under Malthe's watch, before starting the back-bending work of burying each of the slaves' bodies at sea. The dead masters of the plantation will be returned to the Fjern for a ceremonial burial so that they will easily find the gods.

Before we get far, a guardsman hurries down the rocky path.

"Elskerinde Lund," he says, breathless. He catches my eye, and when I look to his thoughts, a wave of his fear crashes into me, dread sinking into my bones. Fear that I'll learn of all his secrets, of the extra goat stew he's been stealing at night, and maybe even of the little boy he watched drown so many years ago—

"Spit it out," Friedrich says.

The man hesitates. "We found survivors." He doesn't look at me as he continues to speak. "One of them has kraft."

We follow the guard back up the path to the burning plantation houses with my nine other guardsmen, waiting in a circle and turning to watch my arrival. A line of the survivors stands in the center of the circle, all slaves. A man, middle-aged and frail—thinner than most, it's clear that he holds a sickness in his lungs, perhaps caught from the last storm season, something he never managed to shake. A woman, her skin a maze of wrinkles, toothless so that her lips sink in like a skull. She watches me. She isn't afraid. She's already so close to death. What could I possibly do to make her afraid? There's another woman as well, breathing heavily as she grips the hand of the girl beside her. The girl is young, perhaps no older than thirteen. She and her mother have the same eyes, the same mouths.

Though he'd been so willing to joke about kraft before, Friedrich takes the matter seriously now. "Do you think the one with kraft caused the uprising?" he asks me, eyes on the islanders.

That would depend on the power, and the strength, of the kraft itself. My chest burns. "Which one?" I ask Malthe.

He marches to the villagers and pushes the girl forward, forcing her to let go of her mother. The girl winces, struggling not to cry, shoulders shaking with the effort. My heart drops. She reminds me too much of my sister Inga, crying as she was forced to her knees.

My mouth is dry, words scratching my throat. "How do you know she has kraft?"

"She tried to use her power on us—confused us for a moment, made us forget who we were, what we were doing here, then tried to run with the others. When we captured them and threatened to kill them all if no one spoke the truth, she stepped forward."

The man in the line of slaves speaks. "She's just a girl. She was afraid, thought you were rebels. They were killing all of us, not just the masters—"

Malthe jams the hilt of his sword into the man's nose. The slave falls with a shout of pain, blood streaming between his fingers as he clutches his face. If he thought he was safe, facing his own people with not a single Fjern in sight, he was mistaken.

"You'll speak when we ask you a question," Malthe says to all of them. "Is that clear?"

No one moves or makes a sound. The woman with her skin of wrinkles watches me.

"Were you fighting with the rebels?" I ask the girl.

She glances up, terrified, before looking at the ground again. She's willing to tell us anything and everything if it means she'll live. Even if she doesn't own her life, she still wants it. "No—I wasn't, I promise you. They weren't of this plantation. No one recognized them. They came here and attacked us. Killed everyone. They weren't from Lund Helle, they were speaking of returning to their ships."

Friedrich gives me a pointed look. I ignore him, glancing Malthe's way, and he nods. The ships will be found and searched.

I ask, "Where were the rebels from?"

The girl doesn't know the answer. She's frightened I won't be pleased. "I—I think maybe Niklasson Helle." She's lying. There's no reason for her to think the rebels came from Niklasson Helle.

I pause. I can feel their fear. Fear that they'll all be killed for failing to protect their masters. Fear that I'll decide they're lying, and that they were all a part of the rebellion. Fear from all—except for the older woman. She stares at me, blue film over her eyes. She's seen more hatred, more evil, than I ever have—probably more than I ever will. The Fjern, who gave me the power I hold, stalking through the plantations in the dead of night when she was a child. Raping her mother and her sister and herself, slicing open the bottoms of her feet and burning the palms of her hands and making her work the fields, threatening death if she stopped for even a breath, hanging her father for daring to meet his master's eye, beating and whipping and tying up a little boy child and leaving him outside in the sun to be eaten away by the salt air, and all because he wouldn't stop crying for his mother after she was sold away. Islanders, tying rocks around their ankles and walking into the sea to escape the hell of Hans Lollik.

To the slaves before me—to all the islanders—I'm the traitor to her own people. My skin might be brown, and my blood might belong to these islands, but I'm no better than the Fjern. My heart thumps harder. I close my eyes. Try to push their thoughts aside—their hatred for me, their fear of me—but I realize that the feelings are my own.

When I open my eyes, the man is still bleeding. The elderly woman still watches me. The girl's mother clutches her hands together so tightly they shake. The girl tries so hard not to cry.

I have no more questions—no way of delaying what I know has to come. Malthe stares at me expectantly. I'd hoped he'd let this pass. No one need know we found a slave girl with kraft in the fields of Lund Helle.

When I speak, my voice doesn't sound like it belongs to me. "The law of Hans Lollik is clear."

The girl's mother begins a low wail. This woman will inevitably feel a guilt I'm familiar with—guilt, that she didn't do enough to save the person she loved. But the guilt will only simmer beneath the rage, the hatred, for me—the one who ordered her daughter's death.

I don't even know the girl's name. "You stand accused of holding kraft, a power that belongs only to your sovereigns of Hans Lollik, gifted as a divine right by the gods that watch over us."

The woman tries to step in front of her daughter, but the guardsmen pull her and the others aside. The girl shakes her head. Her face crumples as she heaves sobs, tears dripping from the end of her nose. I can't save her. The Fjern made it clear when they claimed these islands over hundreds of years before: Only they, with their pale skin, are allowed to have kraft; any slave accused of having the power must be found and killed, no matter the innocence, no matter the age. The fact that the Fjern can't own kraft is one that they despise. My people, descendants of the first islanders before the Fjern ever came, believe the abilities to have come from our ancestors. We whispered that those with kraft were blessed by the spirits. The Fjern disagreed. They don't believe in the spirits of our ancestors; they declare that their gods pass the kraft on as divine gifts to only the worthy, and to the Fjern, my people are not worthy. I was born with my freedom, and so I'm allowed to keep my life, even with kraft simmering in my veins. This girl wasn't born with her freedom, and so she'll die. She'll become a martyr. The hero in every story but my own.

I recite the words memorized, heavy on my tongue. "Anyone who isn't of kongelig descent and dares possess kraft, which belongs only to their benevolent rulers as a divine right, must die by execution."

The woman screams now, fighting against the guards that hold her. I nod at Malthe, and he moves forward dispassionately, pressing down on one of the girl's shoulders so that she'll fall to her knees. I look away when he swings his sword.

Silence, but for the crackling of the fires. The girl's mother has fainted. My hands are shaking. I wipe them on the white of my dress as I turn away, but before I can take another step, the older woman comes forward. She spits at my feet. The metallic smell of blood burning in the heat sickens my stomach, and I feel faint. I don't have the energy or the will to read this woman's thoughts—to feel her hatred. But she wants me to know.

"You're evil," she tells me. "You might call yourself kongelig, and you might wear your pretty dress of white, but you're just a dog taking scraps from your masters."

I could have her executed, too, for being a slave who has shown disrespect to her Elskerinde. The guards, watching closely, will wonder why I don't. I'm already weak, wavering on my feet, but I close my eyes, and I sink into her—feel myself in her veins as her face tightens, her arms and legs cramping. She steps forward, then lowers to her knees. The woman struggles, fights against me—leans forward to kiss my feet.

She watches only the ground as I walk past her.

I return to my horse, Friedrich following closely behind, and pause by the brush. Most days, I'm able to pretend I'm not caught in a horror of my own making. Easy to pretend I'm not the monster who deserves the hatred of her people. Friedrich looks away when I heave into the leaves.

orbit

Follow us:

f **/orbitbooksUS**

🐦 **/orbitbooks**

▶ **/orbitbooks**

Join our mailing list
to receive alerts on our
latest releases and deals.

orbitbooks.net

Enter our monthly
giveaway for the chance
to win some epic prizes.

orbitloot.com